Two Women in Rome

Elizabeth Buchan was a fiction editor at Random House before leaving to write full time. Her novels include the prize-winning *Consider the Lily*, international bestseller *Revenge of the Middle-Aged Woman*, *The New Mrs Clifton* and *The Museum of Broken Promises*. Buchan's short stories are broadcast on BBC Radio 4 and published in magazines. She has reviewed for the *Sunday Times*, *The Times* and the *Daily Mail*, and has chaired the Betty Trask and Desmond Elliot literary prizes. She was a judge for the Whitbread First Novel Award and for the 2014 Costa Novel Award. She is a patron of the Guildford Book Festival and co-founder of the Clapham Book Festival.

Also by Elizabeth Buchan

Elizabeth Buchan

Two Women in Rome

CORVUS

First published in Great Britain in 2021 by Corvus, an imprint
of Atlantic Books Ltd.

This paperback edition published in 2022.

10 9 8 7 6 5 4 3 2 1

A CIP catalogue record for this book is available from the British Library.

Paperback ISBN: 978 1 78649 535 8
E-book ISBN: 978 1 78649 534 1

Design and typesetting www.benstudios.co.uk

Corvus
An imprint of Atlantic Books Ltd
Ormond House
26–27 Boswell Street
London
WC1N 3JZ

www.corvus-books.co.uk

Printed and bound by CPI Group (UK) Ltd, Croydon, CR0 4YY

MIX
Paper from
responsible sources
FSC
www.fsc.org
FSC® C171272

For Alexia, Flora and Finian who have brought much joy

'I thought I knew everything when I came to Rome, but I soon found I had everything to learn'

Edmonia Lewis

Italy
March 1977

HE WRAPPED HIS ARMS AROUND HER AND DREW HER EVEN closer. She knew then that he was telling her that he loved her but could not trust himself to say so.

It did not matter.

For that moment at least, tender and choked with emotion, they were at peace after the turbulence of longing and desire.

They were staying in a hilltop town a short train journey away from the big city. The hotel was inexpensive, clean and discreet. The view from the window was of the plain below, where the spring narcissi massed, and a milky-looking mountain in the distance.

Lying open on the floor beside the bed was her notebook, containing her botanical painting of the narcissi. On the opposite page was a transverse section of its seed head. She had taken her time to select the best specimen and dissected it with the sharpened knife she kept in her bag.

To keep off dangerous subjects – what had taken place between them, the future – they discussed the two paintings they had seen earlier in the morning, sightseeing.

The town's ducal palazzo was run-down and shorn of artefacts. Pacing behind the guide, who was so desperate that he resorted to pointing out the guttering, they had escaped to its museum, which had nothing in it except for the ducal chair and an exquisite miniature painting of Bathsheba bathing.

The label stated that it had been discovered during restoration work in the palazzo and later authenticated as an original from a book of hours commissioned by the then duchess in 1489 and painted by Pucelle *fils*, a celebrated master.

Its subject was Bathsheba bathing in a pool with a fountain playing. It showed her with milky-white, unblemished skin and a slender waist above broadly curving hips and exposed pudendum – a glorious, jewel-like homage to lust. And yet, by placing her in the water, with King David gazing down on her from a distant palace, the painter was cleverly keeping her at one remove. *Beware of sensuality* was the message.

She had studied it for a long time.

Close by, in the church on the piazza, was another medieval painting, this time of the Annunciation. Here, the Virgin sat peacefully in the garden, wearing a cloak of the most intense blue. A rabbit and a mouse sheltered under her skirts. An archangel was winging down, bearing a lily.

She had stood in front of it, and the colour of the Virgin's cloak had shimmered, and grown deeper, burning into her vision: the deep, deep blue of peace and certainty.

Now she stirred in his arms.

'All right?' His breath fell on her cheek.

'The blue makes the heart sing.' She was beginning to feel sleepy. 'It's remarkable.'

'Made from powdered lapis lazuli. Probably.'

'Is it?' She looked up at his face. Since their time together was always short, she liked to take an inventory of every expression. 'How did they convert it into paint?'

'Water and gum Arabic. But it was only applied at the last minute.' He, too, was drowsy. 'It would be used for her cloak, and she would be wearing it at every stage of her life as a mother. Annunciation, birth, flight into Egypt, taking Christ to the temple ...

'The blue that was used for the Virgin's cloak, what they called the *azur d'outremer*, was the most expensive,' he continued. 'A fortune. It was specified in the contract. So much, and no more, to be bought by the painter. It was also spelled out to the artist how he could use it.' The words were muffled. 'No artistic freedom in those days. The artist did what he was told.'

While he had been a student at university, he had read up on the subject, claiming it was a relief from the intensity of his main study.

'A fabulously expensive cloak to wear in the stable,' she said. 'Crazy.'

'Also worn on the flight into Egypt.' His voice darkened. 'Watching him on the cross. Taking her dead son in her arms and draping it over him.'

'Is her cloak ever red or green?'

'Not at that period. Later, perhaps.'

'I bet some of the forgers made that mistake.'

Their hands entwined and they were silent until he said, 'In those days, there was an entire language of colours. Each one had its place in a hierarchy. Everyone understood what they implied in a way that we don't.'

Later, he sat on the edge of the bed staring out of the window, his hands clasped loosely between his knees. A trace of moisture gleamed on his shoulder blades. She reached out and pressed her finger gently on his spine.

'The early representations of Mary usually show her with a flat skin tone.' He turned his head. 'Unless they were taught by a master, the younger painters did not understand that nothing is flat and smooth. But, as they grew older, and if they were not too arthritic, they learned how to extend the colour range … vermillion, yellow ochre and lead white. Pucelle *fils* was one of those painters.'

'How would you paint me?' she asked softly.

He lay down beside her and propped himself up on an elbow. 'Grey skin undertones and … yes, blue shadows under the eyes, long brushstrokes to convey your silky skin. I would command the white lead to be ground and I would mix it with just a shade of black bismuth to capture the movement in your face.' He ran a fingertip over her eyelids. 'Then I could paint the light in your eyes and expose you: both wary and ecstatic in equal measure.'

She pulled him down to her and kissed him lingeringly and deeply.

Regrets? They would be hammering inside his skull. And, she suspected, the beginnings of hatred for her. Or what she stood for.

The church bells sounded in the distance with a silvery shudder of sound. *Vespers*. She felt the ripple go through him. Guilt? Longing? She pressed her head against his chest. 'Go on,' she said. 'Say what you always say. What you must.'

He addressed the ceiling. 'I am … wrong being with you.'

Her heart thudded a little. 'But you say you can't be without me.'

'No, I can't, but I must try.'

It came as no surprise, but it still hurt. 'You're in danger of sounding like a Desert Father. Women's bodies are disgusting and sinful.' She shut her eyes. 'I'll never understand why the views

4

were so pervasive for so long. Or why chastity is considered heroic.'

'Listen,' he replied. 'While I'm lying here with you, I can think only of you and your warmth. Of your beautiful body. I feel sick at the thought someone else might touch it. That you might turn to another and smile at him in the way you smile at me. It would drive me to madness.'

She felt herself melting, dissolving with happiness.

'When I'm here with you there's no room for anything else. That's the reason why.'

What a waste of so many lives, she thought. The battle for chastity took up so much energy and the perceived enemy, which was lust and desire, refused to die. Anyway, surely it was possible to lust and to serve God?

He put his arm across his eyes.

'There are many ways of achieving peace and equality and a good life,' she pointed out. 'They may not include God, but they have everything else.'

He rolled over and looked into her eyes. 'You're talking politics.' His face was magnified above hers. 'If you are, it suggests you don't understand about faith.'

'You're mistaken. I do have a faith. Or rather beliefs.' She was stung into revealing more than she normally would. 'But they're not the same as yours.'

'For the love of God.' The words were pulled from him.

She moved away from him and swung her legs to the floor. 'I don't think God has anything to do with this.' She walked over to the window. 'With you and me.'

There was a difficult silence and she cursed herself for spoiling their brief and precious time together.

'I'm sorry,' she said.

Still the silence.

'Tell me about the books of hours,' she tried again.

She heard him get to his feet, pad over, and she turned to face him and buried her face in his chest.

'They were powerful.' His voice echoed in his chest against her ear. 'They told you how to spend your day: when to pray, how to pray. There were calendars, and texts, and special pleas. Women gave them to their daughters when they were sent from home to marry. Legally, it was the only possession they had the freedom to give away.'

She absorbed the information. 'If I had been a mother, I'd put in private messages.'

'What would you say?'

His gaze disconcerted her. Did he know anything? Did he suspect that, although her life had become his, it was also not his? Her secrets could not be for him and would never be for him. 'I wouldn't know where to begin.'

He touched her chin with a finger. 'I think you do.'

Her unease deepened. 'Remember me. That's what I would say.' *Remember me.*

CHAPTER ONE

LOTTIE ARCHER HAD KNOWN FOR SOME TIME THAT HER nature was divided – she put it down to the fact her mother had given her away at birth and her father was unknown from the word go.

Which life is ever nourished in ideal circumstances? Not many; but Lottie's had fallen short from the start without anyone to guide or guard her. There had been no flowing, and unconditional, tenderness to weep with her over bruised knees, or to apply sticking plaster to the terrors of growing up. No one to say with total conviction: *It will be all right.*

The reasons for her abandonment might have been noble or ignoble but Lottie was never informed, either by the care homes she frequented or by the foster parents who took her in as a teenager and with whom she – sadly – had nothing in common.

She grew to see that her abandonment was hers with which to cope, and hers alone, and she hugged its whys and wherefores to her inner self, no doubt hampering her emotional development in doing so.

There had been dark times.

The scissors.

The uneaten meals.

But the memory of the weapons that she had used against herself had been banished to a dark recess in her mind. Useful experience. Never to be repeated – but something that added an edge, a serration, to her character.

Occasionally, during those years, a counsellor suggested that she unburden herself but, at those times, she was not sure of what she wished to achieve.

It was sufficient for her to understand that one half of her loved order, procedures and clarity – and she was superb at those. The other, wilder half could, on occasion but not always, take risks and had been known to dance around (the permitted areas) of Stonehenge at midsummer and to climb Mount Kenya without a sensible sleeping bag.

Three weeks ago, she had accepted another risk by marrying, and now she was lying beside Tom, her husband, in the apartment in Rome in a newly purchased double bed.

To say she was astonished at herself was an understatement. Marriage had never been part of her plan and, even more astonishing, she had only known Tom for nine months.

Tom arrived in Lottie's life on a hot July day. Her close friend Helena, who was getting married for the second time, had insisted her attendants, of which Lottie was one, should wear pink. Neither the dress nor the colour suited her. But, because she loved Helena, she laced herself into it and resolved to avoid the photographs. Tom had spotted her skulking behind a pillar and introduced himself.

Halfway through their conversation, he broke off. 'I don't think you like your dress. Your idea or the bride's?'

It was a neat insight and she burst out laughing. 'Truthfully, I hate it.'

'It doesn't matter, though,' he said. 'You're lovely.'

She looked at him and her stomach did an extraordinary contraction. 'So are you,' she said. 'And I'm sure that we know each other.'

'That's good,' he said. 'It means there's something there.'

They went to bed that night, a glorious, slightly drunken, surprising encounter in an upmarket hotel with a marble bathroom and a stack of white towels.

The pink dress was abandoned on the floor, never to be worn again.

Partly, Tom snared Lottie with his gift for listening, which meant he paid as much attention to the unspoken words as the spoken ones. Partly, she loved his body, from which she took as much pleasure as she hoped she gave him. Not handsome, with a nose that was a shade too long, his charm came from his lean and rangy energy and it snared her.

He was the only one of her lovers who had got her to talk about her childhood, and she found herself telling him about the care homes and the fostering.

'I survived,' she said.

He stroked her hair back from her forehead. 'Not funny, though,' he said. 'Not for a child.'

'I yearned for the safeness of a mother – except my mother had been anything but safe. I think I wanted relief from being responsible for myself and I was angry that I had to be.'

'Yearning can be cruel,' said Tom. He paused. 'Did you ever try to find your parents?'

She felt the old anguish stir. 'Tom, do you mind if we change the subject?'

He seemed perfectly at ease with her retreat. 'Fine,' he said gently. 'We all have no-go areas.'

One way or another, Lottie's love affairs were always conducted at long distance – *Freudian,* said Helena. Tom lived in Rome and so this affair looked set to conform to the same pattern, but he had other ideas and wooed her with tenderness … and stealth.

There had been many phone calls between London and Rome and those slightly concerning sessions on FaceTime that made her look haggard – 'Rome has so many things going for it, I promise' – and weekend meetings facilitated by budget airlines.

And what of Tom's previous lover, who had moved out three years previously?

'Clare found someone else,' said Tom. 'And she chose to leave. It was bad at the time. I missed her very much. Then one day I didn't.' His gaze raked past Lottie's shoulder into a past – and a no-go area? – about which she knew little. 'It had run its course.' He turned his attention back to Lottie. 'I learned that, at forty, you have to re-educate yourself for the rest of life. Clare's leaving was my lesson that the ambitions and ideals that were good for the first half of my life needed adjustment. The more I thought about it, the more I realised that it was quite normal.'

That struck Lottie as profoundly true.

He took her hands in his. 'We both have baggage from the past. Let's just cut off previous labels.'

'Done,' she said.

Just before Christmas, Tom phoned Lottie in London. 'The post of chief archivist has come up at the *Archivio Espatriati*. Why don't you apply and come and live in Rome?'

Why would she? Her work as Principle Records Specialist at Kew would lead to promotion. She was established and enjoyed her good reputation.

Why would she? The risk-taker asserting herself? Had her feelings for Tom so deepened that a sea change had taken place?

'The Italians are wonderful,' said Tom. 'They are so right about many things and you speak good Italian.' He added: 'I love you, Lottie.'

That was the first time Tom had said it and, to her surprise, she experienced pure joy. Normally reticent, she found herself responding – and the words were almost new to Lottie. 'I love you, too.'

She got the post and, before she took it up, Tom launched the next phase of his campaign.

He took her skiing in Austria. Nothing too expensive, but not cheap either. St Anton was less glitzy than many, but it had an old-world charm and the trails and lift networks linked delightful Alpine villages.

'You can ski all day without repeating a run,' said Tom. 'I like that.'

They skied like there was no tomorrow and, at night, they dined and wined and fell into bed. On the final day, they took the ski lift up the steepest mountain. At the top, Tom sent Lottie a look over his shoulder. *Race me.*

Erotic. Testing. An invitation into new territory.

Lottie pushed herself fast down the terrifying *piste*. Tom was just ahead but only just. The speed was stupidly reckless but she responded to its danger with surging blood and an abandonment to elemental sensations.

The air sliced at her cheeks, her stomach heaved with apprehension and excitement, her legs ached. She caught up with Tom and he turned his head for a second and they exchanged a look of complete understanding.

At the bottom, breathless and ecstatic, stripped of everything except exhilaration, she collapsed into his arms.

'Marry me, Lottie.'

'*What?*'

'Marry me.'

Lottie was unable to respond instantly.

'Say yes.'

Adrenalin coursed through Lottie. Love. New job. Profound change. The tally was seductive. 'Yes. Tom, yes, I will.'

Tom played his trump card with exquisite skill. 'I want to share my home with you, Lottie. You've never had one.'

True: and the reminder made her cry.

As a child, she had had no real home. As an adult, she had lived – along with a vast collection of pot plants – in a series of rented flats that were never quite as she wished them to be because she never stayed long enough. In contrast, Tom had lived in the apartment in the city centre and held down the same job for over fifteen years.

'You can come and go as you please,' he said, blotting her tears with the ball of his thumb. 'The travel is easy.'

He had kissed her in the way that was increasingly familiar and which she had grown to love, and she was taken aback by the strength of her desire to accept what he offered. The decision was not without struggle because her habit of self-containment was so entrenched. *Guarded*, said Helena during one of those talks that were supposed to be cathartic and useful but so very often weren't. *Solitary.*

She could not swear that she *knew* Tom. Not through and through, at a deep level. But her instincts, and everything she had learned about him so far, told her he was kind and honourable.

Plus, she admired the work that he did at the British Council, an institution that had been created to facilitate good relationships between nationalities, and of which he talked with passion.

Helena was hobbled by a rotten early pregnancy and Lottie turned to her other great friend, Peter, for advice. 'Hold the decision until I get there,' he said. 'I'm coming over for the weekend.'

Peter was an actor, a shambling figure who possessed an uncanny ability to appear neat and energetic on stage and considered himself a Shakespearean scholar – Shakespeare was there to be plundered – and he threw quotes around like confetti.

He, Helena and Lottie shared a friendship from university days that had evolved and matured over the decades, the kind that did not ask questions when things were bad. They understood the dark places in each other's spirits, never lost faith and, even under provocation, found reserves of patience.

Lottie and Peter took themselves off to the Campo de' Fiori for a dish of pasta. Lottie willed a cheering aphorism to tumble from Peter's lips. None came.

She poured him a glass of wine. '"Too rash, too sudden, etc., etc. ..." is what you're thinking.'

'I'm not saying anything.'

'You don't have to.'

He put down his fork. 'You've tomato on your chin, but it hasn't ruined your beauty.'

She wiped it away. 'And?'

'OK, how long will you be here for? Until you're carried out feet first? You fought hard to get where you were professionally. Is the new job in the same league?'

'There's potential,' she answered carefully. 'Is my chin OK?'

'More than. What about your Englishness?'

'Englishness? This is not *Our Island Story*. Tom will retire when he's sixty-five. Or earlier, if he wants. We can be flexible.'

'And if you want to return to the UK before Sir retires? What if you find living here difficult?'

'I know, I know,' she said. 'What am I doing?'

He tipped back his chair. Rather dangerously. 'Tell the truth, my darling. What do you know about him?'

'I've told you.' Lottie assembled the correct order of response. 'Brought up in Cornwall. Lived in Rome for fifteen years. Good job at the British Council. Previous relationship but no children.' She reached over the table and placed a hand on Peter's forearm. 'What are you trying to tell me?'

'Is he real? Or the too-good-to-be-true real? You're smart and sharp and you should use your smartness. Have you got past the surface of the affable, intelligent bringer of good tidings to the natives of foreign countries who are keen on culture? What does he actually *do*?'

'Plenty.'

Peter frowned. 'He had a long relationship, which he seems to have got over in a trice' – Lottie made a protesting noise – 'and is proposing to nail you down within months of meeting. Are you sure he isn't Bluebeard?'

'It was three years ago.' She felt a flicker of outrage. 'And anyway, emotions do not conform to timetables.'

'Sorry.'

'But I know you're protecting me.' These days, Lottie's appetite rarely failed, and she occupied herself winding the final coils of pasta on to her fork. 'Do you suspect him of something?'

'Nothing is ever not possible.'

Lottie stared at Peter. 'I think we need more wine.'

After the meal, they wandered the streets fanning off the Campo de' Fiori. 'This is the street of the chest maker, the arrow maker, the hat maker.' She translated the names for Peter, and he insisted on taking her into a boutique selling hats. 'You'll need a proper beret.'

'Why?'

'Because you will look more the part.' He placed an overlarge black beret on her head and stepped aside so she could see her image in the mirror. 'Perfect.'

'I look like a cross between Gigi and a paratrooper.'

'A very stylish one. I'm buying it and you will wear it. It'll be your talisman.'

Wearing the beret, Lottie took Peter the next day to St Peter's and made him stand in front of Michelangelo's *Pietà*. For a few seconds, the crowds around it parted and they were granted a spectacular view.

'What do we see?' He tucked his hand under Lottie's elbow.

A young woman held the body of her dead son in her lap. Her beauty, and its beauty, took away the breath. Even more astonishing was the artistry. To balance an adult body in a lap was difficult enough in life. In marble, it was extraordinary.

'Classical beauty married to naturalism.' Lottie sounded lame and limited, but it was impossible for her to convey how deeply the *Pietà* affected her.

He sent her one of his more actorly glances. 'Yes, but what do you *feel*?'

'What I feel ... what hits me,' Lottie's throat constricted, '...is the grief, all conveyed in stillness. I'm not a parent, but how do you survive something like this?'

Peter shot her a look. 'You don't often say that sort of thing,' he remarked.

It was true. Family. Parents. Children. Lottie had no experience of how they slotted together, or of how the ropes of obligation and affection could bind you tight.

'I sometimes think I missed out,' he admitted. 'Too busy being the actor. Didn't leave room.'

The weekend over, Lottie went with Peter to see him off to the airport. He gave her a kiss. 'Have you made up your mind?'

'You've made me think hard,' she replied. 'Thank you for that.'

'And?'

'I'm going ahead.'

Here she was. In Rome – and it was spring.

Lottie turned her head to look at Tom sleeping beside her, taking delight in his warmth, the long limbs and the snuffle as he hauled the sheet over his shoulder. She reached over and placed a fingertip on his mouth very, very gently.

She moved closer to him, closed her eyes and went to sleep.

Not for long. Tom's phone rang, a noise that tore into the peace, and they both groaned. Tom swung out of bed and picked it up. 'Go back to sleep,' he said, and padded into the next room.

He returned several minutes later and switched on his bedside light. 'There's been an explosion. I have to go.'

Horrified, she exclaimed, 'Are people hurt? Dead? But why you? Won't the police and the authorities deal with it?'

'I need to see if some colleagues are OK.'

'Your colleagues? But it's the middle of the night.'

'Apparently a bomb went off where a couple of them live. They might need help.'

'A bomb ...' she echoed in a stupefied way.

'It's not unknown.' Tom grabbed his jacket, checked over the pockets in a methodical way.

'Let me come with you?'

But he was already out of the door.

Lottie grabbed her jeans and top, struggled into them and followed Tom down the stairs. He was in the courtyard, talking to a man. In the half-light they seemed more ghost than human. After a moment, they loped towards the street where a car waited.

Lottie stood for quite a time in the courtyard, listening to the night sounds. A doubt crossed her mind, followed by a question, neither of which she could resolve.

She made her way back to the apartment and to bed.

He did not return until dawn. Lottie had slept only in fits and starts and watched him sit down heavily on the bed. 'Three dead and one badly injured,' he said. '*Carabinieri* who had been lured to the spot by a phone call reporting an abandoned car.' He shucked off a shoe. 'It's an old trick.' The second shoe dropped to the floor. 'They should have known.' He sounded done in.

'What will happen?'

'A round-up of suspects from whom they will try to extract information.' He twisted round to look at her. 'It's depressing. We thought that sort of violence was over in the nineteen nineties and everyone could get on with peace, Italian style.'

'Not a vendetta, then?'

'It's possible.'

She touched his arm. 'Your lot are OK?'

'Yes.' He slid into bed, pulled up the sheet and sighed deeply.

Lottie searched her memory for what she knew about recent Italian history. 'The bombings in the sixties and seventies? Who was responsible?'

He didn't answer.

'Wasn't the US desperate to stop Italy sliding to the Left?' He didn't answer. 'Tom, I find it very odd that you have been involved.'

He turned away. 'Can't talk now.'

Lottie fell asleep with violent images going through her head. In the morning, she wanted to know the details.

'Nobody knows anything much at this point.'

'Except you were summoned to the scene.'

Lottie was brushing her hair and, glancing into the mirror at Tom, caught him unguarded and was surprised by his expression, which lacked his usual affability. 'I keep thinking about the injured. And the dead.'

His face cleared. 'It's bad,' he said. 'And brutal.'

When they met again that evening, she had decided not to raise the subject of the bombing but to tackle him on a subject that she was anxious to get settled.

When she agreed to marry Tom, Lottie imposed two conditions – and the one led into the other. First, an overhaul of the apartment's Neanderthal plumbing. He had been unexpectedly curt. 'This is an old building. What do you expect?'

'I expect a working lavatory,' Lottie replied tartly, recollecting her tricky encounters with the incumbent one. 'So does everybody else in the world.'

The second was to create a small, urban garden on the balcony. The plumber who had been summoned for a consultation sucked his teeth when she asked for a tap to be installed for the watering and muttered about installing a new set of outside pipes. This would require scaffolding and would be expensive.

Tom said, 'For God's sake, can't we fill the watering can in the kitchen sink?'

But Lottie had become battle-hardened and was prepared. 'We can't live in a city like Rome without plants. Or, I can't.' She ticked off a list, which included lavender, a lemon tree, herbs, roses.

'And to think all these years I've managed.' Tom was at his driest.

'Plants are necessary for a healthy life. Think about eating surrounded by lavender and roses.'

'I do. I do.'

'Good. The soul becomes sick without green around it.'

Tom was aghast. 'I had no idea you were one of those.' Lottie grinned. 'OK. Just take pity on the person, almost certainly me, who'll be carrying the bloody things up the stairs.'

CHAPTER TWO

LOTTIE HAD BEEN SCHEDULED TO TAKE UP HER POST AT THE *Archivio Espatriati* on return from honeymoon but there was a glitch. The outgoing chief archivist (who, it was rumoured, had links to the government) had been scheduled to retire before Lottie's arrival and to disappear gracefully to his villa at Tivoli, but was still in post.

'It's tricky,' Lottie messaged Helena and Peter. 'And complicated in a magical Italian way. It goes something like this … my predecessor has neglected to file tax returns. He can't get his pension without them. In order to hand them in, he has to be at the tax office in person. There are several tax offices but no one can tell him which one he should go to …'

Both Valerio Gianni, the director, and her predecessor were embarrassed and apologetic. They begged Lottie not to consult her lawyer as 'all would be arranged *senza problemi*'. Valerio presented her with a bunch of flowers.

She ignored the request and established contact with her lawyer, Signora Bruni, who could only advise that the process would take time.

An agreement was hammered out. Lottie would be allocated a temporary office, with the understanding she could roam through the archive as part of her preliminary preparations. As soon as the furniture for the office could be arranged, she would start. Valerio Gianni shrugged. 'Maybe a week, maybe not.'

Tom envied Lottie's unexpected freedom. 'This is your chance, Lottie,' he said. 'Go and explore. Enjoy. Get to know Rome. Be seduced by her.' He took her hands in his. 'Be careful, though. There are no-go areas.'

Having lived in Rome for fifteen years and possessed of a sharp curiosity ('nosiness' said his harder-hearted friends), Tom knew a lot about the city and the Romans – her history, her restaurants, feral cats, paintings and traffic bottlenecks.

'To live *da romani*,' he said, 'is to live fully and sweetly.'

He believed it. He really believed it, and Lottie was halfway to believing it, too.

'Come with me?'

He wrapped his arms around Lottie. 'If I can, I will.'

Lottie took to the Roman streets and the tourist buses, and it turned out to be a pilgrimage of discovery – the classical ruin, the elaborate church, the boastful palazzo, the street fountain, the seduction of Roman ice cream, the shops.

'It's quite a feat,' she observed to Tom. 'Those cabin-sized shops can stuff in amazing amounts of sausage, pasta and cheese.'

It was a similar story at the corners and crossroads, where the kiosks were stacked with postcards and publications with eye-watering headlines. In the mornings, the daily pantomime of traffic trying to squeeze through thoroughfares created originally to take nothing bigger than the average Roman chariot got off to a rip-roaring start and was lent a wilder edge by the anarchic Roman parking habits.

Before long, an unfamiliar, almost dreamy, compliance flooded through Lottie's veins. Why be in a rush to take up the job? Signora Bruni would conduct negotiations. All would be well.

However, the summons had arrived and Lottie was now walking to the *Archivio Espatriati*.

Turning left, she encountered a stonemason mending a wall. 'Tack, tack, tack' went his hammer. A dog barked, a child cried, 'Mamma.' And again, with an irritable longing, '*Mamma.*'

She passed a bakery where a row of family-sized loaves, resembling cushions with rounded edges, were arranged on the shelves. A few doors down, she stopped at the café-bar and ordered a coffee and a pastry and ate and drank while the sun played on her back. It was the time of year when the swifts winged in from Africa; Tom had told her to listen out for their calls.

The ironwork chair left patterns on her thighs. The traffic alternately flowed and snarled; a child ran down the street balancing an ice cream in each hand. It was a combination of the transient with the enduring – and it all could disappear with the snap of a snarky Roman goddess's fingers.

Her phone rang. Peter.

'Just checking.'

She laughed delightedly. 'Hang on.' She photoed her half-eaten pastry. 'Sending pic to make you envious.'

'I feel the drama of the city from here.'

'Drama *was* here. A bombing,' she said. 'It was horrible, and Tom had to deal with the aftermath.'

'Is he a Boy Scout, too?' The lightness of Peter's tone hinted that his scepticism about Tom was ongoing.

'Those involved were colleagues.'

There was a small pause.

Pantomime. Noise. Feel. More noise. Ancient stones under her sandalled feet. Toneless and without pulse Rome was not … and would never be. 'I think I'll end up being happy here,' she said.

'Only think?'

'I'm sinking into her.'

'And the rest?'

He meant Tom, the job, the ghost of Clare.

'All very fine.'

'Very or *very*?'

Lottie felt a rush of homesickness and scolded herself. 'I may love Rome, but I *miss* you,' she said.

Later, she crossed the street, dodging a cyclist intent on murder. She stood gazing after the homicidal rider. What if she had been killed like those who had been in the bomb?

Her mood darkened and a shadow cast itself over the scene, and she was reminded of the darker places in any city – its sewers and marshlands. Its tenements. The places, even affluent ones, where screams were not unknown. And the places and times when bombs exploded and extremism thrived.

The Via Giulia had been named after a pope, which Lottie was sorry about. It would have been so much more interesting for it to have been a testament to a Roman matron who had had a wild sex life and a vicious grip on power behind the scenes.

Its surface was cobbled, and substantial pink-, ochre- and yellow-painted buildings rose on either side. She stopped to look at the Mascherone fountain, which was reputed to run with wine at civic celebrations, and at the former jail, now an anti-Mafia headquarters, and spent a moment outside the church of Santa Maria dell'Orazione e Morte, whose funds had been collected in order to bury unclaimed corpses, including those found in the Tiber.

A couple of buildings down from Santa Maria, the burnt-umber *Archivio Espatriati* rose four storeys high. Like many Roman buildings, it was constructed around a courtyard accessed through an archway, and she stopped to ready herself before she passed under it.

A Paul Cursor, from the Medieval department, had been deputed to give her a tour and to show her to her makeshift office.

Afterwards, they bought coffee and took it up to her office. He seemed embarrassed by Lottie's predicament. 'Things can take time here,' he said.

He told her about the retired American general who had set up the *Espatriati*. Rattling with medals, the general had turned up in Rome in the early seventies, a trip he declared had been 'to chase up the memories'. Apparently, these stretched right back to 1948, when he had been in Rome with a mission to hunt down ex-Nazis lying low in the city, waiting for travel permits to be forged in the backstreets to countries willing to offer them sanctuary.

Of middle height and middle-aged, with soft, thinning hair and a terrible haircut, Paul had come across, at first, as nice but a little colourless. But he came to life narrating the story, which Lottie enjoyed relaying to Tom while they ate dinner. 'The Ratline,' she told him. 'It was very efficient. There are rumours that both the Church and the CIA recruited these ex-Nazis and washed their records clean if they agreed to fight Communism.'

Tom helped himself to a glass of wine. 'I like the sound of Paul. He has a vivid imagination.'

What was not in dispute was that, during the Nazi occupation of Rome, documents, of all denominations and provenances, had been thrown into crates, nailed down and stowed in a cave to the south of the city. Over the years, additional records had been piled in with them, including those of foreign nationals.

There they remained, disordered and decaying, until the general rode to the rescue.

An orderly man, as he informed all who would listen, he had been appalled by the predicament of such 'a trove of intelligence', and needed – *goddammit* – to do something about it. His first move was to raise the funds for the establishment and running of a professional archive to house all the papers of British and American ex-pats and to make provision for past, present and future records. Other nationals would have to look after themselves. The funds had been raised – 'it was surprising how many people could spare a dime' – and the *Archivio Espatriati*, a strictly private operation with a mixed staff of Italians, Americans and British, had come to be well regarded and well used.

The building chosen on the Via Giulia had been abandoned since the war. It was easily divided into departments and had the incomparable advantage of a vaulted cellar running the length of the building, which was converted into storage for the archive. Systems had been installed to maintain a cool, stable temperature and to keep the humidity to a minimum.

'Why would a starred American general concern himself with an archive?' Lottie asked Tom. 'And why would anyone give money?'

'That's easy. Read the inscription to him over the entrance. And you can bet your life it wasn't people who coughed up the dimes, it was institutions.'

'I don't blame him for craving a touch of immortality.'

Tom placed a hand on her shoulder. It was one of those moments when she was unsure what he intended by the gesture – a manifestation of the areas of uncertainty in an infant marriage. Things unsaid, inflections misinterpreted, intentions unfathomed.

Reaching up, she entwined her fingers in his. 'That much money …? It's—'

Tom interrupted her. 'Could we move to the bedroom?'

He spoke lightly and with anticipation. Lottie was not going to say no but afterwards, half dressed and brushing her hair in the mirror, she wondered if it had been a deliberate ploy? She raised a bare arm and observed (thank goodness) how the flesh under her arm tightened. 'Were you trying to not answer my question?'

Tom was still prone on the bed. 'Probably,' he murmured. 'You could be a painting by Bonnard. All lush and tremulous.'

The settled light in the room, Tom's rumpled hair and naked legs, the subdued blue gleam of the coverlet also suggested an artist's composition.

Lottie smiled at him through the mirror. 'Back at you.'

The makeshift office at the *Espatriati* turned out to have a large window, a good-sized desk and a well-used office chair.

The building's past was obvious in the plaster work and substantial fireplace. *Good for the general*, she thought, *and his craving for a little bit of immortality*, although she was still intrigued as to why he would choose an archive as his vehicle. Maybe it had been Mrs General who had been on the case. Maybe it had been she (who had been left behind countless times in the boondocks while Herb or Norm strutted the battlefield) who said, 'There's an opportunity here to get your name in lights.'

She unpacked archival polyester pockets and sleeves, plus silver-safe paper for photographs. She held one up between her finger and thumb. Archival records were judged not only as a collection of individual documents but also on their relationship to other records. Which order did they arrive in? Who donated them? Why? These factors were crucial in deciding their significance.

Having stowed the materials, she drank some of the fancy mineral water that had been left on a tray and turned her attention to the documents.

A trestle table ran almost the length of the back wall, positioned away from the direct light, trapping a familiar nosegay of foxed paper, damp cardboard and must. On it was arranged the latest papers to be exhumed from the warehouse.

A temporary label read: *British Nationals, 1880–1980: Mortalities: Homicides, Suspected Homicides, Suicides.*

The documents had rotted over the years, and their stench grew more marked as the room warmed up. The paradox of decay, Lottie reflected, was that it indicated that life had once been present and it should not be vilified. Decay was a process that worked in the shadowlands before the memory of someone, or something, was extinguished.

Homicides, Suspected Homicides, Suicides …

What must Rome have been like post-war? Smashed and sour with violence and enmity like much of Europe? And later, during the sixties and seventies, when political tensions savaged the country, did it shed its stylishness and atmosphere? They were the decades, Tom had told her, in a tone suggesting deep significance, that had been nicknamed 'The Years of Lead'.

'An odd term,' she'd commented.

'It refers to the huge number of shootings. At times, it was bad. Really bad.'

'Fascinating, isn't it, how far belief can push you?'

'Well,' Tom had said, 'all of us are guilty one way or another of small fanaticisms.'

Curious, Lottie had done some research. In 1978, the political divisions and social tensions had culminated in the kidnapping and murder of the former Prime Minister, Aldo Moro, a dominant politician in what was in practice a one-party state. Some called him the 'master-weaver' of Italian politics. The year after his death – 1979 – had been even worse, with over six hundred attacks.

Italians had enjoyed many freedoms, including press freedom, but when they voted it was known that it could only have one result: victory for the Christian Democrats; legitimate opposition, such as the Communist Party, was denied any power.

She had discussed it with Tom. 'But if the Socialists and Communists had made real headway in an election …?'

His answer had been guarded. 'It's likely that Washington would never have allowed it. During the Cold War, no western European country could display even a residual loyalty to Moscow.'

'So,' Lottie had said, 'the realities of power.'

Tom was always pragmatic. 'In its way, it worked in Italy. The Communists ran some of the regions and did so efficiently. Everyone got along until Moro tried to make an agreement with the Communists by which they would support the government in a national crisis. No one liked that.'

Moro wrote to his wife from his captivity and castigated the politicians and power brokers who had failed to come to his aid – including the Holy See, which refused to negotiate with terrorists. In a final paragraph of his last letter, he wrote of 'the inexpressible joy you gave me during my life, of the child I took such pleasure in watching and whom I shall watch to the last …'

Lottie had found it difficult to read. 'It doesn't matter who you are, does it? It's your family you think about at the end and …'

'And?'

'Very often your debts.'

Tom had laughed.

Dust spilled from the papers on the table's surface. Unless unavoidable, materials must never be directly handled. Lottie unpacked her hand-held vacuum cleaner and siphoned it up.

The first task – she glanced at the sun shining outside the window – was to create the Item List as defined by international standards, which involved Reference Codes and precise descriptions.

Allocating the papers a code, she wrote *Mortalities: British Nationals, 1880–1980* on a label, dated it and began.

At the start, she had not understood what had drawn her to becoming an archivist. Older and wiser, she realised that unconscious wishes operated cunningly with the conscious will: she had chosen the profession because she needed its order and rules and it was a way of engaging with humanity without meeting it.

How ironic, then, that this paper engagement turned out to be far from arid and distanced but a daily confrontation with every shade of emotion and behaviour. The documents were a portal into lives and thoughts. In them, Lottie encountered the cruel, the innovative, the violent, passionate, duplicitous, bigoted, corrupt, the altruistic and the loving.

She had learned to interrogate those voices. Who are you? Are you a woman observing from the sidelines? Or are you the man fired up by his religion to the exclusion of sense? Did you live well or badly? Perhaps you are a corrupt leader or a worker who died from careless employer practices?

What people wrote could be quite different from what they thought. What they said could be far from the truth. What they believed on paper could be the reverse of the slippery ambitions in their souls.

Mortalities. She bent over the papers to take a closer look. A puff of dust sifted on to the bench and she wiped it away.

A cursory examination revealed that a percentage of material was too damaged by water and fire for redemption. Isolated words loomed up from the fragments … '*amore*', 'blood', 'political'.

They would be collected up and a decision would be taken later as to their disposal.

Back at her desk, she checked the summary of the file's contents. They included records of homicide cases – sometimes the originals, sometimes copies of what was in the police files. Documentation of circumstantial and anecdotal evidence was also included.

She began.

Shimmering below the statistics and stark reports, a picture emerged of an accomplished and fascinating seductress, aka Rome, whose riches and pleasures could be overwhelming and occasionally fatal.

British Nationals died from natural causes over the decades but, decoding the figures for the early twentieth century, there was a case to be made of 'come to Rome and die'. Some were claimed by 'Pontine Fever' (almost certainly malaria), others had swum ill-advisedly in the Tiber and contracted virulent bacterial infections. There was substantial turn-of-the-century mortality from TB, measles and polio. Later on, the death rate levelled, only to go haywire during the Second World War, midway through which the records went blank.

During the late forties and fifties, the murder rate for British and American nationals picked up. A toxic brew of revenge, vendetta and privation in a feral, post-war vacuum? She checked online to see if there were papers on the subject, and ordered up a promising-sounding one by a professor of epidemiology.

In 1952, the British husband of an American film star working at Cinecittà had been found suffocated by his own socks in a hotel bathroom and his male lover had been strangled with a dressing-gown cord. His widow had immediately flown home, leaving a multimillion-dollar film in limbo. Later sightings of her reported – in the immortal words of Noël Coward – that her dark hair 'had turned gold with grief'.

In 1960, Carol Enderby was driven into a tree by her jealous Italian lover. Both died.

Lottie wrote: *Carol Enderby. 1 Folder. Papers and loose photographs.*

Then there was the fashion designer who had been found suffocated in the therapeutic mud in the beauty parlour that she frequented ... and a couple of so-called American businessmen who had each been taken out by a single shot to the head in the early seventies. *Four Folders. Damaged papers. Possible disposal.*

By the end of the day, she had done an initial survey and categorisation of the material to be allocated to the respective departments.

Two large boxes remained outstanding. A temporary label had been attached to both: *Nina Maria Lawrence, 1940–78. No known contacts. No known issue. No claimants.*

The information checked Lottie. It was bald and unforgiving. To have no one to attend to matters after your death suggested that you had had no one during your life. Therein lay tragedy? Abandonment? Neglect? A hatred of other humans? Terrible poverty and exile? It was a sad dereliction and she was sorry for it.

She thought of her new life, and of Tom, with relief.

Paul Cursor came down from his office on the third floor with a package. 'I'm interrupting ...'

She shook her head.

'I hope you don't object.' Paul was a little hesitant, which, after a second or two, she put down to good manners rather than nervousness.

Lottie dusted her fingers. 'I'm sure I won't.'

'We did a quick check on some of the material before you arrived.' He pointed to the first Nina Lawrence box. 'That one contained what might be a valuable painting from a manuscript.'

'The woman who appears to have had no one?' Lottie was both surprised and intrigued.

'Seems so. It's been put into a frame for protection. I took the liberty of booking an appointment with Gabriele Ricci for you to check it out with him.' He handed over an additional folder. 'This is from a colleague. Take a look if you wish. It's about Bonnie Prince Charlie's daughter. Rather poignant. She stuck by him to the end, despite the drink and his cruelty to her. Ricci's been briefed on it.' Again the good-mannered hesitation. 'Ten o'clock tomorrow,' he said.

She opened the folder. The letter requiring conservation was safely encased in acid-free paper. There was also a second document. 'And this one?'

Paul was almost at the door and turned back, features taut with concern. 'Apologies, I forgot. It had got attached to the painting and is to go back into the Lawrence box.'

Dated 12 January 1976, it was a typed receipt written on crested writing paper.

Commission to landscape and plant a garden
of approx. 2 acres. Detailed drawings to be
submitted.

Overall concept: to create 'garden rooms'

1) English garden to include hollyhocks and
roses

2) Walled medieval one to include regularly
spaced fruit trees (apricots and pomegranates),
box hedging and lavender

3) A cypress avenue

4) Lemon trees in terracotta pots

5) Travertine paving

Paid to Nina Lawrence the sum of 10 thousand
lire for consultation.

The signature was indecipherable, but underneath it was an
embossed ducal coronet and a Latin motto of the Palacrino duchy.

Lottie turned it over. The writing in pencil on the reverse was
dated later and appeared to be a series of jottings. Random thoughts.
Notes. Analysis of the self. It was as if the writer was experimenting
with the idea of creating a journal but had not, as yet, decided on
its shape or form.

CHAPTER THREE

Rome
19 September 1977

Am i frightened?

I am, and I should be, but never enough to step back.

Am I lonely?

There is a difference between loneliness and aloneness (language is important here).

I am … I was used to being alone.

My work involves the piecemeal and the stealthy, but it is also an imaginative act, which I believe – must believe – is for the greater good.

Because I carry secrets, I have a power. Yet, this power is problematic because it takes hold on the psyche and addiction to the process develops.

Italy is in a mess, victim of big social and technological changes. Peasants and labourers are frustrated, the factory workers exploited. Women want divorces and fewer babies and the Church does not like it. There is anxiety about jobs. Students have turned to Communism while the state and its bureaucrats are right wing. Often fanatically.

There have been bombings, terrible ones. Unrest. Violence.

Once upon a time, I would have been on fire with the challenges of watching, reporting, and with the minute analysis of every conclusion, but things have changed.

Now, all I see is Leo smiling at me.

And all I can think of is the way he says 'Nina' when he is trying not to tell me that he loves me.

I am almost thirty-seven, which is old enough to have mastery over the unruly, selfish, greedy elements sewn into our characters. Old enough to know what is true and beautiful.

He is twenty-two and young enough to believe in goodness and duty.

When a disgruntled American buttonholed Benjamin Franklin and informed him that the happiness the new state had promised had not materialised, Franklin replied that the constitution only gave the right to *pursue* happiness and you had to catch it yourself.

So I did.

One way of dealing with trauma, with the unresolved and with loss, is to put them on paper.

There is plenty to mourn, but I will not ignore the gains – the deepening and softening of the inner self, the unsuspected capacity to love the world. Yes, despite everything, it is impossible to ignore the good. Think of the olive tree, I tell myself, after a disappointing rain-lashed spring and an arid summer, yet still producing fruit.

Leo.

'To live is an act of creativity ...' I read that as a young woman and took note. It means that, at certain moments in a life, we must search our creative imaginations, choose a path and launch on to it and, despite weeping blisters and strained muscles, continue the pilgrimage. Getting married, taking on a job, having a child, finding a cause. Choosing is the moment when we make our pattern from the events over which we have no control and impose our own story on them.

The choices also affect our death. They must do.

I know my story.

I think.

NB. The Duke and Duchess of Palacrino hobnob with the family of 'The Black Prince', Prince Borghese (d. 1974), founder of a neo-fascist organisation, *Fronte Nazionale*. During the war, he specialised in tracking down and killing hundreds of Italian Communists. The Palacrinos would like to resurrect Mussolini's Fascism. For them, democracy is a bad alternative.

I am working on their garden.

CHAPTER FOUR

THE VIA DEI BAULLARI, THE STREET OF THE COFFER MAKERS, was in the Campo Marzio district and close to the Campo de' Fiori. Lottie found it without trouble.

Gabriele Ricci's workshop had a stone arch, a large window frontage with bars and an ancient-looking door. A pair of gilt candlesticks and a majolica plate were displayed in the window on a length of green velvet. Lottie peered at them, concerned that, if the majolica plate was antique, which indeed it looked to be, the sun slanting down on to the window might damage it.

'You can't quite categorise him,' Paul Cursor had given Lottie a quick briefing. 'Book doctor, bibliophile, bookbinder and paper conservationist. But good.'

The workshop was a modest space, every wall lined from floor to ceiling with bookshelves. At first glance, it gave the appearance of being crammed, but after looking more carefully, Lottie realised that it was pin neat and orderly, which she liked. Plus, the smell of paper, leather, wood shavings and linseed oil drifting through the warm interior was very pleasant.

The shelves were modern and stacked with a selection of antiquarian and contemporary books, bound documents and files. At the back of the room a workbench was laid out with bookbinder's finishing tools, pots of resin and paint. An easel stood beside a flat-topped table occupying the centre of the room. On a separate table, coffee cups were stacked on top of a state-of-the-art espresso machine. A door at the back led into a second office and an ancient beam with burn marks stretched across the ceiling.

Gabriele Ricci was on the phone in the back room and, while she waited, Lottie inspected the books and the documents, which were in German, Italian, English and Greek.

These included several volumes of French philosophy, two editions of Ovid, three of Herodotus, and a complete set of Charles Dickens, political and religious tracts, plus a modern edition mocked up to look like the original of *Le Lettere di Margherita Datini a Francesco di Marco, 1384–1410.*

She ran a finger along the spines. These books and documents housed the exchanges between lovers, enemies, intellectuals – the men and women struggling with their impulses and tensions, the prejudices and injustices of their worlds.

Many were risk-takers and voices of conscience. Or, passionately religious and brilliantly imaginative. At the time of writing, some of them would have been at the centre of events. Others had waited a long time to be exhumed from obscurity.

How curious then, she thought. In contrast to the insistent and various voices corralled on the shelves tussling with the problems of being alive, the workshop itself felt closed and sterile – as if the richness and polemic of papers and manuscripts had been deliberately muted.

She stood in front of a copy of *The Codex Amiatinus*, an early manuscript Bible, and a voice behind her said, 'Do you wish to look at it?'

Startled, she turned around. 'If possible. I always like to hold a manuscript or book.'

'You can't *know* a work unless you handle it. No facsimile can reproduce that primary contact.'

He sounded hoarse and not particularly friendly.

The *Codex* was a facsimile. Lottie knew, as he would know, that the original was kept under lock and key. 'I agree.'

'Perhaps you have seen the original in the monastery of San Salvatore on Mount Amiata?'

'That would be awesome and, arguably, it belongs there, but it's in the Biblioteca Medicea Laurenziana in Florence.'

It had been a test.

Silence.

Lottie used it to make a snatch assessment of Gabriele Ricci. For a start, he could move quietly. Good looking but very thin. Tall. Angular face with shadows under the eyes and grey hair that had once been dark. A pallor indicated he did not go out much, and the tautly held body looked a stranger to relaxation – and to humour, perhaps.

Reverting to the previous subject, she said, 'Knowing what a manuscript weighs, what's noted in its margins, its wear and tear, the crevices in its construction *is* crucial.'

'Agreed.'

'But not always possible.' She was pleased to note a spark of interest. 'Since the great manuscripts of the world are kept under lock and key.'

'Rightly or wrongly?'

She calculated her response. He would know, as she did, that no facsimile could reproduce the essence of a manuscript. They were useful substitutes but they could never possess the smell or the texture of the real thing. No reproduction mirrored the tears, the overpainting, the patching up, the stitches and the depth of colours or the essence and feel of an original.

'Both,' she replied. 'If we agree that you cannot really understand a manuscript without holding it or inspecting it closely, then lock and key are impediments.' She gestured to his choked shelves. 'It's the great dilemma. Not handling them is to miss engaging with their inner life. Handling them is to put them at risk.'

He took a while to answer and she wondered if her Italian had been too garbled.

'It's none of my business,' she said, 'but if the plate in the window is original majolica, the sun will ruin it.'

'It isn't your business …' Nevertheless, he lowered the blind. Then, he said, 'I take it you are Signora Archer? The new archivist at the *Espatriati*?'

He knew perfectly well who she was.

'Chief archivist.' She added, 'Elect.'

He indicated a chair at the desk and sat down opposite her and said, without more ado, 'Show me.'

'Two projects.' She slid over the folder containing the letter. 'In this case, I'm the messenger. I'm afraid I can't brief you in detail.'

He lifted the tissue paper and peered at the handwriting, which, in places, was illegible.

'It's from a Lady Henrietta Forbes.' She read from the notes that Paul had emailed over.

In accented English, he read aloud. '"If goodness of heart were sufficient for the conquest of the throne, his daughter would occupy it immediately for she is goodness personified."' Gabriele looked up. 'She is?'

'Henrietta is writing about Charlotte, the daughter of Charles Edward Stuart, the Jacobite, who had tried to get back the English crown in seventeen forty-five. She was rejected by him for most of her life but came to Rome to nurse him when he was dying. Henrietta is admiring her sacrifice. As well she might. It's a lesson in forgiveness. He was a drunk and a would-be king, who ran away at a crucial point and behaved badly to his daughter.'

'She thought she would inherit something, no doubt.'

How to defend a despised daughter? Did Lottie *wish* to defend a despised daughter? 'Charlotte was kind. Henrietta says so. She stuck by him.'

He drummed his fingers on the desk. '*Il sangue non è acqua,*' he said.

Blood is thicker than water.

Yes.

Growing up, it wasn't unusual for Lottie to wake up, jaw clenched, stomach churning emptily, in a bedroom that she occupied but wasn't hers, in a house lived in by people with whom she had nothing in common.

'Henrietta died a couple of months later, probably from sepsis after cutting a finger.' Lottie reapplied herself to Paul's notes. 'The letter requires the usual treatment to stabilise it and we hope you will take it on. The terms are these.' Lottie named a sum.

'You're offering less than your predecessor.'

Lottie would not have put him down as a greedy man and she was intrigued by the tactic.

'No,' she replied. 'I checked.'

He acknowledged the point with an ink-stained finger. 'Even so, the price for my services has to go up.'

She half rose. 'The budgets are carefully set at the archive. We offer you good rates but if they are not good enough for you, we'll look elsewhere.'

The thin features tightened. 'You're new to Rome and to Italy, I think.'

'Is it so obvious?'

'Yes,' he said.

'How?'

'You don't believe that all roads lead to Rome. But you will.' He got to his feet. 'You're from the west of your country?'

'You can tell even when I'm speaking Italian?'

'I'm good at accents.'

'How many languages do you speak?'

'French, English, Spanish, a little Hungarian, Italian, of course.'

'For your work?'

'Not entirely. The winter days can be long and sometimes the work dries up.'

Not so. Paul had alerted Lottie to Gabriele Ricci's internationally respected reputation. A conservator and book restorer, he was a man on speed-dial for the major museums. He was not likely to be short of commissions.

'You are looking at me as if I'm one of your documents,' he observed, but mildly. 'Are you trying to sum me up?'

'Yes.' His eyebrows climbed. 'Doctors deal in broken bodies and psychologists in broken minds. But you, a book doctor, operate on vellum, parchment and paper.'

There was another of the long silences and she grew impatient.

Somewhere in the nearby streets, a church bell pealed. At the sound, he went over and shut the door with a bang. 'They *never* stop,' he said. '*Never.*'

'You dislike the church bells?'

'I do.'

There was another silence.

'Are you interested in the projects? Or shall I leave?'

He held out a hand.

Lottie pulled out the package and peeled away its protective covering, giving a small gasp when she caught sight of the contents.

'Beautiful ...' she managed to say. 'How very, very ... beautiful it is.'

The blue of the Virgin's cloak shimmered and burned into her vision as Gabriele Ricci lifted it up and placed it on the easel.

The painter had caught the startled Virgin at the exact moment one of the great stories of the world began, a story that would end with her losing her son in pain and violence.

Impeccable in his sanctity, robed in flowing pink, crowned and bearing a gladioli flower, the archangel winged down towards the figure reading in the garden.

A curious, almost painfully still, hush fell over the workshop.

'Inquiry,' she murmured. *Interrogatio.*

Gabriele's expression did not betray much but she knew she had caught his interest.

No expert, but Lottie knew enough to know that the fifteenth-century painter had expectations laid on him – at this period it was always 'him'. 'Wasn't there a fifteenth-century friar who preached a sermon outlining the precise emotional breakdown of the Virgin's state of mind?'

'That's correct.'

On being told the news by the beautiful, stern archangel, said Fra Roberto, Mary underwent a range of emotions from disquiet and anguished questioning of her fate to eventual submission and contemplation of the divine will.

Here she was raising her hand to ask of him: *How can this be, seeing I know not a man?*

'She's lovely,' Lottie added, admiring the balance between the materials the painter had chosen and the skill with which they were used.

'But in shock.' Gabriele Ricci, who was standing beside her, pointed to Mary's hand clutching her robe in panic.

The Virgin's face was white and shaded with grey tints; her expression reflected her youth, her innocence and submission. Judging by the architecture, the palace on the right-hand side of the painting was Italian, whereas the garden displayed a French influence. The Virgin's cloak of lapis-lazuli blue flowed over a border of periwinkle and acanthus. A rabbit with green eyes and a very white scut played by its hem and a mouse had made a home in Mary's skirts. Overhead, larks wheeled in a bright and joyous sky and, in the bottom left-hand corner where a frog and a worm co-habited under a stone, there was a suggestion of initials.

The past was the greatest of all escapologists and it was almost impossible to experience it viscerally. Taste, smell, the texture of food, stuff under your fingers, fear of God, the warmth of the sun on your back, a caress, the sound of music striking up: the experiences of these five centuries or so back could only be guessed at and never truly felt. Yet there were clues, which, if you were careful and scrupulous, made it possible to take a reading of what was there.

This artist possessed a forensic eye and an artistic sensibility fascinated by the properties of light; he understood perspective and delighted in his subject.

'Fine brushstrokes, gold highlights, unusual lighting effects.' Gabriele Ricci ticked off the points. 'I suspect that the Virgin's cloak is painted in *azur d'outremer*. Ultramarine. Incredibly expensive and only used for the Virgin and saints.'

Lottie's inner ear registered shock. Or yearning. Both? Perhaps Gabriele Ricci found his work a melancholy business?

'If you paid two florins for the Virgin's blue and one florin for the blue used in the rest of the composition you were suggesting a theological distinction,' he continued.

The blue soared.

'This was Mary's colour, chosen to convey benediction to all those who looked on it. The painter's contract would have stipulated a certain sum to buy it and it was not to be used on anything else.'

He was ensuring that Lottie was aware of his intimacy with medieval paint bases, their mixes and application and the iconography.

'Painted on vellum or parchment?' she wanted to know.

'At a guess, parchment; but I would have to examine it to be sure.' He inspected it more closely. 'Bears the hallmarks of a painting from a book of hours.'

The last was muttered, almost indistinct.

She leaned over, careful not to cloud the glass in the frame. 'A classic Annunciation.'

The painting was approximately ten or so inches high and seven inches or so wide and had a *trompe l'oeil* border of a wooden frame on which was written part of a text.

'Yes and no.' He stood back from the easel. 'It's innovative, in fact. The figures are seen in close-up and the painting takes up the entire surface of the page – two things that were still unusual in the late fifteenth century.'

'So, late fifteenth century, would you say?'

'If genuine, I would.' He seemed reluctant to be definite and she did not know him well enough to know if this was just his manner. 'But it's not possible to be sure until it's analysed.'

'And if genuine it's valuable.' She drew in a breath. 'Hugely. Very exciting.'

He shoved his hands into his pockets. 'Where was it found?'

'Among papers being worked on at the *Archivio Espatriati*. A colleague discovered it, put it in the frame and arranged to consult you.'

He nodded. 'They use me on occasions.'

Lottie turned back to the easel.

The painting was beautiful, achingly so, conveying the Virgin's confusion with a touching tenderness. The subject was an old one, had been told countless times, and the psychological drama was easy to comprehend. Unexpected pregnancy. Bewilderment. Uncertainty. And yet, it was also a complicated situation, wreathed in mystery and the perils of belief.

The old demons, and habits of thought, stirred. The ones that made her slow and heavy, instead of quick and strong and positive.

'At least …' and she spoke to herself rather than to Gabriele Ricci, '… Mary was told who her son's father was, which meant she could explain later.'

His dark gaze rested on Lottie and there was a hint of speculation. Hastily, she returned to the subject. 'Are there similarities to the work of the French masters … Fouquet, Bourdichon, Pucelle *fils*?'

He raised his eyebrows as if to say: *So you know about them?*

Lottie judged he was in his sixties – which would account for any tedious prejudices. She was in her thirties and expert in what she did, including ignoring time-wasting prejudice.

'They were much sought after and often highly paid,' she said coolly, raking through her memory, which was generally excellent. 'Three years ago, there was a stir in the art world over a book of hours commissioned by a Renaissance duke; it was hoped that it was a Pucelle *fils* that had gone missing for centuries.'

'There was,' he said, extracting a jeweller's loupe from the drawer. 'I was consulted. The paintings bore no resemblance to Pucelle's.'

'But he was in Italy?'

'Fouquet and Bourdichon worked almost exclusively in France but we do know that Pucelle *fils* was commissioned to paint a book of hours for Chiara, Duchess of Palacrino, in the fourteen nineties.'

'So?' The possibility breathed from her.

'This suggests he was probably in Italy, and records in Paris appear to confirm that he was. But the book of hours that he was commissioned to paint was never found. There are a couple of full-page miniatures in museums, including one here in Rome, a few ascribed to his studio and plenty of forgeries.'

'So …' she said again, calculating the odds.

His loupe inched over the painting and she noticed his fingers trembled.

'And?' Lottie checked her impatience. 'Apologies. I know these things take time.'

He stepped back. 'Some of the characteristics are evident. If it is a forgery, it's a good one. If a pastiche, a respectful one.'

'What about paint analysis?'

'That would be the next step.'

Technically, since it formed part of an archive, the painting came under the remit of the *Archivio Espatriati*. If it proved to be genuine, it would trigger the attention of the art world and, almost certainly, problems. Whatever its status, it would require skilled treatment.

Gabriele passed his loupe over to Lottie. 'Do you know much about Pucelle *fils*?'

'Not enough, clearly.'

'It's never too late.'

'I'll do some research.'

She edged the loupe over the painting. At the bottom right-hand of the page was a minute splatter of red on the painted frame.

'Blood?'

'It happened,' said Gabriele. 'The painter or the scribe might cut themselves, but the painting was too valuable to throw away.'

Water, blood, paint ... Lottie encountered the wear and tear left by human beings on a daily basis. 'All that toil, only to cut your finger and face ruin.'

He shrugged. 'Went with the job.' He peered at the painting. '*Dio*.'

'Is there something wrong?'

'Nothing.' But his knuckles had whitened. 'A twinge in my back, that's all.' Then he fell silent before saying: 'I can certainly look into this for you. I'll fetch the logbook.'

He disappeared into the room at the back of the workshop. She heard him move around. A telephone rang and a quick-fire conversation ensued in an unfamiliar dialect.

She took up the loupe. What had alarmed Gabriele Ricci? Bending close to the painting, she realised she had missed something.

Behind the seated Virgin, a rose scrambled over the garden fence and, behind that, a woman with long blonde hair and a tonsured man dressed in the Franciscan habit knelt on the grass. She was weeping and his hands were raised in supplication. The cartouche issuing from his mouth read: *Obsecro te*. I beseech you.

In the distance, the towers and buildings of the hilltop city were tucked behind an undulating wall. Beyond was a plain consisting of fields and marshes and dotted with classical ruins. The track leading towards the mountain was thickly hemmed with marjoram, blue flax and wild dog rose. Towering in the furthest background was a mountain with flower-smothered foothills threaded through by a path. Toiling up the path were the same woman and the friar.

A white dove circled above them.

'*Paese et aiere*,' said Gabriele, emerging from the backroom. 'A medieval term for landscape and skies. At that period, the painter was instructed to include landscape and sometimes told which animals to include.' He gave the slightest of smiles. 'The olives are painted in *verte de flambé*. The fields are ochre and sienna.'

Lottie was enchanted. 'It's like poetry.'

The lens of the loupe had become smeared with her breath, and the two figures blurred and moved as they ascended towards the solid gold sun in the centre of the sky.

Lottie found herself there, with the stones crunching under her feet, the sunstrike on her back, the sweat under her arms. She sensed their fear and yearning and their desperate need for speed.

Her hand came to a halt and the figures stilled, locking her out from their drama.

'An example of the travel-landscape characteristic, much used during this period,' she said, adding drily, 'That I do know.' She looked up and was struck by his haunted expression.

He turned away to stoop over the painting. 'I think we must agree that this is a sophisticated painter.' He straightened up. 'Where was this found?' he asked. 'Which papers?'

Her finger hovered over the figure of the Virgin. Skill and tenderness rose from the page like perfume. Painted into it was the mighty whoosh of the archangel's wings ... the flourishing city ... the mysteries of the steep, crevassed mountain ... the drama of the woman and the friar, whose flight provided a contrast to the delicate girl's submission in a garden.

'I've only just taken up my post at the archive, but the painting was found in the papers of an Englishwoman. A Nina Lawrence.'

His face was ashen.

Lottie returned to the archive reflecting on the girl sitting in the garden, awaiting a troubled but astonishing future.

Back at her desk, she ignored the waiting emails and did some research on Pucelle *fils*.

The youngest son of the acclaimed French master Jean Pucelle, Pucelle *fils* (as he was always known) was born in Tours around 1457 and died in Palacrino, near Rome, around 1503.

At this period, the Loire Valley was the principal centre for the French court and a cultural powerhouse producing illuminated books. Two master French painters, Jean Fouquet and Jean Poyet, worked at the court, and Pucelle *fils* learned his trade in Jean Fouquet's workshop.

The painter's presence at court ensured that he was exposed to a variety of influences and extensive contact with the royal family and rich and powerful aristocratic families. His work spanned twenty years and included the innovative *Hours of Yseult de Valois*. In demand all over Europe, he was unusual in being able to command high fees from his patrons, who wished to have masterpieces for their collections.

Characteristics of his work included: adopting the device of painting a frame around his paintings, a palette of twelve or more colours, a fondness for highlighting hair and drapery with gold and a marked use of white lead.

So far, so promising.

She ran over future procedure. Authentication. Establishing provenance. If authentic, the decision where to sell it.

The first question must be: who was Nina Lawrence? And how likely was it that she had been the possessor of an original Pucelle *fils?*

Lottie pulled on her gloves and tackled the first of the boxes.

Inside was a mound of dank material, compressed together by age and mishandling. Working with extreme care, she removed each document one by one, prising apart with tweezers those that were stuck together. A photo. Letters. A dried flower pressed between paper. Certificates and reports.

Last to be lifted from the box was a bulging brown-leather A5 notebook, tied up with string. The jacket was stained and foxed, and the pages, plus many additional papers slotted between them, had swelled it to over twice its normal size.

Lottie eased it on to the table. Mould had slid into the cracks, and the string had impressed marks like burns onto the leather.

She prowled around it and took photographs from several angles.

Having cut the knot, she opened it.

Gently, professionally, she turned the pages.

There were close-written entries. Botanical drawings. Pressed flowers. Letters. Photographs.

A life.

CHAPTER FIVE

Rome
1 January 1978

SCRIBBLING NOTES ON SCRAPS IS NEVER SATISFACTORY AND I made the decision to buy this notebook, splashing out to get the best quality I could afford. A beautiful object … it has waited for me. Until I had breath, until I could snatch the time.

What has happened to me was not planned but, because it has happened, I wish to record it, question it. People who do what I do regularly undergo different forms of interrogation and self-interrogation. This will be no different.

Unwise, yes. Dangerous, yes, but I live with the threat of danger. It directs how I live and drives my psyche. It is the black hem that borders my days. I fully understand that I *crave* it. The job I do is for life – and for death.

So be it.

Two years ago a joyous spring rolled into the city and Leo (not his real name) sat down on the steps of a church in a street close to the Campo de' Fiori. Legs out, sleeves rolled up, enjoying the warmth. Everything about him shrieked student liberated from study, free to sit in the sun. As it turned out, I guessed right.

I was on my way to light a candle in the chapel of the Virgin. Why would a robust atheist do that? *God knows* is the answer, unless it offered me reassurance that, somewhere, light should burn in a country that had many dark areas. Italy was in trouble: a right-wing government with no effective opposition clashing with a growing number of Communist voters. Violence, bombings and corruption. There are many good and sane people in Italy, many of whom fought to remain sensible, moderate citizens, but it was hard. My business was, in part, to peer between the cracks and see what lay underneath.

Also, Rex found the church a convenient place to meet and I had grown fond of it. A candle never did any harm, and it could very well be an insurance.

Preoccupied with these thoughts, I failed to notice Leo's outstretched legs, tripped over them and landed on a knee. The jolt made my eyes water and it took me a few moments to get up. I managed to apologise and hoped I hadn't hurt him.

He got to his feet and said it was his fault. On closer inspection, he was indoor-pale and rather beautiful.

We examined the damage. He said he didn't mind being tripped over and insisted I should sit down so my knee could recover.

I needed a minute or two.

The sun was warm, the smart in my knee subsided, but a serious bruise was in the making and we ended up in a café. We drank our coffees and continued talking while the city churned and the swifts came diving in from Africa. He had completed a three-year degree in philosophy in Bologna and had come to Rome for the next phase of his life in the seminary.

A priest? I was startled and disturbed by the idea.

It will be long and demanding, he told me with a relish that made me shiver inwardly.

I looked across the café table and forced myself not to say: *You're far too young and energetic to be locked up behind church walls.*

He appeared to read my thoughts and said that it was not a problem for him and he had always known.

I digested that one and questioned the 'always', and he told me that, in his family, the youngest son was expected to become the priest.

The determinism made it worse.

He said that life's lottery was like that.

I had seen and done many things, but his fate seemed depressing. It was none of my business but I suggested – tentatively – that he could have decided to do something else.

The fact that you are pointed along a way does not necessarily make it the wrong way or one you do not wish to take, he told me. He wolfed the wafer that came with the coffee and I offered up mine.

There was no greater calling, he added … no greater service than to minister to others.

It was a stock-in-trade sentiment but it struck me as odd that he didn't mention God.

I said that his family would be pleased.

He looked at me carefully and seriously and said that he was lucky to have a strong, loving family and to be able to serve it. Didn't I think that too?

I could think of several reasons why not.

He switched the subject and asked me about my work and I told him about a recent trip to a large estate in Tuscany and the garden that was being scooped out of a parched valley.

The plan for it happened to be in my bag; he professed interest and I showed it to him. I told him that my clients were a little bitter about the situation because the land used to be run on the old *mezzadria* system, which suited them fine until the Communists began to demand changes in the 1960s. After that, there was a drift to the cities and, now, they struggle to employ anyone.

He scrutinised the plan, which showed boundaries and sources of water. He jabbed his finger confidently down and said I should plant the olives there. When I asked him why, he replied that it would be the driest area in the garden. He was right.

Had I made friends with the soil? If not, I must get to understand it as I would my own body.

I stared at him.

Take care over the water supply, he warned, and instructed me to guard it because, if not, others would help themselves.

This chimed with stories of water rustling that I had already heard and I laughed and thanked him.

His family were all farmers, working on an estate north of Rome, and his earliest memories were of being taken by his mother into the fields to work with the vines and the olives. At this point, his voice dropped and he let slip that his mother had recently died.

The way he said it suggested a loss to which he was not reconciled and I told him (presuming, perhaps, as I barely knew him) that I could tell that he had loved her very much.

He shot me a look and asked if my mother was still alive.

I told him that I had no family to speak of.

There was a pause and then we carried on talking.

Perhaps we both already understood that we were intrinsically solitary people and destined to remain so. (His vocation. Mine.) Yet he talked at length about his mother and of how he would have done anything to prevent her suffering. 'I was powerless,' he said.

I stopped myself from asking if he found his God had helped.

I thought I was now expert at masking my thoughts but, clearly, I wasn't. Midway through describing his future training, he stopped and said he could see I didn't approve.

I had to give it to him: he possessed the empathy of a good priest.

'My mother used to say it was best to air the room even if the enemy is at the door ...' He played with the wafer wrapping.

I looked at those fingers. Strong ones, but a little pale from long study and in need of the outdoor life.

Why would he give up what is so precious – the right to individuality, personality, the idea of whom one was, or might be – when so many in the world are denied those choices?

Again, he seemed to sense my thoughts and told me that he didn't see it as giving anything up.

I could have told him that I was intimate with the process of taking apart the personality. I could list the tools by which mindset, habit and urges are dissolved and laid out, like so many jigsaw pieces, and what it really means. He had a right to know if his surrender was to be irreversible. Which, presumably, he did? Think of the boat hovering on the edge of a high waterfall, I might say, and what happens next.

I ducked it and remained silent.

Instead, I snatched a look at him. He was brimming with energy, with humour, with life.

I asked him if it was true that, as a priest, he must never ever again claim anything for himself, so that nothing would come between him and God?

He nodded.

It was odd how the clichés tumbled. Our eyes met. I felt the frisson and the untidy yearnings that I would have given much not to feel.

He shifted in his seat. *It's not possible,* he informed me without words. *Not you and I.*

In those days, Leo may have been unworldly but there was also a hint of steel. I liked that and I believed him.

It was peculiar, but the spring air made me feel I was poised to fly and I felt shaky and exhilarated in the same breath. I reached over to the adjacent table, kidnapped the wafer left by its previous occupant and presented it to him, telling him that I wished him the best and that I hoped he wouldn't be lonely in the city.

He snaffled the wafer in one bite, which made me smile, but in the next minute the smile was wiped from my lips because he told me that his uncle, Beppo, worked in the Vatican.

My God.

I remember staring at Leo and feeling nausea stir.

I wished he hadn't told me that piece of information.

I managed to ask him where his uncle worked and he replied vaguely that he dealt with legal matters.

The Vatican City State is the organisation that administers the temporal and diplomatic concerns of the Holy See, which, in turn, is responsible for the worldwide Catholic Church. It has many departments and to have a contact in any of them would be very valuable.

Apparently this Beppo, who is only a few years older than Leo, is clever and trusted and has a brilliant career lying ahead of him.

I grabbed at any old thing to say as I packed the garden design into my bag. Something along the lines that the Palacrino operation would be a big one and I thanked him for the irrigation warning.

His parting remark was the remark of someone born and bred on the farm. 'Water is the most important thing. In the future, the world will go to war over it.'

Rex, to whom I reported, and I had often discussed finding a long-term contact in the Vatican City State. Over the years we had cultivated a couple. The first had inconveniently died and the second had gone to serve in Lisbon. But we still needed to know what was going on in the inner circles and who was pulling the levers.

I knew what Rex would ask me to do. *Get in there. Put a foot in the door.*

I could.

Would I?

CHAPTER SIX

So absorbed was she by this, Lottie had to remind herself that she was in the *Espatriati* office and not drinking coffee at a table with Nina and Leo.

The notebook felt alive between her gloved hands, strong and sentient.

She leafed through the pages.

Rome? Beautiful and wayward, a place on to which you project many longings – poetic, erotic, aesthetic – and hope they will be met. She has allure and seduction and many faces. Lifestyle, fashion, art, sensation. Plenty of sensation. This is where stardust mixes with the sensual. Lies down with it, you might conclude. The chic with the classical. The acme of modernity with ruins that stretch back through several civilisations.

She had a strange feeling that Nina Lawrence was speaking directly to her. *You are here. You must try to live properly. It will take effort. Patience. Mistakes. Understanding.*

Lottie read on.

Ten years ago, when I arrived, I found it harder to settle here than other places. I couldn't put my finger on it. My rooms in the Via della Luce were airy and appealing. They had good bones, lovely proportions and a plaster cornice, and were sparsely furnished, which I preferred.

Maybe, it was the lift, in which I am convinced lives a hostile spirit. (Or the *portiere*'s inability to get it fixed?) Some days, it's mysteriously locked and I am forced to obtain the key from the spiteful teenage girl in the basement. Once, she asked me to pay to ferry my shopping up. You can imagine my answer. Sometimes, it gets the bit between its teeth, spits out sparks and judders to a halt. Usually on the wrong floor.

Perhaps, my unease reflected the political situation in the country.

Leo calls it *dietrologia*. 'It's the theory,' he says, 'that behind all significant political events, acts of terror or even disaster, lies a shadowy network of puppet masters … politicians, secret services, business moguls, freemasons … pulling the strings for their own corrupt purposes.'

Replacing the notebook and the documents in the correct order in the box, Lottie stowed it on the bench.

Slicing tomatoes in the kitchen that evening, Lottie discussed Gabriele Ricci with Tom. 'He wanted more money.'

'He's bluffing,' said Tom, resting his chin on her shoulder. 'It's the way.'

Lottie's instinct was that Gabriele Ricci was not a man who went in for the theatre of negotiation. 'He didn't seem the type.'

'If he's Roman, he is.'

She swivelled around and pressed her cheek against his. Tom was warm, firm and she loved the smell of him – and she wanted to imprint it all in her memory because she knew that you could never take anything good and nice for granted. 'Strange man. He reacted badly to a church bell.'

'Living in Rome is a tricky one,' said Tom. 'You end up half a libertine, half a priest.'

'Do you favour one or the other?'

'Guess.'

Later in the evening, a text flashed up on her mobile: *Your terms are acceptable. The projects are under way. Gabriele Ricci.*

Lottie rolled her eyes at Tom. 'You were right.'

'Of course.' He was enjoying his small triumph.

She was woken in the early hours by him calling out, 'Clare.'

Her cheeks stung as if they had been slapped.

She lay flat on her back and gazed up at the dark ceiling, her emotions churning. Clare had lived and slept with Tom for a long time, and, in sleep, memory, which is at best disobedient, could be wilful.

'What are you thinking?' Tom's voice sounded through the dark.

She turned her head. 'You were calling out for Clare.'

Tom put out his hand. 'Was I? Oh crap. I'm sorry. I don't know why.'

They lay with his hand resting on her shoulder and listened to distant traffic. But there was unease between them and a phantom of his past lover.

Tom said softly, 'Lottie, I'm sorry. Very sorry. Do you believe me?'

It had taken Lottie several wrong turnings, and periods of anguish, before she had learned that the mind took its time to absorb a loss, or a trauma, and that disturbances manifested themselves long after that loss had taken place.

It would be the same for Tom.

Then she remembered Peter and his questions. *Is Tom real? Or the too-good-to-be-true real?* Had she made a muddle by marrying Tom? 'Tom, are you worrying about something? The bomb? Safety? Money?'

He cradled her shoulder with a hand. 'No.'

Lottie punched the pillow and sat up. 'Tom … tell me more about your work.'

'You know the Council works to bring together different cultures.'

'Are you being deliberately vanilla?'

'OK. I'm killing myself to organise the annual Pontignano Conference, which brings together leaders from business, politics and academia. The point is to talk, which a lot of them will, interminably, and to find accommodations, which are few and far between. We are talking human beings here, not sensible animals. But from those small connections we can build.'

She sensed an evasion, a practised one.

Tom sounded sleepy. 'Why don't you come? Clare did once but she was bored.'

Without warning, she was soaked in jealousy. She bent her legs up and hooked her arms around them. 'Right.' She took a deep breath. 'Did Clare leave Rome?'

A cat yowled in the courtyard. 'She's still here,' he admitted. 'She has a good job. So does her new partner.'

'Which is?'

'In the Vatican press office.'

'Ah.' Lottie closed her eyes briefly. 'Thought you had to be a Catholic.'

'She is. Technically. Lottie … I've upset you. But Clare *has* gone.'

He was so full of remorse that she softened. She lay back down and entwined her fingers in his. 'Is it OK etiquette to say that's good?'

'Excellent etiquette.'

His grip tightened. 'My turn. Any regrets?'

Lottie made him wait for her answer. He had hurt her and it would take a little time to fade.

True, deep understanding of each other would take years, many incidents, sharp exchanges, when, no doubt, the love between them would sour and thin and then, if they wished, renew itself. Inevitably, marriage changed the settings of an affair and there would be wounds and longueurs to weather. They might, at times and for long periods, take each other for granted.

'Lottie?' Tom propped himself up.

She reached up and pulled him down and rolled on top of him. 'You're going to have to prove how sorry you are.' She ran her hand down his bare flank, feeling his smooth skin under her fingers.

At the end, it was her name that he muttered into her ear. Covered in sweat and sweetly satiated, she lay back on the pillows and fell instantly asleep.

'Rome is divided into *rioni* and, if outside the old walls, *quartiere* and each comes with its own flavour,' she had emailed Helena when she first came over to stay with Tom. 'For instance, if you live in the Parioli, which is very up-market, you look down on everyone else. The city also has complicated politics. The Left distrusts the

Christian Democrats and vice versa. It's like untangling knotted string.'

What Lottie had grasped was that the Roman city dweller, whatever their stripe, tended to unite in deep-rooted suspicion of incomers on the grounds that, if said incomers cooperated with each other, the Romans might lose some advantage. She had some sympathy.

'We only occupy a small part, but Tom lives in a Renaissance palace,' Lottie continued. 'Very posh, very elegant. It's built around a square with a courtyard. The entrance is a stone pediment with pillars (beautiful) leading into the courtyard, where there's a fountain – a wide marble bowl at the centre of which are three plump women (they do a great service to womankind). Back in the day, it was used for washing clothes. Our apartment is on the first floor, opposite the entrance.'

Within seconds of first setting eyes on the apartment that occupied half of the *piano nobile*, Lottie had taken to it. There were some downsides, such as the dreadful brown furniture, but she reckoned that could be sorted. But, as she also told Helena: 'The sanitary arrangements are gross. I dream of a marble wet room and American plumbing.'

The *piano nobile* was the floor where the original family would have lived, and its main rooms ran the width of the building, with views towards the Piazza Borghese or looking directly down into the courtyard. Its proportions were good and much of its original glory was evident in the plaster and stonework. The ceilings were high – 'Trust me, a bonus in summer,' Tom had said – and the windows spacious. Lottie loved to stand by them, looking over the city and watching the sky.

The view facing south encompassed the pink-tiled church, which had a bell tower with blue mosaics. Originally, the church, now renamed Santa Maria del Divino Amore, had been one of several dedicated to a Christian martyr who had taken three days to die after a botched beheading. Apparently, the saint had welcomed her suffering, a detail that haunted Lottie, who strove, and failed, to understand a mindset that welcomed living for days with a half-severed neck to prove a love of God.

The palazzo housed a variety of people. Lottie hadn't been there a week before she ran slap up against the running battle between the feminist collective on the ground floor (its members distinguishable by their short haircuts and lace-up shoes with ultra thick soles) and the aristocratic family occupying the other half of the *piano nobile* (distinguishable by their excessive make-up and gobsmacking pearl necklaces). They hated each other.

The signora was not to worry, admonished Concetta whom Lottie had inherited. (Concetta referred to herself as the *tuttofare*: 'I cook, clean, take care of you.') She followed this up with: 'They will be suspicious of you because you're from *Inghilterra*.'

'Will I ever be forgiven?'

'Maybe.' Concetta would not be drawn further.

Concetta was an absolute monarch. For the last twenty years, she had worked for the inhabitants of the *piano nobile* and ruled her kingdom with relish, authority and no concessions. Lottie would have to tread carefully.

'Did Concetta intend to reassure me?' Lottie asked Tom later.

'Yes and no,' said Tom.

Before Lottie and Tom married, Concetta had made it clear she had been devoted to Clare and wore this loyalty like a scarf. She also had a habit of barging into rooms without knocking and, if thwarted, she lapsed into a dialect in which Clare's name was thrown around.

'I would like to go over the routines,' Lottie laid before her on arriving back from honeymoon.

'No need, Signora,' Concetta had responded. 'It is all arranged.'

Plumpish, with glossy black hair that she scraped back, she had excellent skin and a wardrobe of multi-pocketed dresses that buttoned up the front. Almost a caricature but not and, certainly, a formidable presence. There was a voluptuousness about her, Lottie decided. A will to power that ran through her dealings with the domestic arrangements and ensured that everything she tackled was immaculate. Tom would not hear a word said against her. Concetta's cooking was superb, he soothed a slightly ruffled Lottie, her ironing masterly and her negotiating skills legendary.

The legendary negotiating skills were put to the test when Lottie embarked on her plumbing projects and relations between her and Signor Bramante, an obstructive neighbour, required smoothing over.

'The poor man is frightened.' Concetta issued her edict. 'I will talk to him.'

'Frightened of good plumbing? I'm sure that can't be true.'

'He's afraid his peace will be shattered.'

Lottie surveyed the ancient lavatory and unsanitary-looking shower with its dripping shower head. 'His peace will certainly be shattered if there's a flood.'

'Does Concetta have a family?' she asked Tom. 'She never goes home until late.'

'We're her family,' said Tom, meaning her employers.

'But she must have *someone*?'

'A daughter, I think.'

'You think?'

'All right, I know.'

The subject was closed.

The plumbing was completed within the week. 'That must be a first,' said an admiring Tom. The following day, there was a knock on the door. A thick-set foreman waved papers in Lottie's face and declared he was under orders from the landlord to paint the palazzo.

This was news to its inhabitants and heated confrontations erupted that could be heard across the courtyard. There were flat refusals to remove furniture and pots from the balconies or, in some cases, to move out. Then, there was the even bigger hurdle of the schedule where, tactlessly, the feminist collective had been placed second to the contessa.

'It is impossible, Signora,' reported Concetta with obvious relish. 'There will be war.'

'What's to be done? Shall I go and talk to one of them? The landlord?'

'Signora, you're new here. You don't know the ways. Not like Signorina Clare.'

Lottie said tartly, 'I'm aware of that.'

Concetta leaned back against stove, planting her feet in their cracked leather lace-ups possessively on the tiles, and fanned herself. It was then Lottie realised that, from now on, in the domestic arena, cunning must be her second nature.

'*You* must sort it, Concetta.'

Which was precisely what Concetta had been angling for. 'It's very delicate,' she said. '*Very.*'

Assuming the posture of a one-woman negotiation team for the nuclear non-proliferation treaty, Concetta departed. Hours later, she returned. 'All is solved. The repairs for the contessa and the women will be done jointly.'

An admiring Lottie could only ask, 'How did you persuade the foreman?'

Concetta's dark eyes seethed with triumph. 'I ask him where he lives, and all is solved.'

'Not sure I follow.'

'He lives near Gabriella,' she explained patiently. 'My third cousin, Signora, which means we are almost kin. It turns out that the poor man has a delicate stomach, which needs great care and attention. I said I would cook him lunch every day.'

Tom and Lottie celebrated their four-month anniversary with dinner on the terrace.

The plants in the recently acquired planters were putting on growth, the lavender was the star of the collection.

Tom speared up the pasta that Concetta had prepared. 'The plants are a success.'

'I'll log that.' Lottie smiled at him.

He put down his fork. 'Have you forgiven me?'

The easy intimacy of the moment was spoilt.

'It's not a question of forgiveness,' she replied. 'But I have to ask the question, Tom. Were *you* asking yourself if you felt you were with the wrong person?'

He flashed back. 'No, absolutely not.'

'You called out in your sleep. From your unconscious. That must be significant?'

'Or just habit.'

'I understand, but it made me wonder.' She turned her head away. 'It was a slap in the face.'

He frowned. 'You have to trust me, Lottie, that's all it was.'

In the best of all possible worlds, she should have told him that she understood the waywardness and unpredictability of the unconscious and of how, at times, its manifestations meant little. But the hurt, or perhaps it was an insult, had hardened and she did not repair the small rupture.

A shout from the courtyard below diverted them and they got up from their chairs.

They looked down to see Sandra, one of the women from the collective, in the act of stringing up political posters along the scaffolding that had been put up for the painting and decorating.

It had been scheduled for removal after the foreman sighed, ate his final Concetta feast and departed for his next – presumably lunchless – assignment. No one imagined for a second the timetable would hold and the scaffolding had remained, offering an irresistible platform for the raging political opinions corralled inside the palazzo.

'Rome=Mafia=Taxes' – Sandra's posters were red rags to the bull of the Contessa Patuzzi, who had descended, with entourage, from the other section of the *piano nobile* and was now overwriting the wording of a despised poster with a marker pen.

Titian haired and voluble, Sandra gave the contessa an earful. The magnificently deaf contessa and her pen carried on.

Half the onlookers clapped.

Sandra squared up to the contessa, during which manoeuvre black marker pen appeared on the contessa's cheek. The contessa called for the police.

The other half of the onlookers applauded.

'The old tensions are still there. It's not done yet,' said Tom, more to himself than to Lottie.

While they leaned over the balcony and watched the small but intense drama unfold, Lottie told Tom about Nina Lawrence and her political comments in her notebook. 'Nineteen seventy-eight, when she died, was a bad time according to her, and she was worried by it. What is so striking, and so sad, is that she did not have any friends or family to claim her body.'

'That is odd,' said Tom. 'Something must have gone wrong. What was her name again?'

Still hissing at each other, the contessa and Sandra retreated to their respective lairs. Lottie found it funny – and not.

CHAPTER SEVEN

LOTTIE SLEPT BADLY AND WOKE EARLY. TOM WAS STILL out for the count, so she dressed, left a note and headed off through the velvety morning to a café in the Campo de' Fiori. Here she drank two cappuccinos in quick succession and watched the light play over the market stalls.

The day's appointments logged in her online diary were sparse, except for a 12.30 meeting with a Signor Antonio, who might, or might not, be one of her new colleagues.

She sent a couple of texts, including one to Gabriele Ricci to settle on the schedule for the work. What a hermit's cave the book doctor's was, and she looked up from her phone and marked the gaudy, noisy, attractive Roman life that was in such contrast.

A shout. Many shouts. The flap of a restaurant awning unrolling. Piled-up vegetables. A flash of a scarlet jacket, a colour so fresh and joyous that she found herself smiling which made her think of the medieval painter with his trove of colour knowledge.

What power he wielded, understanding as he did a colour's significance and the subtleties of meaning conveyed by its different hues. A colour could move, or direct, an audience's responses. It was… Lottie watched a stall holder in the market pile up tawny and plum-coloured dried fruits … unabashed psychological manipulation.

Think of the Virgin's blue. Its task was to signal to the onlooker that they were in the presence of the deity, plus, and this was as important, that the patron who had commissioned it was very rich. Who could fail not to appreciate the deft synergy of religion and mammon?

Yet, there was more. With its pale shallows and deep intensities, blue was the colour of calm, which soothed the disordered spirit. To reflect on its use, and its meanings, was a good subject for a peaceful meditation over a coffee; it helped the backwash from the Clare episode to recede. It was then she remembered that the church where Nina had tripped over Leo, was only five minutes' walk away.

Its classically inspired façade projected faded beauty. Countless feet had created depressions in the marble steps leading up to the huge, brass-studded doors, which, in the days they were in use, would have required several people to open them.

Inside was quiet and Lottie wandered contentedly, assaulted by the giddy, swoony scent from vases of narcissi that had been placed in the niches. She noted the twelve-sided cupula with gilded wood above the transept, the fresco of Christ riding into Jerusalem on his donkey on the south wall of the nave and the mosaic in front of the altar. Votive candles burned on stands at the entrances to the side-chapels, one of which was partially obscured by a pillar.

Churches' interiors varied – of course they did – but they shared the same basic footprint. Lottie was not religious, but she had always appreciated the predictable and reassuring form.

She was inspecting the stone carving of St Anthony of Padua in the north aisle when a movement alerted her. A man, who had been hunched over in a pew close to the altar rail, got to his feet. Under an inexpensive, shiny-with-age linen jacket, every line of his torso expressed tension.

Putting out a hand to steady himself, he edged out of the pew and she recognised Gabriele Ricci, looking as though he could do with a dose of sun. Reluctant to trespass on a private moment, she backtracked towards the exit.

Her footsteps sounded on the flagstones and he looked round. Lottie gestured that she did not wish to disturb him, but he walked towards her.

'I didn't mean to intrude. I've just sent you a text. We can be in touch later.'

'You didn't.' There was a pause. 'Intrude, I mean.' He pulled down a sleeve that had ridden up over his shirt. 'This is a church.' There was a hint of a smile. 'A place where many end up.' Lottie raised an eyebrow. 'Ill, well, happy, guilty. They hope to find the mercy they crave. And if you're a non-believer, you may ask for it anyway as an insurance policy.' He looked over to the stoup of holy water. 'Not that I do. Any more, that is. But the painting you brought in reminded me of the days when such consolations looked reachable.'

She wanted to ask him why, and how, he had arrived at that state of mind but a movement overhead made them look up. A bird had flown into the church and was beating a maddened flightpath around the cupula.

'I'm afraid this sometimes happens. It doesn't end well.'

She watched the frantic bird. 'I can't bear it for him,' she said.

'We have to. And so must it.'

The stoicism chimed better with Lottie than the hunched figure in the pew of moments earlier.

Nevertheless, she sensed he was upset. 'I hope nothing has happened?' She was close enough to hear his intake of breath. 'I don't mean to pry.'

'Nothing that can't be dealt with.'

She cast around for diversion. 'As you say, for some, belief must be crucial.'

She was sure she saw him wince.

Lottie thought about the ways she coped. *This too will pass.* As a nostrum, it worked for her but it was simple and she hesitated to offer it up.

He was looking at Lottie and she realised he was registering her properly for the first time. Her face, her long hair, the plain gold band on her finger, her full cotton skirt and white T-shirt.

'The English are good at not asking the questions they would like to ask,' he said. 'They call it discretion and it is sometimes laughed at. But, at this moment, I'm grateful for this trait.'

Lottie was horribly embarrassed but relieved. Above them the bird dashed itself against a window, its beak cracking against the pane. 'I wouldn't dream of prying. Anyway, I must go.' She slotted the strap of her bag over her shoulder. 'I look forward to our next meeting.'

He breathed in sharply. 'I've done some research into Pucelle *fils*. It will be interesting to talk about him.'

'I've done some research too. Are you any closer to a decision on the painting?'

'There are several possibilities.' He ticked off the points on his white fingers. 'It could be genuine. Or a copy by a junior in his workshop. Or a copy by a later master. Or,' he bent back his forefinger with a savagery that made her wince, 'a modern forgery. Someone who loved his work and understood him.'

'And …?'

'We're still conducting the tests.'

She had barely sat down in her office at the *Espatriati* when her phone rang. 'Signora Archer?'

It was Gabriele Ricci. Given she had just seen him in the church, she was surprised. 'Do call me Lottie,' she said.

'Then, I'm Gabriele.' He cleared his throat. 'I should have mentioned … Pucelle *fils* was known to be in Rome a few years before he died. Also,' there was a marked hesitation, 'I've identified the hill in the painting.'

'Where? Not Rome, surely?'

'Forty kilometres or so north. At Palacrino. A hillside town. You can match the silhouette in the painting against it.'

Excitement stirred. 'Pucelle *fils* died there.'

'There's an area below the town that is famous for wild narcissi in the spring. Pucelle *fils* was commissioned by the duchess to paint a book of hours. I've looked up the contract. There is a particular instruction to include the wildflowers of the area.'

'And did he?'

'We don't know for sure. The duchess had herself walled up a few years later and died of voluntary starvation.'

'She threw her life away?'

'Women's bodies were considered prime targets for the devil to infiltrate,' said Gabriele. 'They were at the mercy of their flesh and unstoppable desires, and their bodies were considered corrupt and wicked. This was probably the only way that the duchess felt she could purify herself.' He sounded resigned. 'It was unusual but not so unusual. It would have been understood at the time.'

Lottie digested this. The duchess would not have viewed her actions as terrible and against nature but as a glorious culmination of faith. 'I hope she achieved what she wished,' she said. 'Is there any more news?'

Her excitement and interest must have danced down the phone and he moved to damp it down. 'I've learned that, in this business, it's best to anticipate disappointment.'

'Where's the painting?'

'Being assessed at the Centre for the Study of Preservation and Restoration. My contact is on the case.'

'Excellent.'

'One step at a time, Lottie,' he said in English. 'Is that how you would say?'

He had let her in. 'Excellent idiom, Gabriele, and I love the accent.' She heard him chuckle and confessed, 'I had my worries about it, but it would be ace if *The Annunciation* is genuine.'

'Thank you.' There was a marked pause. 'You know ... you should visit Palacrino.'

Lottie put down the phone, reflecting on ideas whose potency was so strong that to wall yourself up and starve to death represented a triumph.

Life expectancy was cruelly short in the medieval world. Wouldn't that have sharpened the will to live? Or, as she had sometimes speculated, did its brutalities, and rudimentary medicine, make it so uncomfortable that someone might consider it easier to die?

Lottie worked until 12.15, when she brushed her hair and slicked gloss over her lips.

The door opened and the director, Valerio Gianni, advanced through it with a companion.

He was all emollience – at which he excelled. He enquired if Lottie was settling in and then made for the door. 'I will leave you to your meeting with my good friend Signor Antonio here.'

Lottie noticed the tiny emphasis on 'my good friend'.

Having shaken hands, they sat down on either side of the desk. Lottie offered him a glass of water, which he declined.

Early seventies, she would judge, in a plain black suit with a small badge in the buttonhole, well-cut salt-and-pepper hair and thick-lensed glasses in black frames, his weary air suggested hard-edged irony had been incised into his spirit and he was a man who had seen much and had been disappointed. But for a heavily nicotined right forefinger, she could have taken him for a priest.

'Forgive me for barging in, Signora.'

'You're not,' Lottie replied. 'You had an appointment. But I confess I'm at a loss to know … why?'

'Of course. My name is Giuseppe Antonio and I work in the Vatican. Valerio informs me you are new to Rome,' the weariness lifted for a moment and in its place was sharp appraisal, 'but you've chosen a time when the city is at its best. Isn't it curious how cities often feel things before they happen? Summer is coming and Rome knows it.'

She thought of how soft the shadows were growing, the warm stones, the sun turning more golden by the day. 'Yes,' she said.

'It's a melange city,' he said, and she suspected it was a theme he often trotted out. 'Bits and pieces spliced together from a jumble of civilisations. Romans thrive on ruins. Those left by the Roman Empire, after the Visigoths and Ostrogoths had done their worst and, yes, after the Nazis. Cities survive what terrible human beings do to them.'

The *ennui* was convincing. Intuition, however, told Lottie that it was being directed by a steely sophistication and an agenda was being pursued.

'I came from a poor background, where there was much privation, to work in the Vatican, and I ended up with a very good career.'

It was a clever sketch of his trajectory, which was intended to not tell her that much, but she caught the will and ambition, coupled with a hint of self-congratulation.

'Signor Antonio, I am delighted to make your acquaintance, but would you think me rude if I ask why you are here?'

His gaze rested on the boxes stacked on the bench.

'Of course you must ask. I expect it.' He adjusted his glasses and she glimpsed the operator used to wielding authority. 'I believe that you have been making enquiries about a painting.'

'I'm not in a position to comment. Our investigations are always confidential.' She glanced sharply at him. 'Where have you got this information? Surely not Gabriele Ricci?'

'As you will no doubt learn, in this city, things do not remain secret for long.'

'Clearly.'

An eyebrow shot up at Lottie's tone. 'You must remember that Vatican officials work through hundreds of documents a day.'

Before she came to Rome, Lottie checked up on the Vatican City, which was a shorthand term for the central administrative apparatus of the Roman Catholic Church. Some eight hundred people lived in the square mile of the Vatican City itself, and more than two thousand – mostly men – were employed by it.

Clearly, they would be of all sorts and with differing ambitions. Some driven by faith. Some less so ... rather as she suspected the man now sitting in front of her might be more interested in temporal rewards.

'Day *and* night, if one were being pedantic.' Signor Antonio was measured. 'It never ceases. The pressure is constant. It's the way the Vatican keeps abreast of events. Information about the painting was bound to come out.'

'And ...?'

'But since you are concerned, a contact heard that the painting was being examined at the Centre for Preservation and Restoration and realised it matched a description of one lost from the collection in the Pinacoteca during the war. If that is correct, we would very much like it returned.' He added, 'After due diligence, of course.'

Was he, in fact, a dealer? There were documented instances of dealers donning different personae to track down a quarry. As a class of operators, they were a source of mirth, sneaky admiration and, if they made a successful heist, anger, but they were never trusted.

'By due diligence you mean the correct documentation?'

He gestured as if to say: *If that is required.*

'Signor Antonio, forgive me, but why are you asking me these questions, rather than the curator of the relevant department at the Pinacoteca whose business it must be?'

'I did not mean to put your back up.'

'It's not a matter of putting my back up,' she replied calmly. 'It's more a matter of assessing what the motives might be of a stranger who does not work here asking me about a confidential project.'

'It may not belong where it was found, Signora Archer.'

'Where it was found is not common knowledge and, again, confidential.'

A hint of steel slid into his voice. 'It's a painting crucial to our understanding of the artistic development of the period, and to our understanding of how the Blessed Virgin was seen and portrayed at a pivotal moment.'

'I see that, but there are many Annunciations of the period. You are surely not deprived of "understanding".'

It's a special moment in a life, Signora. As you might appreciate, its value can never be underplayed. Everyone recognises this crucial moment whether they are blessed with children or not.'

Lottie got to her feet. 'Signor Antonio, no doubt the position will be clearer in a few days.'

He had no option but to follow suit. 'Nothing is more important than the Church and the meaning of its message. Keeping it intact is a struggle in today's world. It is our first duty.' There was a touch of scorn. 'The world is troubled and there is always danger of disorder. The Church's role must be that of a peacekeeper and to provide the moral leadership that, in turn, will influence the political leadership. I am totally committed to that.'

This was to veer off the point – which might have been the point?

Suddenly, he switched tack. 'I expect to hear from you.'

'If the painting is authenticated and if you produce the documentation to prove that the painting belonged to the Vatican collection.'

'They can be produced.' He did not specify which papers.

'Nothing can be decided without establishing provenance,' said Lottie, 'as you will be aware.'

'Proof of provenance will be produced at the correct moment, Signora Archer.'

He held out a largish hand with well-tended nails and its nicotine stain. After a second or two, Lottie took it.

'We're interested in what happened to it after it went missing and where it was discovered. It will add enormously to the Holy Father's collection if it is returned.' He released her and stepped away. 'And any other material that came with it? Which we would need to assess.'

'Signor Antonio, if we can help, we will do so.' She conducted him to the door. 'Just to be sure, what is the name of the painter?'

He raised an admonishing finger. 'The painter of *The Annunciation*, of course.'

CHAPTER EIGHT

H E LEFT, LEAVING BEHIND QUESTIONS AND A DISTURBING aura.

Lottie flew over to the boxes containing the Lawrence papers.

> Number: 001768/9. Papers, date to be determined–1978,
> of Nina Maria Lawrence, 1940–78. Condition: damp
> damage and decay. Material exposed to natural light.

It had taken her some years to settle in her mind the true significance of the archival process and she was certain of only one thing: the documents corroborated an early lesson of how little we share with others. The revelations of the solitary souls buffeted by events could be upsetting. On the other hand, the organization demanded by the work suited the part of Lottie that craved the safe and sanitised, order and neatness.

She had been well trained in the system of document management, among other things, devised to track the location of a document at any time, and did not allow herself any short cuts. The protocol was immovable and no one aspect of the process should be shirked.

Throughout her lunch hour and much of the afternoon, she worked steadily, entering the details. Precise and efficient.

The first tranche contained a bundle of receipts and newspaper articles stuck together by damp and mould. Deploying the scalpel and tweezers, she managed to tease them apart, which took a couple of hours.

She turned to a second bundle that was made up of press cuttings.

Top of the pile was a Deaths notice in the *L'Eco di Roma* and dated 1 December 1978:

Lawrence, Nina Maria. Died 15 October 1978.

An appeal followed:

She has no known family or contacts. If anyone is aware of their whereabouts, please contact the authorities below.

The notice concluded with details of her forthcoming interment at the Protestant Cemetery on 9 December at 12.30.

It was warm in the office and Lottie switched the ceiling fan on to low. Its whomp-whomp cut through the still air.

Nina had been young to die. Lottie hoped that her own coffin would be strewn with flowers and surrounded by friends anxious to say their farewells and to press a hand down on its surface with love and affection. It had not been like that for Nina Lawrence – *no known family or contacts* – and it was more likely she had been stowed, solitary and cold, in a mortuary.

Then who had placed the notice in the paper and why did Nina Lawrence have to wait two months after her death before she was buried?

Lottie reapplied herself to the cuttings. Next up was taken from an English news-sheet. Its headline screamed: 'A TERRIBLE MURDER'.

> A thirty-eight-year-old Englishwoman has been found
> by the Tiber with her throat cut …

Truly shocked, and with all thoughts of *The Annunciation* driven from her mind, Lottie's own throat constricted.

Nina Lawrence had been murdered.

Her work was to preserve documents and records and to establish an intimacy with them. A fascinating, stirring and, occasionally, shocking process.

As this one was turning out to be.

Lottie rang Reception and said that she would take no calls until further notice. She switched off her mobile and reapplied herself to the papers, stopping every so often to look up a word or a technical term in the dictionary.

> Respected horticulturalist Nina Lawrence was
> discovered in the Caffè Acqua by the Ponte Sisto on
> 15 October at 7.30 p.m.
>
> It was reported that she was found propped up against
> the stone planter close to the river, covered in blood. One
> witness, Francesco Bianco, alleges that a man dressed
> as a priest was close to the scene of the murder. When
> challenged he had hurried away

The murder scene was described in detail and included a diagram of the café, which was just beside the bridge.

Lottie studied it.

Note: It must have been dark. How had Francesco Bianco known

Nina was there? Had she managed to call out with a severed throat? Surely, not possible?

'The poor lady was still alive,' so ran his account, 'but only just. She looked up at me and I will never forget her expression. I saw a lot of death during the war and I knew when someone was done for. It was useless to get help. I held her hand and said a prayer. It was important that she didn't die alone.'

Note: How could Bianco know for sure it was useless to get help?

She put aside the rest of the cuttings for later. A copy of the medical and forensic report came up next in the pile.

At 2010 a thirty-eight-year-old Caucasian female was admitted to the Fatebenefratelli hospital. Dottor Gennaro, the surgeon, attempted resuscitation but the patient was certified dead at 2220.

The medical report from the hospital gave details:

a) Two transverse cuts on the fingers of her left hand
b) A slash on her forearm, a self-defence injury
c) A stab wound to the thorax
d) A knife slash on the throat from left to right partially severing the airway and the carotid artery

Dated later, a forensic report stated that the killer was right-handed, his sleeve would have been covered with a fine blood spray and it was likely there were other visible blood stains on his clothing.

It also stated that Nina Lawrence had tried to defend herself. There was blood under her fingernails and bruising on her right flank, likely to have been caused by being dragged along the ground.

It went on:

No objects were found at the scene and it has been
concluded that the murder weapon was likely to have been
thrown into the river.

Lottie frowned. It was an uneasy stew of facts. A dark night. A
painful, lonely death. Plus the puzzle as to why there was no one
to deal with Nina's remains or attend her funeral.

She hoped Nina had got a decent grave, with a suitable headstone
and wildflowers planted over it.

She turned back to the press cuttings.

A scandal publication reported excitedly that explicit lesbian
poems had been discovered in Nina Lawrence's apartment in the
Trastevere when the police searched it. Examples from the poems
were given. They were strong stuff and bad poetry.

Other papers feasted on the details.

'Murder of woman guilty of unnatural practices.'

'Unmarried at thirty-eight.'

'Men had been seen going in and out of her apartment.'

A picture came into focus, unexpected and unflattering.

Finally, there was a lengthier feature in a more respectable
newspaper.

A thirty-eight-year-old Englishwoman has been
murdered by the banks of the Tiber. Nina Lawrence had
lived in Rome for ten years and was a landscape gardener
of note who had worked on gardens in Rome, Lazio and
Tuscany.

She was seen leaving her apartment in the Via della
Luce in the Trastevere carrying a bag. A second eyewitness,
who has asked not to be identified, reported sighting a

woman running towards the Ponte Sisto. They said they remembered thinking that, given it was dark, it was unwise for her to be out alone.

No weapon was found at the site of the murder. The police are launching a full-scale inquiry and the British Embassy are handling the formalities.

The police report included with the papers speculated that the killer was either a spurned lover or someone who objected to lesbians. Or, a spur-of-the-moment robbery. (Nina's bag has been retrieved further up the towpath emptied of its contents.)

Lottie rested her chin on her hands.

Nina's spirit seemed to be in the room.

Who are you, Nina? Was your love affair really with a much younger man? Could you have been murdered as a result?

Some of the answers were almost certainly there in the papers, perhaps many answers. People rarely told the whole truth, only their truth.

It was now evening and, being a Friday, the building was almost deserted. Gathering up her things, Lottie made her way down the stairs and called Tom at the same time. 'Sorry, sorry,' she said. 'Will be with you in thirty.'

'It's OK,' he said. 'I'm late too.'

Concetta was in the kitchen browning the guanciale in the *padella* and preparing the *spaghetti alla carbonara* when Lottie arrived.

She indicated the eggs, the bacon, the pecorino and the spaghetti, plus glowing San Marzano tomatoes for the salad.

'Brilliant,' said Lottie. 'Thank you. Now you must go home.'

Concetta took her time to untie her apron strings. 'Shall I cook the pasta? It must be just so. Signorina Clare always said I was the only one who got it right.'

To be fair, Lottie was no expert as to the just-so-ness of pasta. Silently acknowledging her failings on that one, she challenged Concetta. 'The Signorina Clare is no longer here,' she said. 'Could we be clear about that?'

Concetta was the first to drop her gaze. '*Sì.*'

It was a retreat of sorts. Lottie sought to lighten matters. 'Did anyone ring today about the telephone?'

Most of the time, she and Tom used their mobile phones but Lottie, surprised it had not already happened, had suggested they installed a second phone on their landline for extra convenience. 'Sure,' said Tom, 'but it'll be tricky.'

Concetta frowned. A bad sign. 'The landlord rang. He says it's not possible because a second phone means you will have to have another number.'

'No,' said Lottie patiently. 'We just want another phone attached to this line.'

Concetta sent her a look that implied that Lottie lacked a full complement of brains. 'Not possible and it is too extravagant for a second number since you are not going to be here for ever. And, of course, it might mean the Signor Landlord would have to register here as a second home, which is very serious …' She flicked a tea towel under her arm.

Clearly, Lottie should know why it was so serious. 'Because?'

'His utility bills would be higher.' Concetta spoke slowly and clearly. 'In Italy if you have a second home you have to pay more for those bills.'

'I see. But this is just a second phone on the same line with the same number. What could be simpler?'

'I'll pray to St Jude for you, Signora.'

The patron saint, apparently, of desperate and lost causes.

Lottie discovered that her patience had a short shelf-life. 'Tell him that I would appreciate his help.'

Concetta shrugged, which Lottie took to mean that this was one of the serpentine situations many a non-Italian found themselves in. It also suggested that she would never, ever understand the laws and regulations precisely because she was non-Italian.

The pasta was glossy, creamy and very good. They ate appreciatively, Lottie relating to Tom about Signor Antonio and the painting. 'I've discovered that Nina Lawrence was murdered.' She shook her head. 'In the most terrible way.'

He put down his fork. 'It's upset you.'

'I suppose it has.'

'It's not a good story.'

'Are there connections here that I'm not seeing? The painting. Her awful, awful death? Signor Antonio?'

'Perhaps she stole it?'

'Possibly. But maybe she was hiding it for someone?' She stretched her hand across the table. 'Could you spare the time for an outing?'

'Where?'

'Palacrino. Tomorrow?'

'Yup.' Tom's face brightened. 'Mario's restaurant,' he said by way of explanation. 'But why?'

Lottie explained about the background to *The Annunciation*. 'Gabriele Ricci seems to think it is Palacrino and I wanted to snoop.'

They took the car – Tom knew the best routes out of the city – and drove forty or so kilometres north. On the way, Lottie told him about Pucelle *fils* and the duchess who had had herself walled up to expiate the sin of possessing a female body. 'In the eyes of the Church at that time, the female body spelled danger. Women were honey pots exciting helpless men to lustful desires.'

Tom brushed a hand over Lottie's thigh. A light, sexy gesture. 'They had a point.'

'Do that again.'

He obeyed. 'I never thought I would be so happy,' he said.

Lottie smiled at him. 'Me neither.'

Built for defence, Palacrino perched on a steep and rocky escarpment, overlooking plains and woods stretching north and south. Behind it rose a mountain wreathed in a light morning haze, whose summit looked to Lottie's dazzled eyes as if it had been smoothed over with a carpenter's lathe. Driving closer, it came into clearer focus with a sprinkling of trees at its base, rocky and bare at its summit.

She held up a photocopy of *The Annunciation* and her pulse quickened. The curves and steeps of the mountain were almost identical to those traced in the painting. As was the town's wall and the siting of the two palace towers. It felt familiar but, of course, that was an illusion.

At Mario's, they ate pasta and wild boar *ragù*, which was as good as Tom had promised. Afterwards, they walked across the piazza, which had a well in one corner flanked by worn, pinkish marble steps. In the fifteenth century, it would have been a gathering point for the town dwellers. Resting her hand on the stone rim, worn and folded with age, Lottie experienced the frisson that happened when a link between past and present became physical. Maybe Pucelle *fils* would have been among them?

The Palazzo Ducale ran along the entire west side of the piazza, guarded by bronze doors that opened on to a black-and-white paved courtyard. At one end, a stone staircase led gracefully to the *piano nobile*. At the other was a paved area, flanked by marble pillars, where the Palacrino dukes conducted their public audiences. On the first floor, a loggia ran around the perimeter. Funds for its upkeep were obviously in short supply and it seemed, at first glance, dusty and neglected.

Lottie followed the signposts to the ducal chambers. A guide written in hit-and-miss English did its best to interest her in the Palacrino escutcheon, the hooded fireplaces and the *altana*, the covered upper porch, where the servants customarily sat and watched the dukes and their courtiers below.

The duke's bedchamber contained a couple of magnificent bronze wall brackets, a reproduction fifteenth-century bed and not much else. In the duchess's bedchamber it was a similar story, only on a smaller scale.

Lottie lingered by the casement. 'Before glass was freely available,' she read from the guide, 'oiled linen was stretched over the windows.'

Living sequestered lives, the women in that period were not supposed to stand by windows. Yet they must have rebelled against the prohibition. Of course, they would have done, she thought.

And the duchess? Had she always craved oblivion? Almost certainly she would have had no choice about who she married. Was it that, having been presented with a bridegroom whom she found uncongenial, or repugnant, she decided it was the only option she had? Lottie studied the reproduction bed and its green hangings. The sole power a woman of that time possessed was over her thoughts, and her private feelings. In deciding to recuse herself from life and to choose God over her husband, the duchess had, in a drastic, painful way, chosen freedom.

Lottie inspected the wooden shutters, which were secured with iron bars. God would have been as hard a taskmaster as the duke, and she wondered if the duchess had panicked when it was too late.

Tom grew bored and went off to drink coffee in the café on the piazza and Lottie headed for the Memorabilia Room, which was sparsely furnished and as neglected-looking as elsewhere. A massive carved chair labelled *Ducal Seat* dominated it, an unremarkable Nativity hung on the wall and propped open in the display cabinet was a printed Bible from the late sixteenth century.

Capturing Lottie's attention was the miniature painting displayed alongside the Bible labelled *Bathsheba Bathing*.

The text beside it read: *A copy of the original miniature from* The Hours of the Duchess of Palacrino, *c. 1490, by Pucelle* fils, *now in the* Musei Vaticani.

Gabriele Ricci's suggestion of a trip to Palacrino had had a purpose.

The text continued: *The original painting was discovered in the library of the palace during restoration work in 1972 and was on display here until 2010 when it was verified as a missing page from the duchess's book of hours and removed to Rome.*

Lottie took a deep breath.

Measuring approximately 10 ¾ inches by 7 ¼ inches, the size tallied with *The Annunciation*.

The flutter of her professional pulse quickened.

Its setting was a formal garden and, behind it, thrust back into the landscape, a mysterious and magical mountain rose to the sky. The garden was flanked by box hedge and white roses, at its centre a small pool was fed from a fountain in the shape of a cat's head.

Ah, she thought. Traditionally, the cat's head was an allusion to the prostitute.

A woman, submerged to her hips, stood in the pool. Her nakedness was deliberately provocative and anatomically truthful and clearly obvious through the water. A mass of golden hair flowed down her back and her white arms (a little overlong, if Lottie was to be critical) were held loosely by her sides.

A slanted upward glance gave away her secret knowledge that she was being observed. The effect was overtly sexual, strange, voyeuristic, summoning a male vision of female beauty, and conveying the longing and cruelties of desire.

No wonder the king in the red robe and crown watched from a window of a crenellated palace with undisguised lust, while drunken courtiers danced in a courtyard below.

Lottie inspected every detail minutely. Pucelle *fils* was sly, clever and very right. He understood that nothing should be presented as simple or one-dimensional. Yes, we sin … just as the drunken dancers, the leering king and the voluptuous white body are about to sin … and we pay for it. But yet, he was telling us, still we do it.

She traced the nuances. A wry worldliness was counterpointed with a suffering in the girl's eyes and the defensive angle of her white body. How clever it was: for the artist was ensuring that the resonance of the painting reached beyond the erotic and the physical.

Lottie took herself off to join Tom. They sat idling in the café on the piazza while she described the painting to him and he listened with a lazy smile.

A group of schoolchildren of several nationalities took up position on the steps of the fountain. The adults in charge chivvied them into tighter formation and, after a deal of shuffling, they began to sing. Arrested by the sound of their high, slightly fractured voices, passers-by stopped to listen. At the finish, they clapped.

The waiter took their bill. 'They're from a children's village near here which cares for the orphans and abused children,' he told them. 'It's a tradition that they sing here.'

The group disbanded and, shepherded by their carers, moved off. One little boy had been absorbed poking between the gaps in the marble flagstones with a stick. He threw it down. 'Signor Oscar,' he called, scampering over the stones. 'Signor Oscar, wait for me.'

Back in Rome after their supper, she settled down to further research. The evening was a fine one and they had thrown open the balcony doors. Tom was reading in the chair.

Lottie observed him with love and the greedy curiosity of the comparatively new lover. His hair had drifted over his forehead and a window opened on to the Tom who had run feral (or so he said) throughout his Cornish childhood.

Small boy. Shorts. Wellingtons. The boy who decided to hide from his parents for a couple of days to prove that he could.

'And?'

'They had most of the police force out searching but I managed to evade them. Outwitted them, actually.'

'Who came off worst?'

'My parents. They never got over the fright. I just sailed on, causing mayhem.'

Lottie wrinkled her nose. 'I suspect your parents ran you on a long leash.'

'Perhaps. I let off a smoke bomb at a picnic once. A ghastly family one in the rain. Then I did get it in the neck.'

Lottie pictured it. Slippery grass, a bad-tempered sea, damp *dispirited adults, sandwiches curling at the edges and Tom bored out of his mind. A bang, the smoke.*

It reminded her of what she wanted to ask Tom.

'Did you ever find out anything else about the bomb?' she asked.

Tom did not move a muscle but she knew he had gone on the alert. 'Case ongoing. Investigations take time.'

'Any clues?'

He shook his head.

Lottie returned to her research.

In Samuel 2 of the Old Testament, Bathsheba was spotted bathing by King David, who fell instantly in lust with her and, unforgivably, sent off Bathsheba's husband to die in battle. The story was a favourite with Valois kings and many of the artists of the day had tackled it. Almost certainly, Bathsheba had had no say in her fate, but this made no difference to the Church. Viewed as a temptress almost on a par with Eve, her reputation was shredded with gusto.

'Strange,' murmured Lottie, 'how the ultra-wicked Bathsheba is so often dished up in paint as luscious and naked.'

The irony was wasted. Tom was asleep.

She lifted her head and looked through the balcony doors to the evening sky.

A swift screamed through the sky. Tom stirred in his chair.

How lovely the Bathsheba painting was. Even though Lottie only had the reproduction of the original purchased at the tourist kiosk, she was bewitched by its gorgeous palette – the sensuality of pearl white, the golden abundance of her hair, the clear, sparkling water, a sky of cerulean blue.

Lottie propped her chin in her hands. Something was eluding her that she could not pin down.

Then she did. In the Bathsheba painting, there was no additional story taking place in the background.

'Did I fall asleep?' asked Tom.

Lottie got up and knelt by the chair. 'You did.'

He cupped her chin with both hands. 'Was I like an old man?'

She smiled into his eyes. 'Couldn't tell the difference.'

CHAPTER NINE

Rome
30 January 1978

How I love Rome, is a frequent reaction whenever I confess that I live there and it is sincerely, and very often passionately, meant. The city draws out extremes of feeling.

I tell very few where I operate and certainly not my real reason for being here. Being miserly with personal detail is the best practice, the result of good training. Plus, what remains of my uncherished family have no idea where I operate, and I want it kept that way.

Do I miss the intimacies between people?

There are times when I am content with having perfected my apartness. Space around me is my protection and is necessary. Yet I find myself analysing the gap between being alone and loneliness. I reflect, too, on friendship because I'm in need of it, even if friendship is not something that I can ever enjoy.

What an extraordinary thing it is. A friend can know you through and through but does not demand your body or your continual presence. A friendship rolls on and, if you are lucky, is never diluted or disappointed. The true friend can be the last resort – the one that accompanies you to the scaffold.

There are three flights of stairs up to my apartment. In the old days, I would have skimmed up them but no longer.

The façade facing me has a barber's shop, a cobbler and a lunch bar where the food simmers in the window and the interior is stacked with jars of artichokes, olives and peaches. Romans live on the first and second floors, some of them elderly. Close by is the *pensione* through which flit Danes, Germans and Americans, none of whom stay longer than a week. Directly opposite me, on my level, there is a man who spends his day staring at my window. He is harmless and I have almost grown fond of him.

What furniture there is in the apartment is beautiful. Like the walnut table on which I am working, which has whorls of dark, whipped honey in the wood and a deep patina. I've protected it with a length of silk brocade pillaged from an abandoned house. The brocade wishes to pay me back for my looting: however hard I beat it, dust from its former life emerges. My chair … my chair … possesses all the elegance of early-Empire classicism and is a devil to sit on, but I will defend it to my death. Leo and I bought it from a junk shop.

On the shelf are stacked the reports for the gardens on which I have worked. The Vitecello garden, the Palacrino estate.

The Vitecello was an ambitious undertaking and the Renaissance cardinal who created the garden was the loftiest of prelates. NB: Most of the gardens in the Lazio region owe their creation to acquisitive cardinals. No humble stables for the scarlet-cassocked ones, but luscious, shimmering landscapes designed to impress and to shield them from the dirty, diseased, often desperate, existences in the city.

My first task was to disentangle from the neglect and damage of the war the intentions of the cardinal's original designer. I walked around it over several days, and at different times, trying to dive below the surface and to begin a relationship with its structures which were gradually unpeeled from the decades of neglect.

The Palacrino project was of a different ilk. There a garden had to be coaxed out of the dry terrain, using the latest in irrigation methods – and a determination not to be deterred by drought, heat and languor.

I spent a long time thinking about the planting in accordance with my instructions: how to protect and nurture the seedlings with tenderness and will them to strong, luxuriant maturity.

The process will be lengthy, which is precisely what Rex and I planned. Once I knew that General Rasella was a frequent dinner guest, I built in as much longevity into the execution as I could get away with.

My second meeting with Leo was also serendipity.

Rex instructed me to be in St Peter's Square during a papal address. I was to wait there, by the second pillar in the right-hand colonnade, for the contact who would be handing over information.

The crowd was dense, and I had trouble struggling through it. As I got there, I was pushed and I stumbled. My hand brushed against the shoulder of the man in front of me. He turned.

His eyes widened. So did mine.

I remember thinking that he had not yet developed that air of knowing better that so many had. Still in the first stages of the journey, the certainties – and the cruelties and repressions – had not rooted in him. He was still free.

The Holy Father blessed the crowd, which surged towards the balcony. I grabbed on to Leo for support and he held me. At first warily and, then, his hand pressed into my waist.

That was the moment when the sea-change happened. I turned towards him and, such was the press, my cheek touched his. His skin was smooth and warm and smelled faintly of old-fashioned soap. His hand was now under my elbow, willing me to be safe, and I realised that I had never been held so carefully before and by someone so strong. Every cell in my body woke up.

I heard myself asking him if he would like another coffee.

The crowd was splitting into competing cross-currents and I was being pulled away.

He grinned and said he would be delighted, provided there were biscuits.

After that, we met for coffee a few times and idled in the spring sunshine. He had a ready laugh, unusual sympathy and appeared to be happy in his skin. There was no shadow in him. No guilt at these meetings either, because he came to them innocent of anything except friendship.

He wanted to know about my life, which, of course, I was forbidden to tell him.

I made up some family details, something that I had to do for professional reasons from time to time. I had deceived many and not minded too much, but I hated deceiving Leo. To compensate, I tried to be truthful with my opinions on the subjects in which he was interested: religion, painting, farming. It was a way of being honourable.

I questioned him about his childhood, which had been one of hard farm labour and strict family mores. There was bitterness at the hardships and hatred for the landowners who took what they could, he told me. Some were good employers but not enough of them. He also said the landowners were foolish. If they had treated them better there would not have been such trouble.

I asked him why he hadn't gone into politics. To right the wrongs.

I had been clumsy, or spoken too early in our friendship, and he slipped away into the part of him that I could not share and said that politics were for others.

When we knew each other better, I asked him if he had ever had a girlfriend.

Yes, he said. She had plaits, a missing front tooth, white socks and a red satchel and he had told her that he was hers for life.

That was as much as I was permitted.

He asked about me and I confessed to my affair with a married man. His wife knew about it and said she didn't mind. But ... the whole thing was ...

'Was?' He was very gentle.

Skewed, I remember saying.

My hand was resting on the table and, for a moment, I thought he was going to take hold of it. Instead, he observed that he didn't think I regretted it.

I thought about it. True, I conceded and admitted that when I thought about him at all it was with dislike. The discussion stirred up complicated feelings and I added that I hoped that was useful information about the human psyche.

He looked reflective and said that, whenever he was faced with a parishioner in the same boat, he would think of me.

His beauty absorbed me. I found myself sneaking covert glances and drinking it in. Occasionally, I would catch him looking at me.

I learned a lot from Leo, too much to set down, but there was one thing in particular. This was his absolute conviction that life, in whatever form, must be cherished and protected. You must never kill anything, he told me, even if it was an insect, because it had a right to live. A good foundation belief for the priesthood.

Leo was taking the traditional route for younger sons in his family and I understood how difficult it would be to struggle out of the net. Plus, he had this uncle willing to mentor him. The family was large and needy and there were many nephews who required help and he would be foolish to ignore the uncle. I looked at Leo's strong body and clever, feeling face. I remember thinking that, if he chose to enter the world, there was every chance he would fill out and he would acquire more colour. I hated to think of him pale and tortured and confined.

But I was being unfair.

I asked him if the seminary was a way of escaping the world and he replied that it was the way to a rich and deep existence with God. When I asked him when he discovered he had a vocation he said that it had always been there. Waiting.

Was that because his uncle had decreed it?

He took time to consider. 'I think perhaps you don't know how much it means to have a priest in the family.'

And if he hadn't wished to go that route?

He gave me a lesson on family.

This is what he said.

'A family is powerful.' He did not look at me. 'It's like the Church, a living organism that survives weaknesses and corruptions because a divine force is behind it.'

It was fortunate that I had been tamed over the years of doing my work. Otherwise, I might have snapped out something doubting and acid.

1976 was joyous. The spring rolled in. The swifts had never been so numerous, the flowers I dealt with so fragrant, my step so light.

Then summer.

I asked him if he had confessed to his superiors about our meetings.

For the first time, there was pain and doubt in his eyes, which nearly made me cry. He said no, he hadn't.

The omission was crucial in his world – for it meant that the dice had been rolled. Nothing had been admitted between us, but we knew what was happening. It wasn't friendship, although it was based on one. We knew why our heads were choked with thoughts of the other. We knew why our bodies were seized by yearning. I tried to be sorry, but I wasn't.

One aspect troubled me in particular and I eventually asked him. Was I a useful temptation? One that he could fight, win and then declare to his God that he had triumphed.

We were walking in the Circo Massimo in the early morning. Leo stopped in his tracks and said, yes that was true.

The depth of pain I felt took me by surprise.

He turned to face me. 'But you *know* that it's more than that.' I remember the words exactly, spoken tenderly and carefully. 'I'm a novice in this kind of relationship – in the vocabulary, if you like. But you know, and I know, that you are more.'

That was Leo all over. He was honest. He was as honest as I was not – and that hurt, too.

I wonder what people thought as they observed us together. *Older woman and younger man.* Or, perhaps they didn't bother. Rome was filled with misfits and the out-of-the-ordinary. The city had seen so much that the very modest deviation from the norm that Leo and I made in its long history would not raise a ripple.

The first time I fell in love I had been stationed in Istanbul and it had been furtive, desperate, greedy encounters here and there. This is different. This snatched away my soul (as well it might) and I think it has taken his. Neither of us is at liberty to dispose of them as we might like.

He would be joining the seminary soon, after which there would be little free time. But, before he did, he visited my apartment a couple of times. (I won't say he sneaked in exactly but he was discreet.)

I was scrupulous in keeping my distance and he his.

He liked my rooms and the way I furnished them.

He looked around at things I loved and treasured – the table, the brocade, the Venetian wine glasses on the shelf – and said it was like looking into my mind. Then, out of the blue, he told me that it hurt and, sometimes, he didn't think he could survive it.

It was the first time what we felt had been articulated and I said I felt the same way.

Written down, it might sound excessive but when uttered out loud it was anything but.

What is the story? I ask myself. The story is that I tripped over the legs of a much younger man who wanted to be a priest. It was a dazzling early spring day, with a yellow sun and a fresh blue, blue sky, but it was never going to end well.

He said that when he was a boy, he used to imagine making a living in the city and occupying rooms like mine, but had no idea how he could make it happen.

I pointed out that he had ended up in a city.

He laughed. It was the last time I saw him untroubled and serene about his plans.

How is it, I asked Leo, that the ideas imposed by a handful of men are used as nooses and handcuffs to keep us in check?

In the main, I am easy about my inability to give my allegiance to a greater power, but there are times it would be convenient. But, here I am. Detached, resolutely rooted into this earthly life. Only now, I'm aching with love. Aching with lust, too, with a body that won't obey and wishes for nothing more than to lie down and to slake that lust.

The Desert Fathers made one sensible point as they sounded off about their hatred and distrust of women. Sex *does* destabilise. So does guilt.

He and I discussed the guilt.

Isn't it better, I argued, while we are on earth, to cultivate its joys, to occupy the present wholeheartedly, and to accept with gratitude what it offers?

For me, it is a hint of violets, massed narcissi, the softness of an animal's fur, clean ironed sheets and the perfect trust of a child's hand in yours that give life substance and meaning.

Leo countered that one should embrace every nuance of the natural world that is proscribed by God and understand that the darkness is a component of light. All the beauty of life is made up of light and shadow.

We had gone for another of our walks. An innocent pair enjoying a discussion in the Villa Borghese gardens, but there was an unfamiliar tension between us. I kicked the first fallen leaves of the year across the path.

I suggested, unwisely, that his God was, like all gods, indifferent.

Stupid me, because it made Leo angry. Then, he managed a laugh but without his usual humour. 'If you don't believe in him, how can you know if he's cruel or kind?'

Good point.

I don't know what got into me then. I hissed at him that he did not wish to take responsibility for himself. If I was going to fail, at least I knew who was the cause: me, and only me.

He stared down at me and for the first time there was anger, and he snapped back that I would never understand because I had not been brought up in the faith.

He meant I was the outsider. That stung and I told him that he was being deliberately obtuse.

Without a word, he wheeled around and disappeared into the distance, leaving me standing.

There was no contact for a couple of weeks. I was busy on the Palacrino project, which was well under way. Also Rex ordered me to Bari because I knew the town quite well, but I spent much of my time there in a frenzy of longing.

Leo blinked first. He made contact and I flew to the Villa Borghese gardens to meet him.

He was waiting in the Piazza di Siena, a blue scarf looped around his neck, looking like any normal young good-looking Italian man.

As I approached, he turned to face me. At first, we were very grave and unsmiling. Then, both of us grinned at each other like fools.

'Nina, I'm sorry.'

I remember the words repeating again and again in my head: *So am I.*

Our hands accidentally clashed together, warm, shaky, desperate for contact, any contact, and he grabbed one of mine.

Then, in an unprecedented gesture, he stroked the hair away from my cheek.

Scarcely breathing, I looked up into the face that had become dearer to me than anything and asked the question that had been haunting me. If we were ever found out, what would happen?

There was a shadow behind his eyes.

'I would be punished in ways I probably can't imagine.'

The kind of work that I do, the secret work, involves letting part of myself go. That deliberate shedding is axiomatic and beaten into the reflexes.

This interrogation of myself – a health check, if you like – is helping me to piece back together the shreds of who I am. It can sting. Certainly, the muscles of my mind ache.

Working for extended periods experiencing anxiety and, sometimes, fear is a risk on several levels. It is not unknown for people like me to end up with shot nerves.

I had a nightmare last night. I was being chased but I could not move from the spot. Classic.

Studying offers one route to inner peace. Painting my flower illustrations is another. Prolonged application clears the mind. A big project clears the mind.

The Palacrinos wished to incorporate a medieval garden into the larger one – the duke, at his most pompous and dictatorial, demanded to know if I knew what he meant. The not-so-subtle implication is that I am ignorant, but it is absolutely in my interest to let him continue thinking that I am merely a fashionable and rather ignorant designer. He is of the generation brought up to regard those below him on the social scale as deficient and he is unlikely to change. I want the order and discipline, he added, which, I suppose, reflects his political views.

Still, what he wished for his garden was charming and I created it for him on paper.

An enclosed space clustered with trees and plants. Butterflies wing through the air, a frog sits on a stone, a mouse scuttles. A pomegranate dips from a tree, an apricot settles plumply against the wall. Lavender, rosemary, lilies and blue borage crowd the beds. Fragrance that seduces visitors into enchantment.

We began the marking-out and the digging in the autumn. That moment of transition between paper and the earth is always momentous.

I look up, past the clutter of paints and paper, and out of my window. Rome is there, clustered with buildings, seething with its inhabitants. Its colours flash. Its noises curdle in the ear at night. Its beauty is undercut by decay. Living here is a magnificent experience but it can be hard.

Hot skies, the screech of vehicles, faces sheened with sweat, the unexpected and intoxicating scent of a fig tree on rounding a corner, the constant ripple of Romans on the move, a wet piazza in winter, a small fountain in a narrow street ... I have tried hard to pin down the Eternal City but none of these capture its spirit.

CHAPTER TEN

'WHY DON'T YOU LET ME HELP WITH THE NINA LAWRENCE papers?' said Paul Cursor in his charmingly diffident way. 'I've time to spare.'

According to his file, which as chief archivist she had access to, Paul was in his late fifties, had worked at the *Espatriati* for thirty years and had never showed signs of wishing for promotion, which suggested someone who was happy in their skin. 'That's above the call of duty,' she said, not really requiring help but anxious to get to know him.

Paul was in charge of the Medieval department of the archive and an expert on the depositions made by the pilgrims that had streamed into the city.

He had, she decided, a serenity and inner contentment that made him a comfortable person to spend time with. Plus, having been at the *Espatriati* for so long, he knew how to work the system.

'You've been kind to me,' she said.

He seemed neither pleased nor displeased. 'Why would I not?'

Lottie could think of several reasons, not least that it had come to her ears that Joey Haines, who worked with Paul, had railed against Lottie's appointment.

Paul was generous with the gossip.

'Rats were running around here when I first came. I didn't mind them, but they were a danger to the papers and had to go. I got quite fond of one. Mimi ... I *think* she was female. I arranged to trap her and let her go by the river before the Grim Reaper moved in.'

Lottie pried open the flaps of the first box, lifted out the notebook and confessed that she had already begun reading it.

He assessed its size and bulk. 'That'll take a bit of time.'

'Paul,' Lottie began laying out the material in sequence, 'if Nina Lawrence was murdered, how come the police had all her papers? Shouldn't the British Embassy have dealt with them?'

'Who knows?' he replied in his easy way. 'Maybe, if the case went nowhere, there was an agreement to meld what they had and deposit it with other archival material.'

They logged each of the papers on the online records and placed them into the in-house box files, ready to be taken down to the archive in the basement.

'Item: birth certificate,' said Paul. 'Name: Nina Maria Lawrence ... Born in Peterborough General Hospital, 29 September 1940. Mother: Lucilla Maria Risi. Father: Charles Nigel Lawrence, factory owner.' He stopped typing. 'Looks like her mother was Italian.'

Next up was a letter dated 1 December 1981, from a London solicitor who specialised in tracing relatives of the deceased. It stated that no living relatives had been traced for Nina Maria Lawrence but there was a will that had been drawn up in May 1977 and he was including a copy.

It was a minimalist document in which Nina instructed that she wished to be buried in Italy and her effects were to be sold and the money divided between a charity set up to preserve olive trees in Tuscany and the national collection for narcissi.

'Strange,' said Lottie.

Nina's world was almost totally unpeopled. Instead, the drama of flowers and their forms, their scents, their beauty and fragility had offered her sustenance. In death, she had rewarded them.

Other papers included a certificate of residence for Rome, several hotel bills, two for hotels on Lake Como, one for a hotel in Naples and a bill for a restaurant in the port of Bari, dated as far back as 1970. There was also a stack of letters in their envelopes tied up with twine. Finally, there was a fading photocopy of a poem, plus a photograph of a group of walkers in shorts, hats and sticks, one of whom, a small, slight figure with shoulder-length hair, might have been Nina. On the back had been written in smudged biro, 'The Lake Walkers'.

Lottie used her magnifying glass to study the photo. Nina – if it was her – had turned her head away, presenting a tanned shoulder to the camera.

She siphoned dust from a bill for a hotel in Naples … *Double Room with Bath, 2 nights*, dated June 1975. 'Double room. Do you think she had a lover?'

Paul glanced at the photograph. 'Double rooms are cheaper. The group probably shared.'

Lottie recollected the lesbian poems found in Nina's rooms.

Paul grunted as he eased apart two postcards stuck to each other. 'Siena Cathedral.' He held it up. 'And a photograph of a Roman sword.' He showed it to Nina. 'A gladius, no less – the sword that conquered the world.' He placed them written side up on the table. 'To go back to your question, and thinking about it, my instincts tell me that, by sending the papers over here, the authorities were getting shot of a problem.' He sat down at the keyboard. 'Does the case worry you?'

Lottie didn't answer directly. She squinted down at the postcards, which had the same handwriting and were signed, *Your girl x*. 'But it's sad that she was alone in her death. In life, too, it seems.'

Paul's reply elevated him even higher in her estimation. 'It's copeable with.' He stopped typing. 'My partner left twenty years ago and my family and I have not been in touch for years. I like it that way.'

At one end of the scale was the medieval Duchess of Palacrino, who had herself walled up. At the other was Paul, living a peaceful life without a companion.

'What's terrible is dying at the wrong time,' Paul observed matter-of-factly. 'Too young, or with small children. Work unfinished.'

'I'll go with that.'

She read out from the postcard dated 1 December 1970: '"For you, a Christmas song. 'I saw three ships come sailing in with red sails … come sailing in on Saturday in the morning.' Sing my song, my darling." What on earth is all that about?'

'Lovers? They say odd things.'

'She never sent them, though. Otherwise they wouldn't be in the papers. There might have been a wife somewhere in the picture.'

Paul chuckled. 'Could be.' He glanced at the postcard of the gladius. 'Was Nina planning to skewer her?'

They turned their attention to the second box.

'But this has been opened,' exclaimed Lottie. 'Who would that have been?'

Paul shook his head. 'No idea.'

A predictable miasma sifted up from the jumble inside. Inserting gloved fingers, Lottie eased out the top tranche of contents and laid them on the table.

'Police papers,' said Paul.

Lottie did the preliminary sort. 'Mostly. Reports. Diagrams of the murder site. Names and addresses.' She skimmed down the page. 'A list of contacts made by the police. Forensic report. Information about the funeral.'

'Autopsy?' said Paul.

'Can't see one.'

The police report on the funeral was bald, merely stating the date, time and location of the burial. It noted that the Reverend Hayter performed the ceremony in the presence of a representative from the British Embassy and a Bishop Dino Battista and his lay assistant. Attached with a paper clip was a black-and-white photograph of a grave labelled: *Lawrence, Nina Maria. Protestant Cemetery.*

Paul shut down his laptop. 'I've got a few police contacts. Would you like me to try to find out if they still have anything on Nina?'

For a second, Lottie felt powerless to respond.

Imagine dying in the darkness by the river, she thought with a terrible empathy, and the final sensations of being alive … the smell of dank water, of cold earth beneath frantically scrabbling fingers, of hot blood filling up the mouth.

'Lottie?'

Paul was smiling at her: pleasant, helpful, benign. Lottie looked up and his expression switched to concern. 'Are you all right?'

'Of course. Yes.'

Regulatory ropes tied up what could be known about murder investigations. Among other things, this was the basis of ordered existence, of the rule of law … of keeping anarchy at bay. 'Can you do that?'

He shook his head as if to say: *You will learn.* 'I could also take you to the Protestant Cemetery if you like,' he said, holding up the photo.

He left with a friendly, cooperative wave of his hand.

At the original job interview, the director, Valerio Gianni, beautifully suited, diplomatic, rattling with impressive contacts, had explained the funding arrangements. The archive had been set up with dollars and hefty injections of British sterling, a proportion of which had been ring-fenced to fund internships and junior posts. The financial administration was dealt with by professionals and the trustees met on a regular basis.

'We aspire to do our bit for scholarship, the underprivileged and the young,' he had said. 'We depend on you all to set the highest possible standards.'

She had been disconcerted then that Valerio Gianni felt the need to spell out what was engrained into her professional life. Now, as Paul set about shaking his police contacts, she realised she was sailing close to the line.

When Lottie walked in, she found Tom leaning on the French doors chatting to Concetta, who was wielding a professional brush around the pots on the balcony. Her dark hair gleamed, perhaps with a touch of oil.

They were animated and at ease with each other, and to witness it gave her a small pang. They had known each other so well and had been rooted in the same place for so long.

Tom looked round and stretched out a hand. 'Hello, Lottie.'

'You must let Concetta go home, Tom.'

Concetta continued to sweep. 'Signora, I've tried to clean the terrace but it's not easy.'

Tom's hand tightened in warning on hers.

'The lavender, *Signora*, you are not treating in the right way.'

'Really?' said Lottie, torn between irritation and fascination.

The lavender to which Concetta was referring was *Lavandula dentata*, a low-growing variety. 'You should be cutting back all of the growth when it gets dry,' she said, 'leaving only the green shoots. Then, you will always have lavender.'

'I'm grateful,' said Lottie. 'Tom and I can take over.'

Tom released her hand and vanished.

'The Signorina Clare was happy to have me in the evenings.'

Lottie closed her eyes briefly and chose a new tack. 'Do you have a family, Concetta?'

'*Sí*.'

'Husband? Children?'

'No husband. One daughter, Orietta.' She gathered up the broom and the dustpan. 'She has a daughter and another baby on the way.'

Lottie went in for the kill. 'But you work such long hours for us. You can't see much of her. We should give you more time.'

Concetta stood upright. 'She doesn't live in the city. I visit her on Sundays.'

'Have you always lived in Rome?'

'Where else is there to live, Signora?' Concetta removed a pot with a blood-red pelargonium off the table and repositioned it on the balcony.

Lottie itched to snatch it back. 'Did you ever hear about an Englishwoman who was found murdered down by the Tiber? Some time ago. In nineteen seventy-eight?'

'No, Signora.'

Lottie regarded the pelargonium thoughtfully. 'It was all over the press for weeks. Did you hear nothing about it?'

'If she was killed down by the river, she was in the wrong place at the wrong time. But why would I care about an Englishwoman,

Signora, when there are so many Romans who die?' She undid her apron strings. 'I'll go home now.'

She had a smile on her lips, but whether it was malicious or good-natured was impossible to tell.

Tom and Lottie ate dinner and discussed an email from Peter containing a quote from an article. 'My knowledge of Italian politics has rocketed from 0 to 100 per cent,' he said. 'Overnight. Thanks to you.'

In Italy the Republicans emerged after the war, which was providential as the Americans declared they would refuse to give any help at all to any Communist government. Thus, the conservative Christian Democrats remained in power for over fifty years, doling out state largesse and neglecting to collect taxes, until various scandals and crises toppled them. Into the vacuum stepped Forza Italia, headed up by Silvio Berlusconi. Was he a saviour? Many sources allege that the same old carousel of bribery, corruptions, jobs for the boys and sparse tax revenues whirl merrily on.

'Is that fair?' asked Lottie.

'Who knows? Probably some truth in it.'

Switching subjects, Lottie showed Tom a photo of Nina's postcards on her phone and read out the message. '"For you, a Christmas song. 'I saw three ships come sailing in with red sails … come sailing in on Saturday in the morning.' Sing my song, my darling." Rather lovely but odd, don't you think?'

Tom was slow to respond. 'What date?'

'December nineteen seventy.'

He peered at the phone. 'The gladius was the weapon of the Roman foot soldier. Maybe Nina was into Roman history.'

'Paul's taking me to the Protestant Cemetery tomorrow to see her grave.'

Tom got up from his chair. 'Lottie, don't get too hung up on this case, will you?'

'You've met Signor Marcello?' Paul asked Lottie in the taxi.

They were on their way to the Protestant Cemetery as Paul had promised.

'Works in Reception and looks as though he hates the world?'

'That's the one. For years he ran an illicit coffee shop with his son in a room off the lobby.'

She thought of all the papers in the archive. 'What would the insurance have to say about that if something had gone wrong?'

'Insurance is the least of their worries. Father and son bypassed rules and regulations for years. Then Marcello made an enemy who tipped off the authorities, which meant Valerio Gianni had to put a stop to it. There was epic sulking until they ambushed a stand in the shop opposite. Now they have a cracking business.

'The *Espatriati* doesn't have to worry about it, we have the coffee and Marcello makes his money.' He seemed pleased by the neat formulation of the Italian compromise. 'You require obstinacy to live in the UK. In Italy it's humour and toughness. And serpent-like flexibility. Actually, serpent-like cunning.'

A breeze smelling of pine blew over her bare arms from the taxi window and Lottie laughed. 'Love it.'

She turned the subject to Nina Lawrence. 'Did you ever hear anything about Nina's murder?'

They had reached the entrance to the cemetery. 'Yes,' he said, paying the fare. 'There was still a bit of gossip about it when I first arrived. It was a sensation at the time.'

'Justice wasn't done, was it? No one followed it up.'

'Possibly.' He stood aside to allow her to enter.

'No one should be alone in death. Or in life.'

She spoke more passionately than she intended, and he sent her a look as if to say: *Are we really talking about Nina?* 'I do remember it was said she was killed by a jealous lover.'

Inside, the cemetery was cooler than on the streets.

Greeting them were rows of peaceful, lichen-flecked, ivied gravestones outlined against a backdrop of Italian cypresses and pomegranate trees that fringed the perimeter. A watery light filtered silkily over the scene. Save for distant traffic, the cemetery was wrapped in silence.

Perhaps it was having fallen in love with Tom, perhaps it was the essence of the city infiltrating her consciousness, but walking down the path, she was aware of other presences. A protest rose from the graves of those whose lives had been cut short, a silence heavy with a longing for home and the cruelty of being dead.

The legibility of the inscriptions varied. Some were readable, others only just. In the main, the graves were well tended, and their clipped neatness provided a contrast with the sprawl of the vegetation.

Lottie pushed back a strand of ivy creeping across the stone guarding a child's grave. '"Never forgotten",' she read.

'Where are we heading?' asked Paul.

She showed him a copy of the black-and-white photograph and the coordinates for the grave's location, and he pointed to a heavily shaded corner. 'Over there.'

The vegetation massed thickly in that area and they were forced to search for the stone. Eventually, a corner of it became visible and Lottie set about tackling the moss and debris covering it. There it was: *Nina Maria Lawrence, 1940–1978*. No comforting inscription. No genuflection. No promise of afterlife.

Lottie ran her fingertips over the lettering – and a kinship sparked from the carving through to her. 'Why were you killed?' she asked the stone. She looked up at Paul. 'Do you think someone heard that she had a supposedly valuable medieval miniature? Or was it a mugging gone wrong? A rapist who took fright?'

Paul said, 'Lottie, Nina's dead.'

'It's not a bad place to be if you are dead,' said Lottie. 'But, if you are here, it singles you out. Forever the stranger, with a stranger's religion. Them and us.' She looked round at Paul. 'Am I allowed to take photos?'

He nodded. 'And you mustn't leave without paying tribute to Shelley and Keats.'

Shelley's stone was set into the ground, but Keats' was upright. Both recorded shockingly brief existences but, for Lottie, Keats' possessed an extra poignancy. Still, if during their lives the reputations of these wild and gifted men had been shredded or ignored, in death they rode high.

Unlike Nina, she reflected with new-minted loyalty, who also had had a life, a reputation, a talent

On the way out, Lottie stopped to donate money and caught sight of a figure ducking behind a tree. He was shaven headed and wore a leather jacket. Something about his quick and practised movement attracted her suspicion.

'Paul, I think we're being watched.'

Paul glanced in the direction of her pointing finger. 'I'm not going to say you've been reading too many thrillers.'

Lottie shoved a note into the collection box. Looking round as they left the cemetery, she again caught sight of the man standing behind a tombstone. Definitely, he was watching them.

CHAPTER ELEVEN

Rome
15 March 1978

I'M BACK IN ROME.

I have mixed feelings. And nightmares.

I have been away since last autumn and the habit of being in the city has weakened.

I know now that I wish to bring order into my life. Things have changed and, sometimes, I don't recognise myself.

Rex and I slotted back into the long-established routines. To my surprise, he demanded to know where I had been. Home?

That was a breach. Rex should not have asked the question.

I told him it was none of his business, that I had been owed a break, and he snorted that it had been months. He told me in no uncertain terms to get back on it.

I'm not sure he has forgiven me, but that doesn't matter.

At a guess, Rex hailed from an English public school, a minor one that has never produced a prime minister. He has the face of a young Renaissance blood. Search the crowd in Perugino's *Christ Giving the Keys to St Peter*, and there is Rex, with flowing hair and handsome features, observing proceedings – which is what Rex does. Listening, gathering, collating.

I tease him sometimes about the Perugino.

It was safe, neutral territory.

He's an employee of the Vatican City but, of course, he would never tell me which office. That was how it worked, with information kept to the absolute minimum.

His persona is Catholic. Obviously. Hence the meetings in the church. (The rendezvous were varied, though. Some in shops or a safe house or a tourist site. Habit was – and is – the enemy.) Having observed him for several years, he has never betrayed any sign of religious commitment. No making of the sign of the cross, no dipping of fingers into holy water. I always meant to tell him.

The Palacrino connection was an important potential source for us and he required regular updates.

We rendezvoused at the church.

The chapel is tiny and almost always deserted. I made my report and told him I was successful in getting invited to Carlo and Paola Palacrino's dinners, where the guests were a mixture of local landowners, a lawyer or two and a sprinkling of the military, including General Rasella.

The general was a top target. Virulently right wing. Known to be close to the centre of power. Sexually voracious. I had gone to work with flattery and by maintaining an air of aloofness, which I calculated would intrigue him. Quite quickly, he'd determined to have me in his bed.

He had pursued me back to Rome and insisted that we meet for a drink. He suggested a bar in the Via Veneto, which is the craziest place to choose if you don't want to be spotted and you have a wife. I took it he had an arrangement with said wife.

I arrived early to see the general huddled up with a well-known right-wing American journalist who has lived in Rome for years and was well past his prime. The journo was drunk and his lips spittle flecked. In a superbly cut suit, which set him apart from most men in the bar, the general was well on his way too.

I hovered within earshot for as long as prudent, pretending to be searching in my bag. I caught fragments of a discussion about what they called 'The Stay Behind Army', which had run training bases in Sardinia and the Abruzzi mountains for some years.

Rumours of this secret army, backed by the CIA under the control of NATO Intelligence, have been circulating for some time. Almost certainly, our masters back home would know about it, but I filed it away for Rex, before pasting a smile on to my lips and greeting the general, going about the task of charming him witless.

First Rex wanted to know if I was well and that there had been no trouble. Then he and I set about assembling what jigsaw pieces we had trawled from the information seabed over the past few weeks.

Much of it had been obtained by snooping, eavesdropping and, once at the Palacrinos, by leaving a recording device running while my hosts and the general had a late-night drink. Also, Carlo and Paola Palacrino sometimes forgot I was there when airing their views.

CP and PP discuss the well-known secret that the CIA secretly monitors the peccadillos of the Italian elite to gain a hold over them. A couple of their acquaintances are terrified at what scandalous beans might be spilt.

CP and PP agreed that the dossier is now vast and that microphones have also been secretly installed in the Vatican and the Prime Minister's palace.

They are adamantly anti left-wing and believe ex-Prime Minister Moro should not do a deal to power share with socialists.

CP and PP are apprehensive at the growing power of 'ordinary people'. They discussed this at length with General R.

General R is concerned with 'internal subversion', i.e. a socialist working class whose motive is to seize political power for the communists.

In the recording, General R also confirmed the existence of an ultra-secret army, nicknamed the 'Stay Behind Army'. Also known as the Gladio. Allegedly backed by NATO and endorsed by US generals and the CIA. Its mission is to combat a Russian invasion or a Communist government.

General R dropped hints that something big might be happening but did not elaborate.

Rex's chair scraped over the chapel floor.

Did all this seem fanciful? After all, it was 1978 and politics should be less aggressive. Subtler and more conciliatory. Rex and I chewed it over. When I eavesdropped in the bar in the Via Veneto, the general and the washed-up American journalist had referred to the 1970 attempted coup by the secret army.

The coup had been aborted when Soviet ships were spotted cruising in the Mediterranean and NATO and Washington realised that crucial intelligence had been leaked to the Soviets.

This was Cold-War politics.

I reminded Rex that I found out about the Soviet ships when I scoped Bari.

It was one of my small triumphs.

17 March 1978

SOMETHING BIG HAS HAPPENED.

Yesterday, Aldo Moro, President of the National Council of Christian Democrats and ex-Prime Minister, was kidnapped.

Communists, fascists, right-wing or wild-card paramilitaries?

Rex let drop a rare bit of information, which, doubtless, he got from The Office back home. Apparently, no intelligence chatter had been picked up beforehand, which suggests that the perpetrators were 'clean skins'. However, there was no doubting it had been a professional operation, which suggests there were 'sleepers' in the population, lying low until called into action.

Aldo Moro had been about to do a deal with the Communist Party. Therefore, the question must be: why would a communist or socialist bite off the hand that offered a share of power unless it was to split the Left? NB: Non-militant left-wingers are appalled.

Shouldn't the question be looked at from another angle? What if it was the right wing, disguised as left wing, wishing to discredit the left wing?

What if it had been American backed, which would account for the fact the operation had been efficient and clearly well funded?

Whoever has taken Moro will probably kill him.

What a troubled country Italy is at present. Angry, doubting, divided, however much we wished otherwise. Countries go through these upheavals, but the past decades here have been sobering.

The neo-fascists and right-wingers hate the left and are protected by the security services, and many of those who turned to Leninist politics have talked themselves into advocating armed uprisings.

18 March 1978

THE RED BRIGADES HAVE TODAY ISSUED A COMMUNIQUÉ, PLUS a photograph of the captured Moro, claiming full responsibility for his abduction.

I relay to Rex the snippets of opinion (facts are hard to come by) that I gather when out and about.

> *The Red Brigades acted on their own. The Red Brigades are being manipulated by Russia. The Red Brigades have been infiltrated by the CIA. The Red Brigades are actually a bunch of fascists who wish to provoke anti-communist feeling by blaming it on them.*

Take your pick.

The authorities have put up roadblocks around the city and are carrying out house searches for the kidnapped ex-prime minister. Soldiers in full battledress patrol the streets. The sirens scream day and night.

I was stopped on the way back to the Via della Luce from dinner in the Campo Marzio.

The policeman who manhandled me to one side, shouted: 'What the f*** are you doing out? A woman on her own.'

He left a bruise on my arm.

For the record

On 4 January, in Cassino, the boss of the Fiat security services was killed. Leftists?

7 January, in Rome, two militants of the Italian Social Movement were killed by far leftists.

On 20 January, in Florence, a policeman was killed by Marxist-Leninists.

On 7 February, in Prato, a notary was killed by leftists.

On 14 February, in Rome, a judge was killed by the Red Brigades.

On 10 March, in Turin, a marshal was killed by the Red Brigades.

There is also a vague rumour that a seventeen-year-old girl was found murdered in a cellar in the Vatican City. Her name had been linked with a well-known cardinal.

CHAPTER TWELVE

Lottie noted that the window blind had been drawn down over the majolica at Gabriele's workshop when she turned up for their appointment.

On entering, she was greeted with the same odour of ink and glue, the same obvious order and control – tools precisely positioned, books neatly stacked. She spotted two early treatises of Galileo and Isaac Newton and a fancy edition of Euripides' tragedies. A folio-sized book, bound in damaged brown Morocco leather, rested on a foam-rubber book support on the workbench. The display easel stood in the corner covered by a cloth.

It was an unusual place, almost a cave, in which were sequestered riches for the mind and for the senses. Yet when she thought about it, Gabriele Ricci displayed no discernible joy or excitement in his work, nor any sense of pleasure in preserving the endangered.

He emerged from the back room and they exchanged greetings.

'My colleague, Paul Cursor from the Medieval department, will be here in a minute,' said Lottie, 'but before he arrives … Valerio Gianni, our director, was wondering if you and … your wife – or partner? – could join a few of us from the archive for dinner?'

Lottie caught a flash of irritation and something else she could not place. 'How kind. Thank you. It will just be me as I live alone.'

'Then Mirella from the director's office will contact you.' She gestured to the folio on the book support. 'That looks interesting.'

'Late-eighteenth century. Maps of the Rome you never normally see. The city is riddled with tunnels, catacombs and underground passages.' Gabriele pulled on a pair of gloves and turned a page, and Lottie noted that he handled it as gently as a new-born baby. 'It's another dimension to this city. If your stomach is up to it, and you're not afraid of the contents of sewers, you can read about them. There're also fascinating analyses of what the ancient Romans liked to eat and what they got rid of.'

'Oyster shells, I imagine?'

'Yes. Analysis of their excreta tells us they liked to eat local produce. They also threw away a lot of jewellery, probably by mistake, and sent curses down the latrine.'

He turned back to the folio. 'These old maps help conservationists and developers map the risk of collapse in the city. As you can imagine, that is ever a worry for their profits.' He sounded very dry. 'Look up where the *Espatriati* is and you will see that an old street runs under it... Romans like to build on top of other layers. In the war, people hid there.'

She bent over to study it and noticed a pink-tinged stain at the bottom right-hand corner.

'Not blood this time.' Gabriele was at her elbow. 'Wine. At a guess, someone looked through the book holding a glass.'

'What could possibly go wrong?' said Lottie.

He traced the shadowy stain. 'They tried to blot it. But you almost never obliterate the traces.'

Lottie eased upright. 'Did you feel the vocation for books from early on?'

'A vocation?' He seemed startled by the term. 'Yes and no. I had to study hard for the qualifications. I learned to give heart and soul to the work, to … if you like … *interview* my books and papers, to understand them and their secrets and what makes them what they are.'

'But you don't love them, I think.'

The words left her lips and she knew she had trespassed. Of course she had.

For a moment, he looked furious. Then he relaxed. 'If I want to know about you … I give you room to speak, and I listen. I find out where you have come from, who you live with, your thoughts. It's impossible to achieve that crucial and meaningful level of knowledge without studying you. It's the same with the books and the work on them. I need to live closely to them. I must breathe them in, I have to interrogate their pages for the evidence of their past lives, I must observe them as honestly as I am able. Only then can I repair them. Would you still maintain I don't love them?'

'Sorry,' she said. 'Unforgivable.'

His eyes narrowed. 'Don't be.'

At that moment, Paul Cursor arrived and the subject was dropped.

The introductions made, Gabriele moved over to the easel and eased off the covering. The painting shimmered into their respective visions.

Lottie noted that she had clenched her fists.

Gabriele turned around to face them.

There was a moment of anticipation.

'It is a modern copy or, rather, a pastiche,' he said.

'Oh …' said Lottie. She and Paul exchanged glances.

'But with a curious twist. The paints are post-war but, interestingly, the parchment is late medieval. The artistry is beautiful and accurate for the period and, if paint analysis wasn't available, one could almost be taken in.' He pointed to the initials in the bottom left-hand corner. 'But for this. Artists of that era did not sign their work.'

Lottie ran over in her mind what might have been – the fanfare and the negotiations – without too much regret. Harder to let go was the pleasure of handling, of being close to, an artefact so precious and rare.

Paul bent over the painting. 'The initials are E and K.' He looked up at Gabriele. 'Any idea?'

There was a pause. A long one. Gabriele shrugged. 'Your guess is as good as mine.'

'But the parchment?' Paul persisted.

'That's the easier puzzle to solve. It comes from a stash that the trade knows about. When the Allies bombed Rome in July nineteen forty-three, the Basilica Papale di San Lorenzo fuori le mura where some medieval scribes had worked were badly damaged. The cache was discovered in a cellar in a sealed metal chest. News of it leaked out and libraries, etc., fought to get hold of some for repairs. But the black market moved in and forgers got their hands on a quantity. They couldn't believe their luck.' He gave a wintry smile. 'Who knows how many forgeries are circulating as a result.'

Lottie stood in front of *The Annunciation*, narrowing her eyes until the painting filled her vision.

She peered closer.

The background – an example of the travel landscape so beloved of the medieval painter in which small figures appeared more than once – lured her into its vista of mysterious, dreaming rocks and mountain slopes, the wild lushness a counterpoint to the order and colour of the garden that framed the girl below. It was then she noticed what she had previously missed … the woman and the monk had been portrayed for a third time. Here rendered tiny, their figures partly obscured by the misty chiaroscuro, they were approaching the summit and almost on a par with the golden sun.

The painted parchment reverberated with their urgency and fear. Sucked into their flight, she felt the mountain stones punish her feet, the dry heave of oxygen-starved lungs, a terror of falling.

Both men were looking at her. 'OK?' asked Paul.

She stepped back. 'Yes. Of course.'

It came to her in a flash. The flat surfaces and stylised images of the painting – projecting serenity – were deceptive. Painted into them was turbulence and unhappiness.

'Is there a problem?' asked Gabriele.

'Not in a direct sense,' she replied. 'Only I think the painter was unhappy. It's a beautiful work but there's an uneasy element running through it. Perhaps it's the Virgin's unease?'

Gabriele looked away, but not before she noticed that he seemed shaken.

'Thank you for letting me look at it,' he said after a pause. 'The painter is very skilled and knowledgeable about the period. I know we all hoped it was genuine.'

While Gabriele packed up the painting, Lottie and Paul took the opportunity to examine the volumes on the shelves. They lighted on the Euripides, a rare edition printed in Venice, and were discussing the typeface when someone came through the door.

Lottie recognised Signor Antonio, black clad, groomed, a trifle stooped. His phone rang and he stepped back outside to answer it.

'Let's go.' She nudged Paul. 'Now.'

Gabriele handed the painting to Lottie, they said their goodbyes and Lottie and Paul emerged into the street. They passed Signor

Antonio who, having finished his phone call, was smoking a cigarette. He and Lottie exchanged glances but did not greet each other.

They heard Gabriele say, 'You've come about the maps.'

'Why the haste?' Paul wanted to know.

'He's been snooping around the painting. Planned to claim it back for the Vatican museums if it was genuine.'

'Not for the first time. Nor the last,' said Paul.

Lottie raised an eyebrow.

She remained in the office for her lunch hour, reading through Nina's journal.

This entry had no date.

From where did my subversion spring? A remote ancestor who took up arms against a king, or his country, or even God, and infected the family DNA? Not that I fitted into my family in any important respect.

As a child, I pictured myself going into battle with cropped hair, a sword held over my head and a shield clamped to my side. I was the avenging goddess. I was Joan of Arc. I was the wind. I was powerful.

Adulthood did not turn out that way. Any sword waving was disguised, any riding on the wind hidden by darkness and the pall of boredom through which I struggled.

I had one advantage. The romantic child became the woman that holds no moral views on lying, only that it should be skilfully accomplished. The art of the lie is to use it sparingly. I lied to my parents when I left home at twenty-three. I told them I would return but I had no intention of ever doing so. Nor have I. Not even for their funerals.

My mother never rated my looks – the ugly duckling. She called me 'Duck' or 'The Duck' (but never 'the dumb cluck' because I wasn't dumb). But, as I came to understand as I grew older, she gave me the gift of never having to worry about beauty because I knew from the beginning it was never there.

('But you *are* beautiful,' Leo told me. 'Everything about you is beautiful.' And I held my breath from happiness.)

I can pinpoint the day when my life spun on its axis.

Back with my parents in Surrey after graduating, the cherished letters after my name (Fine arts plus Italian) on the certificate resting on my bedroom mantelpiece, I was restless and miserable. What next? How to sneak past the ditches and fences of a childhood patrolled by parents who wished for nothing more for their daughter than the same lives they had led?

My mother demanded to know what I was wearing for the party that night. I asked her what would be the point of getting dressed up.

Because, was the reply.

I knew what my mother was driving at. But I hadn't fought my way through college – my mother shuddered slightly – studied until my hair fell out, starved on the meagre allowance and finally got the degree just to get married, I told her.

She tilted her head, a habit when agitated, and told me it was my happiness that she was worrying about.

That was easy. She had no idea what would make me happy and I told her that too.

My mother felt on safer ground with this one and recited her mantra that a husband, children and a home made a woman happy. She inflected the words as if speaking to a seven-year-old.

I marshalled my knowledge, culled over the years of living with my parents, and threw down a gauntlet, asking her to tell me truthfully if she had been happy.

My mother's increasingly veined hand plucked at her salmon-pink Viyella blouse and she muttered that it was impossible not to have been.

There were many, many reasons why not. Having deciphered the fixed expression on her face, which she would have been horrified to learn suggested ambivalence and not a little suffering, I took pity and went to the party.

Held in one of those glistening white houses in Chelsea, it was hot and crowded. I hugged the wall, trying not to be crushed up against strange bodies. After an hour of torment, I decided to leave.

A middle-aged man with a pencil moustache and very blue eyes touched me on the shoulder. He told me he knew who I was and he could tell that I was about to bolt.

As a chat-up line it was hopeless.

He ignored my lack of response and sent something that went crackling through me. He said I looked as though I could do with an interesting job.

Spot on.

I was careful not to respond too enthusiastically and asked him who he was and he told me that he was friendly with my uncle Richard and that they had been talking about me. He said something else about my brains being unfashionable in a woman, but that he thought they could be very useful, plus my languages.

I remember the thump of excitement. I gestured to the heaving, smoky crowd in the next room. 'Anything but this,' I said.

'Then you'll do.'

His name was Major Trevor and, during our subsequent meeting at his nondescript office off Whitehall, he said he worked for the government, which had need of clever people to make sure its interests were furthered abroad. His eyes were the colour of steel and never swerved from my face as he talked, but I wasn't bothered. It wasn't a sexual predator's gaze, or an admonishing one. It was the gaze of someone who was looking at me. Properly.

Some people are good at sitting at desks analysing and evaluating incoming information, he told me. Some are better at going out into the highways and byways to find that information. An eyebrow lifted as he informed me that he thought I fell into the latter category.

What did he have in mind?

Major Trevor – almost certainly not his real name – gave the kind of oblique answer that became familiar and said he would like to see me brush up my German and Italian, even though I was fluent in both. There were many lessons ahead, he said gnomically. And the first one was: never to leave a trail. Ever.

In a funny way, that was the hardest part: being no one, nowhere, with neither footing nor foundation.

Two years later, I was sent to Istanbul. Major Trevor warned me to go carefully at his final briefing. We were sitting opposite each other with maps arranged between us. I remember his words very well: Our training is just that. Training. It can't replicate what happens on the ground. Be aware, it may take you by surprise. A scrupulous man, I concluded for the nth time. A professional. I wouldn't wish to work for anyone who wasn't.

Istanbul's a den of thieves, he warned. Spooks, smugglers, killers, blackmailers, black marketeers and he never knew whether it was an advantage or a disadvantage sending females. Get yourself to Taksim's, he said. It's run by a White Russian who accepts bribes from everyone without favouritism and arranges for spies to eavesdrop on each other. He laid his hands flat on the table and finished. 'Avoid the Egyptian Bordeaux.'

I took the advice. I was there for a year, did my job, was fascinated by the city and by Turkey and fell in love. Disastrously. He was older – very married – and a journalist. Aware that the affair threatened to destroy me, I asked for a transfer.

I flew home and met Colonel Trevor in a mediocre restaurant in Soho. He scrutinised me over the rim of his wine glass and informed me that I had fallen into the trap of falling in love with another spy. His rueful expression made him almost human and he told me he was sorry I hadn't realised that he was one of the team.

When I thought it over, the pieces slotted together, triggering even greater agony. When I came through, shaken and damaged, I had one aim, which was never to be in that position again.

Major Trevor offered to refill my glass and told me he was sending me to Rome. I was to take a horticulture course because my cover was to be a garden designer advising on the restoration of gardens damaged during the war. Whenever possible, I was to opt for wholesale redesigning, which would bring me into contact with government departments and other possible sources of intelligence.

Here I am, then.

If life was fair, which it is not, I should be running Rex.

My instincts are better than his. I understand about caring for agents, who are almost certainly men and women with wounds: childhood trauma, orphaned, neglected, passed over, pushed unfairly out of the nest. Probe gently and you will find lurking in the background a dominating, belittling parent, abandonment, secret sexual longings, often alienation from the world they inhabit. This ensures they will respond powerfully, often unconsciously, to the invitation to join a secret fraternity and find their wounds soothed by its inclusivity.

Agents are assessed in terms of their *suitability*. In my case? Young-ish, unmarried, unremarkable. Their ability to gain *access* to a given target. It has taken time to penetrate all levels of Italian society. Their *motivation* and *patriotism*. Wounded animals will stick by the one who saves and cares for them.

Sense of humour? Yes. No. Yes.

How to handle agents successfully? It is best to treat them like fledglings, with patience and empathy and not a little stroking. Then the combination of intelligence, modesty and ruthlessness that agents so often exhibit is coaxed delicately into life.

Rex is not that good at it. I think his personality is unstable at times. He becomes ensnared. He has a set vision of the intelligence we should gather and is angered when we can't obtain it. I also wonder sometimes if he is frightened. I would not blame him if he was. I am, too.

How many agents does he run? Quite a few, I guess. Yet Rex never makes you feel special or that your safety is paramount, which would be the most productive way to get the most out of the winged and wounded ducks that we are.

But I am a woman. Need I say more?

In the beginning, I was 'seduced' by the major, that oh-so professional wooer, into this business. He told me that I had a beautiful voice at that meeting all those years ago in London, a statement that both alarmed and disarmed me. It was a compliment – and not many came my way.

That's how I became what I am.

I told Rex about meeting Leo.

I wish I hadn't.

Lottie propped *The Annunciation* up on the bench. Its fate would be decided at the upcoming monthly meeting. No doubt, agreement would be reached that whoever painted it *was* remarkable and impressively well versed in the artistic vernacular of the past. Paint ventriloquism at its most dazzling.

The power of this story was indisputable. Lottie's gaze travelled over the joyous colours, the Virgin's fear and ecstasy, the implacable archangel, the scurry of the animals in their garden, the staggering blue of cloak and sky, and rested on the figures toiling up the mountain— and exclaimed out loud.

The initials were one factor, and it was possible that a fifteenth-century artist had yearned to be recognised, but what she should have spotted was the detail that hammered the nail into the coffin of medieval authenticity, for it would have been unthinkable for that period.

Far up that mountain, the softly rendered woman and the monk held hands.

She caught her breath. Gabriele Ricci must have known that too.

CHAPTER THIRTEEN

Tom was going away for a couple of nights to a British Council gathering in Naples.

'You'll like a bit of peace, I bet.' He searched in the sock drawer while packing. 'Time for yourself.'

Was he willing her not to confess to moments of wishing she were back in her London flat? She glanced at the dressing table, where her things fought for space with Tom's. The honeymoon gloss had worn off a little and she thought of the apartment's dismal decoration. Brown furniture, grubby paintwork and curtains and blinds that had grown ragged in service. A standard lamp with a hideous bilious shade was the final abomination.

'Yes,' she said.

He threw a shirt into an overnight bag. 'Do you think you've settled?'

Despite its rapidity, Tom's packing was practised. He knew exactly what he needed and where to stow it in the overnight bag. 'To being married?'

'I'm learning.'

The adult, and sensible, theory that transparency and honesty were the only way to make a partnership work was not necessarily successful in practice. Tom laughed, but not with any amusement.

'Now, why did I hope you were going to say that it was the best decision you had ever made?'

Contrite, she kissed his cheek. 'Tom, it is. I promise.'

In bed, later, she slid her arms around him. For a few seconds, he relaxed against her before moving away. 'It's too hot, Lottie.'

In Lottie's office, the remainder of Nina Lawrence's archive was laid out in sequence. Selecting the more robust documents, she worked fast to scan the papers and upload them into the file 'Garden Notes', which she had created on her personal laptop.

Transferring them to a private database was not exactly forbidden but it butted up against protocol and, not for the first time since arriving in Rome, Lottie had to acknowledge that Italy was having a strange effect on her behaviour.

The police papers included a list of names typed on to yellowing paper. Heading the list was Marta Teresa Livardo, 31, employed as caretaker by La Cattolica, the landlord of Nina's apartment in the Trastevere.

She rang Paul and was amused at how promptly he answered the phone. 'I suspect you're a master at contacts.'

He laughed. 'Try me.'

Lottie explained she wanted to track down Marta Livardo. Paul was hesitant. 'Is this wise, Lottie? You never know.' Contained in the 'never know' was a multitude of reservations. 'Stirring up things can be complicated.'

'I'll never say you didn't warn me.'

Sweat prickled under her arms. Guilt? Excitement? Her feet had swollen in new, strappy sandals and she kicked them off, enjoying the sensation of a cool stone floor on her hot flesh. It was noticeably warmer. Tom had warned Lottie that summer could be airless, brutal at times and unremitting, and this was the foretaste.

Footsteps approached down the corridor. Lottie shut down the lid of her laptop, slid the leather notebook into her bag and flipped up on to her computer screen a page headed 'Notes on Methodology'.

'It's me.' Mirella, Valerio Gianni's personal assistant, came in the door. 'Signor Gianni's timetable for next week.' She had a habit of speaking slowly and with pauses.

The timetable could just as well have been circulated online, but Mirella insisted on taking it around in person. This had nothing to do with efficiency and everything to do with her desire to remind her colleagues that she was exceptionally beautiful.

Dressed in jeans and a sleeveless white blouse that gave her a magnificent opportunity to show off her toned, tanned arms, she was the personification of chic. 'Signor Gianni sends his compliments,' she said, balancing on a heeled gladiator sandal. She glanced at the piles of documents and a sculptured eyebrow rose.

Lottie scanned the schedule. 'I see that I'm not required at any of these events. Shouldn't I be?'

'Signor Gianni is sorry,' said Mirella. 'These appointments are mostly personal. I'm sure you understand. However, he asks if you would check over the projected running costs for your department.' She slid a file over the desk. 'He regrets the inconvenience.'

This was a bare-faced lie. Neither Valerio nor Mirella cared about the inconvenience.

'Who will sign them off?'

Mirella had the grace to look uncomfortable. 'The director asked if you would be so kind.'

'Since I've had no hand in them,' Lottie pointed out, 'I can't reasonably be expected to sign them until we've discussed them.'

Mirella's gladiator sandal proved suddenly to be unstable. Leaving the timetable in front of Lottie, she assumed a pose in the doorway that granted Lottie a first-class view of her slender figure.

It was so blatant that Lottie smiled. 'I wish I had your figure,' she said, and was rewarded with the flicker of a smile and a polite '*grazie*'.

Lottie was left to survey the scene of her triumph – which was almost certainly pyrrhic but quite funny.

Among the documents scanned into her laptop was a handwritten article on foolscap paper, which, Lottie concluded after some thought, Nina had intended for publication.

The handwriting – black ink on lined paper – was now familiar. The date at the top of the page was 15 January 1975.

How many Romes are there?

Where else will you find style, fashion, art, cinematic innovation, architecture, spiritual comfort, classical memory all contained within one boundary?

Even after the war, which left districts like San Lorenzo devastated and the population hungry, jobless, ill and feeling as battered as the city's infrastructure, it was still the cradle for artistic innovation. Go into any bar or café and the likelihood was a first-class musician would play to you as you drank rough red wine. Look into a shop window and the creations of Italian fashion houses dazzled the eye. Go to Cinecittà and the films that would electrify the western world were being made.

The text was fractured with crossings-out and word substitutions. The article was not, in Lottie's view, important but it gave an insight into how Nina worked.

Next was a page torn out from a book that Lottie found a little shocking. The typography suggested it was from the sixties.

> *Lunaria biennis.* Honesty.
> Not to be confused with *Lunaria,* the fern called
> Moonwort that was credited with magical properties. L.
> *biennis* was introduced into England from Germany in
> the 1570s. It has been called Judas Pence, Money-in-both-
> Pockets or White Satin and Prick-song-wort ...

In the margin, in Nina's favoured black ink, was written, *If only honesty was possible ... If only ... if only ...* Lottie noted the comment.

She turned to an article on the narcissus from a publication called *The Determined Traveller.* Earlier in the week, Lottie had emailed a contact at a press-cutting association and asked if he had ever heard of it. A few days later he replied: 'In-house publication for the Foreign and Commonwealth Office during the seventies. Ceased publication in 1982.'

Integrated into the article were two coloured illustrations. The first was a botanical painting of the narcissi in a typical habitat, plus a transverse section of its seed head with detailed labelling.

The second illustration she recognised as the hill-top town of Palacrino. Narcissi bloomed in profusion on the slopes beneath the town, and foxes, mice and rabbits played around them. On the right of the painting a mountain, dotted with pines and ilex, dominated the skyline. The caption read: *An enlarged detail from a copy of a fifteenth-century manuscript.*

She reached for her magnifying glass. Even with its help, the subtler details were hard to make out, but she willed herself to travel through its portal into the painted world where rabbits had green eyes and very white scuts. They seemed familiar, possibly because many fifteenth-century paintings employed the same iconography.

The artist understood 'atmospheric perspective', which she and Gabriele Ricci had talked about, a device where the foreground was rendered in the vivid colours and the background bleached into near monochrome. 'It's a trick,' he had said, 'to hoodwink the onlooker into thinking they are looking into a hazy distance.'

The magnifying glass revealed a tiny figure in a monk's habit climbing towards a stone building on a rocky outcrop. Its detail was so vivid, so alive, that Lottie was transported into that painted world, listening to the scuffle of sandals on the rocks, the pant of breath forced from overtaxed lungs.

Next, she focused on the crenellations and towers of the hill town. At a top window of a turret, a woman in a plain grey gown gazed towards the mountain. A pair of slender hands clasped the sill and every line of her body expressed longing and a deep despair.

Lottie straightened up.

She thought of the bewildered Virgin in *The Annunciation* and, behind in the distance, the monk and his companion scrambling up the mountain.

She thought of the olive trees and the gold bar of sunlight striking them. And of the initials, EK.

Lottie slid the magnifying glass back into its cover. The idiosyncrasies and leitmotifs of the copyist and of the artist who painted *The Annunciation* had become familiar, much as the submergence of her own emotions into these painted, background dramas had wrenched her responses into unfamiliar configurations.

Puzzled and uneasy, she sat unmoving, with her hands in her lap, for some time, before checking her watch and summoning the porter.

He arrived promptly, muttering he only had half an hour before he left, and she helped load up the trolley, keeping back only the notebook.

In the basement, the lift opened opposite the steel doors into the archive proper. The porter pressed the button, they hissed open and, wheels spinning and creaking with a language of their own, he navigated the trolley inside.

Lottie followed him into the hushed interior.

The barrel-vaulted cellar ran the length of the building and was divided by archival shelving. The surface of the walls had been scraped back to the original dusky-red brick, which, since it was not an ideal material for an archive, had been treated and sealed. Pipes bisected the ceiling and bundled wires ran from sealed junction boxes. The atmosphere was suitably cool and hushed. Uplighters threw shadows up the walls and, except for a central area with chairs, a table and a lamp that threw a circular illumination, the light was crepuscular.

The porter was opening up the designated shelving and Lottie walked down the central aisle to the arch set into the brick wall, which signalled the limit of the archive.

Retracing her steps, she passed an unlabelled door guarding a set of shelving and stopped short. Had she heard something? A footstep?

A few seconds later, a door closed. Soft enough but recognisable.

'Is there anyone there?' she called.

No reply.

'Did you hear anything?' she asked the porter. 'It sounded like a door somewhere.'

'That's the air conditioning, Signora.'

The porter pulled back the sliding steel doors guarding Lottie's section and she began the task of stowing the papers on its shelves.

He tapped a tattoo on the trolley handle, which was distracting, and she told him that she could manage on her own.

She lifted the first box on to the shelf and slotted it into place.

Nina lived in a Trastevere apartment from the sixties to her death in 1978.

She travelled around Italy.

She fell in love with Leo and talked to Rex.

Her last published work was on narcissi.

'Who are you, Nina?'

In part, the answer reposed in these archive boxes and a journal but even the most brilliant historians and archivists would never decode more than one degree of the past. The only thing possible was to build a bridge as carefully and scrupulously as possible – which was precisely what the cherishing of these papers attempted to do.

What better place was there to stow the relicts of unquiet souls and rebels, alongside those who were contentedly dead after long lives, provided they were organised, housed and, against the odds, honoured?

She put this to Gabriele Ricci later as they sat beside each other in the sushi restaurant.

'It's a constructive way to think about the archive,' he said. 'I like the idea of honouring.'

'Nina Lawrence now occupies her space on the shelves.'

'Ah.'

The restaurant was just off the Piazza Navona and their table was by the window. Valerio made a toast. 'This is to our good friend, Gabriele, who helps us so much with our work.'

Gabriele gave a little speech in thanks and Lottie watched him. The customary black had been discarded in favour of dark blue trousers and a white shirt, which suited him much better. He was freshly shaved and wore an expensive watch that she had not seen before. The hermit had been put aside.

He must have known that *The Annunciation* was a modern pastiche. Yet he had said nothing.

He caught Lottie's scrutiny and raised an eyebrow.

Seated on the other side of him, Valerio's wife – an older version of Mirella – was obviously taken with Gabriele and monopolised him as much as possible. He appeared to be enjoying the attention, conversed easily and, from time to time, laughed at Valerio's witticisms.

Lottie watched a family pass by the window. He, tall with brushed-back hair. She, slightly plump but fabulously turned out in a linen shift and big jewellery. Their children beautiful and feral looking.

She turned to Gabriele. 'You're such an attractive people.'

'But living here can be hard, too,' he said in an echo of what Nina had written. 'I hope I'm not stepping over the mark if I say that, when you come to Rome, to Italy, it's vital to understand the levels on which we operate.'

Was he teasing or being – just a touch – patronising?

She gave him the benefit of the doubt. 'Tell.'

'OK, one example.' There was a touch of satire and not a little relish – so that was all right, she thought. 'You're either *statale*, government worker, or *non-statale*. The *statale* enjoy legendary and eye-watering privileges. They're a class apart. The *non-statale* spend their lives scheming to become *statale*. The *statale* consider they have made the right decisions in life. The *non-statale* point out that they occupy the high moral ground because they have set hours, limited opportunity for moonlighting and, unlike the despised but envied *statale*, pay taxes from source.' The caricature was drily done.

She was about to reply but his attention was reclaimed by Valerio's wife, who landed a jewelled hand on Gabriele's arm and demanded to know what was needed to be good at his kind of work.

She sensed his impatience, but he was polite enough with his answer. 'A sense of smell.' The hand taxied an inch up Gabriele's arm. He shifted and it was removed. 'Parchments from Northern Europe can smell warm. Leathery. Parchments from Italy, say, have a sharper, cooler scent.'

Paul sat on Lottie's left; he and Amber Brierley (Nineteenth-Century department) were wrangling amicably over which were the best areas of the city. He turned to Lottie. 'Amber and I agree that the Janiculum Hill is a fantastic place to live.' He sounded nostalgic. 'In fact, I did once – when I first came to the archive. The pay was dire and, in those days, the Janiculum was cheap, and it had the best view over the Trastevere.'

So the American general had been stingy?

'It was a good experience.' Paul sounded nostalgic. 'Not least because I got fit climbing up there every day.'

'Show me on the map.' Lottie whipped out her phone and he

pointed to where it rose on the opposite side of the river from the traditional seven hills.

'It was a hell of a climb and the apartment had not a stick of furniture, not even a cooker. I slept on the floor. But it had wonderful views over the city.' He smiled. 'I used to find shards of red porphyry from Cleopatra's kitchens.'

'Normally, I wouldn't put Cleopatra and a kitchen in the same sentence.'

Paul laughed. 'There were three kitchens sited on the hill and I'm pretty sure the porphyry came from them.'

'Three!'

'The slaves were ordered to produce food at six, eight and ten.' Sweetly, Paul appeared to be thoroughly enjoying the attention of both women. 'Caesar was a busy man. All that dotting about conquering, and she wanted to be able to give him a hot meal whenever he came home from the Senate of an evening.'

'Are you telling me that Cleopatra was a fifties housewife?' Amber laughed.

At the end of the meal, they said their goodbyes. Lottie exchanged glances with Gabriele.

She wanted to confront him. *You knew from the first that* The Annunciation *was not authentic.* Did his behaviour constitute a betrayal? She thought it did.

On the way home, she encountered a Great Roman Traffic Challenge.

Overlooked by a Roman emperor who projected the Roman virtues of discipline and public order (although the emperor had probably been mad and debauched) and by a Church that offered an alternative promise of redemption, a Mexican stand-off between an SUV and a scooter was in train. Horns blared and traffic snarled.

A radio blasted out gangster rap. A sweet, but almost sickly, smell of jasmine drifted from a plant running along a wall.

The scooter won. The traffic snorted into life. Tom had explained to Lottie that the authorities tackled Rome's chronic traffic problem by passing more and more laws to prevent double and triple parking and the blocking of entrances. These were robustly ignored.

Did the city dignitaries who espoused good, logical intentions ever analyse the anarchy that reigned? Did it matter? Somehow, everything kept going.

Lottie searched in her bag for her phone. She must text Tom. She must make it right.

Tom arrived back from the Naples trip the following evening.

Lottie had been ruthless and banished Concetta and, for once, she was in the kitchen preparing supper. She dropped everything and hugged him close.

'It's worth going away,' he said.

Her voice was muffled against his shoulder. 'What *were* you doing exactly?'

'Trying to impress on the Neapolitans that the British Council is their friend.'

'And did you?'

Tom bent over and kissed her. He seemed thoughtful. 'You've just revealed that you've never been to Naples. They don't take kindly to being told what to think.' He kissed her again. 'What did you do?'

She shifted a little in his embrace. 'Eating and working.'

Tom eyed the large lasagne that Lottie lifted out of the oven. 'You know you told me about women starving in order to become saints. Let me categorically assure you that you'll never be one.'

CHAPTER FOURTEEN

Rome
16 April 1978

r
EX AND I ARRANGED A MEETING.

The Red Brigades have issued a sixth communiqué proclaiming that Moro has been found guilty and condemned to death.

There have been eleven shootings in Venice in the past seventeen days.

'Get yourself invited to the Palacrinos', Rex ordered, as if it were the easiest thing in the world. 'Say you have to check something out in the garden.'

The goddess Fortune has been kind in one major respect: I love my work, my parallel universe, which is the garden. When I die, twine ivy around my coffin and scatter rose petals over it.

I once said as much to Leo when we were still together, and pain swept across his features. I wished I had kept quiet.

Looking back.

Ours was not a conventional love affair. Obviously. We rarely touched, except for the time we did. But I look back on it, knowing that I will never be so happy again.

It was slow to develop. In the beginning, we found friendship in a common interest in the land.

I described the woeful condition of formal Italian gardens still languishing even now after the war. Private and public ones had been hit by high taxes and the need to concentrate on other priorities. Every cloud ... he told me. True. The neglect gave me a living.

The way we talked to each other began to change. They were normal exchanges about weather, plants, traffic. Yet other feelings and intentions surged underneath.

This was dangerous, I told him, and he agreed.

That was one of the many things about Leo. He understood without it being spelled out.

When I first knew him, he was relatively free to meet me but, after joining the seminary in the autumn of '76, his movements were curtailed. I was busy, too, travelling around the area and, once, to Bologna and Romagna. (Romagna is known for being the least biddable of the Italian regions and Rex wanted me to take soundings.)

Our walks were important. Exercise is not so easy in a crowded city but, if you are prepared to tackle the spider's web of lesser streets, rewarding. There was the Villa Borghese ... when he stroked my hair. The Circo Massimo. Other parks. We chased down fountains. Not the gaudier ones of the Trevi or the Barcaccia, but the smaller ones and the street-corner *fontanelle*. If you search and have patience and good footwear then there are many. Plump-breasted women, dolphins, lions and amphorae emerging from the stone. Those gleaming animals and humans have nothing more laid on them than to ensure the water is directed in a shining arc and they are happy because nothing ever happens to them.

He described what would make up his future: the rituals, the hierarchies, and who held the authority. It would be a life of personal silence and abnegation while carrying other people's burdens.

In return, I told him about my world, the one I could discuss.

The impoverished prince who longs to bring his run-down villa back to glory but is running out of money. Meanwhile, his wife has run away with a wine producer from South Africa.

The Palacrinos striving to re-organise their estate as a feudal operation and who revere the memory of Mussolini.

And I told him, too, about the living things with which I work: the narcissi, the roses, the salvias and the alchemilla *mollis*.

Leo replied that he preferred the plants that earned their keep. Like ... he was obviously missing the farm ... like an olive grown old in service.

We discussed the parallels between his beliefs and mine. When the garden dies for the winter, I said, it mourns with dead vegetation but the seeds for the next generation are already set. Fertility, death and resurrection are a process.

Leo grinned and said it wasn't so very different.

Sometimes when the heat is almost too much here, I summon childhood memories: the smell of wet earth after rain has swept in, the dry dust-laden scent of summer and the smell of frost-nipped fruit in late autumn. I think of Alba Bourbon roses rising from a bed of old-fashioned pinks and penstemons.

I don't mean anything by it and nostalgia is a dangerous state of mind.

I told him that my clients often favour the English garden and ask me to order chrysanthemums, dahlias and peonies and to plan the vistas to go with them, which include, say, a wisteria pergola, scrub oak, pines and olives.

163

Did he really still wish to be a priest? I asked him once, so swamped by love for him that I feared I was out of control. He said he was unable to give me a proper answer, at least not the one I craved (which was that he was beginning to doubt the vocation).

Your family are everything, I challenged him. He admitted they were. That surprised me. I had expected him to reply that, in the final analysis, it was faith that drove him.

How could I protest? Up till now, I was ignorant of what it meant to be bound by familial fetters. If I ever considered myself as part of something bigger it was my work – those demands and loyalties. Thinking about it, of course, the demands of family and country could be said to mirror each other.

I never imagined how *raw* my love for Leo would make me. How vulnerable, peeled of the protections that I had grown over the years. I worried about how transparent and fragile it made me. How woundable.

On 16 March, a year ago, we ended up taking a train to Palacrino. I had been planning to do some research and told Leo I would be away for a couple of days.

I observed the doubt, the longing and the temptation that burned behind his eyes. I wasn't stupid. Leo was no saint, and in the darker regions of his appetites and desires, there would lurk the purely selfish impulse. And the sexual one.

I remember his words, like I remember most of what he said.

'I love you, Nina. I wish that I didn't.'

I was never going to tell him: *Take that love and use it to develop your vocation, to understand temptation, to understand what the men and women to whom you minister undergo.*

I should have done but I was far too selfish to give up what belonged to me alone.

The words 'come too' slipped from my tongue.

On the train, we sat opposite each other and I asked him how his uncle was and he said Beppo was busy with a big corruption case. Nothing unusual. There was always something big going on. He smiled wryly as he added: 'or being hushed up'.

Leo was becoming more worldly.

Do you think he knows about us, I wanted to know, and Leo replied that it was possible. Apparently, Beppo had remarked to Leo that yearling horses always had to run on a long leash before they could be hauled in but that, in the end, they were always broken in.

I bent my head. The uncle knew.

The new, savvier Leo said that he thought that Beppo might have tried to find out who I was.

I frowned.

The table between us was stained, the plush on the seats was worn, the train windows needed a clean. The future would not be easy. None of it mattered.

Snatching a moment of joy was a luxury, permitted from time to time. To acknowledge intense, ongoing desire was far more serious. It pushed deeper into the spirit and demanded a different response. For both of us, I think.

When we reached the station, he got to his feet and towered over me. I looked up. It was always a source of wonder how he managed to be both elegant and yet strong.

He put out a hand to help me up. After a moment, I placed mine in his.

I tally up the score sheet: the pluses and minuses of the situation. Betrayal. Guilt. That bloody guilt. Grief. Desperate, tearing need. All those.

What I cling on to is the idea of generosity. If we were generous with one another then, if we took nothing else away at the finish, there would be that.

CHAPTER FIFTEEN

In bed with Tom, she asked, 'Can someone exist in a vacuum? Having no one?'

'I detect you're still fretting over the Nina Lawrence papers.'

'I've been reading the journal,' she said, a touch defensively. '*Can* someone?'

He shifted, and a whiff of the starch that Concetta used to spray the sheets before ironing was discernible. It was a reminder of the good things. Clean sheets, newly baked bread, a fire in winter. Normal and sweetly sane.

'Yes, they can,' he said, 'but it takes organisation.'

She propped herself up on an elbow. 'And you know?'

'Of course I don't *know*, but it's obvious that it would have to be planned.'

She lay back down. 'It troubles me to think Nina had no one. It … just troubles me. She writes about how she craves friendship. The true friend who accompanies you to the scaffold.'

'The old nightmare?' he asked tenderly.

She laced a hand into his, feeling his fingers press on hers. 'Yes and no.'

'You shouldn't be doing this,' he said. 'Tormenting yourself. What happened to you in childhood was not your fault.'

'Children blame themselves when something bad happens.'

'Odd but not justified.' There was a pause. 'I'm going to make it my business to make sure you understand that.'

She rolled closer to him.

Lottie woke early. The city was stirring. More precisely, it had never gone to sleep. The night clubs and hot spots catered to their populations through the small hours and the stray cats in the Torre Argentina catted through the night.

Tuesday was Concetta's cleaning-the-floor day and she believed in starting early and could not be dissuaded otherwise. Greeting those mornings was the clank of the bucket along the tiled floors and a dampness underfoot. Lottie had quickly wised up that wearing open-toed sandals on Tuesdays was hazardous.

She picked her way down to the kitchen hoping for breakfast, but Concetta had set up camp. Spread proprietarily out on the table were Parma ham, butter, pasta and green and red radicchio. Two peeled garlic cloves scented the room. The sink was filled with soapy water. This *mise-en-scène* was intended to convey business.

Clank went the bucket in the passage, followed by a cough.

Lottie fought her irritation. Her sandal slid on the wet floor and her big toe slipped out of the strap and banged against the tile.

It took a few seconds for the discomfort to fade but, flexing her toe, she wised up. Be grateful for Concetta and her domestic feats. Otherwise, order and comfort in this apartment would degrade.

Even so – a tiny protest – she positioned her water glass from her bedside table on Concetta's newly scrubbed draining board, where it would almost certainly leave a water stain, and went to collect Tom from the bedroom. 'We're going out.'

A favourite of Tom's was the Caffè Colonna and breakfasting there with him emphasised how quickly Lottie was acquiring new pleasures, not least the intimacies of a peaceful breakfast outside with the person you lived with.

'Did you know that Concetta has a grandchild?'

'Does she?'

'We should give her more time off.'

'If you like,' he said carelessly.

She reached across the table and wiped a fleck of foam from the corner of his mouth. 'It's odd that you didn't know about Concetta's family. You should.' Lottie looked down at her plate and then up at the sky. 'Clare probably knew.'

'Don't,' said Tom.

Lottie's head was aching but she pulled her thoughts together. 'I've been thinking of taking some daytrips. Ostia. Genzano. Tivoli. Perhaps a return to Palacrino.'

'You should,' he said. 'Just tell me when and where,' he signalled for a second round of coffee, 'and I'll see if I can join you.'

While she drank her coffee, Lottie flipped through the paper. *L' Omicidio* ran a headline that was becoming familiar. 'Solved after three months.' She read about the discovery of the body of a known drug dealer, which had been dumped on a roadside in a village south of Rome.

The reporter wrote in emotive prose of how, initially, the police were baffled, of their 'shaming' failure to make headway, the absence of witnesses and the 'terror' of the villagers. He summed up:

Yes, no one ever escapes. Inevitably, a tiny marker
of DNA will give away the secrets of the case, however
hidden, however unobtrusive. A DNA trail is always

present, however hard it may be to locate. It is a question of vigilance. In this case, a junior policeman searched the grass verge and picked up the stub of a cigarette. This has led to the arrest of Tommaso Martino, a respected schoolmaster at the local school. It is thought he took revenge for the drug-induced death of his daughter.

Lottie pushed the article over to Tom. He glanced at it. 'Poor man,' he said. 'I would feel the same if it was my son or daughter.' He looked across to Lottie. 'Do you want to know the real story here? The DNA on a fag is a diversion. The real story is that Tommaso Martino was a humble man. He had no contacts on which to call. Or sufficient influence. If he had, the cigarette butt would have never made it into the lab.'

She folded up the paper. No one ever disappears, she thought. There is always a trace left behind. Somehow, they are there.

In the Via Giulia, she caught up with Mirella, who was progressing down it at a leisurely pace. They greeted each other warily but fell into step.

Since Mirella was a magnet for most, it was akin to a royal progress, which Lottie rather enjoyed.

They halted outside a shop selling cigarettes and Mirella bought several packets. 'It's for my father,' she said, emerging into the street. 'He's confined to his chair and can't get out. It's very hard for him and he likes his cigarettes.' She gave a wintry smile. 'And cake. So I try always to bring him something.'

'And your mother?'

Mirella shrugged. 'She died when I was ten.'

'Who looks after your father?'

'A neighbour during the day. I do the rest.'

This was another side to the beautiful Mirella and Lottie was touched. Clearly, the determination to present a flawless exterior was her way of dealing with the burden of a moribund parent.

The following morning, Lottie called in at Mirella's office with a packet of almond cakes. 'I thought your father might like these.'

A blush – pink and delicate – stained Mirella's cheeks. 'Thank you.' She looked genuinely confused as she accepted the packet. 'No one has ever done that.'

'I hope he enjoys them.'

Paul had been busy tapping up his police contacts and he waylaid Lottie with two trophies – a phone number for Marta Livardo and a black-and-white photograph that had been lurking in a defunct file and had not been used by the press.

It was a professional passport photo in which a woman faced the camera with a neutral expression. She had a narrow nose and an unexpectedly full mouth, with dark hair that was scraped back into a bun at the nape of her neck. She wore a blouse and jumper and no jewellery and looked neat, settled and the sort of slightly colourless person who was easy to overlook. Written on the reverse was; *Lawrence, Nina*.

This was a different facet of Nina Lawrence and did not conform to Lottie's image of the woman who lived so close to the edge, and nothing like the tanned and glamorous figure of the Lake Walkers photograph.

Lottie hid her disappointment. She had wished to see... well, what? Glamour? Charisma? High intelligence? None of those were evident. 'She must have had chameleon qualities,' she said. 'I thought she'd be more sophisticated.'

'Passport photos never tell the truth,' said Paul.

She thanked him profusely and, at the first opportunity, Lottie telephoned the number for Marta Livardo.

The Livardos had retired to Settebagni in the north of Rome, and it was Signor Livardo who answered the call. Naturally, he was puzzled but polite until Lottie revealed why she was making contact and asked if it would be possible to talk to his wife.

Politeness turned into ice. 'Signora, it's too long ago,' he said. 'A sad story. Why do you want to know about her? Are you a relative?'

'No.'

'Then why? You want to make money?'

'Am I right that her murder was never solved? I wanted to know more … Not for the wrong reasons but to try to settle it for her. Does that sound odd?'

'You *are* hoping to make money.'

'Signor Livardo, I've just explained my reasons.'

'You're not an official. This is a case that should be left alone.'

'I am responsible for her papers in the archive; they're being dealt with and I wanted to clear a few things up.'

'She's dead, Signora.'

That was inarguable. 'But her memory isn't.'

'Signora, you know nothing of things as they are here. Trust me, it's not a good subject.'

'But surely one that requires an ending?'

'It had an ending.'

The conversation continued along the same lines until Lottie managed to persuade him to agree to a brief meeting with his wife at the end of the week.

During her lunch hour, Lottie decided to go home to take a shower. Recently, her periods had become more painful and she wasn't clear why. Different water? The building heat? The consequences of a physical and psychological upheaval? Or was it the city, with its light and glitter, its troubles and its beauties, and its satisfactions, that was driving her endocrinal system into malfunction?

The scaffolding and the affair of the political posters was now a memory but the courtyard, which was currently an empty arena, posed an irresistible challenge to the feminist collective.

The target of their latest power play were the empty pots positioned in the corners. When no one had been looking, and almost certainly against regulations, they had planted them up with lemon trees and tied red ribbons around them.

The largest was directly in Lottie's line of sight and she walked over and sniffed at the flowers; the scent was almost dizzying.

A familiar voice made her look round.

Tom was running down the staircase from their apartment, addressing remarks over his shoulder to a couple of women. One was Concetta. The other was tall, dressed with boho elegance in a flowing skirt, with hair pulled back into a chic and untidy bun.

At the bottom of the staircase, the trio stood talking for a few seconds, obviously saying their goodbyes. The woman hugged Concetta.

Concetta returned the embrace with enthusiasm.

The women stepped away from each other and Concetta went back upstairs. Tom slipped a hand under the woman's elbow and she smiled at him. Still linked, they walked through the arch from the courtyard and out into the street.

An emotional hurricane – anger, dismay, and an old terror – barrelled in and Lottie ran upstairs.

Needing quiet, she headed straight for the bedroom and sat down on the bed. Clasping her right wrist with her left hand, she pulled hard and concentrated on the cracking of bones.

Years ago, when her life appeared to be at its worst, she used to tell herself that it was a dream and would pass.

The tactic was no longer appropriate, or effective. Plus, Lottie would despise herself if she fell back into those weary thought patterns and behaviours.

Tom's nail scissors lay on the dressing-table top. Lottie picked them up, ran her finger along a blade and dropped them back.

She undressed. Shoes. Linen wrap dress. Underwear. Normally, she would have placed them on a chair. In this instance, she abandoned them to the floor.

In the shower, sluicing with water brought relief to her body but not to her disordered thoughts.

The woman must have been Clare and, judging from the easy intimacy they displayed, it was likely Tom and she still saw each other.

There was no reason why Tom should not see his ex. They had parted amicably, and they were adults.

Why hadn't he told her?

The towel rasped over her skin as she dried herself, her bodily discomfort contributing to her sense of destabilisation. Dressed in fresh clothes, she checked herself in the mirror and was reassured. Whatever she might be feeling, she looked fine. Just fine.

She touched her hair and her reflection did the same.

What is happiness? she enquired of her own image. *Can you expect it?*

As a child, she had decided it was something she only read about in books. Or saw on the TV – but not that often. She read descriptions of wonderful, choking moments experienced by the writers when listening to music, standing still in the sun, stroking an animal. As an adult, she came to understand it was the most fleeting of experience and could not be ordered up.

Lottie felt it when she had achieved a good piece of work, or when Tom bought her a pink T-shirt with 'Dolly Mixture' written on it and made her laugh helplessly. Or, when he turned to her in bed and said: 'You are the best thing.'

Unhappy was different. Never an aspiration like happiness, it had a habit of seeding itself and of being destructive, and the grown Lottie had promised herself never to allow herself to sink into that state ever again.

Picking up the nail scissors, she opened the top drawer and stowed them in the leather case where they belonged.

Before she left, she sought out Concetta, who she found hunched over the kitchen sink.

'Was that Signorina Clare I saw you and Tom with?'

Concetta turned on the hot water tap. 'Yes. She came for coffee.'

The next question betrayed a certain vulnerability but ask it Lottie must. 'Does she come here often?'

Concetta positioned two of the cups on the draining board. 'Not often,' she said, and made a play of placing the third cup beside the other two.

Lottie tackled Tom after their evening meal, which they ate on the balcony. Tom talked at length about the Italian political situation in the 1970s which she listened to in chilly silence.

Eventually, she asked, 'Why are you going on about this, Tom?'

'Because of this Nina Lawrence you're interested in.' He was echoing what she had already read in the journal. 'It's thought a right-wing coup was planned in December nineteen seventy, headed by the Borghese Prince – an awful man – but someone took fright when intelligence revealed that Soviet ships were cruising in the Med.'

'You mean the Americans took fright.'

He stared at her. 'What do you mean?' His good humour switched off.

'Wasn't the US keeping a watchful eye?'

'Best not to speculate.'

'Why?'

'I'm not sure,' he said, 'but some things don't get discussed.'

'Because governments are misbehaving.'

He said gently: 'It's never black and white, Lottie.'

She shot him a look. 'Tom, you're more political than I thought.' It was warm and the aroma rising from the lavender and herbs was delicious and she was reluctant to break the spell. 'I saw you with Clare here at lunchtime.'

He was taken aback. 'I didn't spot you but, yes, she was here.'

'Concetta tells me she's visited several times.' He nodded. 'Why didn't you tell me?'

'Because I thought it would cause trouble.'

'And it wouldn't cause trouble if I found out? Which I have.'

He shifted in the chair and she knew he was annoyed but she could not tell whether it was with himself.

'I told you we parted on good terms.'

'I'm delighted. But shouldn't you warn me when you are planning to meet?'

'Clare was fond of Concetta and drops in to touch base.'

Lottie appeared to be observing this exchange from a great height, detached from it and taking notes, rather as the sociologist might. Simultaneously, she was plunged into deep and complicated feelings.

'Lottie, don't look like that. There's no need.'

'I should meet her, then.' She looked directly at him. Thin, beaky nose, kind mouth. Preoccupied. 'I would like to.'

Tom inhaled audibly. 'You know I love you. And only you. Clare and I are history. It ran its course.'

They had lived together for ten years. They had enjoyed it but then, it was over.

Funnily enough, Lottie understood the psychological sense. During her twenties, she experienced a similar arc with Bill. Love for him hit her with a mallet and nothing else mattered until she was exhausted with sensation and emotion. Then, it changed for them both. She and Bill struggled to acknowledge it but, eventually, broke free and thrived.

'Of course you must see her if you wish, but you must *tell* me.'

'Lottie, I'm sorry. It was innocent.'

She leaned over and pinched a sprig of lavender between her fingers. *The calming aroma.* 'Being married and living together is different from just making long visits. But there are things I *know* will threaten us.'

'I agree. For you, it's Clare and we will sort it. For me, it's worrying that you are becoming too involved with the case of this dead woman.' He thought for a moment and then said in a low voice, 'Lottie, you must not be frightened of being abandoned. That part of your life is over. There's no need for a substitute. We'll make this marriage work.'

Only Tom would ever be allowed to say anything like that to her.

'Then don't go behind my back. Don't deceive me. It's better I know.'

He made no move to touch her. 'I promise.'

'OK,' she said after a moment. 'We have cut the labels off the baggage.'

She got up from the chair and went to bed, leaving him on the balcony with the swifts.

Over the next few days, Tom went out of his way to be tender and considerate, but the contentment Lottie had experienced on first arriving in the city was no longer on tap.

It had consequences. She and Tom rowed over the lamp.

'I hate it,' she said. 'It has to go.'

'That's ridiculous. It does its job.'

'Even if it did, and it doesn't, it's so ugly. Is it a family heirloom or something?'

He was reluctant to answer. 'Clare and I found it in a junk shop.'

Her breath was suspended for a second.

'It must go,' she said. 'Don't you see? Especially after our last conversation.'

'For God's sake, Lottie. What's happened to you? It's a *lamp*.'

Later, as she lay sleepless beside Tom, sadness crept through her.

'Lottie.' His voice sounded extra loud in the hush.

'Yes.'

If she was hoping Tom would offer a resolution, or even a diplomatic treaty, perhaps touch her gently, lovingly, she was disappointed.

'Be careful with the Nina Lawrence business.'

Bunching the sheet around her shoulders, she rolled away from him and stared into the dark.

Walking to work the following morning with Nina's notebook in her bag, she found the traffic fumes were stifling and the sun too hot. Tourist numbers had swelled overnight and there were too many of them.

Perhaps it was the still unsorted job situation at the *Espatriati*, which she was beginning to find intolerable. Perhaps she had too much time to chase after Nina Lawrence's story. Plus, her feet were sore and her stomach painful.

Analysing unhappiness was difficult. It had many shapes and feelings. Many manifestations. In the past, she had been unhappy, deeply so. She recognised its grip.

CHAPTER SIXTEEN

Lottie caught a late-afternoon train to Settebagni, alighted and walked up a street lined with small food shops and cafés. The hibiscus was in full flower, jasmine threaded through iron railings and an umbrella pine reared up at the end of the thoroughfare. It struck Lottie that her one-sided acquaintance with Nina had borne fruit. She was beginning to take notice of flowers and shrubs.

A man, whom she took to be Signor Livardo, was settled at a window table in the Caffè Alighieri. Stocky, wearing a checked short-sleeved shirt and baggy trousers, he looked amiable enough. At Lottie's arrival, he stood upright and extended his hand.

They exchanged greetings. On sitting down, Lottie was subjected to an inspection so penetrating that she revised her impression of his being amiable. She asked: 'The signora?'

He raised both hands. '*Scusate.* My wife had to attend her cousin at the last minute. She's not well. They are close and need each other.'

Lottie would have bet good money that he had never mentioned this meeting to his wife.

They settled on an early-evening *aperitivo*. As an opening gambit, she produced her business card and handed it to him over the table. He placed it in his shirt pocket.

She studied him. Someone – his wife – ensured that his hair was well cut, his eyebrows trimmed and his shirt impeccably ironed.

'You wish to talk about the English signorina? She was a very nice woman. Very nice nature. Always helpful. A good woman. She and my wife were friends. Good friends. They … we … helped each other. We were shocked. Very shocked.' He let a pause elapse before adding, 'But, you know, these things in the past … they really should be left there.'

The *aperitivo* was served, along with a bowl of heavily salted crisps. Signor Livardo took a large handful. The crisps were soon a memory and a crumb lingered on his chin. Lottie sipped her drink, taking in as much detail as she could without alarming him. He drank and ate and greeted acquaintances, giving off every appearance of a man who enjoyed retired life.

She pushed an enlarged copy of the passport photo towards him. 'Is this Nina Lawrence?'

He made a play of dusting salt off his fingers and looked everywhere but at the photograph.

'Signore?'

The slight widening of his nostrils as he studied it informed Lottie that it must be Nina. To be sure, she produced a similarly enlarged copy of the Lake Walkers and placed it beside the first one. 'Is this Nina?' At first he tried to deny it but changed his mind. '*Sí.*'

'The smaller girl with dark hair?'

He slid the photograph back to Lottie. 'I don't know who the other people are.'

She waited patiently.

'My relationship with the Signorina Lawrence was formal,' he said. 'Not friendly. It was my wife who knew her best.' He retrieved her card from his pocket and read it. 'I had to be careful with the women lodgers.' He shrugged. 'You will understand …' The gesture was intended to include Lottie in a collegiate conspiracy.

The waiter fussed around the table. Laughter sounded from the next table and ice chinked in a glass.

Lottie was interested to note that he was sweating.

'No one was ever charged with her murder. Either then or later?'

'How would I know, Signora?' He shifted irritably.

She considered pointing out that the Livardos had lived in the same apartment block, but had no wish to compromise this delicate exchange by annoying him further.

'Nina Lawrence is owed some justice. An explanation.' She produced a newspaper cutting dated May 1979, which stated that the case had been closed and no further action would be taken. 'Nobody tried to keep up the momentum.' She took careful note of his reaction. 'Why would that be, do you suppose? Why was she not worth bothering about? Was it because she was foreign?'

Signor Livardo had polished off his *aperitivo* with some speed and ordered a second. 'The foreigners,' he said. 'There are a lot of them. But she was a nice girl and it was terrible what happened.'

'Girl?' Lottie was puzzled.

He checked himself. 'A slip of the tongue. She was young when we first knew her. Late twenties, perhaps. My wife and I had just got married and we moved into the apartment on the ground floor; she was already living there.' The tended eyebrows drew down over the bridge of his nose. 'We were there ten years or so before she was … murdered.'

'If you knew her for ten years, you must have known her reasonably well.'

'We knew the signorina …' He extracted a packet of cigarettes from his pocket. 'And we didn't know her. That's how it was.'

Evasion lay behind the bland gaze, but of what exactly? 'Yet you considered she was a good woman, and your wife thinks of her as a good friend.' Signor Livardo was silent. 'Did it strike you as a dereliction that the police didn't do more?'

'It's easy to criticise the police, especially when you don't know the details.'

She acknowledged the point but pressed on. 'But they interviewed you and your wife.'

He shifted restlessly. 'You don't know that.'

'It's recorded in the papers we're archiving.'

The moment the words left her mouth, she felt a chill. A touch of menace.

The waiter appeared with the second *aperitivo*. Signor Livardo fussed with the ice cubes. 'You were asking about the police. Naturally, they asked us a few questions but nothing more.' Lottie made a gesture to prod him on. 'Whether we had seen her that night.'

'Wasn't it odd they didn't question you more closely? She'd been brutally murdered.'

'I know nothing about police matters.'

'That's odd, too,' said Lottie, 'because when I was researching who you were, I learned that you worked in the police records department for thirty years.'

On the train back to Rome she watched the landscape rattle past: the umbrella pines, overhead lines, a huddle of buildings. A flash of burnt umber and ochre on houses. Each detail seemed to want to impress itself on her memory, and she put this down to the fact she was living in a landscape, both exterior and interior, that was still strange.

At one stop, a bunch of teenagers spread noisily through the carriage, each wearing a uniform of tight jeans and grubby trainers. At the penultimate stop a mother and her small son got on and sat down opposite Lottie. The little boy found Lottie fascinating and stared. Lottie returned the scrutiny, touched by his beauty and innocence.

After a while, he extended his hand to Lottie. Glancing at the mother, she took it and they sat for a few seconds with her clasping a small hand in hers.

What do you want? Signor Livardo had demanded, all bonhomie incinerated.

He was on the back foot. Yet she was fully aware that she had only one shot at getting anything out of him.

Leaning forward across the table, she asked for the second time why there was no full-scale inquiry into the murder and who took the decision to bury Nina in the Protestant Cemetery.

He dusted his fingers and shook his head. 'I have said enough. That's all.'

At the earliest opportunity in the office, Lottie wrote up her notes of the encounter. One, Signor Livardo had lied. Or, tried not to tell the truth. Two, he had access to information. Three, he *had* given her something before he clammed up entirely, albeit in coded form.

'Those who took the decisions went to the funeral,' he had finally admitted.

The Anglican priest was to be expected – just as a representative from the British Embassy might be. But what were Bishop Dino and his assistant doing there?

Turning back to the documents, she studied the dog-eared, faded witness reports from other occupants of the Trastevere building that she had scanned into her laptop.

'A modest person …'

'She wasn't the sort you noticed …'

'She was very quiet. I can't remember any visitors …'

Lottie began to rough out Nina's life.

Nina Lawrence lived in the Via della Luce in the Trastevere from 1968 in a second-floor flat. She had been a landscape gardener, working to restore plants and gardens that had been destroyed during the war. She completed projects in Rome, Lazio, Tuscany and Umbria. Her last publication had been an article on the narcissus *N. poeticus* (apparently mentioned in Ovid and Pliny), which had been well received by her peers.

There was also a photograph of the body. A battered and frail-looking Nina had been laid out on a mortuary gurney, a sheet drawn up to her shoulders. It did not hide the throat injury or the bruises on her face. Lottie found she could not bear to look for more than a few seconds. It was a violation – an ultimate no-go area – and the sight was pitiful and shocking. It also poked a finger into the stew of her own anxieties.

Mirella phoned with a summons to Valerio Gianni's office. 'Would it be possible to come now?'

'Give me five,' said Lottie.

'Lottie, my father liked the cakes very much,' Mirella added. 'It was kind of you.'

'I'm so pleased.'

Valerio was ensconced in his state-of-the-art office chair behind a desk covered by office accessories in exquisite leather: diary, penholder.

At her entrance, he got to his feet and fussed over Lottie. Was she happy? Comfortable? The wait for her to take up her full position was inexcusable, but it would soon be over …

He took five minutes or so before he got to the crux. 'Such a pity about the painting,' he said. 'There is much regret.'

'Why don't we frame it properly and have it on display?'

Valerio frowned. 'No,' he said. Flatly. 'No.'

The dismissal seemed over-emphatic and she was curious to know why. 'Then I will stow it with the rest of the papers.'

'Please do.' He nodded. 'On the subject of the papers, did you come across anything that struck you as … contentious?'

Lottie's protectiveness towards Nina's secrets continually surprised her. 'Depends what you consider contentious.'

Valerio fiddled with the penholder. 'Her lifestyle, perhaps.' He was clearly annoyed. Or was it rattled?

'Would you care to go through them yourself?'

His gaze evaded Lottie's. 'No, no,' he said. 'I trust your judgement.'

He did nothing of the sort, thought Lottie as she left his office, wondering if it had been Giuseppe Antonio who had asked Valerio to find out information.

Which suggested information was there. Either she had not looked in the right place or she had not looked in the right way. Both were possible.

Back in her office, she decided to keep the journal under lock and key in her desk drawer.

The now familiar and pleasing leather and paint smells in Gabriele's workshop greeted Lottie as she let herself in and skirted around a partially opened box of books on the floor. A jacket was draped over the chair back and a shabby briefcase parked by the bookshelf.

Surrounded by papers, Gabriele was at his desk; he looked tired and irritable.

They exchanged greetings. Lottie enquired if he was working on anything special. 'A history of the world.' There was a trace of humour. 'I'm shelving it under "tragedy".' He noted the package Lottie was holding. 'A project?'

She unwrapped *The Annunciation* and the photocopy of the illustration from *The Determined Traveller*. 'I have some final questions before it goes into the archive. You've concluded that it's a modern pastiche but I—'

'Are you questioning the conclusion?'

He had taken the half-uttered query for criticism. 'No, but—'

'Perhaps I didn't make it clear. The old masters only had earth, stones and organic berries and plants to make their paints. The pigments here,' he pointed to *The Annunciation*, 'contain metal oxides that came much later.'

His touchiness was revealing. 'I'm not questioning your judgement,' she said. 'You *are* the expert. I'm here because—'

Again, he did not stop to listen before launching into an extemporary lecture on medieval painting, larded with references to the techniques of the period.

A professional wound had been prodded. Pride? A mistake in the past that had sensitised him to even mild criticism. Or … She observed that his hand was not quite steady … was it a personal wound?

'Furthermore, the depiction of the Virgin *Interrogatio* was not fashionable at the time Pucelle *fils* was painting. Painters were instructed to show her either submissive or rejoicing,' he said.

Everyone had their secrets, of course. Their areas of vulnerability and their flash points.

'Gabriele, could you stop? Please.' She indicated *The Annunciation*. 'It isn't authentication that I wanted to talk about.'

He breathed in sharply. '*Scusi*.' Obviously nonplussed, he went over to the expensive-looking coffee machine in the corner of the workshop. '*Scusi*.'

She placed the illustration from *The Determined Traveller* beside *The Annunciation* and addressed his back. 'Tell me if I'm wrong, but monks … priests … do not consort with the opposite sex other than in a pastoral way?'

He fussed with the dials on the coffee machine. 'In theory, in the Catholic faith a priest or a monk has to be totally open to God and strive to have no outside interference. They become his vessel. Nothing and no one should get in the way. Money, power. Sex. Love for someone else.'

'But it happened, of course.'

He swivelled to face her so abruptly that the paint pots on his desk rattled. 'Then temptation has to be resisted.' He ferried the coffee to his desk. 'Please, sit.'

She shot him a look. 'It must be very hard when times are difficult.'

'As always, when rules are set they are often broken.'

'So … is it coincidence that these paintings both feature the monk and the woman with the blonde hair? Could it be the same painter? Our EK? Or are the pair of them a well-known story that's often painted?'

Catching up the loupe, he studied it. When he stood upright, the pale, taut look was back. 'Do you know where the original of this might be?'

'The caption in the magazine cites it as from a fifteenth-century miniature. But I think it's the same person who did *The Annunciation* and not an original.' She ticked off on her fingers. 'The woman and monk in the background. The unusual green-eyed rabbits in both. The same setting.'

He barely glanced at the illustration. 'The background is Palacrino.'

'I thought so.'

'Famous for its narcissi in spring. Families go there to picnic. I've been there in the past. To escape.' He dropped the loupe into a drawer and shut it. 'But I haven't been back for years.'

Lottie gathered up her things. 'At your suggestion, Tom and I went to Palacrino. It's a gem of a town. We ate at Mario's.'

'There are similarities between the two,' he admitted, after a moment, 'which, as you say, suggests the second one is also a pastiche.'

'You know that a genuine Pucelle *fils* was discovered in Palacrino during the seventies and put on display there until the early eighties when it was brought to Rome?'

'I did.'

'If it had been on display, our EK might have seen it and copied the style.'

The exchange faltered.

She drank her coffee. 'Gabriele, did you know from the beginning that *The Annunciation* was not genuine?'

There was a startled silence before he replied. 'An instinct may be powerful but it's not always correct. Everything should be investigated.' He frowned. 'You're doubtful.'

'I wondered if you've been straight with me.'

'Did you?' There was a flash of anger. 'You will understand as well as I that assumptions must be challenged and I could not be sure until the investigations were done.'

Did she believe him? She did not know him well enough to make the judgement.

Gabriele pushed aside his cup. 'Are you still working through those papers?'

'Almost completed.'

'I wondered about her. Her death.'

'Which was awful.'

'Yes, it was.'

He was almost inaudible and her antennae sharpened. 'Do you know anything about Nina Lawrence?'

He placed a fingertip on the illustration from *The Determined Traveller.* 'Only that she was murdered.'

'It's strange how no one claimed her. And why the virtually secret burial?' Gabriele's expression was blank and she sensed he had withdrawn into himself. 'Yet there's an inscription on her gravestone. Someone must have organised that.'

Gabriele picked up a small pot of paint and turned it round and round.

'If you *did* know anything about her,' Lottie went carefully, 'I would like to know. I would like to honour her—'

'The *Espatriati* is a good archive,' he cut her off, 'with plenty of space. That's a kind of honour.'

At the doorway, she turned back. 'You couldn't explain to me why Bishop Dino Battista, a Roman Catholic, would have been at her burial? Is that customary?'

'I have no idea,' he replied.

CHAPTER SEVENTEEN

Rome
20 April 1978

I WAS WORKING ON THE ARTICLE ON NARCISSI WHEN THERE WAS a knock on the door.

I ignored it.

The plant derives its name from the narcotic quality of its scent – *narce*, which effected numbness and made the senses swoon – and not after the self-absorbed Narcissus, and that probably accounts for the tradition that says narcissus scent is harmful.

The narcissus is one of the flowers longest associated with men. Centuries before Homer, flowers of the species were used by Egyptians in their tombs. The Greek Furies wore narcissi in their tangled locks, the scent of which stupefied those they were punishing.

Second time, the knock was impatient.

I knew who it would be.

I hated to be interrupted when I was working on an article or illustration, but it was no surprise when Signora Marta Livardo, caretaker, nuisance and enemy, took the silence as permission to barge into my room without an invitation.

On this, she had form. Still a youngish woman, but bossy and nosy, she was never seen without an ostentatious gold cross around her neck. A woman of contradictions? She shouts at her husband with language that would make a sailor blush (he gives as good as he gets), but the flamboyant cross suggests devoutness.

She was stopped in her tracks when I confronted her and blustered that she had heard a cry and came to see if all was well.

Her eyes darted around busily. Snaffling up information. The clutter of paint pots. The botanical drawing I had been working on. A pile of clothes on the chair that I had thought about ironing but had not got further than the consideration.

She dislikes me very much – as much as I dislike her – but, agog to know what I get up to, frequently buttonholes me on some pretence or other. I suspect she has a second key to my rooms and snoops around.

I am careful. As I should be. Leaving the indicators in place. Hiding my journal and papers in the cache under the bath that the men from The Office constructed when I moved in.

She wanted to know if I would be going away again. I asked why she needed to know and she replied she was obliged by the landlord to keep her records up to date.

I heard her walking back down the passage, her rubber-soled lace-up shoes emitting little squeaks, and I smiled. At least the two of us know where we are. It's a straightforward, honest situation of mutual distrust.

Many wild species of the narcissi are to be found around
the Mediterranean, especially around the Iberian
Peninsula, but not exclusively.

The Mediterranean littoral is heart-stoppingly beautiful. Powdery
shape-shifting sand. Hard stony beaches. Patches of red, ochre
and yellow. The glitter of the sea. A sea that can turn sullen and
menacing. The heat at midday. The darkness of the night sea.

I ached to return. I don't know why this should be, as I come
from a different place.

Narcissi …?

For convenience, they can be divided into half a dozen
major and some minor sections …

Not too scholarly … I checked myself. The dullards at the mag's HQ
might miss the embedded messages. Not that I mind leading them
a dance. Quite the reverse – but it wasn't professional.

I rounded off the narcissi article with a quotation from the
herbalist Gerard, who explained that Sophocles named the narcissus
'the garland of the great infernal goddess, because they that are
departed and dulled with death, should worthily be crowned with
a dulling flower'.

The next stage was always fun – obtaining the illustrations to go
with the article. Back at *The Determined Traveller*'s HQ no one has
a clue and, if I don't do it for them, they usually choose something
witless.

So I 'find' it.

I packed it up and sent it on its way by the usual route.

22 April 1978

YESTERDAY, REX ISSUED ME WITH INSTRUCTIONS.

The Red Brigades have – allegedly – shot a prison warder in Milan and published a seventh communiqué declaring that Aldo Moro is alive and they are ready to swap him for communist prisoners. They have also issued an ultimatum that if this has not taken place by today Moro will be executed.

Whatever you think of Moro, it is appalling. To be held captive, knowing a death sentence has been passed, must be excruciating. Even the toughest of men, and Moro is tough, must be reduced to terror and anger, knowing that the police are not doing the best job at finding him. Even worse, his political colleagues are being slow to act.

Rex and I discussed the stage management by the RB, who proclaim hostility to the press but use it to trickle information out to the public.

Amnesty International has appealed to the Red Brigades.

Rex ordered me to contact our military friend, who we suspect has insider details about the kidnapping, and offer him the usual frills.

Does he ever think about what 'the usual frills' entail? I wondered. Has he ever endured the boredom, the hot breath, the distasteful aftermath? Well fed, glossy, impatient for results as Rex is, I suspected not.

The mark of an adult is to accept and absorb the distasteful and unwanted during their existence. No life is ever free of either.

Discuss.

He was anxious that I understood what was to be done. Obediently, I parroted back at him that I was to make contact with the general as soon as possible.

When we said goodbye, Rex told me to take the utmost care, something he had never done before.

Was I affronted by the warning? No, Rex was anxious, which was an indicator as to how tricky things had become.

I had my persona and it was a convincing one. Landscape gardeners stick to vistas and contours, bulbs and blossom. Their arena is not political. 'I'm a garden designer who's good at her job,' I say sweetly and earnestly. (The earnestness is crucial because it makes me look a little stupid.) 'Nothing more.'

The real danger came from a different quarter, but Rex was ignorant of that.

Yet, on reflection, I have concluded that I was wrong. Gardening does have its political dimensions.

Writing, thinking, *being* the gardener is to understand that the power of the harmonious garden dwindles if an alliance is not made between death and decay and new life. If he or she is a true gardener, they must understand that the secret activity under the surface is as significant as the theatre of plants above.

28 April 1978

Moro is still alive and the RB issue their eighth communiqué demanding the release of thirteen Red Brigades prisoners in exchange for him.

As instructed, I went into the field.

The Palacrinos live their lives in a permanent state of astonishment, lamenting the fact they are neither as rich as they think they should be nor as well looked after as they think they are entitled to be. But they possess superb taste in gardening, which I know exactly how to satisfy.

The planting of the box hedges and the scrub oaks and, beyond them, the pines had been completed. The vista I had planned was now assembling. They insisted that a dinner was held to celebrate that the bones of the garden were in place. It dovetailed nicely.

We ate in the room overlooking the valley, with the mountain in the distance. As a setting, it could not be bettered but it was a long way from the kitchen, giving the staff no end of trouble. The table was laid with silver and white napery and lit with candles in crystal candelabra.

We were ten in all.

'Dear Signorina Lawrence … Nina …' Paola Palacrino raised her glass to me at her end of the table. 'We hope that you will design many more gardens, but we think that there will never be one as beautiful as this one is going to be.'

She raised her glass and the other guests toasted me. If I had not disliked their politics heartily, I might have been touched.

I had been placed next to the general, a chore for which I had prepared myself, wearing the black dress that left my shoulders bare.

He was exactly as before: puffed up and gleeful at how closely he was embedded into the powers running the country. In a way, I understood. To be close to the epicentre is addictive.

We discussed the Moro kidnapping. Of course. He told me how the house-to-house searches were increasing, and roadblocks were springing up. He said there was no question that the left-wing terrorists would be trapped in the end and punished.

God help them.

He knew more than he was telling me but, because he was vain, he could not resist dropping a hint or two to keep my interest piqued.

My training kicked in and I knuckled down to my task.

However, later, in bed with him, I was forced to grit my teeth. It took all my resolution not to throw him off me. His smell, his laugh, his ludicrous self-regard.

I never allowed myself to think about Leo while it was in train because that would have been a kind of blasphemy. It would have spoilt everything that was good and true about him and me.

The general's defences lowered, his talk was less guarded, bordering on the careless. He let drop that Moro had packed the documents of 'historical compromise' (the ones with which he was going to face the Italian Parliament) into the car from which he had been kidnapped.

(Discussing it with Rex when I returned to Rome, we picked that one apart. How had the general got hold of this detail, which had not been released?)

Not even the Pope was able to help, he told me when I began work on him again.

Surely it wasn't in His Holiness's bailiwick, I said, and waited for a moment before asking him who he thought had done it.

He was enjoying himself too much to answer immediately, then muttered that the Red Brigades were claiming the honours but I should not take everything at face value.

No I won't, you old goat, I thought.

In an offhand way, I remarked that the Red Brigades weren't as clever as they thought they were and the general said that most zealots were blind before ordering me sharply to continue what I was doing.

I decided to bide my time and to only ask follow-up questions when he was at maximum vulnerability. Instead, I murmured that, whoever they were, they were brave.

He muttered something that sounded like … 'Gladiators' training'.

I paid special attention to the spot that made him almost shriek with pleasure.

Afterwards, we lay quiet. He heaved over towards me and said he had not had such a good evening since he visited a well-known nightclub in America.

I told him I longed to visit the US. I let a second elapse before murmuring that I believed it was very anti-communist over there.

'*Sí.*' He was drowsy but not too drowsy to explain how the US opposed Communist governments anywhere in Europe and how many people in Italy approved.

I closed my eyes.

Later, Rex and I go over what we know.

> *Multiple suggestions, to be verified, that armed opposition to the left wing in Italy is directed by the CIA. Members of the Italian government working with them.*
>
> *Their mission: to sabotage any gains made by the left wing and to create an Italian Nationalism capable of halting any slide to the left.*
>
> *The methods: to organise terrorism and blame it on the Communists. Spread fear and pass restrictive laws.*
>
> *Strong possibility that the kidnapping of Moro was, in fact, orchestrated by CIA operatives who have infiltrated the Red Brigades.*

Before he fell into satiated sleep, the general murmured that I should bloody well remember there was no proof of any of it.

I went on the alert, sensing that, when he roused from his stupor, he would register that I had been asking questions.

He snored away beside me and I considered Moro's possible fate.

Was he resigned? Fearful? During his captivity, he must have thought of his wife and children. Did he regret trying to bring together political factions? I hoped he had the energy to achieve some tranquillity of spirit. There can be no greater tragedy, I think, than going to your death unresolved.

When the general woke, he seemed surprised to see me still occupying the bed. I could have gone but I calculated taking flight might have made him additionally suspicious. He was as sour as a lemon. Draping an arm across my breasts, he told me I was a small girl with a large curiosity.

The hint of danger brushed cool air over my flesh.

I slipped out from under him and reached for my clothes. I told him that last night had been very special and he must go back to sleep.

It was early and nothing stirred as I returned to my bedroom. I shut the door and sat down on the edge of the bed.

I was bereft.

I yearned for Leo and counted the months since I had seen him. Six, seven, eight, nine … Each one heavier to live through than the last. I thought about everything that was good, bad, maddening and wonderful about him.

I wondered if he yearned for me.

Time flows at different speeds in different places. The night with the general had been achingly long. My night with Leo – our night – fled in the time it took for him to run his fingers wonderingly down my body.

CHAPTER EIGHTEEN

r EADING THAT ENTRY MADE LOTTIE CRY BECAUSE SHE KNEW
how it all ended.

Paul – who else? – helped Lottie to track down Bishop, now
Cardinal, Dino Battista at San Pietro, a retirement home for priests,
in the Trastevere.

'It's run by an organisation within the Catholic infrastructure,'
he told her. 'A sort of Catholic freemasonry. They're a world to
themselves.'

She looked it up. Not everyone approved of this particular
movement which had a reputation for elitism and secrecy but many
did. It espoused modern management methods with conservative
ideology and ran its own university and college for student priests
in Rome.

Cardinal Dino's biography revealed he had worked for a time in
the Curia, which was the government of the Holy See, supervising
Church works in the Roman districts and was familiar with all
aspects of the Curia's administration.

'Why would a Catholic bishop have participated in Nina's
burial?' she asked.

Paul had no more idea than Gabriele Ricci. 'It's unusual, I would think, but not unheard of. Maybe there was a personal connection. Or he heard about the murder and felt it would be a charitable act.'

This was a game of grandmother's footsteps. One step forward, two back. Thinking it over, Lottie realised that Tom had been clever to spot that she had been ensnared by its sly compulsion.

It had taken several phone calls to firm up the appointment, and she reflected ruefully that she still had to learn a thing or two about putting her hands on the right levers.

Her choice of clothes needed to be judicious and she unearthed a long-sleeved blouse and a full skirt. Since she was planning to walk, she added flat shoes, a hat and a shoulder bag.

Halfway across the Ponte Sisto, she halted and looked down to the towpath where the dying Nina had been discovered. A few people – tourists, at a guess – strolled along it. A couple of booths selling drinks had been erected and birds surfed the water.

Having crossed into the Trastevere, she navigated her way to the Carmelite monastery of Santa Maria delle Scala. Old and austerely beautiful, the retirement home stood next to the church, surrounded by a businesslike wall.

Entering via a gate set into the wall, she found herself in a medieval cloister planted up with herbs and lavender. The bees were busy, their humming loud in the quiet. Two grey-clad nuns with string bags stuffed with vegetables glided around its perimeter.

No one here would ever break into a run, or shout. There was no need, for a powerful organisational presence was embedded into every stone, every sprig of sage.

The porter ushered Lottie into the visitors' area, a thickly whitewashed room in which a few chairs had been placed. She knew better than to expect to be taken any further into the building.

She studied the pamphlet set out on a table, which stated the objective of the home was to ensure the comfort of elderly priests in the final stages of their lives.

Minutes went by.

The uncomfortable chair became more so. The silence felt heavy and unwelcoming. She thought about the Roman Catholic Church and its seeding into Rome. If this had not happened … if St Peter had not stamped his presence on the ancient imperial city one way or another… there was a chance that Rome might just be an antique and half dead.

Twenty minutes elapsed and she wondered if it was deliberate. Almost certainly.

'Signora Archer.' Cardinal Dino entered the room.

She rose to her feet. 'Your Eminence.'

A handsome man with swept-back white hair, spare and stooped, he was dressed in a soutane with a sash and scarlet facings so immaculately pressed it suggested vanities.

He moved stiffly towards a chair and levered himself into it. His shoes were small mirrors – polished by the nuns, no doubt. Once settled, he indicated in the manner of a man used to compliance that she, too, should sit. 'Signora Archer, how did you get my name?'

'I read about you in a newspaper article and I traced you to here.' She had decided not to bring Paul into this.

'So, a detective?' The tone was neutral, but the expression was not. 'And an able one.'

'Your Eminence, I wanted to ask you about a woman called Nina Lawrence. You attended her funeral in December nineteen seventy-eight.'

His reply was slow in coming. 'I do not recall.'

'That's curious,' Lottie said. 'It was only when I mentioned her name that you agreed to see me.'

He regarded her from white-lashed eyes. 'Signora, I'm sure you don't mean to be offensive?'

'Not at all,' she replied calmly, her instincts informing her that this was a prelate who did not like women. Antediluvian. Tiresome. Reductive.

'Well, then,' he said, 'you had better tell me.'

She gave him the photograph. 'This is Nina Lawrence. I wondered if you knew her.'

The cardinal studied the photograph. 'Should I?'

She gave him a prompt. 'Signorina Lawrence was English, living in the Trastevere and murdered under the Ponte Sisto in October nineteen seventy-eight. Her case was in the papers for weeks.'

'What makes you think that I would read papers, Signora?' He sounded impatient. 'What is all this to do with me?'

'You really don't know, Eminence?'

The hard gaze did not modify. 'You'd better explain.'

'Eminence, you attended the funeral with your assistant and a representative from the British Embassy.'

'I've been in the service of God for many years and presided over many funerals.' His gaze was unsmiling, instilled with certainty. 'Many.'

'Perhaps I could help?' Lottie read out a newspaper report of the murder and Nina's burial. Looking up from the text as she finished, she observed his resistance crack. There was no point in denying his presence at the burial, but whether he would choose to remember or not was still in the balance.

'Signora, it shows Christian spirit that you care about a dead woman after so long a time. Do you have a personal connection?'

'No.'

He positioned his hands on the arms of the chair. 'Why, then, are you interested?'

He had every right to pose the question, to which there were several answers. She glanced around the white and forbidding room. 'Justice was not done and I'm interested to know why.'

The cardinal smoothed the soutane over his knee and said nothing and, despite the warmth, she felt his icy disapproval.

'Nina Lawrence was abandoned in her death, which was a horrible one. No one seems to have minded about it. Or cared enough,' she said. 'Or, perhaps, they weren't aware.'

'Aware of what?' The question was softly posed. 'Are you suggesting that proper procedures were not followed?'

'*Was* there something being hidden, Eminence?'

His hands fell into his lap. 'Signora, it's refreshing to meet someone with such an active imagination. I don't know for certain because I told you I do not remember, but I fear there's nothing to tell.'

This was like digging in a heavy clay soil. The voice of prudence murmured in Lottie's inner ear; she ignored it.

'I believe those were difficult years. There was unrest and violence.' She allowed a second to elapse. 'Church and politics were caught up in the troubles. Individuals were. Could Nina Lawrence have been so too and, somehow, she crossed your path?'

An angry red stained the cardinal's cheeks and Lottie felt marginally encouraged that she was getting somewhere.

'Signora, The Holy Mother Church is above politics. Let us be clear on that. Yet, I must own you are persistent and, since you have made it your business to pry into the matter, I will be frank.'

He removed a speck of whitewash that had drifted down on to his soutane and his gaze shifted to the small window set into the white wall. 'I'm reluctant to speak about this, but the woman who interests you was a lost soul and a sinner.'

Really?

'Would you be prepared to give me some details?'

His disapproval could not have been more marked. 'It is not your business to ask for details or for me to reveal them. Discretion has kept me silent to this point. All I will tell you is she had a bad lifestyle and her death was not surprising. Many others like her have ended that way, may God rest their souls.'

A quick anger fired in Lottie. 'Are you saying Nina Lawrence was a prostitute or a criminal? A lost sheep?' She chose the Biblical image deliberately.

'God instructs us not to speak ill of the dead, but her lifestyle was questionable. She got herself mixed up in a sin and the wrong society and with people who are not merciful.'

'And the Church is?'

He fixed a cold gaze on Lottie. 'Signora, I must insist. The Holy Mother Church is merciful.' He got to his feet and, after a few seconds, Lottie rose to hers. 'This woman lived an immoral and selfish life, which set a bad example to all who knew her. She merited punishment on earth and her end was part of the punishment. But God will pardon her if others cannot.'

Lottie was shocked into silence. Eventually, she said, 'Eminence, I am grateful.' She picked up her bag but could not resist one final attempt. 'Your assistant. Would I be able to talk to him?'

Cardinal Dino shook his head. 'No.'

The answer was unexpectedly fiery and contrasted oddly with the froideur that had characterised the interview. It was also intended to be final. 'I think you should go now. This woman was murdered. That inescapable fact will have influenced other lives for the worse and they need, and are owed, peace. She should be left ... she *must* be left to the silence of the grave.'

'I do see that point of view,' said Lottie politely. 'But fresh eyes are always useful. I am sorry to disappoint Your Eminence, but I will continue my enquiries.'

He raised his arm as if to give a blessing but, spying more errant flakes of whitewash, gave a bad-tempered exclamation and brushed them off.

He did not look up as she left the room.

Lottie emerged into sunlight strong enough to make her eyes water and she searched for her sunglasses. She pushed them up her nose and took stock.

Encountering misogyny was not unusual but this had been blatant. From what she had seen – and she conceded there would be other sides to him – Cardinal Dino was a myopic and rigid man mired in attitudes of the past.

Yet, she must concede that his point about leaving the dead to rest in peace had virtue, and any rational person would advise Lottie: *Stop this crusade. You do not know this woman.*

Lottie understood she could only empathise with what the journal revealed. As with the cardinal, there would have been other sides to Nina, aspects of her life that would remain hidden, and it was impossible to achieve genuine intimacy with the dead.

Perhaps in searching for Nina, she was searching for the answers about herself?

'Lottie ...'

Startled, she looked up and all the edginess of the past days fell away. 'Tom!' she said, delighted. 'How did you know I was here?'

He was dressed in his not-so-smart linen suit, which tended to be his office garb. 'I tracked you down.'

'How thrilling.' Kissing his cheek, she sniffed the familiar aftershave. 'Why?'

'Can I talk to you?'

She shut her bag. 'Has something awful happened?'

'Nothing like that. Nothing bad.' He reached for her hand, which, since it was hot, she was reluctant to yield to him. 'Are you up to walking?'

'Of course.'

They retraced the route that Lottie had taken earlier, past a row of cramped-looking medieval buildings with outer steps leading to the upper floor. Past a substantial house with an impressive *portone* through which she peered. At the centre was a marble well with well-worn steps surrounding it and lacy ferns sprouting from its base. It looked old, settled and slightly forbidding.

It was becoming commonplace for Lottie to try to see the city as Nina must have seen it – in the twist of a street, the shadows, the fall of water from a fountain, in the closed shutters. This was unwise and she shook herself mentally.

'What's this about, Tom?'

'The Nina Lawrence case,' he replied. 'We've discussed it already. But ...' His grasp tightened on Lottie. 'You're at a loose end. I understand, but it's not a good idea to take it any further. It's an old murder. Stirring up old history can be awkward in a city like Rome.'

Lottie repossessed her hand. 'Not good reasons.'

'I have to ask you to trust me.'

'A murder is a murder.'

Their pace had slowed.

'It wasn't an important one.' His voice held an edge.

'Did I hear correctly? Did you *mean* that?' Tom shoved a hand in a trouser pocket. 'Anyway, you've contradicted yourself. If Nina's murder does not matter very much why are you acting like the Grand Inquisitor?'

'Italian politics are complicated.'

'*Are* we talking politics? Or the unspeakable death of an English-woman who nobody seems to care about? Which, as the cardinal has just told me, she probably deserved.'

'Lottie, Church affairs can be murky. There's sometimes a line running between them and political affairs.'

She sent him a sharp look. There was something here that she was not getting. '*Sometimes …*' She halted. 'As far as I can gather, they each sleep in the other's bed.' She repeated her original question. 'How did you know I was here? And why couldn't this have waited until I got home this evening?'

'In his day, the cardinal was a powerful figure in the Church. Still is. And anyone who goes to see him gets checked out. I was a first port of call.'

They were now standing under an umbrella pine. Its sharp sappy smell was almost dizzying, particularly combined with the heat and the dust.

'You came all this way to tell me some gauleiter at the Vatican didn't want me asking a few questions?'

Tom shifted and his face fell into the shadow.

'And you *let* them?'

'Lottie, calm down. Please? I've been here a long time. They know that I know how it works and you're my wife. Of course, they contacted me.'

'Jesus,' she said, more appalled by this revelation of how Tom operated than the rebuke he was dishing out. 'Let me get this straight: the Church, bless it, in the guise of the cardinal, doesn't wish the story of a murdered woman to be aired. You agree with them and came running to tell me to keep quiet.'

Her hand shook with a combination of fury and shock.

Tom focused on the treacherous shakiness. 'I know you're not used to this way of doing things, and you're not the only person to object.'

'So you don't think it's peculiar,' she said.

'I think you should stop ferreting.'

She looked up at Tom. 'When they discovered I wished to ask questions, they ran a trace on me and got you involved. Would they do that for the average visitor?'

Tom was silent.

'Would they? No. I'm thinking there must be something about this case that worries the Church.' She checked herself as a hard, painful doubt pushed itself forward. 'Or is it you behind this?'

Tom had beckoned – 'Marry me?' – and she had followed him down the dewy path of desire, and the natural urge for companionship. Looking back – had Peter been right? – she had disobeyed her own rules and neglected to question exactly what he had done in the past, what he did now. *His provenance.*

'Tom, who told you where I would be?'

He shrugged.

'Tom, where did … *does* Clare work?'

He took a while to confess. 'The Press office, the UK section.'

'Did she tip you off?'

Again, the answer was not immediate. 'Lottie, it doesn't matter.'

She looked squarely into his eyes and realised that trying to fathom out Nina was one thing but to understand that she did not know her husband was another.

Tom returned her gaze with the seeming honesty that had now become equivocal.

They parted acrimoniously and went their separate ways.

Hot and jangled, Lottie returned to the *Espatriati*. There Paul was waiting to take her to his apartment for lunch, which had been arranged a couple of days previously.

He took one look at her. 'That went well, then.'

Lottie managed a smile. 'What am I missing, Paul?'

'Who knows?'

Paul's one-bedroomed flat was a bus ride away from the archive. 'It's not so far from Cinecittà,' he said. 'Sometimes I walk down to the studios' entrance and peer through, hoping to see the ghosts of Burton and Taylor.'

'Or Fellini?'

'I crave spectacle.'

The flat was cool, airy and book filled. An ambrosial aroma greeted them as they went in. Paul explained that he had got up early to make the special *ragù* that had been slow cooking during the morning.

It was excellent and Lottie begged for the recipe, which Paul handed over. 'It was given to me by a friend who had it from a friend of his. This means you have joined the chain. It's for people who belong here.'

'I love that idea.'

Lottie watched while Paul made coffee. 'Nina Lawrence knew it was dangerous to be writing things down but she risked it because she wanted someone to know about her life. Probably Leo?'

Paul turned off the heat under the coffee pot. 'From what you tell me, she was living a double life. That brings immense strain, and writing the journal offered release.'

Lottie returned home in the early evening to discover the hated standard lamp in the passage outside the front door, with its flex neatly coiled and tied.

She went in search of Concetta, who she discovered rubbing its vacated patch of floor to eye-watering brilliance, using the polish she favoured whose smell reminded Lottie of school dinners.

'What's going on?'

Concetta sat back on her knees and dusted her hands on her overall. 'Signor Tom said the lamp was to go.'

Lottie's stomach lurched. 'When did he say that?'

'He telephoned at lunchtime. He said you did not like it.'

'I don't and that is nice of him.' She glanced down at her hands. 'I gather he and Signorina Clare bought it together.'

Concetta sent Lottie a shrewd look. 'It was a long time ago,' she said, surprising Lottie with her diplomacy. 'It's a good lamp and it works.' The duster was being wielded with hard swipes. 'Plenty of people would like it. They don't have money to throw out good things.'

What possessed me, wondered Lottie, to hand over to Concetta a just cause on a plate? The lamp's right to life was now a battle of moralities.

'It's a good lamp,' Concetta repeated.

In a flash, Lottie got it. Concetta wanted the lamp but could not possibly ask for it. 'You're right,' she agreed with utmost tact. 'Do you know someone who might want it?'

'No,' said Concetta.

'Why don't we leave it outside our front door for the time being and see if anyone takes it? Then, someone else will be able to use it.'

Concetta's gaze shifted this way and that, but it appeared Lottie's suggestion was a master stroke of diplomacy and a solution that would work. The lamp would be carted away to Concetta's place, Lottie would not enquire who had taken it and proprieties would be maintained on either side.

Concetta nodded. 'Sí.'

The matter settled, the atmosphere improved.

Lottie sat down on a vacant chair. 'Concetta, we have discussed Signorina Clare coming here ...'

'The signorina is nice ...' Concetta got slowly and perilously to her feet. 'A good person to work for.'

'I'm sorry that you miss her, but I will make sure that I am a good person to work for too.'

Lottie could have done with a little more enthusiasm in response, but she had to make do with Concetta's: 'certamente'.

There was a pause while options were weighted up.

Concetta plumped for prudence. 'You know, Signora, the lamp *was* difficult to clean.'

'I'm sure that whoever takes it will cherish it very much.'

A silence followed, which, to Lottie's surprise, was not hostile, merely one in which an acceptance of the status quo was acknowledged.

Concetta picked up the polish and duster.

'I had a wonderful lunch,' said Lottie. 'Cooked by a colleague. Pork loin cooked very slowly with red onions and juniper berries, olive oil, butter and white wine eaten with rigatoni pasta.'

Food. Italian food … cooking. It was the trigger. A spark ignited.

'I know it.' The duster disappeared into Concetta's pocket. 'Very good. Not everyone can cook it. If you would like we can make it together.'

Lottie smiled. 'I *would* like.'

Tom was staying late in the office preparing for a conference. Lottie phoned him. 'Thank you,' she said.

He knew what she was talking about. 'You were right. It was a dreadful old thing.'

'But it was generous of you.'

'My second nature,' he said, and Lottie laughed.

'Tom, I'm sorry about this morning. Please forgive my outburst.'

'I'm sorry, too.'

They finished the conversation with matters between them not exactly back to normal but satisfactory.

The following morning, on the way to work, Lottie asked for a kilo of pork loin at the butcher and arranged for it to be picked up by Concetta.

'*Eccola.*' The butcher wrapped the parcel and labelled it. He shot an appreciative look at Lottie, who had a new dress on, and asked what she was going to do with the pork. 'Ah, you must cook for four hours,' he said when she told him.

'Rubbish,' called out the woman behind Lottie. 'At least six.'

An argument erupted with not a few in the queue turning into ardent partisans. *Yes. No. How dare you.* Lottie watched and listened, intrigued by how confident in themselves this random group of Romans were. Alive. Opinionated. Feet on the ground.

She emerged into the warm street. This city was something. A glorious fusion of beauty, luxury and ease, married with scornfulness, style and an old, old history. And, yet, of the moment.

If she were willing to build a marriage … if she immersed herself in this new setting … there was more than a chance that the melancholy that lurked in her would retreat to backstage.

In the office, she unlocked Nina's notebook, placed it on her desk and readied herself.

CHAPTER NINETEEN

Rome
27 April 1978

THE VATICAN SQUARE MILE HAS A DIFFERENT FEEL TO THE complex city outside of it.

Any noise is subdued. No one runs. The gardens are cleaner. No laundry flaps out of windows. No graffiti.

The Vatican pharmacy is always crowded and, so too, is Annona, the well-stocked supermarket. Here the goods are exempt from most taxes and a *tessera* pass, which permits shopping there, is prized more than gold dust. Naturally, a black market thrives in them.

Annona's biggest seller is gossip. A lot can be overheard when queuing up to pay. Financial scandals. Sexual scandals. Church politics.

I have not been there very often. It is not an ideal rendezvous for the simple reason everyone is watching everyone else and jealously guarding their privileges.

But I did meet Rex there in June of 1977.

I found him scanning the fruit juices as arranged. If he picked up a carton of orange juice, I was not to approach. If an apple, it was clear.

He placed an apple juice in his basket.

We stood a few feet apart. I scrutinised the cheeses that I was not able to buy because I was not in possession of the worth-its-weight-in-gold *tessera*. I moved past him and, in a classic manoeuvre, dropped a piece of paper into his basket.

At the end of the aisle, I glanced back to see him shifting the carton of apple juice over it.

The paper gave Rex the details of where I would be that evening.

Leo wished to introduce me to his uncle and Rex wanted the contact. It was a bad idea all round, but I had to go through with it.

As I calculated might happen, Beppo had confronted Leo about me and insisted on a meeting.

Leo and I talked it over long and earnestly – I, pretending I did not want the meeting, but knowing I had to meet him because of Rex.

In the end, I told Leo that I would do my best to persuade his uncle that we were friends and I wanted to consult him because I was thinking of becoming Catholic.

His face cleared.

I booked a table at the *Eau Vive*, one of the chain of well-known restaurants that stretch through the Catholic world. I had been curious to eat there.

The Roman branch is close to the Pantheon and occupies two floors in a sixteenth-century palazzo. It is frequented by diplomats, priests, prelates and Vatican personnel and their families who wish for pasta-free dining as the cuisine is mainly French.

I chose my clothes carefully for the encounter, thinking well-off socialite needing to find a purpose in life. Hair in chignon. Big earrings. Dress with a swooping neckline, but not too tight, and strappy high heels. A bag that suggested designer. It was a disguise intended to nudge Beppo into seeing a woman with too much money and time, and too lightweight, to be a threat to his nephew's future.

Nowhere but in Rome is it possible to buy a simple dress, a bag, a pair of shoes and achieve a transformation. Argue with me if you like, but Roman – Italian – clothes possess innate witchery. Wearing them is to acknowledge the importance of the *bella figura* and a belief in life-enhancing elegance and form. Beauty is a moral duty.

When I arrived at the restaurant, Rex was sequestered at the back of the room. I did not look at him, nor he at me, as I was ushered to the table.

Leo's uncle was already there and rose to greet me. He took my hand and gave a little bow. I knew that my preparations had done the trick because I was an almost exact copy of the soignée, discreetly jewelled women at the other tables and he had clocked it.

Wearing a dark suit with an insignia badge in the lapel, he was in his late twenties, of medium height and, at first glance, a benign aspect. On second glance, I suspected he was watchful, possessed of hidden energy and a ruthlessness. Unlike my beloved Leo, Beppo had traded in youthful illusion for realpolitik. His name did not suit him.

Wary, but polite, we introduced ourselves. I asked where Leo was and he lied convincingly that his nephew had some last-minute family duties and sent his apologies.

I made no comment. The message had been conveyed. Leo was controlled by his uncle.

We regarded each other over the table and I asked him what I should call him and he replied that his friends and family called him Beppo and he would be honoured if I did too.

I almost choked on my wine.

During the excellent meal, I asked him about the girls who were serving, some of whom were in the traditional garb of their countries. I'll say this for him: he was worldly, knowledgeable and amusing. Apparently, the girls hailed from all over the world and took temporary vows of poverty, chastity and obedience, but they were not nuns.

I envied them. They exuded a serenity and calm that, I imagined, was explained partly because they were safe and fed. At 9 p.m., as was the custom, the girls gathered around the statue of the Virgin and sang 'Ave Maria'. Some priests and a couple of professed nuns in grey habits who were also dining got to their feet and joined in.

Over dessert, I launched a reconnaissance of Beppo's views. It was so nice to see that not all traditions have been abandoned, I said.

His gaze slid over my face, a scrutiny that I disliked but I knew how to deal with. Then he relaxed and exerted himself to be charming and said it wasn't wise to be stuck in the past but, yes, sometimes it was too hastily abandoned.

I gave him the benefit of my best smile – not too confident but inviting confidences – and said that if you believed in something then one must stick to one's guns. (Sometimes, I surprise myself with what I find possible to say.)

Out of the corner of my eye, I watched Rex make for the exit while remarking that I believed Beppo came from a big family.

He explained that he was brought up on a farm – olives, goats, vines – in a family of six brothers and sisters. It could never have been said that they were well off, but, unlike many others, they didn't starve.

He was impressing on me how far he had come from that rural upbringing.

I said I believed he worked on legal matters in the Vatican which suggested he was a lawyer, and he said he was, specialising in compliance with Catholic doctrine.

And some financial matters, too, he added.

Intriguing. (The talk circulating at the moment was of opaque accounting at the Vatican and of Vatican cash – allegedly – being handed out to fund the building of luxury apartments in London.)

I remarked that he must have been highly ambitious. He agreed he had been, still was, and told me how the local priest had arranged for his education. His parents had been wary until the priest suggested that he finished his education in Rome, whereupon they changed their minds.

I could picture it. The eldest brother, who – apparently – was a fool, would take over the farm, and it was obvious there was history between the brothers. The other siblings needed to make their way, political unrest and poverty were deepening and the communists were causing trouble. Rome, he said, looked even more desirable.

He looked down at a packet of cigarettes lying between them and said that unrest such as he had just described left its mark. Either you went under or you went.

The story, dropped easily from his lips – which suggested it had been told more than once – was designed to convey that he was ambitious but also principled.

So ... woven into the power plays of his family were obvious rivalries, and the younger brother had set out to prove he was the equal of the older, plus a mover and shaker with influence to boot.

I asked if he had married and he replied there had been no time, but he had devoted his energies to his many nephews and nieces.

By the coffee stage, I had him more or less pinned down as a man with fierce right-wing political views.

I dabbed my lips with the napkin. Any second now, the business of the evening would commence.

He went in carefully, saying that he believed his nephew and I had become extremely good friends. I concurred and offered up the information that Leo had been helping me with problems of belief.

He was regretful, he said, but in the future Leo would be expected to concentrate on his studies and he would have to give up certain aspects of his life.

I plucked at my discarded napkin and asked if that was a warning. 'Yes,' he said.

He managed the feat of saying it bluntly and, yet, silkily smooth.

His gaze travelled over the frock and the jewellery, and I knew that I had succeeded and he had made an error of judgement in concluding that I was an unmarried woman hungry for sex, and only that.

It was, he suggested, time for me to move on before the situation became complicated.

This was exactly what I had expected, but it angered me – which I should not have allowed, although I managed to hide it. Still, I could not stop myself suggesting that it was up to Leo. It was his life, his future.

He gave me a look: *You know better than that.*

Patiently, he explained that Leo was young and inexperienced. He was not saying – he cleared his throat – friendship with me was not useful and, of course, some experience was a good thing. But friendship could change and it could give Leo unnecessary problems at a moment when he needed a clear head. And a clean heart for his vocation.

He leaned over the table towards me and appealed to my sense of what was right and kind. 'You see,' he said in that awful way, 'he will go far.'

I made the equation. The worldly uncle reckoned that it was OK for Leo to have a sexual experience, but not an emotional one.

Plus, he was grooming Leo to rise through the Church ranks, where those occupying the higher echelons were often powerful figures who dictated Vatican politics and strategy. They had a finger on foreign affairs, a diplomatic say-so, and influence on governments.

I stared at the unobtrusive insignia in the buttonhole of his dark suit, frustrated that I could not quite make it out.

'I think we understand what we are talking about,' he said.

'And if I choose not to understand?'

Underlying the silky reply was a threat. 'Then, steps would be taken.'

I let a silence elapse. I hated his casual betrayal of Leo and, at that moment, I hated him too. Above all, I longed to let this urbane, seemingly charming man stew in his terrible ambitions.

I smiled gently and understandingly – the woman of the world – and told him that I agreed Leo was very talented and he would go far.

I rose to my feet, filled with shame for the way Leo had been discussed and bartered and that I had been part of the transaction.

He leapt to his feet and said if I ever cared to repeat the evening, it would be his pleasure.

It took all my self-control, all my training, not to turn on my heel. Instead, I inclined my head and said that I would be delighted to think about it.

He held on to my hand for longer than he should have done. 'You see, there are bigger interests than you, than my nephew, than I.'

I caught the hardness, the inflexibility, the drive that lay behind the urbanity and I hated him.

If Beppo had known, it was too late.

We had been together in Palacrino that magical March weekend and it was far, far too late.

When we returned from Palacrino, Leo wrote me a letter he never should have written.

> I love you and I'm consumed as if by fire. What I can do
> about it I don't know, but I am mad with it.
>> Do we think alike?

The handwriting was rushed and rapid.

> The answer is we do on most things. I know little about
> you and I know you keep hidden from me parts of your
> life, but I can say with certainty that you hold the key to
> who I am. It has never happened to me before and when I
> consider how often we fail to understand others, I find it
> astonishing.

I cried thinking of what it would have cost Leo to write it. Breaking every rule in the life he had agreed to follow. How typically generous of him to do so.

Unwisely, I wrote back, but I was wise enough not to send it. It would never have got past the sentries in Leo's life and might have reached his mentor uncle. Also, it would have added to the burden on Leo's conscience.

I had once read a letter from an eighteenth-century woman. I think she was French but what she wrote is how I felt.

I owe you everything. Love, tenderness, a lesson in how
to feel. I never knew that I could walk through my life
filled with such beauty and feeling. A new sun rises for me
every day. Since I have met you, and loved you, my life has
become dearer, the sounds and scents of the world more
precious.

I copied it into the letter that was never sent and added my own words.

You will think me narcissistic, but I want you to know
everything. The light and the dark of my mind and soul. I
crave the same from you.

The memories I carry are like the change in my purse. The one of us drinking coffee together was lovely, but of a lower denomination. The one of Leo turning to me for the first time, his face blazing with passion, is of much higher denomination. And the memory of us that one time, together, in the hotel room comes highest of all.

And the memory I have of myself. Weeping with joy, with discovery, with lust and tenderness and with the knowledge that we had indulged in what is forbidden and, yet, regretted not one step.

CHAPTER TWENTY

LOTTIE RAISED HER HEAD FROM THE JOURNAL.

How slow she had been.

Vatican legal matters. Compliance. Financial affairs.

Opening her laptop she typed in the name 'Beppo' and, within seconds, read that it was a diminutive of 'Giuseppe'.

Giuseppe Antonio, the man who visited her office, was almost certainly Leo's uncle. He must have heard *The Annunciation* had been found in the Nina Lawrence papers that had been retrieved from storage, realised that they contained clues in them to an old scandal, and wanted to protect the reputation of his nephew, who might, or might not, be a notable Church figure.

Furthermore, Antonio was a friend of Valerio Gianni, whom it was said had big, meaty connections in the Vatican – Giuseppe Antonio obviously being one of them.

Nevertheless, if Lottie was correct, there was something corrupt and cruel about the desire to keep Nina Lawrence's history quiet.

The *entente cordiale* struck between her and Concetta was holding and Concetta had invited Lottie to visit her daughter with her.

Orietta lived twenty-five kilometres or so from Rome's city centre in Genzano, where the spring *infiorata* was about to take place. 'It's the tradition ...' Concetta explained. 'Very old. The bigger one is later but this one is for the schoolchildren.'

She bustled between table and stove in the kitchen and, every so often, Lottie was forced to edge out of her way.

Since The Affair of the Lamp, a colonisation of the kitchen had taken place. A crucifix now occupied the shelf above the pans and a mirror framed in candy-pink plastic adorned (hardly the correct term) the wall adjacent to the fridge.

Concetta tipped a heap of plump and glossy early broad beans into an earthenware bowl.

'*Infiorata?*'

'A carpet of flowers is laid along the main street and everybody comes to look and to have a good time.'

Lottie looked up the *infiorata*. Themes were allotted for each year: 'Botticelli Paintings', 'Roman Emperors', 'Mythic Monsters'. She showed Concetta the photographs on her laptop. 'This year it's Dragons.' Concetta fanned herself with an oven glove. 'For the children, you know? They draw the designs with chalk on the road. Then they work with the flowers. Very difficult. Very hard. But good for them.'

Would Nina have known about the *infiorata*? So far in the journal, Lottie had not come across references to it, but Genzano was close enough to Rome for an easy outing. It was a not unreasonable assumption that Nina might have visited. With that in mind, Lottie offered to drive Concetta over to Genzano on the appropriate date.

The weather was shifting into a higher gear and the bright blue sky was suggestive of the high, hard heat of summer to come when she said goodbye to Tom and got into the car. Negotiating

Roman traffic was tricky at the best of times, and Lottie, subjected to Concetta's distracting running commentary on other drivers, only just managed to avoid a couple of collisions.

Even so, being out of the city and the *Espatriati* was unexpectedly liberating and fun, and her grip on the wheel gradually relaxed.

Turning off the main road into Genzano, a car shot across their bow. 'The man has the face of a crocodile,' hissed Concetta, 'and the manners of a pig.' A woman in tight capris on an electric bicycle dipped and swayed beside the car, seemingly at ease with the risks she was taking. Not a stray lock fell from her dark ponytail.

Lottie felt weak.

Once parked, Concetta hurried off, leaving Lottie to enjoy the spectacle of flowers unrolling down the main street.

A full, floral palette, from the palest to the darkest of greens, to reds and purples, pinks and blues, had been sculptured into every form of dragonage. Horses bore armoured knights on their backs and fought scaly ones. A medieval queen had one coiled at her feet. Dragons sat at the mouths of rocky caves. They spat fire, were impaled on lances and clashed with fellow dragons in symphonies of ochres, olive greens and browns.

Lottie wandered happily.

Yellow was a dominant colour. There were fiery suns and, scattered throughout, representations of sunflowers picked out in golds, Chinese yellow, russet-yellow and canary, growing in the backgrounds alongside rocky caves and mountains.

Nina wrote about the sunflower. Native to Central America, they were held in high esteem because they were believed to have been the emblem of the Sun God. Pioneer folklore had it that, when the Mormons left Missouri to look for a land where they could be free to worship, sunflower seeds were scattered over the Utah plains by the vanguard wagons so that the women and children following on the next summer would know where to go.

Picture the Mormon women. Frazzled from travel and the not-knowing, almost certainly hungry, scanning the stony prospects, and nerving themselves to push onwards, their gaze ever searching out the splash of yellow to tell them that their menfolk had gone that way.

Lottie halted beside a fine example, where a bright yellow sunflower bloomed behind a prancing horse.

Was it a coincidence that Nina wrote about the sunflower in the notebook?

In the café behind, a woman was shouting across the road to a friend and sweeping the pavement. Lottie waited until she had finished and took a photo of it.

Two doors down from the café, a boutique sold lingerie in oyster satins and black lace. Beautiful, luxurious things. Lottie admired a nightdress hemmed with satin. Moving on, she noticed a man on the opposite side of the road who had stopped to fiddle with his phone. He was middle-aged and, except for his shaven head, unremarkable.

Further on, the delicatessen offered up a spectacle: jars of goats' cheeses in oil, black olives in cream earthenware bowls and salamis hanging from ceiling hooks like stalactites acted like magnets. In she went and, pot of the olives in hand, emerged ten minutes or so later to find the man was still there talking into his phone.

Stopping to photograph here and there, she found her way to Orietta's house, which was set two streets back from the main street. Semi-detached and modern, with big picture windows, it had a wire fence running around the garden.

Concetta sat in the garden under a vine-smothered pergola absorbed by her two-year-old granddaughter. Lottie was struck by the image she presented – the soft smile and protective pose was a side of Concetta with which she was unfamiliar.

A dark beauty, which suggested the family originated from the south of Italy, Orietta was six months' or so pregnant and looked like her mother.

'Does she bully you?' Orietta wished to know, her smile revealing beautiful teeth.

'Yes,' said Lottie. She glanced at Concetta, who was whispering to the toddler. 'But I could not manage without her.'

Orietta was no fool. 'She's choosy, my mother. But she has a heart, and, if it's given, there's nothing she wouldn't do.'

'My husband has benefited. Very greatly.'

'Yes.'

Tea was served under the pergola from a tray patterned with ripe cherries. There was no milk, only slivers of lemon and almond pastries. The toddler played at their feet. The three women gossiped. A scooter roared up the street followed by a car driving too fast, releasing a stink of fuel. Concetta clicked her tongue against her teeth. 'Barbarian.'

Since coming to Italy, Lottie had acquired phrases and idioms and they slid off her tongue with pleasing alacrity and ease. A modest achievement, perhaps, but one that suggested that she was beginning to blend in to Italian life.

Released from the chores and the kitchen – or, perhaps, it was the stimulus of being with her daughter – Concetta turned talkative. 'The signora,' she turned to Orietta, 'works with the dead. That's her business.'

'You could put it like that,' Lottie defended her work, 'but in some ways, I keep them alive.'

They ate the pastries, and Orietta told them about the participating schools and the designs. 'The children have to learn what the messages of the flowers are. They all have meanings.'

Lottie accepted a third cup of tea. 'The sunflowers are great.' She showed them her photograph of the impressive sunflower in the final section, standing tall behind a dragon. Its colours were of the darkest ochre, dipping into rust.

Orietta consulted the leaflet that Lottie had brought with her. 'That's the school run by my cousin,' she said. 'They have a good art teacher.'

But Lottie was not listening. She was staring at the photograph. In the background, in the right-hand corner, lurked the man with the shaven head.

She recognised him now as the man she had seen in the Protestant Cemetery.

It was late when Lottie backed the car into its parking place, a tricky manoeuvre that left her covered in a faint sweat.

The apartment was silent. Tom had left a note on the table to say he had gone to bed. Lottie poured herself a glass of wine and let herself out on to the balcony. Cradling the glass, she stood there for some time. There was a whiff of lavender, the sound of a door slamming and darkness punctured here and there by lights in windows and doorways.

Later, she lay beside Tom shrouded in his sleep and his secrets. However long she lived with him, however close they grew, she would, of course, know only a percentage of what he thought.

Ill at ease, she sighed. Shifted. The old serpents, the wily doubting ones, slithered into her thoughts.

Who was the man with the shaven head?

Always at such moments, she was thrown back on the memory of being abandoned, cold and hungry. 'Think of it as the sea wall that you have built against them,' advised a therapist that Lottie had once consulted when she was struggling to forget them. 'From time to time, those defences grow fragile, any defences grow fragile, and they will need rebuilding. Just rebuild them.'

She grasped at her wrist – the habit learned from the times when she felt she belonged to no one and nowhere. Laying a finger over her pulse, she counted its beats. 'That's me,' she said to herself, followed by the mantra that had seen her through. 'No one can take that away.'

Once – a couple of glasses of wine in – she had confessed to Helena that she almost wished she had been mistreated by the foster parents who plucked her out of the children's home. Then her anger would have had a legitimate and concrete target.

Helena's frown had reproved Lottie. 'You're crazy. You wanted to be beaten up? Or abused? Or any of those appalling things that happen?'

'Sorry.'

'I know what you're trying to say. Mike and Rachel didn't love you. And that's not enough for a child. But …' She had laid a red-nailed hand on Lottie's arm. 'Sweet pea, get over it.'

'I'm trying to say that just being tolerated leaves a … hunger.'

Helena's frown had lifted. 'You do know you're a fool and I love you.'

Did it matter? There were worse things than a lack of unconditional love. Yet, she knew, her experience during that time had laid a cold finger on her spirit and blighted her capacity for joy.

Tom's breathing deepened. He was very warm, and she shifted further away.

A light outside projected a pale circle on to the wall.

Sleepless.

A man with a shaven head had been following her. The rational calculus in her mind clicked through possibilities and decided that it was coincidence.

She decided to stick with that, slid out of bed and crept into the sitting room.

The darkness was softening at its edges and there was the peaceful hush before the dawn.

Seated at the table, she began to construct a timeline of Nina's movements around Rome, Lazio and Tuscany, using the journal and consulting the files in her laptop.

Nina's handwriting was tricky to decipher, particularly as a few of the journal entries were in French and Italian, but her habit of dating her writing was helpful. Certainly, the dossier of her garden commissions was impressive, as was the roster of clients. Palacrinos, Tavianis, Gellis ...

At the window, pink now stained the sky.

Lottie worked through the material: letters, bills from professional colleagues, ideas for a garden design and several formal commissions – a garden near the estate of La Foce in Tuscany and an estate south of Rome.

Nina also had the slightly curious habit of annotating receipts from her clients. On the bill from the Tavianis, she had written:

In the evening, the sun positions itself precisely above the
mountain peak, poses so all can admire and then slips
down like Thetis into the water ...

On another she had written:

236

They talk nonsense … Spoilt, demanding but
disadvantageous to cross. They inherited money or made it
by means that's best not to ask about and they believe that
their ill-gotten money entitles them to be superior.

The final papers from box number two had not yet been scanned
in and she spread them over the table.

A carbon copy of a letter to a Celestine Grazia in May 1978 read:

I promise to visit every month, more often if I can.

Lottie's expanding log recorded that Nina returned to the Palacrinos'
garden at least three times in 1978 to check up on the planting.

The lead urns must be planted up with nepeta and set
against the olive trees. The orange trees should be on the
sunken terrace in front of the house and their pots should
be painted light green …

This was a copy of another letter to Paola Palacrino:

It is important they are sited in exactly the right position
and I suggest I come up and stay for a couple of nights to
make sure.

The reply was also there:

Come immediately, Nina. Stay with us and we can talk
about everything. Bring a nice dress. The general was
asking after you.

Landscape gardener. Living in Rome. Travelling in Lazio and Tuscany. Having an affair with a man with whom she should not have been (almost certainly a priest). Working undercover. Botanical artist.

Who was the man with the shaven head?

The unanswered questions washed to and fro. Lottie dropped her head into her hands and peered through latticed fingers. It was a struggle to find Nina but there was also the struggle with her own psyche – and, she guessed the two connected to each other.

When she looked up Tom was standing in front of her, having padded in from the bedroom in bare feet.

'Lottie, what *are* you doing?'

'Trying to assemble a jigsaw puzzle.'

He placed both hands on the table and leaned over towards her. 'I won't ask again why you are so obsessed. I just have to accept you're mad.'

Their eyes met. His were alive with irony and his customary humour – and she felt relief so great she was almost dizzy. She dismissed her irritation and went to fetch a glass of water.

On her return, she found Tom bent over the papers. He looked up at her entrance and the mood had snapped into something else. 'These shouldn't be here.'

Tom disliked mess which Lottie understood. 'I'll clear up later, don't worry.'

He tapped the letter. '*This* shouldn't be lying around.'

She skim read. '"The garden faces south …" What's odd about that?'

'Go on.'

Underneath Paola Palacrino's signature could just be made out in pencil in Nina's handwriting: 'Rough Notes.'

Lottie read out aloud: "'Rex and I discuss the Roman Sword. Running a secret army and funding an unaccountable intelligence service is a risk to democracy. Creating hidden forces that can be called into play against the Soviets has turned out to be a Pandora's Box. In almost every country, these cells are being activated for peacetime political activity and are protected by the very highest.'" She tapped the paper. 'So ... Nina was politically aware. She had to be.' She glanced up at Tom and was taken aback by his expression.

Fury. Astonishment. Fear? 'What the fuck was this woman *doing*?' he muttered.

'Tom, explain.'

There was a second of silence.

'You must stop this.' Every iota of humour had been stripped away. 'Leave this stuff alone. Get it into the archive. She's dead and gone.'

'Not gone,' said Lottie stubbornly. 'Not gone.' Ironically, she agreed with Tom. It would be better if the papers were stowed in the archive as soon as possible, but she was angry. 'What are you doing talking to me like that? What's got into you?'

At odds and deeply awry, they stared at each other. It was Tom who blinked first.

'I'll get us a drink ...' he said. 'Wait there.'

Lottie heard him moving around in the kitchen. He reappeared carrying a loaded tray, put it down and passed over a mug of tea. 'It's got a dash of brandy in it.'

Rattled by their misunderstanding, she looked down at the mug and debated whether to shove it back at him. Then she saw that, having calmed down, he was back to the old Tom.

'Why only a dash?'

'Sorry,' he said. 'It's the middle of the night.' He sat down opposite her. 'Did you know I was an expert on jigsaws?'

'I suspect that's a brazen lie.'

'Maybe. Here's the thing. Choose the right space in which to solve your puzzle. Turn the pieces over. Sort the edge pieces. Sort by colour. Work on small sections. And ...' He tapped the lid of her laptop. 'Top tip: never give up.'

She leaned against the chair back. 'I thought you'd just told me to do the opposite.'

'I can help, Lottie, and it would be nice to do something with you.'

'Why so? You don't approve of what I'm doing.'

He picked up a couple of the police papers. 'It was a tricky, complicated time when she was murdered.'

She smiled wryly. 'And I don't understand? Is that what you're telling me?'

'I'm telling you that we're a partnership and partners look out for each other.'

There was the faint taste of brandy on her tongue. 'OK.'

'Let's go over what you do know.'

Lottie gave the details and Tom listened.

'The painting was found in her papers. Gabriele Ricci and the experts all agree it's fake but painted on original parchment obtained on the black market.'

'The artist had underworld contacts,' said Tom.

She spread her fingers over the surface of the table. 'The question is why would Nina Lawrence have the painting?'

'Payment. Think of all those *duchi* and *principesse* for whom she worked. There's a fair bet they had one thing in common: lack of cash.'

'Then both parties would have known it was fake.' Lottie was enjoying this. 'A *duca* or whoever would never have handed over a genuine one knowingly. It would have been worth thousands and thousands.'

'Maybe they needed to get rid of it.'

She ticked off additional possibilities. 'Was she acting as a fence ...? I don't think she would have stolen it, but maybe she was helping someone out. And, perhaps, she knew it wasn't genuine.' She clicked on to the file on her laptop that contained the article for *The Determined Traveller* and its illustrations and pushed it over to Tom. 'Or was it Nina who made the copy? She could draw and she knew about paint. She had seen an original in Palacrino.'

Tom peered at the illustration. 'Why the initials "EK"?'

'If you're forging something you don't use your real name.'

'In my experience, if you use something as a decoy, it generally contains a clue.'

She was intrigued. 'You know, do you?'

'Observation is good.' He gathered up the mugs. 'First piece. Were there any bank statements?'

Lottie checked over the documents on her laptop and pushed it over to Tom.

He ran an eye down the screen. 'She was in credit at the time of her death. A couple of payments were made immediately before.'

Lottie stood behind his chair. 'Clients,' she said. 'I recognise the names.'

'She had also arranged to pay someone on a regular basis.' He pointed to the entries. 'The equivalent of two hundred pounds every month to a Celestine Grazia.' He twisted around and looked up at Lottie. 'A fair old sum at the time. Maybe she was the forger? Or knew something and had to be kept quiet?'

She peered over Tom's shoulder. The payments to Celestine Grazia began in January 1978 and continued up to October 1978, the month of her death.

'If you give me a printout of this,' said Tom, 'I'll do a bit of ferreting.'

Lottie put her hands on his warm, solid shoulders. 'That's nice of you.'

'I am nice,' he said. 'Very.'

They returned to bed. Tom wrapped his arms around Lottie and cradled her to him. They were, Lottie thought, so close, so full of emotion, so delighted to be with each other.

'Forgive me?' he said. 'More than anything, I want you to settle and to be happy.'

Deeply touched, she swallowed the lump that rose into her throat.

He whispered to her, 'Lottie, when I met you my life knitted together. I hope very much you feel the same and that you don't feel you have to spend your time with the dead.'

She touched his cheek and thought for a moment. 'I love what I do. You have to trust me, Tom. As I trust you.'

Something flickered momentarily behind his eyes. Then, he reached over and turned off the light. A dawn light crept around the blind. 'It's a bit late to go back to sleep.'

She laughed, for he was already rolling the T-shirt that she wore in bed up over her head. 'That's blatant,' she said.

'So it is.' He bent his head. 'It's meant to be.'

CHAPTER TWENTY-ONE

Rome
29 April 1978

THE GENERAL DEMANDED DINNER AND I RECKONED HE WOULD enjoy the quirkiness of *Eau Vive* and took him there.

'It's very proper,' I warned him. 'You have to behave. No naughtiness.'

That perked him up.

He ate heartily, approved of the nine o'clock cabaret and wanted to talk about sex.

We were drinking our coffee when Leo's Uncle Beppo was ushered into the restaurant.

I avoided eye contact but he halted by our table. There was no help for it and I had to introduce the general, who was just getting going on what he planned for later and bristled at the interruption.

Then something caught the general's eye and, I swear, it was like a light being flicked on.

A message had passed between them, an acknowledgement they belonged to the same tribe. The general invited Beppo to join us for a drink and they talked for half an hour or so about acquaintances in common, the shooting of the prison warder in Milan by the

Red Brigades and the latest letter written from his prison by Moro addressed to the Christian Democrat Party.

All stuff that was common currency.

Once or twice, Beppo drew me into the conversation, but in a way that indicated that his impression of me as a good-time girl still held. In the end, I got up, said I was going to the Ladies, went outside to smoke a cigarette and tried to work out what they had spotted in each other. When I returned every survival instinct crackled into life. They had agreed on something and it was probably over me. I could tell from the way they welcomed me back. Very polite. Very false.

Never allowing your contacts to meet is a good principle and should be observed. I blamed myself for not thinking through the location of the dinner carefully enough.

The general came back to my apartment for 'coffee'. I had tidied meticulously. Not a scrap of paper or any of my artist materials in sight. Everything compromising in the cache under the bath.

He has no finesse, not an iota, and I gritted my teeth while he had his way. Hoping to get some more inside detail, I was very careful with my questions about the Moro kidnapping, but he was jumpy.

Whose side was I on, he demanded, and I told him 'his'. Of course.

I left it at that. He sent me a mean look and said that he wondered about me.

Wonder away, I advised him, and forced myself to trace a line of kisses down his torso. Lower and lower.

He fell asleep and I waited until he was well and truly snoring and got up. Very carefully, I lifted his jacket from the chair and took it into the bathroom.

Wallet, keys, a letter from – I think – his wife, who lived in the country, and a lapel badge with the insignia of a sword. The Gladius.

I replaced everything carefully and slid my way back into the bedroom with the jacket.

He was on the case and demanded to know where I had been and I told him that a girl needs the bathroom.

In bed, he reached over and grabbed me by the throat. 'Do I believe you?'

The grip was painful and vicious. I saw flashes of light and fought for breath.

It was a warning.

Did he do this to his wife? I managed to gasp.

The grip slackened and he told me to leave his wife out of it and I said I would if he treated me properly. It seemed to do the trick and he released me.

That hurt, I told him, and it wasn't the deal.

He blustered and told me he could hurt a great deal more and it was obvious he was enjoying his little reign of terror.

I fingered my throat, which felt bruised and swollen, and asked him if he would ever tell his wife about interludes like this one. It was high risk.

I remember the threat in his voice as he said: 'Women like you ...'

I pulled myself together and told him that women like me were here to serve their country, and ran my hand over his chest. He was not to worry. I had no hidden depths.

To butter him up I asked him to tell me all about his days in the field (only one or two, I suspect), about his prowess, and he rattled on at length. 'When you've killed once,' he said, 'the line is crossed. Next time is easy.'

The general left my apartment in the early hours and I lay awake.

245

The misery I experienced most days washed through me. I have not seen or heard from Leo since our final meeting last year. That terrible day in early autumn. Missing him does not get easier.

I wanted him.

I wanted him and – for every possible reason that he might think of and not think of – I needed him and I could not have him.

Rex visited the apartment. *Not* good practice but we needed to go over the situation and to take our time.

I drew the curtains closed. We drank coffee and ate the best *cantucci*, dipping them into Vin Santo.

He and I agreed. Neither the Italian state nor the US wanted Moro alive, although they would never say so and everyone would fall over themselves issuing statements of profound shock and horror. Given Moro's push to do a deal with Italy's large and powerful Communist bloc, many in his party – and in the Parliament – view his kidnapping as a godsend.

However, a few of the more thoughtful are asking: how come the Red Brigades were so much more efficient at this sort of operation than the state was in finding him?

Without doubt, the operation has been suspiciously well funded and planned. We mull over the theories.

Under international law, it is an offence for an outside country to meddle with the internal affairs of another nation, but the Americans and, almost certainly, the Brits are doing so. They are concerned about NATO security. The last thing they wish is for the Communists to have any leverage in an Italian government.

Did the general intend to let the information slip, or not? He hinted that indeed it was a secret, right-wing paramilitary group that was hell-bent on preventing the Communists having any power. (We must bear in mind he might have been feeding me false leads.)

On the other side of the argument, a secret, left-wing underground group is working to put the Communists in power. Moro is the ex-prime minister who mediates between the two. Who acts? Who takes advantage? Who loses?

I had never seen Rex so on edge or noticed worry lines on those Renaissance features. Over the years, I had grown fond of him, and I wondered about his life. His home. His emotional stability. How long *he* would last?

Ours is a strange relationship. It would never be called a friendship by the observer, but it is. It is.

Naturally, I have no idea who Rex's other sources are, but I wondered if he pushed them as hard as he pushes me. He orders me to keep going with the general just in case we can feed something more to HQ. They will be working on their responses.

I kept my expression neutral. In the past, I have treated my body as resilient, yes, but friable and disposable. It did not count for that much.

In that past, I would have had no problem. My body was easily deployed if it was necessary. My spirit, too, was willing. It had been part of the game, a portion of the undertaking I took all those years ago.

That had changed. My body and spirit have been re-stamped and newly tempered in a different fire, which makes that easy, obedient disposal hard.

Metamorphosis was something I had only read about until I met Leo. But it has happened to me. I have dived in deep as one person and come up another.

I imagined that I knew myself. But it was far from the truth and I must learn about the new me.

I made fresh coffee and filled up Rex's cup. It was bitter and bracing and he gulped it down.

I sat down opposite him and told him that, when I took that time off earlier, I had done some thinking and I would be leaving as soon as I could arrange matters.

He gave a start and said he bloody hoped not.

I cannot be the first, nor will I be the last to leave his stable – or indeed The Office – and his reaction surprised me.

Among other things, you have to be lucky in this work, I pointed out, and I worried my luck was running out.

Curiously, Rex understood. As a tribe, we are supposed to be logical and calculating, but there is always an element of superstition. He asked me what I planned to do.

I said I was already packing up my papers, and that I was thinking of training as a teacher.

Rex laughed so hard that he knocked his cup over.

I cupped my chin in my hand and gave him some advice, which was to treat his flock more gently. We need encouragement, I told him. We need to feel wanted and loved.

'*What?*' he exclaimed and I told him to remember my advice when I had gone.

He turned serious and warned me that I couldn't leave yet. Not until the Moro affair was done. We needed the general, he said.

To be fair, Rex didn't know what he was asking of me.

Several days later, I was sitting at the table with my journal. Lacking the energy, I had not written anything in it for days. It lay on the table. A once ultra-smart accessory, now battered, water stained and, because I had inserted so many letters, dried flowers, sketches, unable to close.

Leo disliked cars. Loved olive trees.

I was thinking about the future. I *had* to think about the future and I was making plans.

The phone rang. I let it and it went on and on. Finally, it stopped.

In the corridor, Marta Livardo was kicking a bucket along the tiles in a bad-tempered way and music blared from the pocket transistor radio she always had with her.

The phone rang for the second time. Second time around, it was easier to ignore.

She banged on the door. 'Signorina, are you all right?'

I didn't answer.

Prying was a way of life for Marta Livardo. Given the job, it was inevitable. People coming and going. Love affairs, quarrels, mortalities, debts and their fallout, are all compressed under this roof. A microcosm of human life. There are so many telltale details on which to feast. Extra laundry, raised voices, late payments … To observe is to accrue power.

I should know.

In another existence, Marta and her nosiness would have been amusing. I might even have felt affectionately about it. In her position I, too, would want to watch the endlessly fascinating comedies and tragedies played out under this roof.

The door handle rattled. In a flash I was on my feet and flung open the door.

The lightning change in her expression from cunning snooper to startled innocent was masterly. She shoved her keys back into her apron pocket and muttered that she had heard the phone go and was worried that I was ill.

That made me angry and I pulled her inside, accused her of trying to find out if I had a visitor and invited her to open the cupboards and look behind the curtains.

I had to hand it to Marta Livardo. She did look round, her mouth set in its customary mean and miserable lines.

Then I recollected what has happened to me. How the experience has loosened the emotional sinews, how judgement of others has become softer, how love makes it possible to suggest alternatives.

I captured one of her hands in mine, told her we had known each other a long time and wouldn't it be better if we were friends? Her fingers felt rough and swollen in mine, and I thought of all her years of thankless work. I told her that I knew how hard she worked and how sad she was.

The fingers between mine jerked and she spat at me that I knew nothing.

But I do *know*, I insisted. She turned her head abruptly away from me but I held on.

We can help each other, I told her. If we choose to.

CHAPTER TWENTY-TWO

Anticipating her new role, Lottie was reorganising her days and readying herself for the work ahead.

At the time the *Espatriati* documents had been extricated from the warehouse in the south of the city, it had been assumed that all the material had been reclaimed.

Not so. Valerio Gianni rang Lottie to say that the warehouse had been slated for development and four boxes of documents had been discovered in a cellar. The entrance had been hidden by machinery that had been installed when the warehouse had been used as a wholesaler. Arrangements had been made to send them in.

When they arrived, Lottie made a preliminary reconnaissance.

What wonderful people.

She read on a sheet of lined paper torn out of an exercise book.

The Fatebene Fratelli, the Do-Good Brothers (a name to
which they live up), have taken me in to their hospital.
When the Germans ask to question all the patients,
they are told that there is a special isolation wing where
patients, which include me and several Jews, are suffering

from the highly infectious Syndrome K, and it would be dangerous to inspect it. So far, it has worked …

The note appended to it read: *Written by Guy Peters in May 1943 at the Fatebenefratelli hospital.*

With a pang, she remembered that Nina had been taken there. Lottie checked the map. The hospital was on the Isola Tiberina. She hoped the reason the letter had never been sent was not the worst. It was followed by:

The coffin was so very small … It was easily covered by the roses. When I laid them on it, I did not think it was possible to feel such pain.

At the bottom of the page, the same handwriting stuttered to a final sentence:

My heart is now closed. For ever.

The note accompanying it recorded that Louise Burlington soon after died of grief in May 1880 and was buried beside her son.

Next up provided a sparkling antidote to the sadness. A clutch of black-and-white photographs showed a group of magnificent-looking women modelling clothes: form-fitting sheath dresses, a huge round hat, a strapless satin ball gown, trousers with figure-hugging blouses and billowing sleeves. All were labelled in a sloping script with the initials of the client for whom they had been made in the top right-hand corner.

The accompanying article read:

The 1950s was the moment to be a fashion designer in Italy and, when he arrived penniless, Harold Welsch sensed a female yearning for beautiful and frankly uninhibited clothes. 'You can only dress a woman perfectly when you know what's going on in her head,' he said. 'Desire permeates her bones. Desire for men, for attention, to be free to be herself ...'

Where had Harold got his expertise and energy? Or the louche, wild vision that resulted in clothes that ached with sex and style, cocked a snook at the establishment and made him enormously rich? Harold died from liver failure in 1961 and, at his funeral, the female mourners dressed in his creations turned out en masse and caused a sensation.

She saluted him.

Several documents required work and, before they were allocated to the relevant departments, Lottie rang Gabriele to ask his opinion.

They discussed the projects and, then, he asked, 'Is the work completed?'

Lottie did not need to ask what Gabriele was referring to.

'I'm pretty sure it is. As far as I know. But I'm still reading through the journal. I thought you might look at the cover, which needs attention.'

At the other end of the phone, Lottie heard him moving around. A restless, awkward tread.

'Is everything OK?' she asked.

'Perfectly OK.'

The conversation ended with Lottie none the wiser.

She was scanning the final entries of the journal into her phone when Gabriele rang back and asked if he could meet her later that afternoon. He had something to say about the murder and could she meet him at the Ponte Sisto.

'So you have a theory about who did it?'

'Yes. And no.'

His voice was thin and troubled.

The Ponte Sisto linked the Via Giulia on one side of the Tiber with the Trastevere on the other.

Sublime architecture, Lottie thought as she approached it. Even the graffiti contributed to its spell.

But this was where Nina died. As such, the scene carried extra resonance and she had come armed with the police diagrams of the murder scene in case Gabriele wanted to consult them.

She crossed the bridge. On the Trastevere side, she ran down the steps from the embankment, her hand brushing over the heated stone. The river was grey-brown, and the air above the line of tents straggling up the towpath in the direction of St Peter's shimmered in the late-afternoon heat.

In the baggy shirt and trousers he wore in the workshop, Gabriele waited at the bottom of the steps, his customary pallor tinged with colour.

'Gabriele—'

He did not bother with preliminaries. 'I knew her.'

The confession was painful.

The sun hit her four-square in the face and her heart began to pound.

'You *knew* Nina Lawrence?'

'In the notebook … the journal … does she refer to a trainee priest?'

Lottie closed her eyes for a second, the better to absorb her feelings and the punch that came with the revelation. 'Yes.'

'With whom she had an affair?'

'You're the man she fell in love with.'

'I am.' His features were a mask of distress. 'I loved her. Very, very much. Her murder changed my life.'

The river, the birds coasting on its surface, the sun, the straggle of booths and tourists … the bright scene took on a tragic quality.

'And *you* were the nephew.' Lottie trod carefully. 'But you're supposed to have forged your way through the Church hierarchy and be a cardinal by now.'

'I never took my vows.'

She could see it now: the hermetic workshop, the hidden history, an old anguish that she sensed so often when she was with him.

'Was that your punishment? You wouldn't have been the first trainee priest to have an affair.'

'I lost my faith.'

'I should have known,' she said. 'But I didn't see. Now I do.'

'I have always taken care to hide it.'

'And your uncle is Giuseppe Antonio?'

'Yes.'

'I have been stupid. I thought your uncle's name would be Ricci. Like yours.'

He seemed surprised. 'He's on my mother's side.'

They were silent.

'This is where she died,' was wrung from Lottie. She wanted to say: *Almost certainly, she was thinking of you.*

'Where she died is where I felt … I feel … I must confess to you.' He looked across the river to the opposite bank. 'You don't mind me doing this?'

255

'This might sound odd,' said Lottie, 'but no. It helps. I've been living with Nina.' She looked down at his arm, which had a paint stain on it. 'What made you decide to tell me?'

'I knew I could trust you,' he answered.

She absorbed the compliment. 'Did you know she called you Leo?'

'She told me that, whatever she did, she would never name me.' They fell into step. 'She knew the fallout if we were discovered and what it would do to my family. She also argued that absolute secrecy would give me the space to think about my future.'

Lottie said nothing.

'This is a shameful admission. I avoided reading about her murder and I never came here.'

Grief and guilt were past masters at digging their teeth into the flesh, and she understood.

Lottie said: 'I was knocked off my bicycle once and woke up in hospital. I never knew what happened. Still don't. The point is, I don't want to know.'

'Exactly that.'

Traffic screeched on the embankment above. They passed a huge block of stone that had been dumped at the river's edge. At its base bloomed a clump of poppies, blood-red and pink. A tangle of reeds straggled down into the water.

The path was uneven and, in places, stony. Lottie trod carefully and was equally careful not to probe Gabriele too hard or fast.

They walked in silence.

'Nina broke it off,' said Gabriele eventually. 'It's strange, but even after all these years, I have trouble saying it. At the time, I thought I would go mad. I was young and imagined all kinds of things. I thought she had met someone else ...' His laugh was bitter. 'Imagine,

I was a priest in training and I wanted to kill whoever the man was.'

'But not to kill Nina?'

'What do you think?'

'Of course you didn't kill her, but I suspect you *think* you know who did.'

Two cyclists edged past. 'Nina …' The way he articulated the name suggested it was a luxury he had long denied himself. 'I don't know if you will understand, but I loved her so much that I ended up half deranged.'

Ah, thought Lottie, *a fellow traveller*. 'If you mean knowing what it is to be buffeted by emotions so savage you find it difficult to maintain control, then I do know.'

'She was extraordinary. Not beautiful, but lovely. Lovely in herself,' Gabriele said. 'When I was younger, I managed to shake her memory off for long periods. It took some doing and I lost my vocation, but I refused to live as a haunted man. But these past few years … perhaps after wine … I find myself asking her ghost for forgiveness. She's with me much more.' He walked on for a bit. 'Do you believe in ghosts?'

'Of a sort.' She thought of the mother she had never known. Of the father she had never known. 'I encounter them in the documents most days.'

'At least your ghosts cannot accuse you of abandoning them.'

Despair. Doubt. Disbelief. Gabriele must have become intimately acquainted with all of them throughout his long penitence. 'You seem to blame yourself for her death, but her murder could have been a robbery or mistaken identity.'

'Nina and I had caused a scandal and quite a few people got to know about it. At that time, there were disappearances and murders in the Vatican. Two young girls … you may have heard of them. One of them was known to be having a sexual relationship with a priest and it made me wonder if the Church wasn't above exacting punishment.'

'Murder?' She was startled.

Gabriele fiddled with his watch, the expensive one Lottie had noticed previously. 'I wasn't in a good state of mind. I had all sorts of wild ideas.

'I found it impossible to continue.' He glanced at Lottie. 'That's the irony. Nina was dead. I knew I would never feel about another woman as I had for her and the way was clear to take my vows. But I had a breakdown and was hospitalised for a short while.' He smiled grimly.

'How can I help, Gabriele?'

'The footprints in the sand will have been covered over, but you have been through the papers. Can you tell me anything? Anything at all?'

She regarded him thoughtfully. 'I think it would be better if you read them for yourself. It would be easy to arrange and you will be able to take as much time as you need.'

He came to a halt. 'You do know something … What is it?'

Was she being fair? Was she being wise? Surely it was better, more honest, if he encountered Nina directly on the page?

'Nina was not straightforward. All I can say is that I know nothing more than you might have suspected.'

Gabriele gave a short laugh. '*Dio*, that's life.'

By now, they had traced the bend in the river and, lapped by a pearly heat haze, the dome of St Peter's dominated the view.

They turned back.

'About your uncle,' she said. 'He knew about you and Nina and he always protects your interests, then and now. I bought *The Annunciation* to you, which you must have told him about. Yes?

When he realised that I was working on Nina's papers, he was alarmed and … I think … I think he tried to put me off the scent by making a play for *The Annunciation*. He was terrified that I would work out what happened.'

'He was right. You did.'

She wanted to be truthful. 'Papers required cataloguing. I was at a loose end. It was obvious that there was something unfinished about Nina's life and death. I confess … I … confess it really hurt me that she had had no one, and no justice …' A faint groan issued from Gabriele. 'What surprises me is that you weren't put on the police list.'

He gave a typical Italian shrug. 'Easy. Antonio has contacts and can arrange matters. He insisted on negotiating with the police and with Bishop Dino, who was in overall charge of my seminary.'

'You mean the *cardinal*?' She stopped stock-still. 'I should have known. Under any stone …'

Gabriele smiled. 'The Vatican is home to the humble, the saintly and the ambitious. Bishop Dino aimed to become a prince of the Church and made sure that he did so. No scandal would be permitted on his patch. The deal was that if my connection to Nina was hushed up and I agreed never to mention her, then I could remain in the seminary.'

'But you left.'

'In the end, I did.'

Lottie held out the diagram of the murder scene. 'Are you ready?'

'Yes.' His gaze travelled over the arches of the beautiful bridge. 'I've been a coward.' He made a disparaging gesture. 'I've called myself many names over the years but I never *did* anything. That's what astonishes me.' He was silent. 'That's what I hate about myself.'

Lottie thought she understood all too well. Often with bad or dishonourable behaviour, her instinct was to distance herself. Or ignore it.

They had drawn level with the starlings of the Ponte Sisto, where a crude but vivid graffiti of a she-wolf suckling Romulus and Remus reared up the embankment wall.

She looked up into Gabriele's weary face. 'I know exactly what you're saying.'

He turned his head away. 'I need a few more minutes.'

'Would it help if I tell you something? Personal?'

He nodded but without enthusiasm, for which she had sympathy. Dealing with the past demanded energy, and it was difficult to find extra energy for the lives of others.

'Tom knows about this but not many others do. I was given away at birth.' The old unease, the companion of her growing years, raised its head. 'It's something I don't want to think about … but I often do when my defences are down. In my twenties I tried to find my parents. I discovered my father was untraceable and my mother had left instructions she was never to be contacted.'

She now had his full attention. 'Go on.'

'I never tried again.'

'Yet it's not finished.' He was very gentle – and she caught a glimpse of the priest he might have been. 'It's a primary rejection and you still carry it.'

True.

'And a cruel one.'

'Discovering my mother abandoned me made me hate myself, and I saw the world as harsh and very bleak. I got over it, but there's a stubborn part of me that still hopes that, one day, the phone will ring.'

She had only told a few people, but the confession was more

draining than usual. Perhaps it was the disquiet on Gabriele's face – to which she was adding.

She looked down at the path, where a millipede scurried between the cracks and a rustle suggested there was a tiny animal in the patch of reeds.

'No child should grow up not knowing who they are.'

'But they do. And survive. Yes, I despair easily and I'm often told off for it by the people who love me. What you call the primary rejection sits squarely at the back of my mind. It's like a wall that is too high and too thick to get around.'

He touched her on the shoulder. 'Perhaps it's useful to think that she wasn't rejecting you but trying to preserve herself.'

From the direction of the Trastevere a church bell sounded. Momentarily, the grip on her shoulder tightened. The bell ceased and his grip loosened. A bird landed in the water with a soft splash.

Lottie smiled. 'I met Tom. How lucky was that?'

'And you're making a success of it.'

There was a short silence. 'I hope.' She smiled. 'That's what I'm trying to offer you. An affirmation, I suppose.'

There was a further silence. The heat hammered at their temples. The brightness of the day and the vivid summer vista of river, trees, weathered stone, the chatter of the passers-by, the smell of coffee coming from the booths and occasional cigarette smoke was in direct contrast to the dark and the terror of what had happened here.

His gaze veered past Lottie to the bridge. 'The café closed down,' she said. 'It didn't like the publicity.'

He looked down at the diagram. A dispassionate record, dotted with measurements and figures.

'Would you mind if I did this on my own?'

'I'll take a walk.'

She passed a flood marker – a relic of the time before the embankments were constructed. Then the Tiber could, and did, rise to unprecedented levels. Today, it flowed peacefully. She stood on the riverbank and watched the swirl of water, with a cargo of flotsam, make its way to the sea.

She glanced back. Gabriele was standing stock-still beside the towpath, staring at the ground. While she watched, he dropped down on to one knee and rested his hand on the earth.

When she rejoined him, he looked completely done in but composed. 'Now I have come here, I'm reluctant to leave.'

On their way back to the Via Giulia, Gabriele talked about Nina. 'She was a realist. I remember her saying that a vocation never really loses its grip, but the experience of sex would help me do my work because most people think about the flesh most of the time. She wasn't shy about talking about those kinds of things.'

Lottie liked the idea of the practical Nina.

'Above all, I wanted her to say that she and I would last for ever,' he said, 'but she never did.'

'Do you ever regret that you gave up on the priesthood?'

He took off his sunglasses and polished a lens. 'Yes. No. To succeed, your belief must be greater than any other thing. It has to surmount any longing for affection, for power, for people.' He gestured to a group of students walking down the street. 'Or for the small things. A mozzarella from your hometown, a dog at your feet, good shoes. The rewards, however, are enormous, but at a cost.' He lifted his gaze to Lottie. 'But, to answer your question, no I don't.'

'Gabriele, did you ever question what Nina said she was?'

He frowned. 'Why should I do that?'

It wasn't her ground to trespass over. 'You must come into the archive and read her journal.'

A client rang Gabriele on the mobile and she listened in to his side of the conversation. Important auctions and large sums of money were mentioned, and she grew increasingly uneasy.

They passed a corner fountain in the shape of a dolphin.

'Nina …' Gabriele articulated her name as if he was practising how to say it. 'Nina loved plants and wildlife. She kept a record of what we saw when we went on walks. She was generous and paid for everything because I couldn't. But I never knew anything about her family. Except once when she told me how she used to take refuge in an orchard when things were bad at home. She spent hours observing the natural world. Didn't I know there was a universe in just a few square inches of grass?'

Lottie negotiated a broken paving stone. 'From the start, you knew she was the painter of *The Annunciation*?'

He nodded. 'I'm sorry about that, too. I had never seen it before. But I took one glance. I was too poleaxed to say anything.' He grimaced. Again, she was reminded of the deep, hard wounds Gabriele had suffered. 'Apologies.'

She thought of the anticipation and the fuss it had caused – and forgave him.

'The parchment,' he said. 'The seminary had managed to obtain several sheets with which to restore a couple of their manuscripts. I had volunteered to work in the library. I took delivery of it and recorded one less sheet than there was. Simple.'

'Ah.'

'It was my present to her.' He was back in the past, 'It was a sin, but I never thought about it once.'

A woman pushing a double buggy bore down on them and they stepped aside.

'Did you never wish to marry and to have a family?' asked Lottie. 'After Nina, I mean some time afterwards, of course.'

He smiled broadly – which was a first for Lottie. 'Once. But she decided that my life would not suit her and married a cheese-shop owner on the other side of the city. I saw her from time to time. She used to give me hunks of pecorino; I think she felt guilty because she was the one who called it off. You know something? I was relieved. I'm better on my own.'

At the entrance to the *Espatriati*, Gabriele kissed Lottie's hand. It was an unexpected gesture and it touched her greatly.

'You've been a good friend,' he said. 'And I trust you.'

'Thank you.'

'I'm glad you came to Rome. One more thing … promise to try to knock that wall down?'

A balance shifted in Lottie. 'I will.'

'Good.'

Possessed by a rage to know, Lottie raced up to her office and opened the journal.

At first, she could not locate what she felt should be there – the account of how it ended. She found it underneath a pamphlet, paper-clipped to the page, with a fuzzy black-and-white illustration of a house and garden that advertised an open-air midsummer concert to be held at the Palacrino gardens.

CHAPTER TWENTY-THREE

Rome
3 May 1978

AFTER THAT MOMENT IN PALACRINO, LEO VANISHED BACK INTO the seminary. We had told ourselves it was where the physical between us began and finished – the Alpha and Omega of Leo and Nina.

The summer seemed endless. Preoccupied and fatigued, I had decided to leave Rome in August and did not plan to be back until March. I yearned to say goodbye to him one last time.

I thought it over endlessly. Selfish? Unproductive? Unprofessional?

I gave in and invited him to my apartment. It was risky. Marta Livardo would almost certainly spot him, but, I think, I sensed that Rome and I were finished with each other and it made me reckless.

He ranged around the bookshelves and told me he remembered every one of my books. He told me, too, that my botanical paintings were beautiful. He looked at the journal lying on the table and I know he knew that I had written about us.

We sat at the table with the rug and drank tea in large white china cups (I persuaded him to try it with milk) and discussed how the painter's role had evolved. In the fifteenth century the patron ordered the painter to paint the picture as he wished it. The artist of today produces what he likes and then sells it.

It was not the moment to be at odds, to acknowledge that we had parted, or to think of our futures. That moment needed to be just as it was and filled with love.

It was.

Yet, tension gathered. The memory of our night in the hotel in Palacrino was between us.

The tea had been drunk. He stood up and, for a breathless second, I thought he would move towards me.

'Nina ...'

Nina ...

If he lapsed once and gave into lust, then he would be forgiven, Leo explained. Even a few times with someone who didn't matter very much. The problem came if he gave heart and soul to another human.

I grew angry as I picked my way through the logic. A one-night stand with some poor girl and the soul was not imperilled, I hissed at him. But a loving relationship was a ticket to hell.

He drew himself up, which meant he towered over me, and told me it was the easiest thing to reduce things to the absurd.

Leo was flexing his intellectual muscles, which was good. I could feel the strength gathering in him, that mental discipline, the intensity he would need. But emotion as tangled as mine was dangerously selfish. I had been foolish to get myself into this situation and now I was bitter that I had run up slap bang against his God.

Even if his faith was as solid as the Rock of Gibraltar, I said, could he not understand the ironies of that position?

The question should have been answered by Leo – as all who

lived and thought by his chosen creed should answer. But, because he was involved and he loved me, he struggled with it and I, soft and weak, could not bear for him to suffer.

Don't say anything, I told him. You have chosen. You are a good man and will live a good life for others.

He confessed that the future would be daunting. Tough and lonely. Listening to him, my heart contracted with pain. Part of the process would be to find God during those times, he said, but it would be hard.

'I thought He had already found you,' I couldn't help flinging at him.

I knew that it cost Leo to admit to anxiety, but I was still angry that he demanded my sympathy for choosing a way of life that – I believed – was to cut out so much that was deep and true.

He was standing by the window, his figure bathed in light filtering over him like an old master painting. At that moment, I realised the ironies applied to me, too. I had chosen a way of life that also demanded a straitjacket and the loneliness of a vocation.

'I wish you understood,' he said.

I remember his exact tone.

Looking back, I could have told him that I was exactly the person who would understand, but the words refused to take shape and I bitterly regret that. It would have been a small grace emerging out of the mess we had made.

Instead, I wanted to wound him and I told him I wanted him to go. That second.

He was not surprised and was, perhaps, relieved.

What price his vocation? What price my professionalism?

We were inching towards the edge of the cliff and the resolution we had promised each other would not be easy.

I felt my nail dig into the ball of my thumb. I told him we were done. Finished. I said that the situation meant we could neither sleep nor think, and it was best to get it over with. Then, we could be peaceful again.

He looked sceptical and, as it turned out, he was right. Being at peace would take a long time.

He sounded like a drowning man who had only a twig to grab on to.

He bowed his head, a habit that must now be ingrained but which infuriated me. His bag was on the floor and I bent down to retrieve it at the same moment that he did. We stood up. His hands were on my shoulders, a touch of his flesh on mine. I backed away, stumbled, and he caught me up against him.

Un-orchestrated, clumsy, shorn of grace, the power that drew me to him, I freely acknowledge, rendered me helpless.

He muttered that if he couldn't have me, he didn't want anyone else to either.

It was illogical, stupid, possessive, atavistic ... everything that was wrong, but it lit in me the fire that crackled through my flesh.

All that was mean and stupid took possession of me and I flung the question at him: was I one of those forgivable one-time lapses, the one that wouldn't damn him?

He looked into my eyes, and his were dark, dark with anger and lust. And love. He told me not to be stupid.

That was it.

In times past, the act had always been pleasurable and, with my first love, feverish and addictive and guilty. Until I was in bed with Leo, in Palacrino and at that moment, I had not understood that it could be sublime, rhapsodic and so full of feeling that words could not describe it.

I cried at the finish.

Leo did, too.

As he had done once before, he pulled me close and my hip encountered his. He made me laugh by telling me that he was pleased I had put on a bit of weight. It used to worry him, how thin I was.

Many hours later, we got up from the bed and dressed, considerably more slowly than we had undressed.

Leo was quiet and I did not press him. He needed space – and peace, if he could get it. I needed to steady myself.

I wanted to remember what happened in clear, pure colour vision. I wanted to relive each movement, hear each murmur, reprise the moments when the sharpness of desire was accompanied by an almost transcendent sense of love and of awe.

He gathered up his things, including the bag that had triggered our downfall. He had taken a shower and slicked his hair back, making him look much older, and it was a different man who said to me that he didn't know what was going to happen. I sought his free hand and held it. His fingers tightened over mine and he told me that he would never regret us. Or what had happened.

I searched his face. I hope not, I told him, determined not to cry, and demanded that he honoured us.

He said he hoped I would manage. He *knew* I would.

Fine, I thought, hovering on the edge of the cliff. *Go back to your vocation. Indulge in the pitilessness of it and burn and yearn.* 'I will manage,' I told him.

Even at that last moment, when I railed against the idiocy of a Church that would not let its priests be normal, I wanted to spare him, to give him the choice to make lightweight luggage of it.

I had to allow him the grace with which he could repair his torn ambition, his riven loyalties. So I reminded him that he had not taken his final vows and that, in the scale which he counted so important, what he – we – have done was not so heavy.

I think he understood because he paused in the doorway. 'Thank you.'

He let himself out of the door without a backward glance, leaving me with tears slipping stupidly down my cheeks.

I have not seen Leo since.

I think about him every day and find myself cataloguing what made him.

Leo was a socialist through and through. 'The rich should be made to help the poor. It is their obligation.'

I remember telling him off and not to air extreme views. It was best to be careful.

Leo smiled his beautiful, but slightly haunted, smile and replied that what he believed could be found anywhere in the Gospels.

Once, I asked him if his uncle shared his views and he replied that he didn't think so.

It was obvious that he disliked the question and I wondered if the connection between uncle and nephew was as solid as he would have it.

Leo liked strong coffee in the morning.

Leo loved his mother and his family.

He was a good man.

He will never know.

CHAPTER TWENTY-FOUR

AT THE *ESPATRIATI*, THE SITUATION HAD INCHED FORWARD.

The outgoing chief archivist declared himself to be happy with the arrangements for his retirement and the vacated position awaited Lottie. Twice, Valerio Gianni telephoned to reiterate his apologies for the time it had taken.

Naturally, there was a complication.

Valerio explained how the archive's finances came under Italian tax and VAT laws. At the same time, the American general had negotiated a special status for the archive. Did Lottie appreciate that, although she was an employee, she was officially freelance?

'But I am a full-time employee,' Lottie pointed out. 'At least, I was until five minutes ago.'

Valerio was apologetic about the anomaly and wanted to reassure her that these categories were in name only. 'In that case,' said Lottie, treading through this fiscal minefield, 'it won't matter if I'm registered as an employee.'

'Lottie, what can I say to put your mind at rest?'

Lottie replied he could very easily put her mind at rest with the reassurance, plus documentation, of course, that she was an employee. 'You can also put on paper that I am not breaking the tax laws and therefore I am not contravening the tax and VAT authorities.'

She was not sure she interpreted his answer correctly, but it was along the lines that that would depend on which tax office was approached.

'Surely I just pay my tax according to how much I earn?'

The director offered a bewildering overview of tax slots to which Lottie might be assigned as an employee of the *Espatriati* – slots that seemed to have nothing to do with her income but depended on into which category of worker she fell. He reassured her that she could be perfectly sanguine but it might be wise to get an accountant, and he hoped that all these difficulties would be quickly resolved.

An undercurrent surged beneath this conversation, a suspicion that he was trying to juggle competing and complicated factors. Lottie had to hand it to Valerio: he never permitted it to surface. 'He wants me to keep quiet about the financial arrangements,' she reported back.

'Of course,' said Tom, as if it was the most normal thing in the world. 'He probably relies on the *bustarella* for the tax arrangements …' He took in her bewildered gaze. 'An envelope.'

'You mean a bribe.'

'I couldn't possibly comment.'

Lottie stared at him. 'You've gone native.'

'If that's what you call it.'

'I'd better learn about envelopes,' said Lottie.

In the end, it was sorted. The paperwork was registered and Lottie was free to take up the post.

Tom insisted on accompanying her to the *Espatriati* on the first morning in her new official capacity. 'Solidarity,' he said airily. 'Partners.'

Partnership was a prosaic word, lacking the fire of the divine and the Dionysian, yet tucked into it was the suggestion of comfort and reliability, which Lottie appreciated.

The route from the apartment to the archive was now familiar. Tom carried her bag and suggested they had a cup of coffee together at a favoured café. They didn't talk much, just enjoyed the time of day when the crowds, the traffic fumes and the noise had not become irksome.

'Nervous?' he asked as they got up to leave.

'Should I be?'

To Lottie's surprise, Valerio Gianni was waiting in the *Espatriati* lobby to greet them. He shook Tom's hand enthusiastically, made encouraging noises about the British Council and personally handed Tom his pass.

'You appear to have a galvanising effect on people,' she said as they waited for the lift. 'Valerio rarely leaves his office except for lunch.'

'Just think of me as a magnet,' said Tom.

Pleased by his interest, she had planned to take him down first to the archive.

The doors hissed open and she switched on the lights.

Shadows immediately painted themselves up the walls and darkened the aisles leading between the floor-to-ceiling filing cabinets.

'You should have better lighting,' said Tom, sounding concerned. 'You could kill yourself in this gloom.'

Lottie led the way down the central aisle to the section where Nina's papers were stowed. She twisted the wheel and the doors slid back. 'Welcome to my world.'

He prowled the length and breadth of the archive, asking a lot of questions about the layout and where each department had its shelves. Tom could never be called a sentimental man, but to patrol these shelves was surely to be struck by the contrast between the expanse of an individual's life and the small dimensions of the box where the records of it fetched up.

'Future generations might not bother to do this ...' She was having a Cassandra moment. 'They might even destroy archives as impractical.'

'Not sure what evidence you're basing your gloom on,' he answered. One of the boxes stuck out and he shuffled it back into perfect line. 'Ending up represented by a few pieces of paper is never the whole story.'

'No, but it's frequently the best one can get.'

'But, from what I gather from you, it's best not to feature in one of your documents. It means a nasty end.'

'Some of the deaths in there are natural and at the end of a long life,' she pointed out.

'If you say so.'

'Is something the matter?'

He shook his head.

Glancing over her shoulder, the contrast between the murk of the unlit areas and the circles of light on the brickwork suggested they had strayed into a film noir.

Tom's unease infected Lottie and, for a mad moment, the shadows in the archive seemed threatening. 'Tom, think me crazy, but I'm pretty sure I was followed when I went to Genzano.'

He attempted a joke. 'Unlikely. You're not a person of interest.'

'*Grazie* for the compliment.' She nipped his arm. 'He was shaven headed.'

'In that case, you definitely weren't being followed. Marking yourself out like that means you're not a pro.'

'So I am crazy?'

'Without doubt.'

She thought of the shaven-headed man and of how someone with ill intentions could conceal themselves in this hushed, dimly lit repository of life and death.

'I'll take you upstairs,' she said.

Her new office on the first floor was spacious and airy.

'You'll be getting ideas,' said Tom, casing the joint. 'Plus, you have the biggest desk in the world.'

'Good.' She sat down in the new office chair upholstered in lime green.

'Not sure about the colour,' said Tom.

'The label says it will flatter most complexions.'

'Really?'

A tray with coffee and biscuits wrapped in gold foil had been placed on the desk. 'I love the Italians,' she said.

The bench had been moved down from her temporary office along with the latest batch of papers on which she was working.

She unlocked her drawer, extracted Nina's journal and placed it on the bench.

Tom strolled over. 'Is this it?' He touched the leather cover. 'Very good quality. Suggests she had money to spare.' He stood back. 'Bit tatty. Like a schoolgirl diary.'

She endeavoured to see it through his eyes. 'Tom, would there be Foreign Office records on this case? Somewhere? Surely they would be involved in the death of a British national?'

Before Tom could respond, Mirella appeared at the door carrying a stack of files.

Today she was wearing a pencil skirt and a sleeveless blouse that revealed more than a hint of lace underwear, a detail which appeared to rivet Tom.

Heels clicking on the floor, she walked over to the desk and placed a file on it. 'These have been on Signor Gianni's desk.'

Lottie threw them a casual glance and then a startled second look. 'Those are from the Nina Lawrence cache.'

Mirella shrugged. 'He asked for the boxes to be brought down to him when you were out of the office. He took a look through them and sent them back up.' She gave a creamy little smile. 'These got left out somehow.' She seemed unsure how to make a friendly gesture. 'I know you were working on them.'

'That's lovely of you,' said Lottie.

'He won't notice.' She placed them in front of Lottie. 'His memory is … short.' They exchanged looks and it seemed to Lottie they understood each other perfectly.

'How odd,' she said, 'that it wasn't logged that Valerio had them.'

'Yes,' said Mirella.

Mirella assumed her characteristic side stance so Tom could, if he wished, take in every detail of her svelte body. Throwing a look at him, she left the room.

'Quite something, isn't she? I love her. She knows she's magnificent.'

'If you say so,' replied Tom warily.

Lottie dropped her chin into her hands. She would bet a substantial sum that Valerio Gianni did not do hands-on archive work. So why was he looking through the Lawrence papers?

Networks of contacts, vested interests and self-advancement existed everywhere. Back home, she had been caught up in it occasionally. But here? She shot a look at Tom. He knew Rome through and through, and he would know about the networks.

'Interesting.' Tom rifled through the papers. 'Bank receipts, etc.' The rustle of shuffled papers sounded loud in the room. There was a pause. 'Was there an autopsy report in the stuff you've dealt with?'

'No, there wasn't, only a hospital doctor's report. And the photograph and some forensic analysis about blood spatter, etc.'

'Then you won't know,' said Tom, 'that the autopsy here cites that she had had a child?'

Lottie grabbed it from him with shaking hands. 'So that's why Nina went away. To have a baby.' She sat down in the lime-green chair and read it through. *The details of a woman's body*. What she had last eaten, her lungs, her heart, the structure of the pelvic girdle indicating she had delivered a child. 'It must have been his. Gabriele's.' She looked up at Tom. 'That would have changed everything.'

She imagined Nina discovering she was pregnant. The catch of the breath as the news sank in. The cotton wool in the knees.

At thirty-seven Nina might well have given up on the idea of motherhood – or never contemplated it.

'I'm sure she wanted it.'

'You can't know,' said Tom. 'She might have been terrified and furious for nine months.'

But I do know, thought Lottie, with the empathy, the transference, perhaps, that had been growing in her.

Nina had had a baby with Gabriele, the man she loved against the odds, and Lottie felt a joy for the woman she had never known, followed immediately by an intense and disconcerting dart of jealousy.

Tom was watching her. 'You look all dewy,' he remarked.

'I was imagining her pleasure.'

'It might not have been the priest's.'

'Don't spoil it.' But Tom had a point. 'Yes.'

'You said that the reports claimed she got about.'

Lottie persisted stubbornly. 'It doesn't matter whose it was. She will have wanted the baby.'

'Are there any clues in the papers? In the journal?' She shrugged. 'Then you can't be sure.'

But I am, she wanted to say, although it ran cross grain to her training and years of experience. 'I just know.'

'Really?' He smiled to take away the sting.

'Nina was not a woman to flinch.'

'She would have had to have been strong and very sure,' said Tom. 'I bet you, if he was the father, Nina's priest did not step up to the plate. He would have been terrified that his superiors would get to know about it and he'd be in line for a punishment. Penance and privation. Plus, the history of the Church and inconvenient pregnancies is not pretty.' He paused. 'Think Magdalene Laundries.'

She shifted in the lime-green chair. 'I've read the notes and diary entries, Tom. She was too powerful a personality to give up her baby unless she wished to.'

Tom paced about the office. He seemed to be making up his mind about something.

'What is it?'

He grasped the edge of Lottie's big, flashy desk and leaned over towards her. Their faces were on a level. 'Lottie, you need to know something: Nina was almost certainly working in intelligence.'

Lottie looked into Tom's troubled countenance.

'I realised that early on,' she said impatiently. 'It's obvious she was gathering intelligence to give to Rex, whoever he was.'

Tom was tight-lipped. 'Why didn't you say?'

Her eyebrow lifted a fraction. 'I thought you would have known.'

There was a small but difficult silence.

'What do you mean by that?'

She tried to remember what she had, or had not, told Tom. 'Only that I've talked to you often enough about her.'

'You have. So what do you make of her being a spook?'

'It's interesting, slightly dubious and it complicates her life. But she obviously felt strongly about her country, otherwise she wouldn't have run the risks.'

'So you don't condemn her?'

She was astonished. 'Why would I?'

Tom straightened up. He seemed taller and rather remote. 'The question is who for? The UK, the FBI, the Italians, the Soviets?'

'The British. I don't doubt it.'

'Doubt is a professional tool,' he said. 'You must hover always on the edge of scepticism.'

'Then what do you think?'

Tom said, 'I don't know. Probably the Brits. But a pregnant agent isn't a great idea. Gives headquarters headaches. Do they pull them back while they have the baby? If they do, all the contacts built up and the flow of information might be compromised.'

He continued, 'If you're in deep and you change your mind about working in intelligence, it's hard to get shot of it. Vested interests don't like it. Very often there are vendettas. Scores to be paid off. It's possible that was Nina's fate.' He was very dry. 'It's not only the Church that would be livid at one of its sons being mixed up in a sex and baby scandal.'

The room had grown warm. Lottie poured two glasses of water and handed him one. 'Are you saying that's why she was murdered?'

'Who knows? The possibilities exist.'

'My God, I hope the baby was safe.'

Tom moved over to the window and looked down into the Via Giulia. 'If it lived.'

'*Don't* say that,' she said. 'Don't.'

He turned around and sent her a long, thoughtful look.

Lottie said: 'It's true Signor Livardo never mentioned a child, which suggests it was never in the Trastevere apartment. But her pregnancy would have been noticeable, unless she went away before it began to show.'

Lottie retrieved the journal from the locked drawer and leafed through its pages. 'Yes, I'm right. She says that she went away the late summer of nineteen seventy-seven and came back in the spring of 'seventy-eight. She could have concealed it.'

Tom came and sat down opposite her. 'Lottie, I've been thinking about this for some time. You, me, all this. What are we talking about here? This preoccupation with a dead woman.' He placed his hands on the desk. 'Don't fly at me, but is it really about you? Are you searching for something that I don't know about yet?' It was not unknown for Tom to retreat into the ultra-logical when faced with these kinds of conversations. But here he was verging on the emotional. 'Am I wrong?'

Her laugh sounded brittle. 'Cod psychology.'

'Maybe. Doesn't mean the point is invalid.'

'What are you trying to get me to admit?'

'That's for you to say, not me.'

She cupped her chin in her hands.

Would Nina's response to the world have altered? Would the blossom have been whiter, the bees louder, garden aromas drowsier and more seductive? Marking what was happening to her body, did she observe the tiny vulnerable shoots of new growth and think:

This is me?

The noise in the Via Giulia crescendoed. A street argument was in full train, reminding Lottie of where she was.

Rome was built on seven hills and all roads led to it, but underneath ran catacombs and passages, cities of the dead and the covert.

'Lottie ...' Tom was pressing. 'Tell me what it is.'

She remembered the moment when desolation drilled down into her, took up residence and never left.

In a room with a broken bunk bed with grubby sheets into which she had been shown and told to make no noise. Nothing else was there. No pictures, no books. No curtains.

No past.

This was her future.

She understood then that she belonged to no one, and never would. And if she ever had a child, she would never give it away so that it could be led into a room with a broken bunk bed ...

'Lottie ...?'

The moment had passed. 'I want to know what happened to Nina.' She looked up at him. 'And I will find out, Tom.'

CHAPTER TWENTY-FIVE

A BUNCH OF LILIES IN ONE HAND, LOTTIE RANG THE BELL OF the Livardos' apartment.

Amply tested over several phone calls and several cancellations of appointments, Lottie's powers of persuasion had finally prevailed and this visit was happening. The flowers were to sweeten the pill.

Marta Livardo was taller than her husband, with white hair and dark eyebrows. She was dressed in a flowered overall and brown lace-up shoes that had seen plenty of use. But for the fractious set to her mouth, she would have been handsome.

She greeted Lottie without smiling, accepted the flowers, and led her inside. 'My husband is out,' she said, indicating where Lottie should sit.

The room was sparsely furnished with a coffee table, a sofa, a single armchair and a cupboard. A small rug sat on the tiled floor. There were no pictures except for a framed reproduction poster of Piero della Francesca's *Resurrection* with a palm cross slotted into one corner.

There was not much discernible comfort. No colourful cushions or a table with knitting and glasses on it. No sense that this was a place of refuge. Rather it suggested a lifetime of hard work and limited savings of which the best was being made.

Marta Livardo was nothing if not direct. 'I don't want to see you, but my husband has persuaded me that I should,' she said. 'Discussing the signorina is to rake up difficult times. She should rest in peace.'

'Your husband told me how much you liked her.'

A flash in the other woman's eye alerted Lottie that old antagonisms had not faded. 'She was a good tenant and always polite. Some tenants aren't. They take liberties.'

Lottie accepted a cup of tea with a lemon slice, sat down in the chair and opened her laptop. The signora perched on the sofa and pulled her skirt down over swollen knees.

'Did you know Signorina Lawrence for long?'

'She was already living in the building when my husband and I moved in. In nineteen sixty-eight, I think. I was responsible for the apartments. I cleaned for them and ran a laundry and repair service. It was a lot of work.'

It did not take much imagination to agree that it would have been hard work. Hauling cleaning materials up and down floors, washing the communal stairs, carrying bags of laundry, listening to complaints about blocked drains, broken kettles, late delivery of laundry.

'But if that's your place,' said the other woman, 'that is your place.' The fatalism was edged with bitterness. 'I always ask God why some have to work so hard and others are granted leisure at no cost to themselves.' She set down her cup in the saucer so hard that a crack sounded. 'I have no answer.'

The signora's past, and its privations, wrapped her in grievances. Perhaps her present circumstances did too? Lottie was sympathetic. She knew to the last degree how long fingers from the past could squeeze pleasure and meaning out of the present.

'I agree. It's not easy to justify.' She opened her laptop. 'Your husband will have told you that I'm an archivist and I'm supervising the archiving of Signorina Lawrence's papers. We would like to clear up certain things before the report is written.'

Marta Livardo sighed. 'After she was ... there were a lot of things we had to deal with and got no thanks.'

'Like what?'

'I was asked to clean her rooms after the funeral. They were in a dreadful state. Having been left so long. Some of it was horrible.'

'Horrible?'

'Poetry. Written about women ...' Marta Livardo flushed. 'You know. *Women*.'

'Ah, I see. Did women come to the apartment?'

'I can't remember any.'

'Did the police ask you about them?'

'I couldn't help them on that.'

'Then perhaps the poetry was not significant?'

'Maybe. Maybe not.'

'Do you know what happened to her things?'

'Such as?' She was cautious and wary.

'Her furniture?'

Signora Livardo folded her hands into her lap. 'A man arranged for it to be taken away. A table. An old chair, not worth much. A piece of carpet, which I threw out. I never knew his name but the telephone number he gave in case something was missed out was a Vatican number.'

'Her papers?'

Again, a noticeable caution. 'The police asked me to collect them up and took them away.'

'All of them?'

The question triggered an aggressive response. 'Why would I keep the papers?'

A guilty conscience?

Lottie glanced around the joyless room. 'And did you? Find anything else.'

'No, *niente*,' she said. 'I scrubbed those rooms from top to bottom. The next tenant would have no reminders of what had happened.'

'Signora Livardo, we have found out some details about Signorina Lawrence and I don't wish to pry too much but there is one that requires clearing up. Do you know … did she have a child? Or ever refer to having one?'

The hands in the signora's lap clenched so strongly that the knuckles whitened. 'Is that any of your business? Matteo warned me.' The hard mouth tightened. 'You are wanting to make money.'

Lottie explained, as she had done previously to the husband, that no money would be involved. Marta Livardo's other accusation was more pertinent. Was Nina's baby any of Lottie's business?

'My investigations are purely to put the records in place for the archive.' Calculating that a short pause in the questioning would work in her favour, she put aside the laptop and took a mouthful of tea.

The two women eyed up each other over their cups.

'Let me tell you what we know,' said Lottie. 'The autopsy reports that she had had a child and we need to know if that child survived. If he or she is alive they are entitled to make decisions about the papers in the archive.'

Marta Livardo observed the expensive laptop and a lifetime of resentment – and something else Lottie could not place – was kettled into her expression.

'Your husband told me that you were friendly with the signorina and it occurred to me that, if you had been, she would have asked you for help if she was in trouble. The situation would have been difficult for her. She might have turned to another woman. She might have needed advice.'

'How could I have given advice? It would not have been possible.'

Lottie pressed on. 'The signorina would have had to make some choices. What to do, where to go, how to present her condition. She would have needed good counsel.' She allowed a small pause. 'I thought maybe you would be the person to help.'

Marta Livardo held up a gnarled finger, the result of years of cleaning and washing. 'It was not my place to give advice. I was only a caretaker. The signorina was a professional woman. Why would she turn to me?' For a while she was silent, and it was evident that an inner struggle was taking place. Eventually, she blurted out: 'We didn't like one another.'

The admission seemed to drain her.

Lottie put down her cup and decided that it would be politic to ask for a refill. 'It's such excellent tea,' she said, with the result that there was a tiny diminution in the hostility.

The older woman heaved herself to her feet. 'I'll make some more.' She stood four-square in the shoes, which were too heavy for the warm weather. 'It was a disgrace … Unmarried. With those men who visited.' The malice, which, clearly, had been ripening over the years, burst forth. 'I warned her. "Signorina," I told her, "you're getting a reputation. Your rich clients won't like it." She never listened. "It's none of your business," she would say. Or, "What if I tell people that you are snooping? What then?"'

She sighed. The malice had petered out and, in its place, was obvious regret.

'All the same, you worried about her,' said Lottie, rather touched.

'She called me "Signora Livvy". "You have nothing to tell, Signora Livvy, because you don't know the story," she once said to me. I didn't like that name. But I knew better. I recognised that look women have when they are first pregnant. The difference in how they walk and talk. I've studied it.'

'Yet you must have talked from time to time?'

'Yes, about her work. You know, doing the gardens. Once or twice, she told me stories about the people she worked for.' She picked up the tray. 'They were grand people who permitted themselves to take liberties but didn't like other people doing so. "Beware," I told her, "they will drop you."'

She disappeared into the kitchen and returned with a fresh pot of tea.

Was the signora's disapproval political or religious? Probably both. They could get mixed up with each other.

'Did you know any of her visitors?'

A shoulder lifted. 'I grew to recognise them. There was the young one. He came a couple of times. He was nice but very anxious. Wouldn't say anything but ran up the stairs fast.' She lapsed into a reverie and gave a gusty sigh. 'Ask my husband. He might know.' She added, 'A *lot* of men came and went.'

'How many do you mean by "a lot"? Four? Fifteen?'

There was a reluctant admission. 'Two or three. Perhaps four.'

'Were any of them priests?'

Signora Livardo almost dropped the teapot. 'A *priest? Dio*. No, never. Only after she died. Then a priest did come to counsel us. We prayed for the signorina's soul.'

In the background, a door opened and closed.

'Anyone else who might be important?'

Lottie was conscious of holding her breath.

'No.' It was a percussive denial, but as she handed over the tea, her hand shook slightly. The emphasis changed. 'Yes. Perhaps. When the signorina went away, trying to hide from us that she was having a baby, a Signor Antonio came to see us. He said he was a friend and looking after her interests and could we let him into her apartment as she needed some books. I asked my husband and we agreed he could but he didn't find them.

'He came back once or twice, always bringing me a special salve for my hands because he said they looked bad from too much cleaning. He was a nice man, very well dressed, with a badge in his lapel. He asked that if the signorina returned we could let him know if anyone visited her and who they were.'

'Did you tell him about the baby?'

'No.' Marta Livardo looked desperately around the room. 'I may have.'

'You *may* have?'

'He said that if I helped him, he would help me.' She looked away. 'Apparently, there were funds available for people like me and he might be able to arrange something. He could also arrange for prayers to be said for us.'

Lottie fitted together the fragments of information.

'The child?' There was a long, long pause. Lottie's stomach tightened. 'Do you know when it was born?'

'She went before anyone could tell and was away for Christmas,' her words drifted, 'and didn't come back until she had got her figure back.' She frowned. 'Yes, just before the kidnapping. You know... of Moro.'

So ... Nina *had* gone away to have her baby.

'The child?' Lottie repeated softly.

'She never mentioned it. Then I got her in a corner and demanded to know. After a bit, she told me it had been born. I never saw it.' Marta Livardo's expression was bleak. 'I would have liked to have done.'

'Do you know what happened to it?'

Her gaze now fixed on the *Resurrection*. 'She said the baby had died.' She made the sign of the cross. 'Died, and she didn't seem to mind. I *couldn't* forgive her for that. Not caring. I didn't see her cry once. Not even when her breasts were leaking. I could spot that detail, too, however hard she tried to hide it. If she had been a proper woman, she would …' She reached for her tea. 'To not mind about your child dying is monstrous. *She* was a monster.'

There was the anguish of an old history hanging over the room. It was then Lottie understood. 'Do you and your husband have children?'

'No. God did not see fit.' A history of blighted hopes was written all over her face. 'We tried. We prayed. We spent our money on doctors. No good.' She rubbed a swollen knee. 'I begged God to tell me how I had sinned and what I could do for him to make my body work, but it didn't happen.'

'That's why you wished to be prayed for …'

Marta Livardo uttered a panicked cry. 'Stop!'

'Please leave.' Signor Livardo stood in the doorway and cut into their exchange. 'My wife is upset. You've no right to come here and ask these questions.'

Lottie rose to her feet. 'I understand. I'm much clearer about the signorina and I'm grateful. I will add the following to the records: the signorina went away to have a baby. A Signor Antonio checked on her apartment while she was away and, after she was murdered, helped you to arrange the disposal of furniture, etc.'

Marta Livardo held out a shaking hand to her husband. 'Matteo, she wanted to know about the men that visited the signorina. It's for the records.'

He sat down on the sofa beside her and she whispered into his ear.

He laid a hand on the swollen knees. 'I can't do that.'

Lottie packed up her things. The atmosphere in the room was leaden and tragic, and she regretted stirring up the other woman's unhappy history.

'Matteo ...' The appeal was low and urgent. 'Give them. Then she will go and leave us in peace.' She gave a shuddering breath. 'Our consciences ...'

He heaved himself to his feet and opened the cupboard to reveal shelves stacked with files of different colours. Having rifled through, he pulled out a torn and elderly-looking buff folder from which he extracted some papers.

He held them out to Lottie. 'I was trained to keep records,' he said, 'like you.'

Lottie ran an eye over it. There were four ruled columns, each with a heading: *Date, Time In, Name, Time Out*.

She looked up at the Livardos. They were not bad people, far from it – and yet they had been prepared to do this sort of thing.

From her fortress on the sofa, Marta Livardo launched her final volley. 'She laughed and told me I was a busybody when I warned her about her reputation. But she didn't laugh when she found out she was having a baby. Oh no, she was crying then.'

The first entry read: *16 March 1977, 3.30, Unknown male.* The last read: *29 October 1978, Noon, Bishop Dino.*

'Is this the priest who visited you after the murder?'

Husband and wife exchanged glances. 'Yes,' said Signor Livardo.

'But why would Bishop Dino visit you? Did he say?'

'He was a friend of Signor Antonio's, who had spoken to him about us. As a man of God who knew our sadness, he said he liked to think he might be of some comfort and was happy to make use of his contacts and influence to get us an invitation to attend a papal service in St Peter's. On condition we never spoke about it.'

So... the bishop ensured that his care and consideration for some of the humbler in the flock would be known in the Vatican. Was that goodness? Ambition? Vanity?

'Did you go?'

'Yes, we did.' A hint of animation appeared in the other woman's face. 'We had some of the best seats. I wore a black veil.'

Signor Livardo glanced at his wife. 'There's something else.'

'*No*,' cried Signora Livardo. '*Please.*'

Ignoring his wife, he disappeared into the next room, returning with a framed picture under his arm.

He stood in front of Lottie and held it out, face down. 'You must not judge us.'

His wife was crying silently. She fumbled in her overall for a handkerchief and pressed it to her mouth.

Lottie began to understand. 'Did this belong to Nina Lawrence?' She turned it over and her stomach contracted.

The professional voice spoke in her head: *Large-scale miniature, dimension echoing those pioneered by Pucelle fils.*

A nocturnal nativity. Of the type sometimes favoured by Northern artists of the late-medieval period because it gave them a chance to show off their skills.

Undamaged.

Wooden frame. Modern.

A beautiful, slightly bewildered, exhausted Virgin in a blue cloak knelt beside her son in a manager. The golden rays emanating from the baby fell on to the noses of the donkey and ox who had pressed up close. In the sky, the Star of Bethlehem beamed down bright starlight and spilled over Joseph's face.

How to describe it? A painter's symphony of blue, gold, light and deep rich midnight. Its delicate shimmering beauty recording the astonishment of a mother at what had overtaken her, illuminating the new, complicated love shining down from her on to her baby.

'Did she give it to you?' Husband and wife were silent and she hazarded a guess at what had happened. 'You *took* it?'

'It's not for you to judge,' insisted Matteo Livardo. 'My colleagues … the police … said there was no more to be done …'

'No, Matteo …' His wife fussed with a strand of hair. 'She *did* give it to us.'

Lottie sat back down. 'Please tell me,' she said gently. 'There is no blame being apportioned here. We need to know what happened.'

Marta blew her nose. 'I said we did not like each other, which was true, but … in the end … she seemed to understand what I felt. "Livvy," she said, "we are both in difficulties. We must help each other. We must forgive each other." I believed her. She asked me to look after the painting. "Will it comfort you, Livvy? I hope so." She said if anything should happen to her I could keep it until someone came for it. She didn't say who, but she trusted me to know who the right person would be.'

Tears slid down her cheeks. 'I liked that she trusted me.'

'Marta …' said her husband. 'Don't.'

'But …' She glanced at her husband. 'We held on to it. That was wrong.' She wrapped her handkerchief around her hand. 'We were owed it. After all the difficulties.'

'Perhaps the right person didn't come and Nina's trust in you was borne out?'

She pressed a fist against her cheek. 'No, he didn't.'

Lottie went over to the sofa and sat down beside her. She held out her hand and, after a moment, Marta Livardo took it. Lottie held it tightly in her own. 'Thank you.'

Signor Livardo held out *The Nativity*. 'Take it.'

'Wait ...' Marta Livardo heaved herself to her feet and bent over *The Nativity* and with one of those swollen fingers traced the outline of the Virgin through the glass.

Her husband pointed to the door. 'Please go, Signora Archer.'

Lottie obeyed. Her feet slapped hollowly over the tiles as she left the room. The door closed behind her.

Tom caught Lottie poring over the framed *Nativity* and weeping.

'What?' He gathered her into his arms. 'What?'

'I don't know,' she managed.

'Yes you do.'

He looked down at the painting and saw what she saw: blue, gold, light and deep midnight. He must have also seen that the painter's delicate and forensic skill in revealing the astonishment of a new mother and her fear.

'You're not to grieve or hope any longer,' he said into Lottie's ear.

'I'm not,' she lied.

CHAPTER TWENTY-SIX

Rome
8 May 1978

AT OUR NEXT MEETING, I PASSED A WRITTEN REPORT TO REX
via a dropped prayer book. It was risky to talk to him directly.

> *General Rasella has been working with the Ministry of*
> *the Interior. He alleges records of phone calls, contacts and*
> *negotiations of the crisis committee working on the Moro*
> *kidnapping are being kept.*
> *According to him, the US sent only one expert on hostage*
> *taking, who worked under the direction of the interior*
> *ministry. Why only one?*
> *General Rasella has visited the US on several occasions*
> *and has contacts.*

At the bottom I wrote: *Being followed.*

They had varied from day to day: a youth in a leather jacket, a
man on a scooter with a bag of vegetables. Today he was elderly,

surprisingly slow, neatly dressed. I had already spotted him hanging around in the Campo de' Fiori. Rome is not that small and the probability of coincidental meetings low.

My training snapped in. *Continue as normal.*

I was right. If I quickened my pace – or slowed it – he clung on and kept me in his sights.

I was close to the Pinacoteca in the Vatican City. Diversion was necessary and I did a smart about-turn and joined a hefty queue for the entrance, from where I watched him walk away.

Good leather shoes, clothes neat and pressed.

Noted.

Inside, I loitered by the ticket booth and read a pamphlet before heading for the gallery for some painterly therapy.

I need it – for I am truly desolate.

I think about the Bathsheba that Leo and I saw. Did the artist know that he had taken a revolutionary step by devoting a whole page to his miniature? He must have done. Was he conscious that in doing so, he had introduced a new drama and psychological depth? That might have surprised him.

A reproduction is useful. It works in the way that studying a road map before the journey ensures you are aware of the lie of the land although you have not yet experienced it. Nothing, but nothing, prepares you for encountering the genuine work. No reproduction can convey the artistry, the delicate suggestion, the texture, the *spirit* of a piece.

Nor can it grab you by the throat and leave you breathless, as the Bathsheba did that magical spring day in Palacrino.

Aflame with love, I remember studying it, inch by inch. Its sly insinuations, its remarkable depiction of clear water, its presence, its unflinching understanding of lust.

Yes, the technical achievements were breathtaking, but the Bathsheba was astonishing because it marked the beginning of a journey of the artist as realist and psychologist.

In 1492 a Dominican friar preached a sermon about images in churches and paintings. 'They are there,' he said, 'for anyone who cannot read.' In a society where words and numbers were not as important as those images, they offer a direct pathway into our understanding of that past.

'It is one thing to adore a painting,' the friar continued, 'but it is quite another to learn from a painted narrative what to adore and what is their purpose.'

So many things escape our untutored, contemporary eye. Women gesticulating in a painting, rather than resting their hands decorously on their girdles, indicate to the viewer that they are light of morals. Venus's raised hand in Botticelli's *Primavera* is not beating time to the dance of her maidens as might be supposed, but extending an important invitation to you, the onlooker, into her kingdom.

How iconography was used during that era, and how powerfully it worked, is an understanding easily lost by us.

One must look. Always look and the truth will be there.

CHAPTER TWENTY-SEVEN

THE SUN WAS HITTING THE WINDOW OF GABRIELE'S WORKSHOP when Lottie turned into the street carrying *The Nativity*.

Less welcome was the sight outside the entrance of black-suited Giuseppe Antonio talking to a companion resplendent in a cardinal's black and scarlet. Cardinal Dino.

The two men were deep in conversation. Giuseppe Antonio placed a hand on the cardinal's arm. The cardinal surveyed him from his superior height and interposed a few words. Observing them, Lottie concluded, was to witness secular and religious vested interests in collusion.

They went into the workshop and Lottie followed.

Gabriele greeted the cardinal, and Lottie was shocked to see his hostility. 'It has been a long time, Eminence.'

Cardinal Dino inclined his head. 'A long time, my son.'

It was obvious that the history between them was as troubled and unresolved as ever.

Gabriele pulled out chairs and gestured the two men should sit.

'I'll come back later?' said Lottie.

'No,' said Gabriele.

The now-seated cardinal fixed Lottie with the adamantine stare that she remembered from their previous encounter. It made her question if his flock had ever been the beneficiaries of his compassion and understanding. Sneaking a look at him from under her lids, she saw a man who had hoped to be better than he had turned out to be and was aware that he had failed.

One hand, with its substantial cardinal's ring, lay on the arm of the chair, where its symbolism could be admired.

'Your Eminence, I have been impolite. I should have written to thank you for seeing me,' she said.

The cardinal crossed his legs, revealing highly polished and expensive-looking shoes. 'Yet you did not take my advice. It happens. Those who are foreign to this city frequently don't understand.'

'I apologise for not being Italian.'

He did not like that. 'You wished to stir up the unsavoury facts about that unfortunate woman.'

'There are aspects about the case that are puzzling. I wondered if she got herself mixed up in Church politics?'

The cardinal frowned.

Giuseppe Antonio interposed himself. 'Signora, it is good to see you again,' he said. 'Are you bringing in a special project?'

She made her answer vague. 'I wanted to show Gabriele something beautiful that I've come across.'

'Gabriele?' An eyebrow did an acrobatic lift at her use of the Christian name. 'From somewhere interesting, I should imagine.'

'I'm so sorry, I'm not at liberty to say.' With that, she retreated to the back of the shop, plucked a volume from the shelf that turned out to be a biography of Percy Bysshe Shelley and browsed through it.

Gabriele emerged from the back room with a tray of glasses and water in a frosted jug, which he handed around.

Giuseppe Antonio held a handsome-looking prayer book between his hands; he placed it on the table.

The cardinal pointed to it. 'I'm aware that the last words we said to each other were, on my part, ones of deep reproach. And on yours, anger. But time has elapsed. I'm now old and your uncle assures me that you'd be willing to work on this project. It belonged to the founder of the institution where I now live and they would like it restored.'

The prayer book looked in reasonable condition and was more likely to be an excuse and a peace offering. Probably thought up by the master tactician Giuseppe Antonio.

The two men measured each other up. Eventually, Gabriele picked up the prayer book.

He gave it a cursory examination. 'It can be done.'

'Can I take it that we have arrived at a peaceful place?' The cardinal was peremptory as opposed to conciliatory.

Gabriele looked up from his examination of the prayer book's binding. 'Eminence, I am surprised that you are concerned about matters between us. But since you are here, I can say that I don't mind one way or the other how we regard each other—'

His uncle cut him off. 'What Gabriele is saying, Eminence, is he is pleased there's no enmity between you.'

'Why now, Eminence?' asked Gabriele.

The cardinal got to his feet. 'My time is limited and it's God wish that we make our peace.'

'If I remember correctly, Eminence, your last words to me all those years ago were that my loss of faith and vocation would dog me all my life. It was hardly a peaceful parting. Why would I wish anything from you?'

With reluctance, Lottie ceded admiration to the cardinal's answer. 'We're older and wiser.'

'Yes,' agreed Gabriele, 'we are. We can see things more clearly.'

Giuseppe Antonio addressed Lottie. 'To return to our previous conversation, the woman made the wrong decision to go out at night by herself. Very regrettable. It is known that the river at night is not a safe place.'

The workshop had grown very warm and the heat crept over Lottie's skin. 'Perhaps,' she said.

She heard Gabriele's intake of breath. 'Her name was Nina,' he said. 'It's unworthy of you not to name her, especially as you knew her.'

The reproof was not intended to be gentle.

The cardinal inspected his ring. 'So, the episode has not been laid to rest.'

'I had hoped …' said Giuseppe Antonio. 'But whatever we feel, now is the moment to bury it.' He gestured to the prayer book. 'Will you let us know about this?'

The two men departed, and Gabriele pulled down the blinds and cleared the table of paints and books.

'The cardinal was not the man to help you all those years ago,' said Lottie. 'I see that. I'm sorry if I angered him.'

'Don't worry,' said Gabriele. 'It doesn't alter anything.'

She pulled herself together. 'But this might.'

What was she doing? The right thing or a destructive one?

She began: 'Gabriele, I have something of Nina's that I think was intended for you. It wasn't among her papers, but somewhere else, so I feel I can hand it over. But I warn you… it might open… wounds.'

She placed the parcelled-up *Nativity* on the table.

He glanced up at Lottie as he tussled with the Sellotape.

'Nina …' He let the wrappings fall away, caught his breath held it up. 'Wonderful Nina.' He then examined it inch by inch. 'It's stunning. Almost an original master.' The professional in him added, 'But it's not on the parchment. It's on canvas.'

'And not entirely faithful to the old masters,' said Lottie, and her apprehension sharpened. 'Nina always gave the paintings her own stamp. Gabriele, look.' She pointed to the background.

Illuminated by the moon, the now familiar monk and the woman walked towards the stable. He carried a staff, and the moonlight revealed she was wrapped in a blue cloak of a gentler, paler hue than the Virgin's. Miniature though the figures were, it was possible to make out that the woman had tears on her cheek.

'Aren't they you and Nina?'

'Yes.' He put out a hand on the desk to steady himself and looked up at Lottie.

'You knew that from *The Annunciation*.'

He nodded. 'I can't bear that she's weeping.'

She positioned the painting directly under his nose. 'Gabriele, consider what this painting is. What does it show?'

Shocked? Disbelieving? Angry? 'A Nativity.'

'That's Nina's message.'

It took Gabriele many moments before he could talk. Sinking down, he froze into the chair.

Lottie sat down beside him and put her arm around his shoulders. He did not resist.

'Nina had a child?'

'So the autopsy report states.'

'Mine?'

'It's possible. More than possible. But we don't know. It could have been earlier in her life. But ...' She paused and felt the tension of a lifetime locked into those shoulders. 'The painting suggests otherwise.'

'My God.'

The old habit of calling on God had not been discarded.

He began to piece out the logic of what had happened. 'Nina didn't tell me because it would have made it all harder. She did everything she could to make it easier.' He looked up at Lottie. 'I should have supported her. I didn't.' He glanced at *The Nativity*. 'But it does explain why she disappeared.' Lottie nodded. 'And no one knew?'

Lottie said, 'Marta Livardo did.' She removed her arm and ticked off the names on her fingers. 'She told your uncle after Nina was murdered, who must have told the cardinal. When I went to see him he informed me that Nina had been a fallen woman, which is the usual way of putting it.'

He pulled himself upright, walked over to the bookshelves and ran a finger along a line of books. 'I abandoned the priesthood because I thought I had sinned too badly and let it down. I thought that the mixed-up parts of me would never come together and it would be impossible for me to save souls.' He glanced around. 'Which, after all, is the sacred obligation of a priest.'

'But you also lost your faith?'

A bottle of brandy stood beside the espresso machine and he reached for it, pouring two slugs into glasses. He shoved a glass towards Lottie and leaned back against the shelves.

'All wasted, wasn't it? The sacrifice and effort. Carrying the guilt. Worse, Nina's life.' There was a pause. 'She must have suffered. She must have been angry and lonely. And, God forbid, frightened.'

'I think she was, but I'm not sure why.' She touched his arm. 'Look, Nina took her own decisions.'

The brandy did its work and he sounded less riven. 'Bishop Dino as he was then was an ambitious man. Everyone knew that. He got angry if there was trouble on his doorstop. Beppo warned me.'

'Did Nina and your uncle meet more than once?'

'I don't know. He told me to be wary of her. He said she was a bird of paradise and would fly away.'

She looked again at the painting. Here was the Virgin kneeling in front of her new-born son, endeavouring to make sense of what had happened to her. As Nina would have done?

Medieval women were taught to regard the Virgin's experience as the most significant event in creation. They would scrutinise a nativity in a book of hours and reflect on the miracle that a mere female could have found such favour with God.

Powerful and suggestive, it was an image used to concentrate a medieval woman's thoughts and to bend her will into emulating Mary, the perfect woman.

'Lend me your loupe, Gabriele?'

He opened a drawer and passed it to her.

Bending over the painting, she scrutinised the monk and the girl. Under her brandy-softened eye, their outlines were hazy.

But ... it was there, the clue that Nina wanted to leave Leo.

The stick carried by the monk was a large gladioli and clasped tight in the woman's hand was a narcissus.

She needed a minute or two to think.

Gabriele was saying: 'Bishop Dino summoned me and demanded that I give her up. He didn't know we had already parted and told me that he would take steps to make sure that she was kept away.'

'Not murder, surely?'

'No.' Contempt for the cardinal was still there. 'But he was – he is – that interesting paradox: a man of God with few scruples. He might have said something to someone who took the matter in hand.'

'You're not talking about your uncle?'

'Beppo is a fixer and smoother. He's not capable of that.' Gabriele sat down and buried his face in his hands. 'My child ... if it is ... had no parents. That's a heavy, heavy cross.'

Lottie found herself concentrating anywhere but on the painting.

'I must find him or her.'

The kaleidoscope of conjecture and possibility that was being turned over in her mind came into focus.

'I can help you, Gabriele.' Sweat prickled her upper lip and she brushed it away. 'You know all about the iconography in paintings? Yes?' She passed over the loupe and pushed *The Nativity* over to him. 'The flowers in their hands. What are they?'

'The narcissus and the gladioli.'

'Gabriele, if the child ... your child ... survived, the flowers are the key to where Nina took it. She painted the clue into her picture. The message was meant for you.'

Poleaxed by the shock of the discovery and its implications, Gabriele told Lottie he needed to go away and think. Brandied up, they said goodbye and promised to be in contact very soon.

Lottie understood his need for silence. It was, she told Tom later, a revelation so sharp and loaded that it almost hurt.

'The monk was holding a gladioli?'

'What of it?'

'Listen to me,' said Tom. 'I'm going to do a bit of digging. OK?'

'That would be good.'

A day later, Gabriele made contact and asked to meet Lottie at what she had come think of as Nina's church.

On her way out of the *Espatriati* she spotted Mirella, who was searching for something in her bag. Almost certainly she had chosen to do so at the entrance, thereby giving passers-by a chance to admire the silk Pucci pantsuit into which she had been poured.

Lottie waved at her. Mirella's single-mindedness was an object lesson and it made her smile. Mirella waved back.

It was a hot day and the cool inside the building was welcome. A mass was in train, with worshippers occupying several of the pews. She and Gabriele retreated to the tiny Lady Chapel, whose entrance was partly obscured by a pillar.

They sat facing a small altar dominated by a highly coloured statue of the virgin and a pot of lilies. Votive candles burned on a stand and their smoky, waxy smell mingled with the incense.

'Lottie, *The Nativity*... I would like permission to keep this after you have catalogued it.'

'I won't be cataloguing it. It belongs to you.'

He nodded and Lottie settled herself to wait.

The church microphones crackled. Mass had finished and the priest could be heard instructing his assistant.

'Giving up the priesthood was painful,' Gabriele said at last. 'Death throes usually are. Losing Nina was one thing, but her death was another. That made it impossible for me. It was difficult for a couple of years, but I was lucky and found another vocation as the so-called book doctor. It has given me much in return. I have not missed the Church.'

'But I met you here once.'

'I know. Strange that. You had brought in the painting and it was like ... having a disordered stomach. I needed to come here and to settle it.'

'Why are we meeting here now?'

'Because ...' He steadied himself. 'I lied to you when I said I never saw Nina again. I did. One more time. The day she died.'

'Gabriele...'

'I'd been lost for months,' he said. 'No sleep. No appetite. My will to learn had vanished and my spiritual state was a lost cause. I could no longer see the point of being on this earth. I had sinned in the eyes of God and the Church, given up Nina and distressed my family.' His lips twitched and a touch of self-deprecating humour crept into the confession. 'God didn't see fit to advise me on that one. My uncle did, though. He urged me to keep on in the seminary. He kept dangling the prospect that, one day, I could be a powerful man of God. He said ... that even if I had lost my faith, it would be a good life with many compensations if I rose in the hierarchy.'

Not for the first time, Lottie wondered why, if he felt so strongly and ambitiously, his uncle had not chosen for himself the path that he urged on his nephew.

Gabriele read her thoughts. 'His role was to be the secular arm of the family. Mine the religious. It might have worked.'

He looked up at the chapel ceiling, where plaster cherubs sat on the beams. 'I don't know what I was expecting. One day, I woke up and realised I was on my own.'

Lottie knew this was not an easy place to arrive at. 'Hard but necessary?'

'Actually, it cheered me. I may have been without the underpinning of my vocation, but I knew where I was at last. I knew never to have expectations of any deity of whatever stamp.'

Lottie extracted the timeline she had drawn up for Nina's movements from the folder in her bag. 'Nina left Rome after you broke up, and she didn't return until just before Prime Minister Moro was kidnapped.'

'When she first vanished, no one had any idea where she'd gone. I began to look for her in our usual places. I even asked the *portiere* at her apartment. No help there. A year later, I was still consumed by her and her disappearance. It was almost winter, and I felt so bleak that I walked in here and sat down in a pew over there.' He pointed. 'I was struggling at the seminary and everything – body and soul – was out of step. Thinking back, I had probably already decided to give it up, but I had not yet admitted it to myself.'

Lottie thought of what came next: a shuttered, shrouded workshop and the retreat into it.

'I had got up to leave when I saw Nina coming in through the door ... It took me a moment to realise that it *was* her. When the penny dropped, I was flooded with happiness. I knew she wasn't religious. In fact, the opposite, and I was gripped by the idea that she had come here because it was where we first met.'

Lottie bit her lip and kept quiet.

Nina had come here to meet Rex.

'She looked different,' continued Gabriele. 'Very thin. Her hair was longer and her coat was too big. She looked so small ... lost.'

'Did you speak to her?'

Gabriele did not reply for a few moments. When he did, it was with a halting admission. 'I did not move.'

'Because?'

'I've asked myself that a thousand times. I had longed for her day and night for all those months, but when I saw her in the flesh I was paralysed. But … but …' He looked past Lottie. 'But the truth is … I also kept quiet for those crucial seconds because I couldn't bear to go through it all over again.

'She didn't see me. She came here into the Lady Chapel and knelt directly behind a man I didn't recognise. She said something to him. The pillar was in the way and it was impossible to get a clear view. Then she left and I gathered my wits, followed her out of the church and called her name. She knew at once who it was and turned around. Her face lit up in the way it used to do. I ran towards her but she smiled and shook her head, as if warning me to keep my distance. Then she vanished.'

Lottie knew something about baptisms of fire. 'I'm so sorry.'

He glanced at her – and Lottie knew he trusted her to listen and to understand.

'I will never forgive myself for not saying anything to her when I saw her here. Ever.'

'Did you get a look at the man she was talking to?'

'Not really. He wore a hat. But no amount of going back over what happened is going to change anything.' He picked up the timeline from the chair. 'Lottie, I ask myself every day why I hesitated. Why didn't I tell her that I was thinking of giving up the vocation? It might have stopped her going out that night.'

Lottie said, 'Logically, it might not have done.'

'Logic doesn't have anything to do with it. I blame myself and that is it.'

'But logic should tell you that the probabilities tell a different story. Whatever you might or might not have said or done, Nina would still have died.'

He looked around at the edifice that dealt in sin, suffering and the promise of forgiveness. 'You mustn't try to exonerate me.'

'But *you* must try. As you advised me,' she said gently. 'Forgive me, Gabriele, Nina was an independent, professional woman who wouldn't have taken risks unless there was a good reason.'

He was not convinced.

'I've been thinking over what we talked about by the river.' She focused on a candle. 'You might not remember because I was trying to divert you. There was a woman who had a baby and didn't want it. The baby was given away and put into a care home. Later, she was fostered out to a couple who were kind but alien. As a result, that girl grew up blaming that mother for her sense of unease and her loneliness and thought of herself as a lost child and lived her adult life thinking that there must have been something wrong with her for her mother to have done such a thing.'

As always, disquiet washed through her – rough, stinging, a known antagonist.

'Then she met someone who issued a simple instruction. "Knock down the wall."' She smiled at him. 'Which was you, as you know. So I will. So must you.'

'I get it,' he said.

'You and I, both.' The candles on the altar guttered. 'You made me understand that what my mother did was to do with her, and her predicament, not me. It didn't make it easier, but it was a good foundation on which to rearrange the mental furniture.'

He shifted restlessly and old secrets and past suffering were obvious.

'Nina's death was almost certainly not your fault, Gabriele.'

He cupped his hands, as if her words had landed in them and he was weighing them for size.

'You have something better to do now,' she said. 'It is never too late to find a child. Believe me.'

After a moment, he nodded. 'So, the search begins.'

At the doorway, they turned to look back down the aisle – and both were summoning the shade of Nina in her overlarge overcoat.

Lottie's relief on stepping back into the Roman streets was marked. Here, human transactions might be dangerous and complicated but not crushed by the almost impossible demands of a religious vocation.

Back in the office, she booked in Gabriele for a lengthy session to read through Nina's papers and the notebook.

She felt, she knew, it was crucial that Gabriele made contact with the original. The online facsimile would offer only a fraction of the experience of the real thing. To feel the weight of the notebook, to smell the must and dust of the past, to note its marginalia and inserts, to see where paper clips had left marks on the pages would be to enter Nina's world.

Just as she, Lottie, had done.

CHAPTER TWENTY-EIGHT

Rome
8 May 1978

IT TURNED OUT THE GENERAL LOVED BALLET.

Anyone who loved ballet – any of the arts – must be on the side of the angels, which gave me a meaty conundrum because it was impossible to consider the general anywhere near approaching an angel.

We were going to an open-air performance of *Romeo and Juliet* in the ruins of a Roman villa. Before that, he was driving me out of Rome to a (indifferent) restaurant in a village to the east of the city. I wondered why. To tap up a contact? To bribe a local police chief (always prudent to have onside)? Maybe to check over an arms cache? What was not in doubt was the general's deployment of me as a cover. The wining and dining of a woman he was currently bedding looked perfectly normal.

I took a long look in the mirror.

You're too thin. A stick … Marta Livardo informed me. She should know because, since my return, she has been keeping a closer eye than ever on me.

We speak to each other as little as possible and our exchanges are short and sharp. She looks me up and down in that way of hers – hostile, assessing – and she is bursting to ask, *What happened to your baby?*

She won't ever know because I won't ever tell her.

In my absence, I had asked Marta not to touch anything in the apartment because the dust, disturbed or otherwise, would give me clues if someone had snooped.

Sure enough, the papers in my desk have been rifled through. Marta was not a professional and I left a collection of handwritten poetry that would put her off the scent.

I wish you and I, Maria and Pearl, were dead.
Sappho would know how terribly we suffer …

It was enough to suggest that I loved a woman and it amused me to consider her expression when she realised the implications.

The nights are not easy. Nightmares prowl around their edges, which is a new element in my life for which I blame what has happened to me. Maternity has opened doors into rooms that are dark and empty and I do not know yet how to furnish them.

I am learning, every minute, every second. Greedily and with dedication.

I have changed. In the past when I was terrified, I used to will on the worst to happen to get it over and done with. Now my fear is of a different order. I tremble to think that something may go wrong and it is a sharper, crueller fear than anything I have ever experienced.

I told myself that my life was shattered when I first came to Italy. Looking back on that episode, I see that it was a test and had nothing on the experience of deep and proper love.

Part of that love is for Italy. It is a country that is far more anti-establishment than I imagined – anti systems, anti elites – which is one of the reasons that socialists and communists have taken such a grip on the politics. I salute that. It is when they run to extremes that the problems begin.

Italy is beautiful. In its art, architecture, style and elegance can be found the secret of living well. They may differ greatly in their opinions but its people understand that instinctively.

My hair is still glossy and my skin clear but there are circles under my eyes and my lips are dry. I must remake myself. Smarten. Visit the hairdresser and the boutiques in the Via del Corso.

My outfit was carefully assembled. Which earrings? What perfume? Which shoes would last a day and into a warm evening without killing me? Which blouse would hide the sweat stains if it became too hot?

After lunch, we walked around the village and, well-oiled and overfed, the general suggested I should go and see a fine medieval wood carving in the church while he smoked.

It was an order.

Indeed, the carving was exceptional. I expended precisely five seconds on it before I nipped down the aisle to the vestry, which had a separate entrance, and prised open the door a crack. From here, I could see the general unpadlocking the door to a brick building opposite the church.

Almost certainly, this was an arms cache. I took a couple of photos, removed the film and sealed it in its tube and slotted another one into place in the camera. Outside, I pushed the tube down into the earth at the corner of a grave under an umbrella pine. Rex would arrange for it to be retrieved later.

Later, we were seated in the garden of a Roman villa for the open-air performance of *Romeo and Juliet*. Ballet in Italy ranks second to opera, but the costumes are always superb and the beauty of the dancers set off Juliet's girlish muslins and the ornamental silks of the Capulet and Montague households.

It was warm and dark, the air scented with herbs, ripening figs and cigarette smoke. Juliet was gathering the courage to drink the friar's concoction and a full moon rose behind the stage.

It was so beautiful, so unmatchable, a perhaps never-to-be-repeated combination of beauty, sensation and joy, and it choked me to consider that, if I died, I would never feel, or see, those elements again.

The general's day having been so successful, he took it out on me in bed that night.

I flattered him and told him he was in fine form and asked him if something particular had happened.

He smacked my bottom and – and I had to resist the urge to kill him – told me that I was in bed with a powerful man.

There was no need to tell me, I said. I knew I was with a powerful general, a leader of men.

He grew philosophical. Armies don't disband at the end of wars, he said, but continue in various shapes and forms. He then said: *I am that army.*

How preposterous he was and how dangerous, not least because he was stupid.

Which army would that be? I asked. Not unreasonably. He grabbed my arm so hard it hurt and said it was secret and it was none of my business.

I thought of making the joke: *I'll just imagine your uniform,* but thought better of it.

He launched himself on to me so heavily that it was difficult to breathe and warned me to keep my mouth shut. He added he would be watching …

I lay quite still and said that I wouldn't ever be so foolish or disloyal.

He read me the lecture. I was to remember that he was very powerful and he didn't want me going around being loose mouthed.

His hand crept over my breast and squeezed hard.

I made no sound. I did not move.

He whipped his hand away and declared he was being playful.

I told him that I had got used to it.

Back in Rome, the police were everywhere stopping and searching. An Iranian neighbour down the street has been dragged off for questioning.

Report to Rex:

> *The general continues to drop hints that he belonged to the secret army, known as the 'Stay Behind Army'. It is operational but never, ever acknowledged. The doctrine of deniability is sacrosanct.*

Rex and I analyse whether the general is using me to set up eventual useful contacts should the situation get too tricky for him and he needs to bail out of Italy. I am reasonably certain that the general has not cottoned on to who I am, but the discussion is the trigger for me to take more precautions.

The last few weeks have aged Rex. We touched on how to keep healthy and sane and he studiously avoided any reference to my situation. I remind him that I won't be around much longer, which he doesn't like. Do I know, he asked me, how much effort it requires to bed in someone new?

Not exactly professional but I forgive him because it is a compliment.

As I walked back to the Trastevere, I stopped to listen to a radio blaring through an open window.

After fifty-five days of captivity, Aldo Moro has been found stuffed into the boot of a Renault.

He is dead.

CHAPTER TWENTY-NINE

LOTTIE HAD BEEN PLAYING SAFE AND STOWING THE JOURNAL in the archive each evening. Tonight, it was late and the archive was empty.

The atmosphere challenged her, as it sometimes did, and the uplighters, which she now saw as a little sinister, contributed further to her disquiet and she fancied she could hear the pent-up voices corralled in their boxes and files. Eccentrics, villains, the saintly and those who resented dying prematurely   Nina among them, protesting her death.

At the appropriate section, she inspected the shelves, deriving a keen professional pleasure in seeing the Lawrence files now stowed in situ.

A noise checked her. A footstep? A soft click of a door closing? It took Lottie a few seconds to work out that it had come from the wrong end of the archive.

She patrolled down the aisle, right up to the stone wall that signalled the archive's limit. All was in order.

She had noticed before that the shelving unit at this end was unlabelled but had made nothing of it. The unit had no handle and was, presumably, empty and awaiting future material. She placed a hand on one of its doors to test it. As well maintained as everything was in the archive, the pressure caused the two halves to roll apart.

Inside was empty shelving and very dark. About to beat a retreat, Lottie pointed her phone torch down the defile and exclaimed under her breath.

Set into a stone archway was a door. It looked old but, as the oiled lock clearly revealed by the torch's beam suggested, in use.

The arrangements in place, Gabriele was due at the *Espatriati* the following morning.

'I'm coming with you,' said Tom when Lottie told him.

'Why on earth?'

Even so, she was happy to have him alongside.

A pale and impatient-looking Gabriele waited for them in the lobby. The formalities over, they took the lift to the basement to fetch the papers and the journal.

With the now familiar hiss, the doors inched open and they filed in. A couple of the archivists were at work in the Medieval section, including Paul, whom Lottie introduced to Tom and Gabriele.

Tom said: 'Am I right, this area has only quite recently been in operation?'

'Ten years or so,' replied Paul. 'Originally, the records were kept upstairs. Then, with better technology for preservation available, they were transferred down here. Which was always the plan, I think.'

'Ah,' said Tom.

Paul excused himself and vanished towards the lift.

Lottie instructed Tom and Gabriele to wait by the reading area and went to check if the porter had left the trolley as requested.

He was not there but the section was open.

A touch alarmed, she stepped between the shelving and was brought up short. A figure with a torch was rifling through one of the box files.

'Giuseppe Antonio ...'

In the gloom his clerical black appeared deeper and blacker and matched his expression.

She switched on the light. '*What* are you doing here?'

He blinked. 'I could ask the same of you.'

Lottie indicated the badge on her lanyard. 'I'm the chief archivist. You're the intruder.'

He shrugged. 'I'm finding out what I should have investigated years ago.' He held up a postcard. Lottie squinted at it and caught the word 'Palacrino'.

Pieces of jigsaw slid around, searching for their slot.

One: Nina worked for Rex, feeding him snippets of intelligence during a time of extreme turbulence that would have been channelled back to the UK.

Two: the US and Gladio units were working to provoke anti-left-wing sentiment in Italy.

Three: the Palacrinos were on good terms with a general known to be ultra-right wing.

Four: Nina slept with the general.

A dank odour of corralled underground water sifted up from the floor. She smelled it alongside her own apprehension.

The space was small enough to induce claustrophobia and, as she edged towards him, he shrank back against the shelves. 'When did you find out about Gabriele and Nina and who Nina was?'

The avuncular, if enigmatic, presence that he had taken pains to cultivate had been dropped and his tone was icy and bitter sounding. 'Early on. We realised that she was relaying information to a handler.' He dipped into sarcasm. 'They should have brushed up on their fieldcraft.'

'So you ran your nephew to find out things from Nina.'

'If you like. For a little while, until it was time for him to buckle down.'

'Imperilling his future. His happiness.'

He nudged the open box file with an elbow. 'Gabriele's situation was not unknown. Young men at the beginning are often tempted. It is survivable. We had a bigger arena to consider, larger objectives than a small love affair.'

'I would be willing to swear Nina never said a word, and you never found out a thing.'

'You don't have to open your mouth in order to say things. But I will concede, she was brave.'

Lottie sat on her fury.

'Where did Cardinal Dino come into this?'

'Cardinal Dino?' Antonio was taken aback. 'He's a man of the Church who had ambitions and liked to showcase his charity in order to get preferment. What you might call a "useful idiot". Nothing else.'

'Then, you're the link ...'

No denial was issued. 'And you're the stranger, Signora. Best to be careful.'

'As has been pointed out,' she said coolly. 'Please replace that material.'

He took his time to do so. Lottie closed the box file and slotted it into the shelf. 'You will leave her in peace.'

'You may think this brings this episode to an end.' She was surprised by his obvious regret. 'But politics does not work like that. There is still much to be done.'

She acknowledged the point silently and gestured for him to move into the aisle.

'You've been here before,' she said. 'I've heard you. You were here last night. I reckon you're worried, otherwise you wouldn't take the risk of being discovered.'

He clicked his tongue impatiently. 'There are arrangements. Provisions.'

'Provisions for what and for whom?'

'Valerio Gianni will brief you.'

Lottie understood. *Under every stone, etc., etc.*

He pointed a finger at Lottie. 'Your generation think you have it sewn up. But you've no idea how precarious civilisation is. What is required in sacrifices to shore it up. It takes only a war, a plague, the wrong political movement and down goes the house of cards.'

He appeared to be having some trouble breathing and banged his chest with a fist. 'I need to sit down.'

She hoped that he realised the depth of her contempt. 'You'd better come with me.' She led him over to where Tom and Gabriele waited.

'What are you doing here?' asked an astonished Gabriele.

Antonio grabbed hold of his nephew's arm. 'A chair. Please.'

There was a fuss as they lowered him into it. Antonio took out his handkerchief and pressed it to his lips, which, now they were in better light, had noticeably paled.

'Your uncle is wishing to destroy evidence about Nina Lawrence.'

From his sitting position, Antonio gave an audible sigh.

'That's all finished,' cried Gabriele angrily. 'We had a love affair. It was a disaster and we paid for it. It was a long time ago and long forgotten. Why resurrect it?'

The handkerchief again came into play. 'She was not what you thought, my foolish Gabriele.'

'What did I think? You have no idea.'

What existed between this uncle and nephew had directed their lives, for good or ill. *Il sangue non è acqua*. Deep ties of blood and history.

'I protected you, remember?' said Antonio.

Tom intervened. 'Gabriele, your uncle is anxious for other reasons … He's searching for leaked intelligence about the murder of Aldo Moro in May nineteen seventy-eight.'

'Shut up,' said Antonio.

Gabriele looked blank.

'Nina was engaged in gathering information,' said Tom.

Lottie looked at him. She was not familiar with this Tom.

'*Nina?*' There was no doubting Gabriele's intense surprise.

'I warn you not to say anything more,' said Antonio. There was a faint line of sweat on his top lip.

Tom paid no attention. 'Moro was kidnapped by the Red Brigades. But there is plausible evidence that the Red Brigades were being controlled by agents who belonged to the "Stay Behind Army", the Gladio. And, behind them, the CIA. Possibly. It's not proven. Nina was trying to assemble the picture.'

Lottie stared at Tom and tiny threads of suspicion began to plait themselves into an explanation – the bomb he had gone to investigate, his anxiety about her work on the Nina Lawrence papers.

Gabriele rounded on Antonio. 'How did you know this about Nina?'

'I took her to dinner. I wanted to meet her. Remember?'

So?'

'She had a minder there. Checking up. I happened to have spotted him in the Annona and it was easy to find out what was going on. Easy to make the connections.' A spot of saliva appeared at the corner of his mouth and he dabbed at it. 'Rome was – is – stuffed with spies. Every country had a string of them reporting back home.'

Tom seized his moment. 'The US saw the kidnapping as an opportunity to stabilise the centre-right and to encourage voters to turn against the left wing. Am I correct, Signor Antonio?'

'Again, I suggest you shut up.' Antonio's suaveness was splintering.

The jigsaw pieces shuffled into place.

'You know this place well.' Tom continued to address Antonio and it was not a question.

'Tom ...?' said Lottie, angry with herself for taking so long to understand what had been going on.

He ignored her. 'It's quite a story, you will agree. Originally, the *Espatriati* was the front for an ops-room for the Americans, who saw the fight against Communism as their primary task. The general would have held meetings down here, and the concealed door allowed agents and government figures to come and go in secret.'

'*That's* where the funds came from,' said Lottie. 'The CIA dollar.'

'Did you kill Nina?' Gabriele demanded with such ferocity that Antonio's head snapped back. 'Or did the Church have something to do with it?'

'The Church?' Antonio was genuinely shocked. 'You thought the Church would murder?'

'I've learnt anything's possible.' Gabriele dragged a second chair over to Antonio. 'You know as well as I do.'

Uncle and nephew squared up to each other. 'Have you turned so much against something you were once part of?'

'Yes,' said Gabriele. 'I have and I did.'

'I thought I had your measure,' said Antonio.

'You don't.'

The archive's air conditioning shifted into another gear, giving off a subdued asthmatic wheeze.

Antonio turned to Tom. 'This is none of your business. I could cause trouble for you.'

'I don't think so.' Having issued the sharp put-down, Tom continued, 'I put it to you that it would be difficult for you if your snooping was made public.' Antonio did not move a muscle. 'But, as always, there's a deal to be made. Tell us what happened to Nina Lawrence and nobody will say anything.' He was cold, insistent and flinty. 'Why search the Nina Lawrence files?'

It was a curious place for an interrogation. Or perhaps it wasn't. Lottie glanced around her. The hush, the dimness, the shine of the treated brick walls could double for a prison cell.

'That wasn't her name,' Antonio admitted eventually.

'No,' said Tom. 'It was Estelle Keyes.'

'How do you know that?' demanded Lottie.

Tom glanced at Lottie. 'I warned you I would look into the case.'

Antonio shifted. 'I see you have surprised your wife. I wonder if she understands.'

What?

'I understand perfectly,' said Lottie, knowing there were important things she had missed. She addressed Gabriele. 'The EK of the painting?'

'Nina Lawrence was not who she said she was. Beginning with her name,' said Antonio. 'Not unusual. Rome is that kind of city.' He spread out his well-kept hands. 'Gabriele, the woman who you consorted with … Estelle … worked for intelligence. She found out some things and went too far.'

Gabriele sat down opposite his uncle. Their faces were shrouded in the half-light, their body language tense and hostile. Yet they were similar and there was no question that they were cut from the same cloth.

This, then, was the drama of a family's power over its members – and its downfall.

'Tell me,' demanded Gabriele, this time with menace. 'You tell me she did not die because she and I were lovers. She died because …?'

His uncle met his gaze. 'I've told you what I know.'

'Liar.'

Antonio raised an arm, as if to defend himself against the words coming his way – and Lottie perceived that, if he did not know it himself, losing his nephew once and for all would be a body blow to an ageing man.

Over the years, Lottie had wrestled with documents under her remit to arrive at the correct answers. She had learned the pitfalls and, more than once, had been deceived and waylaid. It was a matter of knowing how to interrogate the material, using every scrap of knowledge at her disposal.

She did so now.

'You met Nina and General Rasella at a restaurant in the summer of nineteen seventy-eight?'

Antonio's expression was blank. 'I've no recollection.'

'You and the general talked,' said Lottie. 'She recorded it in the account she kept.'

Antonio's gaze flicked towards the archive's shelves.

'Nina kept accurate records.'

'Where are they?'

'Well hidden and well guarded.' Tom placed a restraining hand on Lottie's shoulder. 'Did you tell the general that Nina Lawrence ... Estelle ... was not who she said she was? Information he would have had no compunction in using.'

'Supposition. The general knew the game. He would have been on alert.'

'But you both shared the same right-wing political beliefs and it's possible that you supplied the information that would harm her. One, she was intelligence-gathering at a time of maximum upheaval and was getting close to discovering who was involved in the Moro affair, including possibly the general himself. Two, she had a child.'

'He did,' said Lottie. 'It's in her journal.'

'I've nothing to add.'

Tom said: 'Records show the general did not come to a good end. He was shot in his own garden.'

'Is that a threat?' Antonio tapped his chest with a fist and breathed audibly. 'How crude.'

'You tipped off the general,' insisted Lottie. 'At a dinner.'

'Gabriele,' his uncle's voice softened, 'I hated that you were a dupe.'

Gabriele was having none of that. 'How did you do it?'

Lottie summoned up Nina's shade, placing herself in Nina's position – a woman who had a baby to protect and was frightened by her situation.

Despite this, and knowing the dangers, Nina went out to complete her mission.

Wars were fought in many guises. What characterised them were their hatreds, vendettas, uncertainties and violence and, paradoxically, the way they had of drawing out what was best in people. In Nina's case a heroism and a gift for silence.

She glanced at Tom. *What did he know?*

Gabriele was incandescent. 'Nina was careful about going out after dark. She always had a car pick her up. Or a taxi.'

Antonio slumped back in the chair. 'I'm too old for this,' he said. 'And tired.'

'Giuseppe, you're no longer my uncle. You're no longer Beppo. After this, we will never speak again.'

Antonio dropped his hands into his lap and stared down at them.

'How and when did you lose your moral sense? Before I met Nina?' Gabriele glanced at Lottie. 'I think it was when you came to Rome and were corrupted by what you saw. I didn't understand.'

'I did what I thought best for you, Gabriele.' Antonio shifted in the chair. 'You had a future to be thought of. I tipped off Rasella that Nina Lawrence was using him. Told him about the child. Obviously, he and his confrères had no scruples about what they did to neutralise her. He reported afterwards it was simple to arrange to send a message saying that the child was ill and she had to come at once.'

'The priest that was said to have been at the scene?' asked Lottie.

Antonio shrugged. 'It's a good disguise. It throws lots of dust in the eyes.'

A stillness had captured the group as the secrets struggled into the light.

Antonio added, 'He was clever, the general. Or someone was. That's all that was needed. To rely on maternal feeling.'

Gabriele had dropped his head into his hands. 'My God.'

'But I did not arrange her death.'

Lottie and Tom exchanged glances. *Nina's death* – a deeply troubling and heinous act.

And yes, some men were capable of luring a new mother to her death for the sake of political gain. Everyone knew that. It was of an altogether different measure to be faced with it.

Without warning, Gabriele reached over and slapped Antonio. It sounded like a gunshot. No one moved, not even Antonio, but, hard and vicious, it must have hurt.

'That's for Nina,' said Gabriele.

Gabriele's reserve, to which Lottie was accustomed, had burnt off and he blazed with anger, a savagery even, which she trusted would not spill over into serious violence.

The doors to the archive whooshed back and a porter with a trolley creaked down the passage.

Again, Gabriele slapped his uncle. Harder this time, and even more brutal. 'That's for my child.'

A single lick of moisture slid down one of Antonio's cheeks. He put up a hand and wiped it away. 'I did not deserve that.'

'Yes, you did,' said new Gabriele. 'And still do.'

'An error of judgement,' said Antonio, the hand on his cheek trembling from shock and strain. 'You would not have made a priest.'

'Tell me where the child went.'

It took an effort for Antonio to heave himself to his feet. Once upright, he surveyed the group with a mixture of malice and resignation. 'You'll never know.'

Gabriele went white.

Tom barred Antonio's attempted exit. 'You don't know? Or won't tell?'

'I had no interest in what happened to a baby that should not have been born,' said Antonio, and the refusal to make his position more palatable was almost impressive. 'It was not my business. Then, or now.'

'But it was mine.' Gabriele spoke in a low, passionate voice. '*My child.*'

'If you insist on it,' said Antonio, and unleashed the final insult: 'But you can never tell with some women.'

He looked at Lottie. 'Please give my greetings to Valerio Gianni.'

Unsteady on his feet, panting and forced to frequently steady himself, he managed to make his way down the passage to the double doors. No one helped him. The doors whooshed open and he was gone.

'May he never sleep easy again,' said Gabriele. 'Ever.'

He ran his fingers along the edge of the table, tracing its contours as if he could draw strength from them. 'Sometimes she'd look at you,' Tom and Lottie did not need to ask who, 'and it felt as though she was looking right through you. You knew you could have no secrets and I didn't. I was too naive. I had not learned how to hide things. But Nina had.' He was silent. 'But she would have told me if she was having another man's baby.'

'But not yours,' said Lottie. 'She would never tell you that.'

He looked up at Lottie. 'That's precisely how I know it's mine.' His eyes were shadowed. 'And that's how I know she loved me.'

The seconds clicked onwards, falling into a silence.

Finally, Lottie said, 'I will fetch the journal for you, Gabriele.'

331

CHAPTER THIRTY

BLINKING IN THE BRIGHTNESS, TOM, GABRIELE AND LOTTIE emerged into the daylight.

Gabriele stabbed at the lift button. 'I would like to say I'm sorry about that display but I'm not.' He wheeled around. 'I think I'll take the stairs.'

Tom put his hand on Gabriele's shoulder and squeezed it. 'No need for apologies.'

The lift arrived and bore Tom and Lottie upwards, an uneasy silence stretching between them. *Who are you?* Lottie questioned silently.

Back on the ground floor, Tom bent over to kiss Lottie goodbye but she took a step back. Tom's eyebrows shot up. 'Right.'

Gabriele had climbed the stairs in time to observe the interchange. 'I hope I'm not the cause of problems.'

She shook her head and, carrying the journal, she and Gabriele went up to her office.

Throughout his career he would have been faced with similar objects on which to work, but this would be of a different order of experience and Lottie had taken care to make it easy for him. There was coffee, water and a ban on the phone ringing.

Gabriele sat down in the lime-green chair.

'I generally spend a day examining a project,' he said. 'Assessing the foxing, the staining, the marks, the burns, the wear and tear.' He rested his hands lightly on the journal. 'This is different.'

He leafed through the pages, pausing to look at an entry or an illustration, before settling to read, an intense process which Lottie felt she should not be witnessing. At one point, he got up and paced over to the window before resuming.

Lottie occupied herself with looking through reports from various departments.

When Gabriele reached the final pages, he looked up. 'I didn't know the half of it,' he said. 'I was blind. Very.'

'Nina took care that you didn't. She wanted to protect you.'

'Listen to this ... "To keep whole in the face of fear is almost too much. But I must do so. Fear is a terrible destroyer of confidence and ability. It muddles one and blurs the objective. Curiously, you can feel more fear for other people than you do for yourself."'

'Nina was brave,' he said. 'I hope she knew that.' He pushed back his chair. 'I should feel easier after reading this,' his hand rested on the journal, 'but I don't. Sadder. And furious. With myself especially.'

'It was Nina's other life that brought about her murder,' said Lottie.

'Maybe.' He came to a halt. 'But I'm good friends with guilt. When I'm at a low ebb, it doesn't take much. Lovers in the street, a garden, a biscuit served with coffee, and Nina is there. You could accuse me of being addicted to it, dependent on it, even to enjoy it, however painful. As I told you, there have been periods in my life when I haven't thought about Nina. But when I do ...'

'I understand,' said Lottie. She set aside the reports. 'Gabriele, if there had been no family urging you on, would you have wanted to be a priest?'

'I thought so at the time. I was young and I liked the idea of a cause, but, after I left, I never had any yearnings to return.'

Compare and contrast, she thought with a touch of hilarity. Gabriele's family had worked on him in one way. Her lack of family had worked in another.

She pitied Gabriele's wounds. Old they may be, but they had been deep and terrible. And she pitied her own.

'I'm sorry about your uncle.'

'We had a long relationship. Now we don't.'

She hesitated. 'You must look for your child.'

He placed his hand on the journal – as if to draw sustenance from it. 'He or she will have a life. I'm worried I'll do damage by making contact.'

Lottie leaned over the desk. 'You haven't been listening to me.'

Again, the wry smile. 'I have. I have.'

'The need to know *who* you are never leaves you, however good the life you have.'

He frowned.

'My birth certificate has no father on it,' she said. 'Only the name of the woman who gave me away for good. It is a big space in me.'

Lottie would probably never decide if her mother had taken one look at her new-born features and experienced repulsion. Or if she could not bear to give up the good times. Or if it had been a desperate and principled acknowledgement that she could never look after a child.

'I'll never know my mother's reasons, but Nina, on the other hand, was generous,' she said. 'Cleverer and clearer headed than my mother, and she has laid a trail for you.'

She flicked up *The Annunciation* on her laptop screen.

She sat down beside Gabriele and caught the now familiar scents of leather and ink, with the faintest trace of paint.

'First *The Annunciation* ...'

The perfect maiden, the startling blue of the cloak and the luminous landscape behind the garden.

He looked at it for a long time. 'It's a superb pastiche. Nina knew what she was doing.' He paused. 'I should call her Estelle.'

'You knew her as Nina. And Palacrino is your place.'

He pointed to the backdrop in *The Annunciation*. 'My father had been ill. He never got over my mother's death and I asked my supervisor if I could spend the night away to see him. I didn't go home. Nina and I took the train to Palacrino. They say the first lie is the worst and it was a bad one. But I was never a good liar and my supervisor must have guessed. I sometimes wonder if it had been policy to allow their trainee priests out on a lunging rein, the better to bring them in.' He shrugged. 'Antonio's approach.'

Lottie traced the outline of the undulating city wall, corralling delicate spires and sloping roofs, and the mountain beyond.

'Our room overlooked the mountain,' Gabriele continued. 'It was warm, very warm, and it was often hazy. We promised ourselves we'd climb up it. We never did.' He smiled. 'I don't think we left the room.'

He indicated a window in one of the white-stoned turrets.

'I'd never had a lover. Nina had. We were nervous and made bad jokes. Nina said she worried because she might be too old for me and I said she wasn't to worry as I had no one to compare her to.' He was silent for a moment. 'We were both happy and nothing else mattered. You don't often have that feeling. A true intense experience and wishing to be nowhere else. I wish she had told me.'

'How could she? You were going to be a priest. She gave you the freedom of not knowing. I reckon she planned to finish her work in Rome and take the child home with her. The baby had changed her.'

'And the other clues?'

The Nativity lay on Lottie's desk and she picked it up and turned it over. 'Gabriele ... I believe Nina laid a painting trail. She was under pressure and it was unlikely she could think of any other way at this point. It's possible it's in here.'

The frame, which was of excellent quality, had small metal clasps on the reverse that had rusted and sunk into the cardboard backing.

Lottie began to prise up the first. 'Let me.' Gabriele reached into his bag, produced a micro-spatula. 'Never without one.'

His hand was unsteady, which made easing open the clasps awkward. He lifted off the cardboard and Lottie gave a soft exclamation.

An envelope addressed to Gabriele lay underneath. Using tweezers, Gabriele prised it away and laid it on the table.

Lottie got up and went to the door. 'I'll leave you to read that in private.'

Twenty minutes later, she found him with his head in hands. Sheets of paper were spread out in front of him and he pushed them over to Lottie.

Rome
15 October 1978

Gabriele,
He arrived in this world after many hours close to
midnight on 23 December 1977, accompanied by a cry
from me.

337

There is comfort in remembering and I try to remember every second.

He was placed in my arms, a wailing, nuzzling enemy of my peace. A milky angel winging into my psyche and taking possession of my body and spirit.

I loved him.

I loved him, my Christmas baby.

The days were cold and dark, the nights colder and darker. I held him for hours, willing his eyes to open and for him to look up at me. He was, *is*, blood of my blood and bone of my bone. And of yours.

The pillows in the refuge were narrow and stuffed with hard wool. I lay back against them and contemplated the shift in everything I knew.

Nothing had prepared me for birth. Its power. Its relentlessness. Its mastery over the body. Towards the end, I thought I had already died except I remembered that, if you are dead, there is no pain.

I told him about his father, about his mother, about the life that I planned for him. He listened and then got down to the business of his existence, which is to feed. In the let-down milk reflex, I felt life transferring from me to him and it is the most extraordinary privilege.

After I was able to sit up, I would not let them take him away. I told them that I must do everything for him while I could. They looked at me and warned, 'Don't get too attached.'

The weeping arrived a few days after and I cried for hours, holding him close to my heart so its beat would comfort him.

The aftermath of giving birth is like gasping for breath in a stormy sea. I am post-partum. I grieve for his father, who is you. I am ever more conscious that our lives are surrounded by a darkness, which conceals I know not what. Give birth and it creeps closer.

I will shield my son.

I had no idea I could feel like this.

He is now in the safest place I could find and cared for by the perfect people. I visit as often as I can. At first it was every month. Then, because I could not bear it, every week, however difficult it is to arrange.

In between I yearn.

What would you say, my loved Gabriele, if you knew? I suspect you might take one look at your son and, in that single pulse of recognition, you would be divided from your vocation.

I know this because it has happened to me.

I wish I could see you. I love you, Gabriele. I love you. But I know it is over.

It's a good thing, a necessary thing, to have an episode in a life when someone else matters more than you do. In that way, we become proper human beings. While we were together, although hidden, you were more important than anything else. I told you and you pretended otherwise but you were pleased.

Now?

To have a child is to be pitched into a new level of empathy and terror. It cannot be a brief episode. The child is for life. Is life.

Gabriele, we differ in the matters of our faith, the

religious and secular, but in one way I believe absolutely in yours. The birth of a child is about hope.

It is to climb the mountain – our mountain – towards the sun. It is to understand boundless and unconditional love.

I want to thank you for everything, including our son. I do not blame you. Nor do I have any claim on you, which leaves me free to act, and I will do my best to arrange matters so you are not implicated in any way.

I don't blame you for your choices. They are hard ones. So are mine. That is life and they must be faced.

I confess that I am afraid, which makes me a little ashamed. Not just about the practicalities but about how being afraid affects the spirit. Fear is not a good companion. It's always ready to inflict a wound.

I wish, I wish things were different … but it had been set in stone before I met you. Long before I met you.

When I can, I will fetch him and take him away somewhere safe.

My Oscar.

Your Oscar.

'Oscar …' Gabriele looked up at Lottie.

He seemed completely winded.

'It's dated the day of her death. She must have written it after seeing you in the church.'

'You and I know each other much better now,' he said. 'But I don't know Nina any longer. Where would she have taken him?'

She thought of the acquired skill and experience necessary to interpret the silent documents in the archive, silence broken only when the files were opened and the reading room filled up with their presences, often more telling than in life.

'You *do* know her,' she said.

'Where would she take our son?'

'I might be wrong.' Lottie looked down at her hands folded in her lap. 'Will you take that risk?'

'Go on.'

She pointed to *The Nativity* and the weeping woman carrying the narcissus.

'The place of the narcissi. Your place. The place you told me about.'

'Palacrino.'

She added carefully, 'Did you know there's a village close to Palacrino where orphaned children are cared for?'

Gabriele picked up his phone. 'We'll begin with the birth certificate.'

'What name will you give?'

'Oscar Keyes,' he said. 'Nina would have wanted him to have his own name.'

'Or Oscar Ricci? He is Italian. She would have been careful to make things easy for him.'

His eyes narrowed with emotion. 'Possibly. Yes.'

'Gabriele. I'm pretty sure there's a Signor Oscar who works with the children in the village near Palacrino. Long story, but I heard one of the children call out the name when Tom and I were there.'

Signor Oscar, wait for me.

She went home to face Tom.

She found him nursing a whisky on the balcony. In the courtyard below an argument had broken out between two women, each informing the other they were useless.

She stood in front of him, blocking the view. 'I need to know who you are, Tom.'

He swirled the whisky around the glass. 'You mean you want to know where I get my information?' He looked up. 'I've lived here a long time. I've got contacts. Information is part of my business.'

'Political contacts?'

'All sorts.'

'MI6 contacts?'

'Who doesn't?'

'I don't.' She prised the glass out of his hand and set it down on the table. 'Tom, do you pass information on to them?' She stared into his eyes and got her answer. 'You *do*. What sort of person does that?'

'Nina Lawrence, for one,' he said, holding her gaze. 'At any point, there are listeners and watchers.'

'Nina was operating at a time when there were real fears in certain quarters that Italy would turn Communist. You're not.'

'Jesus on a bike,' said Tom. 'Listen to me, my obstinate Lottie. *Listen.*'

He spoke fluently and with authority and she listened to a different story, at the end of which she interrupted, 'We've been over this. Post-war everyone is scared witless that Communism would make headway in Italy in particular. The right wing, or elements of it, wanted to ensure that the working classes were kept in their place. So they devised strategies to create chaos, blame the left wing for it and unleash state repression. But, Tom, *that* is in the past.'

'Is it?'

'That bomb ...' she said, realisation dawning. 'The one you went to investigate ...'

'Admirable,' said Tom.

He gripped her by the shoulders. 'The right-wing organisations and the Gladio were very, very secret for all sorts of reasons. Documents are redacted, files swept clean, and people have lost their lives if they got too close. Now, do you see why I was anxious? Even now.'

Lottie shook him off and took herself to the kitchen, and Tom followed her.

She filled a saucepan with water for the pasta and lit the gas under it. Her hand trembled as she threw the match into the saucer.

'Tom, let's go over this again, *are* you British Council?'

'I am. Through and through. My life's work.'

'But you work for that other organisation too?'

'Shall we say, there's some dovetailing?'

She swivelled around and leaned back against the sink. 'You've been lying to me.'

'Not lying.'

'Just not telling me everything.' She ran over the implications. Secret services had their people everywhere – agents and stringers. Whole structures.

'So you're a Nina,' she said flatly. 'And you've deceived me.'

Tom remained stock-still and the small kitchen seemed very overcrowded.

'Not exactly. But I'm sometimes asked questions by contacts.'

'I don't know how to handle it,' she said. 'It's like an infidelity.'

'No, it isn't,' he said. 'Don't personalise it.'

'If discovering that your husband is probably working covertly

343

doesn't come under the heading of personal, I don't know what does.'

'Lottie, put it in another box.'

'How very male. And a convenient moral equivalence.' She pushed the pasta into the boiling water and poked at it with a wooden spoon. 'Did Clare know?'

He did not answer at once. 'Perhaps,' he said.

'My God ...' The notion struck her. 'She's in it too. Working in the Vatican.'

'She's a contact. That's how we met. What are you going to do?' He was frowning and had gone pale.

She thought about the information he always seemed to have at his fingertips, the tip-off when she visited Cardinal Dino. 'I'm not sure. This changes ... not everything but the balance between us. We haven't lied to each other, but we haven't trusted.'

'I'm not allowed to trust in that way. It's not wise.'

'Have you been having me followed?'

'Yes,' he said simply. 'I was worried. Probably wrongly, but I wasn't going to take the chance.'

She was staring at him, not sure whether she was going to burst into laughter at the absurdity. The laughter was still-born because it *was* true Nina had died and there was nothing laughable about that.

'Jeez. Is there a stock of men with Number-one haircuts behind the woodshed awaiting a command to go out and follow?'

'It's not unknown. It's sometimes necessary.'

He made a move towards her. 'Don't,' she said sharply.

'Lottie ...' Tom was reining himself in. 'You can't let this become a problem. I won't let it.'

Her brain felt hot with shock, and with the questions that were swarming in. 'I've been very stupid.'

'I'm sorry.' He dug his hands into his pockets. 'We agreed once before that nothing is ever black and white. Is it?'

The pasta was cooked and she hovered, almost poleaxed by the desire to down the spoon and rush out of the flat.

'What are you going to do?' he said again.

The small bubbling sound of the cooking pasta was oddly soothing. She turned her head and her eye was caught by Concetta's pink plastic mirror.

She thought about what she had gained by living in Rome, which she had never expected. She recollected how, in the past when her circumstances had become uncomfortable, she had moved on and it had never solved anything. She glanced up at the mirror, its pinkness now enhanced by a rosary that had been draped over it.

She bit her lip.

The idea of throwing away the accommodations and the unfolding sweetness and intrigue of this new life was to be wanton with opportunity but … Tom had not been transparent. Not honest.

He stuck his hands deeper into his pockets. 'Lottie, you will have secrets, and private thoughts, about which I will never know. I don't expect to. But you must know that, whatever I do in my work, I will never betray you.'

'But you might have to choose between it and me,' she pointed out.

'Yes. And I don't want to think about that.'

'No pretence, then.'

'Then there are no lies.'

An area of unknowing stretched between her and Tom of which she had been ignorant. It hurt but, to her surprise, not unbearably so. Perhaps, in a marriage, the trust waned and waxed and could never be a constant measurement. The only guarantee being that it was there, a thread running through.

'Lottie?'

Silence.

'You know that I would accompany you to the scaffold. Lover and friend. I'd help you up the steps and then I'd come with you.'

Despite herself, Lottie was listening.

'I would,' he said. 'No question.'

There was time ahead to negotiate and to understand.

'Oh, for God's sake,' she said, 'chop the parsley, will you?'

CHAPTER THIRTY-ONE

As arranged, Concetta was waiting for her first thing in the market, a basket over her arm, wielding a fan. She did not actually greet Lottie with: *You're late*, but she was almost certainly thinking it.

She looked Lottie up and down. 'Good.' Lottie had taken care with her choice of pencil skirt and sleeveless blouse and very strappy sandals because she knew stylish presentation would benefit Concetta's standing.

Concetta was wearing one of her many pocketed dresses, her hair was glossy and she smelled of the rose oil she favoured. She snapped the fan shut and dropped it into the basket. Crooking her finger, she indicated Lottie was to follow her.

She led the way and performed a series of introductions to the best places to buy fruit and vegetables. 'It's important to know, Signora Lottie,' she said, ploughing a furrow through the crowd.

It was the first time 'Lottie' had been appended to the 'Signora'.

For a good half an hour they moved from stallholder to stallholder with plenty of chat. 'This is my signora and she will be buying from you often and I know you will treat her well.'

Three peppers here. Mushrooms there. The best cheese across the square.

Lottie was aware she was being shown the pathway through a maze. Surreptitiously, she texted Tom: *It's very touching*.

A church bell was ringing when she joined him for lunch. 'There's someone I want you to meet,' he had told her at breakfast. 'Please will you be there?'

The restaurant had gaily striped green and white umbrellas and Tom and another figure were already sitting at their table.

It was Clare: in an olive linen dress, hair pulled back, large earrings.

Tom said, 'I thought you two could pull my character to shreds.'

As well he might, thought Lottie. 'Tom, I hadn't agreed to this.'

'That's why I didn't say anything.'

Nevertheless, Lottie wished to make the point and hovered.

Clare got to her feet. 'I asked Tom to do this. I thought we should lay the ghosts. And we should have everything out in the open. There can be such trouble if it isn't. Don't you think?'

Lottie found herself shaking hands with her predecessor. 'To be fair, I had said that I wanted to meet you.'

I certainly wanted to meet the woman that the confirmed bachelor married.' A smile tweaked the corners of Clare's mouth. 'It was quite a feat.'

They ordered lunch and a glass of wine. Clare was politeness and warmth itself, asking detailed questions about Lottie's work and how she felt about coming to live in Rome. 'It's a culture shock and it took me a while. But now I wouldn't live anywhere else.'

'I haven't landed yet,' Lottie found herself admitting. 'It takes time, more in the head than anything else. But I'm getting there.'

Clare looked at home, accustomed, rooted, and she and Tom exchanged gossip about British Council activities and bantered amicably. There was no bitterness, or the suggestion of shadows. If anything, they appeared to be long-term, well-tried companions.

'And your family,' Clare wanted to know, 'where do they live?'

Lottie felt Tom's eyes on her. 'I don't have any family to speak of. Or, if I do, I don't know them.'

Clare was no fool, sensed the subject was tricky and changed it. 'Concetta tells me that you have wrought miracles on the balcony. I bet it's beautiful. And Tom tells me you have been interested in the murder of an English girl. Some time ago.'

Under the table, Tom's hand rested briefly on her thigh.

'Tom's mentioned that I work in the Vatican. Yes? I asked one of my colleagues to have a quick look at the files. Tom says that you reckon the murder wasn't investigated.' She flicked a look at Tom. 'You're right. There's a note from the legal department stating that, if there are implications that might involve the Church, no records are to be kept and to keep it out of the media. Here's a copy.' She passed over a piece of paper.

'Thank you,' said Lottie. If the order was signed, she knew who it would be. She glanced down at it. Correct.

Tom went in search of the cloakroom. Clare leaned over the table. 'I'm sorry if I've made you uneasy.'

'It goes with the territory,' said Lottie.

'Yes. But you mustn't worry about me. Worry about Tom and his work. We had a good time living together and we're good friends, which worked until I fell in love with Sylvia. Then, it had to change. Obvs.'

She was laughing and Lottie found herself joining in.

How very Roman it was to solve a problem over an al fresco lunch.

Lottie put two and two together. 'Was it you who tipped Tom off about my visit to Cardinal Dino?'

Clare turned serious. 'Yes. Tom had warned me that you were pursuing the cold case. There've been one or two other unexplained and distressing murders, as you'll know, and the Vatican can be sensitive. A lot of accusations, past and present. Mafia. Right-wingers. Communists. Tom was anxious about your interest in the case becoming so public.'

When they rose to leave, Lottie said to Clare, 'You were right about bringing the ghosts into the open.'

'Come and have dinner with me and Sylvia,' she said. 'Soon.'

She and Tom watched Clare go off down the street. At the corner she turned and blew them a kiss. 'I should have asked more about you and Clare but I didn't like to. Had you become friends by the time she met Sylvia?'

'Yes and no,' he said. 'At one point, I thought I was mortally wounded, but I wasn't and Clare knew it. It was the same for her. There's no blueprint for co-habitation, although people like to think there is.' He cupped her chin with a tender hand. 'Because I hadn't met you, Lottie. When I did, I realised I was waiting.' He squinted down at her. 'I didn't *know*.'

''Tom, that's the nicest thing.'

In the evening, walking home from the *Espatriati*, she sensed a presence.

A shaven-headed man?

Twice, she swung around but could see no one.

The third time, she turned around it was to see a small boy lugging a pet rabbit in a cage. The rabbit was heavy and he was red-faced from exertion.

She smiled at him.

Everywhere possible there was a scramble of flowers and plants. In pots, over walls, forcing their way through crevices, a sapling pushing between pavement flags or a bush slyly rooted in a gap between walls, offspring of the unseen force that did battle to survive.

As she rounded the corner, the evening sun struck like a spear between her shoulders. She was walking down a Roman street, with a medieval church on her left and a Renaissance archway ahead, sights complemented by cooking smells, a hint of jasmine and rubbish, a whiff of feral cat, a glimpse of discarded coping stone or balustrade, peeling paint, ochre walls.

For that moment, Rome's many pasts seemed so clear, so immediate, so present, layered up on each other like fabulous patisserie.

The nape of her neck was damp with sweat and she searched in her bag for a band to tie up her hair. Pulling it back, her scalp prickled and she expected to see a phantom of a would-be saint with a half-severed neck rise from the stones under her feet. Or the small figure of Nina Lawrence flit through the shadows towards the river.

She came to a halt. She was wearing thin-soled sandals and the warmth of the pavement percolated through to her feet. Almost, almost she was tempted to shuck them off and to make direct contact with the ground. Then, it might be possible to feel she was growing into those ancient stones, and a connection to Rome – her connection – would run through her, from top to toe.

But she did no such thing. Instead, she laughed at herself and continued on her way.

'And the Gladioli?' asked Tom later as they sat on the balcony with their evening drinks discussing Gabriele and the search for Oscar.

'That's the clue to her death. She put it in because she feared her life was in danger.' She looked up at him. 'As you said.'

He was silent for a long time. 'I have something for you,' he said eventually.

'Another drink?'

'Your turn.' He placed an envelope in front of her. 'You don't have to open it.'

The swifts were swooping above her head. It was warm and, for once, peaceful.

'Tom?' She was apprehensive.

But he had turned away and was standing at the edge of the balcony, looking down.

Lottie opened the envelope and drew out a folded piece of paper. It was a copy of a death certificate for Kathleen Charlotte Black.

'Where did you get it?'

'The usual channels,' he answered. '*My* usual channels.'

'So, my mother died ten years ago.'

'She did.'

She put the certificate on the table and went to stand beside him. 'That's that, Tom.'

'If you wish it.'

She nipped a sprig of lavender between her fingers and inhaled the cleansing aroma.

'I think I wish it. I do wish it.' She took his hand and his fingers tightened on hers.

Lottie was drifting to sleep, with Tom beside her.

She imagined Marta Livardo banging on Nina's door with a piece of paper in her hand and handing it over.

The two women eye up each other and Nina reads the message and cries out. 'My baby is very ill. I'm to go at once.'

'Dio. Your baby? Then you must. What do you need?'

'My bag.'

Marta Livardo gives it to her. Nina looks up and around the apartment – at the brocade on the table, her journal, which she shoves into a box and piles papers over, the lamp casting light over a half-drunk cup of coffee, the drawings of sunflowers and gladioli that she was working on. The anchors to her life. There is no time to make her usual preparations before going out.

It will be a dark, cold journey, but she must get there.

She turns to Marta Livardo. 'We haven't been friends. But can we be now?' Their eyes lock. 'For the sake of the baby.'

After a moment, Marta gives a stiff nod.

Nina picks up the envelope and inserts it into the back of the framed Nativity *and clips the backing into place. 'If anything should happen to me, will you guard this? Please. It's for the baby. Don't let them take it. Someone will come for it in the end. You will know if he is the right person. You are to give it to him.'*

Marta Livardo takes the painting. 'You must be careful.'

'I'll go by the Ponte Sisto. There's a taxi rank on the other side.'

Snatching up her coat, Nina picks up her bag and runs downstairs.

Lottie sighed and turned over. She would never know the exact details of Nina's last hours. Yet she was certain she knew her way into Nina's heart and of what she was thinking.

At the doorway, Nina hovers for a moment. She knows it's possible that she is poised between life and death, but she also knows that her non-negotiable, overwhelming love means she must run into the darkness that was – that is – Rome to be with her son.

ACKNOWLEDGEMENTS

There are many wonderful and absorbing books on Italy and Rome and it was difficult to choose on which to concentrate. However, the following proved to be goldmines. *Painting and Experience in Fifteenth-Century Italy* by Michael Baxandall (Oxford Paperbacks), *The Vatican's Women* by Paul Hofman (St Martin's Griffin), *The Best Gardens in Italy* by Kirsty McLeod (Frances Lincoln), *A Traveller in Rome* by H. V. Morton (Methuen), *Notes from a Roman Terrace* by Joan Marble (Transworld), *NATO's Secret Armies* by Daniele Ganser (Frank Cass), *Italian Neighbours* by Tim Parks (Vintage) and *The Moro Affair* by Leonardo Sciascia (Granta Publications).

In addition, *A Masterpiece Reconstructed: the Hours of Louis XII* (The J. Paul Getty Museum and the British Library) offered invaluable essays by the late Janet Backhouse and a reflection by Thomas Kren on the provocations of Bathsheba in illuminated manuscripts. Last, but not least, a huge thank to Henry Hemming for giving me permission to use his list of agent must-haves, which I have taken from his superb *M: Maxwell Knight, MI5's Greatest Spymaster* (Arrow Books).

I have taken details and scenarios from all of them and hereby acknowledge my debt. Any mistakes are mine.

Those who know Rome will realise that I have invented the *Archivio Espatriati* and its location. I hope the Via Giulia will forgive me. Nor does Cardinal Dino's retirement home exist in the Trastevere and nor does the church where Rex and Nina rendezvous.

A huge thank-you to Sarah Hodgson for her needle-sharp and tactful editing, to Hanna Kenne for her patience and professionalism and to the star team at Corvus. Homage is owed also to Alison Tulett, who pulled together the manuscript so skilfully, with additional thanks to Fabiano Fabiani for his excellent fine tuning. Also to my agent, Judith Murray, and all at Greene and Heaton.

As always, my friends were on standby and were rocks. With especial thanks to writers Fanny Blake, Marika Cobbold, Isabelle Grey. They know what they do to keep the process going.

To my family: Benjie, Adam and Lucinda, Eleanor and Henry and Alexia, Flora and Finn. You put up with everything but you make it all possible.

Don't miss Elizabeth Buchan's stunningly atmospheric

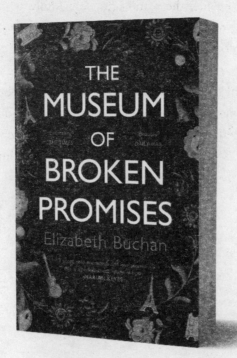

'A gem of a book ... beautiful, elegant'
MARIAN KEYES

'Intricately plotted and beautifully written'
KATIE FFORDE